A REALM OF FIRE AND ASH

AGGONID'S REALM

KATHY HAAN

ISBN 979-8-9855077-7-5 (eBook)

ISBN 978-1-960256-01-0 (paperback)

First edition March 2023

Book cover design by Asterielly Art

Published by Thousand Lives Press, LLC

Edited by Fervent Ink

To those who grew up despising love triangles and tossing books across the room, shouting, "Why can't she have them both?" This one's for you, because in this story, not only can she have both, but she can have 'em all. Eventually.

BE ADVISED

This is a **dark fantasy romance** with elements that *will* upset some readers. Please read CW/TW at kathyhaan.com/triggers.

CHAPTER ONE

MORTE

Convectus

A phoenix rises from the ashes of her remains. A symbol of rebirth, and a promise of the return of the gods. I remember the myths, but I don't believe. Not anymore.

The first time I died, I was a toddler. Trapped underground in Castanea—our world below the realm of Bedlam—my mother didn't have access to the life-saving medicines of the surface, and I'd been struck with the same fae fever that had swept through our colony via the trees.

My mother had wept as she watched me writhe in sweat-drenched sheets in our one-room treehouse high atop a canopy. The sickness came on fast and strong, devouring my body until it withered to nothing. Two months later, long after they'd buried me beneath a willow, my name carved into its trunk, I'd crawled into her bed, asking for a cup of water.

It takes minutes to resurrect now.

The Tolden—the name of my people in Castanea—thought I was a child of the gods. A gift. The sickness could've kept me, but it didn't. Instead, it left a mark on my soul, a sign that I was theirs. For

1

hundreds of years, I lived in fear they would come for me as they did every other child. I'd embraced the nights and hated the days. In the shadows, I discovered a different kind of beauty, while the brightness of the sun revealed its own terrors. The sickly yellow light of day was the burning of my flesh. The cold, dark night offered me safety.

That'd been millennia ago. I no longer live in fear, having spent thousands of years rising from the ashes. And I no longer believe I belong to the gods. I am my own person, writing my own destiny.

As there was, and always should be, a new beginning. That's my battle cry. A promise I made to myself, to my friends, and to the realm. It was the reason I lived: to rise again, to protect the innocent, and to bring justice to the wicked.

As a fresh gust of wind blows against the windows of my tree-house, I slide my bed a little to the left and feel along the floorboards until I find one with raised corners. After unscrewing the flooring, I pull out a wrapped bundle of well-worn letters. I bring the stack to my face, inhaling its musty scent of ink and parchment that stirs the memory of a distant ocean. The smell overwhelms me, crashing against my senses like a raging tide, bringing with it the roar of waves, the salty tang of the foam and the far-off horizon of an endless sea.

But even beyond all of that, all these years later, I can still breathe in the scent of Wilder and all those days we spent together before he left. Our best days were spent far beneath the surface, exploring the depths of the ocean where the light never reaches. Days when we'd forget about the war that waged above us and just revel in each other's company. But those days were long gone.

And now, there are no more letters. No more visits. No more combing beaches for shells, making out under the stars, or sneaking in and out of Castanea.

I've only got a graveyard of memories and these scraps of dead trees tattooed with his sweet words to keep me company now. This morning, I'd needed a glimpse of them more than ever. No part of today is going to be easy, as it's an anniversary of sorts. Almost two hundred years since I've seen his face. Two thousand since the day he told me he loved me.

I take one last deep breath of the bundle's scent before tucking it away and standing up from the floorboards, just as my house begins to shudder.

I hurry to the doorway, peering out at my second-in-command. For a phoenix fae, Noct sure doesn't have a quiet tread. She rushes down the footbridge to my treehouse, shaking the entire structure with her bounding steps. Despite my annoyance at her quaking the whole place, I can't help but admire her beauty.

When she shifts, she becomes a two-headed phoenix. However, in her fae shape, Noct appears as a striking figure with one head—like the rest of us—and her maroon hair falls in gentle waves down her back. Despite her unnatural beauty, her strength and power are evident, emanating from her very being. Her silver eyes are bright and piercing, with a keen intelligence that marks her as a warrior, ready to defend her people at a moment's notice.

It's rare she and I have the same two days off in a row, and we plan on practicing shifting from our fae forms to our phoenix forms while in-flight. We're going to do it just below the cave walls to give us an even bigger challenge.

As I open the door, Noct greets me with an excited grin so wide it nearly touches her pointed ears. She's dangling a flask between two fingers. "Look what I brought!" She pushes her way inside. But as she turns around to get a better look at me, her smile fades, replaced by a look of concern etched deeply into her features. "You okay, Morte?" she asks, her voice laced with worry.

I can see the concern in her eyes; feel the warmth of her hand on my arm. But I can't find it in me to smile.

Not today.

"Yeah." I grab my bag by the door and sling it over my shoulder. "Just thinking about him."

No one knows the details. Just that the man I love is someone I can never be with.

I can still remember the first letter Wilder gave me. He'd been nervous all day, fidgeting and avoiding eye contact. But finally, as the sun was setting, he stopped me before I could fly away and handed me a small envelope with my name written in scrolling ink. I'd flown to the top of a nearby oak tree and read the letter, tears streaming down my face as he confessed the depth of his love for me, but how his kind can only be with their *anchor*.

It's their version of a soul-bonded mate, and I wasn't his.

It'd wrecked me, knowing we could never be lovers or anything more than best friends. Still does. Especially after what he did for me.

For us.

But the letters he sent me every week were something to look forward to, something to tide us over until we saw each other again on the weekends. I cherished each and every one, reading them over and over until the paper was worn thin. And even though we were only apart for a few days at a time, it was hard. It was always hard. But we made it work because that's what best friends do.

Even if I was his anchor, I made a huge mistake. One I've spent my life trying to correct.

I step out of my treehouse, the cool air ruffling through my hair, carrying with it the scent of ash and smoke from last night's bonfire we'd had by the river as a squadron.

We'd had fun.

As a phoenix, fire and ash are a part of my existence, a constant reminder of my rebirth.

But today, it's the memory of Wilder's letters that weighs heavy on my mind, tugging at my heartstrings. The thought of him, of what we could have been, fills me with a sense of longing.

Noct follows me out, her excitement for our training now subdued by my somber mood. We make our way to the nearby clearing, where we can practice our shifting without causing any damage to the surrounding trees. I watch as she takes a swig from her flask, the contents sloshing around with her movements. She offers me some.

"Unless that's absinthe, I don't want it." I shake my head. The memory of my first taste of the spiced liquor comes rushing back to me, the bitter sweetness of it filling my mouth. I had found a jug of it abandoned in the Wastelands when I'd been without water for days. It had been enough to help me get through a rough sandstorm that made the journey much longer than normal, and I'd been grateful for it.

I push the thought away and focus on Noct, who's staring at me curiously. 'What's up with you?' she asks.

"Nothing," I mutter, but even as the word leaves my mouth, I wonder if there's more to it than that.

Absinthe always seems to find me just when I need it, and it's about the only time I ever indulge. It's rare, and no one seems to know who makes it.

"Might not kill you to live a little." Noct grins.

I roll my eyes at her, even as a smile touches my cheeks. "That's all we ever do."

Live.

Releasing her wings, they glitter in the dim light of the underground ecosystem, her feathers catching what little illumination is provided by the glowing lichen that clings to the walls. Her wings are matte and ashy, as if she'd been rolling around in soot, but they still retain an otherworldly allure. Her feathers shimmer with a mix of dark blue and violet hues, and the tips of her wings are tinged with fiery orange.

Fae flies illuminate the path, and as we move towards the clearing, the distant sound of falling water grows louder, and the air is filled with the fresh scent of damp earth and mossy trees. The clearing is a small patch of soft grass surrounded by towering pines, willows, and glowbarks that reach up to the ceiling of the cavern. It's peaceful here, away from the hustle of our daily lives, and I feel a sense of calm wash over me. Noct takes another swig from her flask, and I can hear the sloshing of the liquid inside as she moves.

I stretch my wings, feeling the power within me. Shifting from my fae form to my phoenix form takes focus and control, but I'm confident in my abilities. Noct and I stand facing each other, ready to begin. I close my eyes, taking a deep breath and centering myself. When I open them, my phoenix form bursts forth, flames flickering at my feathers. I take flight, soaring above the trees, feeling the rush of air beneath my wings.

My wings are a glossy crimson, like a bloodstain on white cotton. There are tiny bumps in the colors, as if they're filled with a network of miniscule, iridescent scales. Up close, they're not scales at all, but downy feathers that seem to glow red, like embers caught by candle-light. Or firelight, as it were.

Noct follows suit, her two heads streaking through the air with a fierce determination.

We fly in tandem, weaving around each other in a graceful dance. I can feel the thrill of the moment, the exhilaration of being alive. For an instant, I forget about everything else. It's just me, Noct, and the rush of flight. But as we come in for a landing, the weight of my thoughts crashes back down on me. The same thought that always sends me hurtling down to the floor.

My mistake.

Noct notices the change in my mood and lands gracefully beside me, shifting into her fae form. "You want to talk about it?" She toes the rock near her, kicking it into the trees.

I appreciate her offer, but I shake my head. "Nah, I'll be alright."

"Maybe you just need a good lay. Isn't the old saying that the best way to get over someone is to get under someone else?" She plops onto the grass, digging into her bag and pulls out her phone. "I can text Ronin's friend, Quinn? He thinks you're hot, and I heard he's got a big di—"

"No," I interrupt, falling beside her to steal her phone. "Isn't he dating what's-her-face?"

"They broke up," Noct sing-songs, winking at me suggestively. "Trust me, he's available."

I roll my eyes, tossing her phone back to her, the thought of being with someone else only making me feel worse. "I appreciate the offer, but I don't think a random hookup is going to solve my problems. Besides, I'm pretty sure I'd eat him alive."

She's my closest friend in Castanea, the only one who knows the shit storm brewing inside me.

My parents are long dead, lost in the war with the werewolves. Their hearts were used to cure two werewolves of their affliction long before I ever met Wilder. The pain of losing them is easily one of the worst things I've ever gone through, and knowing the Tolden no longer need to live in fear of werewolves helped solidify why I'd ever agreed to form a squadron in the first place.

Yet, I can't muster the courage to confide in Noct my deepest, darkest secret. The insurmountable guilt of my recklessness weighs heavily on my conscience, knowing that it landed the one person I love more than anything else in this godsforsaken world in prison.

A life sentence.

It suffocates me like a noose around my neck, and I can't shake it off no matter how hard I try.

Before she can respond, the sound of laughter echoes through the woods, and we turn our attention towards the path at the far end.

Ronin and Quinn appear, and I turn a scowl towards Noct. "You set me up!"

Noct just grins at me, showing off her dimples. "I didn't set you up. I only hinted we might be here." She stands and dusts grass from her shorts. "Besides, Ronin and Quinn are good company. And who knows, maybe Quinn will be able to take your mind off of things for a while."

I sigh, but eventually get up to join them. Ronin greets us with a smile and a wave, and Quinn grins when he sees me. I can't deny that he's attractive, with his messy blonde hair and bright green eyes, but I just don't *feel anything*.

"Hey, trouble." He pulls off his shirt, flashing me a smirk as he uses one hand to tug his belt free.

"I didn't realize you'd be joining us." I sigh, averting my eyes from where he's undressing.

Quinn is an eagle shifter, and always makes a point to undress before shifting, rather than buying clothes he can shift in. It's almost as if he expects me to be impressed with his skinny legs and oversized arms.

A loud chirp goes off, and I pull out my phone to see a message from the general.

EMERGENCY MEETING IN 5, MEET AT
CASTANEA COMMAND

I mutter a curse under my breath, then show the message to Noct. She nods at me gravely, her expression mirroring my own sense of dread.

"Sorry, boys," she says. "Duty calls."

It's not unusual for a top-secret mission to call us away. Work is about all I do anymore. Anything to keep my mind busy, away from my obsessive thoughts about Wilder.

We keep to our fae forms as we take air, flying towards command. The flight itself will take four minutes, and we could sift—or teleport —but Noct needs to get the alcohol out of her system before meeting with the boss.

If he's here, whatever it is—it's big.

I CALL MYSELF MORTE, but that's not my name. My name is lost, but my title is not. I am the First, the leader of the Great Company, commander of the last remnants of the God Wars. My people have forgotten the truth, and it's up to me to correct them, so I tell them stories of the old times. I tell them about the gods and the wars and the lands of the old. I tell them about the first war, when gods and mortals fought against each other, and when gods stood on the thrones of man.

I wasn't there, of course. I'm not that old. But while fae are immortal, they can be killed, and I cannot. So I tell their stories. They used to call me to battle. Not to fight, but to hold their hands as they're read their last rites. To ensure they're not forgotten when the sun sets, their bodies lie cold, and Luna's beams kiss their cheeks as she guides them beyond the veil.

That's a burden I no longer have to bear. It wasn't long before more of us were born, each bearing long, flowing manes of hair that glow in shades of fire: whites, blues, reds, oranges, and yellows. Most of us have hues of red hair, and we're all female. My crimson tresses mark me as leader, though all our beasts—beautiful birds with long wings—are fiery red.

Since High King Finian Drake retook his throne, my legion of eight phoenixes has joined the royal guard. We don't fight on the front lines. We're a special ops division, only sent to the worst conflicts. Suicide missions, where death is inevitable.

After decades of trying to get into the prison—to right the wrongs of my past—my new role might do just that one day.

In the Castanea command room, we stand before General Risç, who commands all the royal squadrons. He's a giant of a man, with muscles bulging out of his armor and his wingspan almost as wide as he is tall. But his eyes are bright and light yellow, like the sun has kissed his corneas and never left, setting them aglow.

The general's footsteps thud in the room, like a battering ram on a castle gate. The solid thunk of his footfall is a stark contrast to the quiet din of the cave walls. Each room at command is carved into bedrock, and though we're underground, flora and fauna flourish, showcasing the magic at work to keep this underground sanctuary running for all the Tolden. Vines have snaked their way up the walls, giving them a lush and verdant look. Wildflowers bloom in patches, a riot of color set against the dark stone.

Tiny points of luminescence reflect off the walls, as if stars filled up this cavernous space. A sweet scent fills the air, the subtle aroma of damp earth and petrichor that linger in the background, giving a sense of safety and home.

The cave walls emit a gentle hum, like chimes in the wind. A low rumbling can be heard in some places, presumably coming from the magic keeping the sanctuary alive and functioning.

The General's eyes hold a touch of pride as he surveys us. When the Great Company joined forces with the guard, their military casualties plummeted, though we've been busier than ever.

My heart stutters as I hear General Risç's words, the chill of dread freezing the blood in my veins. "Bedlam Penitentiary," he growls, "has a rogue inmate who's wreaking havoc on the island."

Terror grips me with icy claws. My deepest fear isn't that they'll uncover my secret connection to one of the inmates, but for his safety. My fear sharpens, taking hold of every nerve in my body, pulling it taut.

Those who say you quake with fright have never felt true dread before. It's a primordial force that seizes you, rendering you completely immobile as your body comes to terms with the magnitude of your impending danger.

Noct jabs me with her elbow, and it's then I realize the general is in front of me, trying to hand me something.

I blink hard, clearing my sight.

I take the thick manila folder from the General, infusing as much magic as I can into my hands to keep them from trembling, while flipping through the pages and photos inside.

The first page is a data sheet with inmate information.

CLASSIFIED
01 MAR 2023
NAME: Noah Tackwater
ALIAS: No-No
ORDER: Hydra
SEX: Male
INMATE NO: 00626
AGE: 2,072
HOMETOWN: Gala, Convectus
MATE: Cora Drashor [DECEASED 01 JAN 1704]
SENTENCE: Vita damnationem [12 JUN 1704]
CLASS: Extremely dangerous
CELL BLOCK: H
CELL NO: 16WL
CONVICTION: 42 counts, 1st degree murder; 3 counts, attempted murder; 16 counts, assault; tampering with evidence, 19 counts; resisting arrest, 1 count; torture, 316 counts; kidnapping, 45 counts; false imprisonment, 45 counts; rape, 1 count

CELLMATE: *None*
PREVIOUS CELLMATES: *Priscilla Musgrove [DECEASED*
    FEMALE 28 FEB 2023]
EYES: *Hazel*
HAIR: *Brown, shoulder length*
HEIGHT: *6'9"*
WEIGHT: *290 lbs.*
TATTOOS: *Star on right cheekbone*
BACKGROUND: *Inmate escaped holding cell while in beast*
    form, no known accomplices, sixteen guards killed, 302
    inmates injured

My breathing stalls, and it takes everything in me to remain standing. Three-hundred-and-two injured? Gods, let him be okay.

I flip the page, reading our assignment.

MISSION: *Contain or exterminate*

Attached is a mugshot of him, a picture of him in his fae form, and a photo of him as a hydra. He's one of the realm's most prolific serial killers and is said to be a master at manipulating his body. There's a grainy screen capture from a video of him ripping off the head of an inmate, his hydra form replacing his arms and neck.

"What can he do?" I glance at the General before returning to pages detailing the guards he killed.

Small mercies none of the inmates are dead.

"Besides kill?" He snorts. "He can manipulate his body in a variety of ways." The General paces. "He can tear himself apart into many small parts and reform nearly anywhere, or shape shift his fae form into a hydra. The target can be in many places at once, or singularly. He can be a serpent, a dragon, a demonic-looking thing, or even a mist."

Dread consumes me. Hydras need water. So do merfae. They're likely in the same sector, which means that either way, I'm likely about to see the man I've spent my life pining for today.

Whole or otherwise.

"The man is phenomenally dangerous." He stops pacing. "And as of twenty minutes ago, he's killed six more than what's listed on that sheet. All of you will die. Multiple times, and likely in painful ways. I recommend extermination."

"Permission to speak, sir," Bow calls from her formation behind me.

"Permission granted, private."

"Are the other inmates separated from the target?"

"The target is currently moving about within the prison, though we've confined most of the other inmates. And one more thing: you won't have the use of your magic, as they have to keep the suppressant deployed or the other inmates will revolt."

I nod, stepping out of formation to call the squadron over to a map the general lays out on a nearby table.

I point to the last marker, near the water. "He won't venture far from here, because he'll need to dip in and out of the pool to maintain his shifted form."

Noct regards me with a curious expression but refrains from commenting on my knowledge. I learned this information from Wilder's mother, who'd casually mentioned it ages ago. She spoke of how fortunate merfae were to possess the ability to exist both on land and in water, unlike some water-dwelling creatures who could only maintain their form on dry land for a brief period before reverting to their fae form.

"Should we sift to here, then?" Noct points to just outside the prison walls. "We'll have a better vantage point for the attack, and we'll be closer to the physical and magical wards that seal off the buildings from the sea."

Sabine quickly notes down an entry point on the parchment with a streak of blue ink. "Theoretically, if we can slip past the wards without being noticed, we can corner our target."

"If we can do that, it's a matter of eliminating him by use of fire." I roll up the map, barking off orders before turning back to the general. "Give us a portal stone and we'll be there in fifteen minutes."

12

CHAPTER TWO

MORTE

Bedlam Penitentiary

*W*aves crash at our feet. The smell of old copper fills my nostrils, and lockdown sirens blare from the sentry towers; a high pitch screech, like nails scratching across stone. Scarlet lights flicker in rapid succession, keeping time with the flash of lightning that illuminates the largest cell block. The howling wind reminds me of the cries of wolves, while the rain hitting the prison walls echoes like a thousand boots marching in cadence. Thunder cracks louder than the alarm.

"Nothing in block D," Noct calls to our group via the tiny walkie-talkies attached to our collars.

Freezing rain bites into my exposed skin, and the ground shakes as the sky opens up. We've separated ourselves into different buildings. Mine is a stone, three-story structure with a courtyard in the center. In the middle of the courtyard is a giant lake where water-based fae can paddle, swim, and recharge their magic. Fae go insane if we can't use our magic after too long, so all inmates have an hour every day to expend it.

I'm in my fae form three levels up, sitting on a bar of iron that juts out over the grotto. The water's inky surface ripples with each boom of thunder and pelt of rain. Splashes paint the inner walls of the grotto, disrupting the reflection of the black iron bars on its smooth embankments. The sight of the water stirs something deep inside me, a hollow ache at what it's lost.

Where are you?

I can feel him. As sure as I know the kiss of fire on my skin when I die, his presence stirs inside me, drawing me closer. My beast paces inside me, desperate to find Wilder. To keep him safe from this hydra.

To feel his arms around me again.

But first, I've got to make sure this monster can't hurt him. It's my fault Wilder is here. If something happens to him ...

"Checking out block C now. Over," Harmony's tinny voice breaks through my half-formed thought.

Above the din of the rain and wind, and the blare of the siren, I hear a commotion in the distance.

"What was that?" I reach for my radio.

"Came from your sector, Commander."

Rising from my crouch, I back along the edge of the plank until I reach the stairwell leading to the barred entrance. The ancient metal and oak door bares its splintered and rotted teeth to me, and the thin screech it emits grates on my nerves. The hairs on the back of my neck stand on end, but I force myself to ignore it.

"I'm on my way," I say into the radio.

If Noct knew about Wilder, she'd help me see him, even if it were a few minutes, but I can't put another friend at risk.

Never again.

I hurry down the long, narrow, black-tiled corridor, passing other inmates in their cells until I get to the corner where the prison's heartbeat is loudest. The first cell is silent, until a thin and low cry breaks from behind the steel bars, then another louder one. A half-dozen prisoners run past me, their boots and magic suppressant chains clanging on the metal stairs when they descend three flights to reach the ground level.

The corridor is a beehive of activity. Guards file out of other rooms to head toward the private sector. A few attendants join them as I skid to a stop at the end of the hallway that leads to where all hell has broken loose.

I squeeze through two male guards wearing blue shirts with an X emblem over the breast pocket. They pass me and head toward one of four cells near a steel door leading outside. Rising from my crouch, I back along the edge of the plank until I reach the stairwell leading to the barred door. It unlocks with my irises, allowing me to squeeze through.

Harmony is there, and she's holding onto the arm of a large female inmate who's attempting to escape during the commotion. The muscles on the prisoner's arms bulge, and the tendons in her neck strain when Harmony clamps the magical binding around her wrists.

Two male guards stand over a heap of bodies, kicking to turn over an inmate. But it isn't a convict.

Noct.

She screams, her voice like a trumpet of death. Blood pools from a jagged wound on her stomach, blackening her navy uniform. Writhing in agony, her shrieks claw at my eardrums, and I shove the guard away and kneel at Noct's side. I want to end her suffering as quick as possible, otherwise it could be another hour before she dies, so I do what any good commander would do. What any good friend would do.

I pull a lighter from my pocket, flick the wheel, and hold it to her sleeve. It catches on the thick material, the yellow-orange flame sputters out of the nozzle, and the fabric pops. My lighter gleams in the darkness, the small flame spreading across her clothes like a deep blue, licking snake. It engulfs her entire body, and within minutes, she's ash.

The horror-stricken faces of the guards turn to bewilderment as the ashes take shape. Not a single inmate makes a sound as they watch, wide-eyed, as Noct's body re-forms. Her pale flesh blisters, red, then dark, as the skin stretches over her form. The smell of burnt flesh permeates the air, and the ashes trail down her arms when she lifts her head. Her large grey eyes, the color of pewter, fix on mine.

"I'll never get used to this," she whispers as she scrambles to her feet, naked as the day she entered this world, and I toss her a pair of clothes from the pack on my back.

"You and me both." I grimace as I stand in front of her, trying to shield her from the open-mouthed shock of the strangers in the room.

She pulls them on with quick, efficient movement, and all the while the room stares, transfixed.

"Target spotted in Block B, moving in," Arwen calls.

Slipping the map of the prison out of my pocket, I search for the area on the grid, finding a room at the end of the row. "This way," I say to Harmony, who's still binding her prisoner with magic.

She nods, and we push through the crowd gathered at the entrance to the corridor.

"All right everyone, we'll regroup at the rendezvous point. Let's make it quick." I motion them along, and shepherd the bewildered prisoners out of our way and into the waiting hands of guards.

The corridor is dark, dimly lit by a few bulbs in each cell illuminating the bars. Metal clanks against metal whenever someone passes, echoing down the hall. Screams, moans, and laughter trail us as we hurry through the cellblock. We skirt a set of stairs, hug the wall around another block, and come to a stop at a locked door marked BLOCK B.

"I've been hit," Arwen's pained voice calls through the communicator. "Estimated exsanguination, three minutes."

I wince. That's a painful way to go. "Roger that," I answer as I flip the latch on the scanner. It flares as it scans my eyes, malfunctioning and searing my irises.

"Fuck!" I shout, slamming the lid and jumping back. Throwing my elbow over my eyes, I suck in deep breaths, counting to thirty. "Noct, can you open it?" My vision flashes red behind my closed lids, and I can't see a damn thing.

"It isn't working at all," she growls. "Won't even turn on now."

I lift my hand to the door and bend my fingers around it, seeking the tumblers by feeling alone. By the time the metal screeches and buckles, I've gained some of my sight back and forced the door to part, revealing another door beyond. I yank it open and duck through, not seeing the massive hole in the floor. I'm mid-shift to fly, but my wings catch on a jagged scrap of iron, shredding them like a hot knife through butter as I tumble several stories down. Shouts from Noct, Harmony, and Arwen ring out above me, their faint words broken by the wind blasting against my body.

Through my haze, I use my elbows and knees to slow my descent. Sharp, jagged edges tear through the fabric of my uniform as I skid across the twisted wall. My back slams into a concrete floor below me and I collapse with a groan. Something is broken, and my adrenaline surges. Resting against the wall, I pull out my communicator from a pocket in my uniform. Cursing the darkness, I squint and press my thumb to the glowing ring at the front. I shake the device, but nothing happens. It's dead.

Somewhere during the fall, I lost the backpack with extra clothing, a flashlight, and other supplies for surviving in hostile environments. It's going to be a long night.

Catching my breath, I slump against the wall, running through scenarios in my head. I can't see well, on account of both the darkness and my damaged eyesight. Who knows how far I fell, or where I'm even at?

The easiest thing would probably be to light myself on fire, resurrect, then climb my way out of here with a perfectly healthy body. After reaching into my pocket for the lighter, my fingers poke through a large hole.

Shit. Where ...

I groan. The damn thing is gone.

Feeling around for anything portable and sharp, I come up empty. There goes impaling myself to death. My breathing comes in desperate pants, and the only other sound is groaning metal, and far-away shrieks of agony from prisoners who no doubt have been caught by the hydra.

Gods, don't let that be Wilder.

My fingers feel for injuries, and come across a wet, tender gash in my leg. Below it is a jagged tear through my pants and the skin beneath. My jaw grinds as I palpate it, trying to check the extent of the damage. I could always yank the metal out and hope it nicks an artery.

Gripping the jagged metal fragment between my fingers, I take a shuddering breath and pull with all my might. A desperate howl rips its way out of me as pain crashes into me, followed by a wave of warmth that suggests something deep within me has been torn open. I gasp for breath as I fumble with the metal, accidentally dropping it into the dark depths below before I collapse, blood still pouring from my wound and my only chance at death now out of reach if this wound doesn't bleed me dry. I could be here for days.

My hand nudges a small, round bit of concrete and I grab onto it, feeling above my head for the slab of iron I know I'd felt just before I hit the ground. My palm meets the cool metal and I begin tapping the concrete against it, trying to make noise so the team can find me.

Tap. Tap. Tap.

The sound echoes through the space above me, but it still isn't enough to be heard over the bloodshed taking place in the main part of the building.

Fuck.

I shift into my phoenix form, hoping my body has repaired itself enough to allow me flight. The transition is excruciating; whatever damage took place in the fall is exacerbating existing injuries and, in all likelihood, giving me new ones.

Closing my eyes, I take a moment to compose myself. Then, spreading my wings as wide as I can with the space I have, I prepare to take flight, only to plummet down, down, down.

Disappearing into the darkness of the pit, something bands around my midsection, wrenching me from my free fall. The motion knocks the wind out of me, and I'm crushed against a broad chest. Still unable to see, I use my other senses as I shift back into my fae form.

The scent of mint and faraway seas comes to me seconds before I feel a warmth over my eyes and hear the crunching of glass. My lower lip trembles with emotion, cutting off my breath.

He's here.

Just as I know I'll rise again from the dead, so, too, do I know his scent.

Seizing my wrist before I can do more than gasp in surprise, he pulls me back to him, his nose nuzzling against my neck, the breath stirring against my pulse.

"Little Bird," he coos. He's the only person who gets to call me that. The sound is a mixture of heartache and disbelief, and I don't need to see him to know the pain we share.

2,000+ years ago

I'VE TRAVERSED this unforgiving landscape countless times, but this journey is different. With Wilder by my side, I'm both exhilarated and terrified. Bringing an outsider into Castanea is a risk I've never taken before. Before we get there, it's two days of the worst conditions you'll ever encounter, as The Wastelands were designed to keep my people safe from the werewolves who would stop at nothing to kill us for their cure.

The sandstorm rages on, whipping grains of sand into a frenzy that blinds and suffocates us. We've been walking for hours, and I can feel the grit grinding between my teeth. The wind howls like a beast, and the stinging sand scours my skin. But Wilder keeps up, never once faltering or complaining.

The blistering sun pounds down on the barren landscape, heating the ground until it's almost too hot to bear. Darkness descends, like an oppressive cloak that only brings with it a frigid chill on our sand-ravaged skin, our bodies pushed to the limits in this inhospitable expanse.

Finally, we reach a small cave carved into the side of a rocky face. It's a meager shelter, but it's better than nothing. I light a small fire, using my fae magic to protect it from the gusting winds. The warmth is a balm to our battered bodies, and we settle in for the night.

There's something so draining about spending the day traversing across scorching desert only to be freezing at night.

"Are you okay?" He pulls me close, and I press my face against his chest, shivering beneath the blanket that barely covers us both.

His arms are my sanctuary as I inhale his scent, like mint on the ocean breeze. I feel myself melting into his embrace as though he is not only my escape from the cold evening desert air, but a destination. Home. His touch is more comforting than any drug, and I never want to let go.

I've always been possessive of him. My phoenix, too. She rears her head any time someone lingers a little too long in his direction.

"Better with you." I peer up at him, brushing a smudge of dirt from his brow. His eyes are like the color of the deep sea, where creatures with bioluminescence glow in the darkness, and the water is a mysterious blend of navy blue and emerald green. It should feel unnatural to have his gaze on me, but it has only ever felt right. "Usually, I have to do this by myself."

Our bodies are crushed together, my heart pounding against his chest in a fierce rhythm. I can feel the heat emanating from his skin, enveloping me in warmth. I'm desperate to kiss him, but I restrain myself, scared of the repercussions.

I may not be his anchor, but I can't help the longing that fills my chest. We've never had sex, but I've thought about it. He's starred in every single one of my fantasies, and then some.

The steady thump of his heart under my ear soothes me, and mine beats in time with his.

To fae, saving yourself for a mate isn't an unusual thing. Even if it takes thousands of years for you to cross yours, if you're lucky enough to have one, you almost always will know it ahead of time.

I'm the last of our kind to not have a mate at all. But if I can just spend time in his orbit, basking in the bliss that it is to be near him ... it might be enough.

Wilder's fingers trace the shell bracelet around my wrist, a comfortable gesture he does every time he lies next to me. In turn, my fingers find their way under his shirt, resting on the elevated area near his heart. I like being close to the space beneath his ribcage where one of my own feathers was imbedded during a ritual. It now sits inside his skin like a raised tattoo.

Fae feathers can bring people back to life if they're killed, provided they aren't children, so mine will keep Wilder safe. A phoenix feather can grant anyone immortality, and I'd given him mine in exchange for the beautiful shell bracelet that sits around my wrist. He'd told me that the gift of a shell from a merfae is the sign of a vow, but he still hasn't got around to telling me what his promise was.

He rests his chin against the top of my head, his breath heavy and deep, as if every part of him is consumed with worry for me. His warmth radiates through me, and I can feel the intensity of his emotion as he whispers, "You don't have to do this alone anymore. I'll come to you. If I'd known it was like this for you ..."

I laugh softly, but the sound is stifled by the weight of the moment. His grip tightens on my chin as he lifts it up, so that our eyes lock. His gaze burns into me and I can feel the fierce commitment behind his words: "I want to."

"Maybe we can take turns." I smile up at him. "I've spent my whole life below ground. I want to see the rest of the world."

He grins at me, the corners of his lips quirking up slightly. "I'd be happy to show you," he says, his voice low and silky. "But first..." He leans in, his breath hot against my cheek as he brushes his lips against mine.

I melt into the kiss, every fiber of my being surrendering to his touch. His lips are soft and insistent as he deepens the kiss. The warmth emanating from his body intensifies as he pulls me closer to him, molding our bodies together until there is no space between us.

I moan into his mouth, my body responding involuntarily as he runs his hands down my back and over my hips. I feel a hunger building inside of me, an urge to take him deeper, to feel every inch of him inside of me.

For months, he's been my only friend outside of Castanea. My secret. The one my beast craves to make her own whenever he's nearby. Our magic intertwines, feeling so right. This.

I want this, forever.

But merfae only sleep with their anchors.

As though the thought reaches him the same time it reaches me, he pulls away, all my senses still alive with the sensation of being his. With a low, throaty purr he utters the words, "I've been waiting an eternity to do that."

"What took you so long?" I grin against him, burrowing further into his chest. Though I already know the reason. I am not his anchor. We must remain content with our friendship.

"I must've been lost in my own kind of wasteland, waiting for you."

Present Day

A WASTELAND. That's what it's felt like since he's been gone.

A firm hand strokes my hair, his touch reverent, seeking. "You're hurt," he whispers into my ear before he places his lips there to deliver a lace of heat.

"Wilder ...?" His name is nothing but the faintest of whimpers. "Am I dead? Truly?" It's the only explanation.

His chuckle reverberates against my chest. "No, Little Bird. You're in the basement level of the prison. Someone's beast is on the loose, but you probably already know that. That's why you're here, isn't it?"

I nod, unable to muster any more words. Tears fall in earnest as I wrap my arms around him. He holds me, pressing gentle kisses against my forehead as I sink to my knees, my injuries not even a factor, but my pain soul deep.

"I'd heard about the fierce little warrior they send in to eliminate dangerous targets. You don't know how proud I am of you." Wilder takes a deep, steadying breath. "I thought you still hated me ..."

The quiet admission is tinged with such agony that the balance inside me shifts.

"Never in my life have I hated you." My voice breaks. "They wouldn't let me come see you. I promise, I try every week." Not even my status as Commander of our most elite squadron gained me entrance, and not for a lack of trying. Inmates don't get letters here. And only mates can get a visitor's pass.

"Every week?" he asks, incredulous. "I've been in here nearly two hundred years, Morte."

"I know." Silence stretches between us, an overwhelming sadness decaying inside my chest. It threatens to drain the life out of my soul. Until six months ago, I'd come daily. That was before I'd made the squadron.

Wilder pulls me into his lap, the brush of our magic tangling together, embracing at last.

"What time is it?" I ask.

He stills. "Um, just past midnight, I think. They don't give us clocks in our cells." *Another way to make them pay for their crimes.*

"Seventy-thousand, four-hundred and forty-six days." I breathe, but barely. The walls I've built around me crumble in his arms. That's how long I've gone without his touch. The number on the other side of it, infinite.

Vita damnationem is his sentence. That's the rest of his life, and for an immortal, it's forever. And it's all my fault.

I'd been so reckless. He shouldn't be here, rotting away.

Grief clings to me so tight, I choke on it. I've known this man since I first ventured out of Castanea as a rebellious twenty-something, thousands of years ago. We weren't allowed to leave, but I did. I sneaked through the watering hole portal to the surface, traversed the barren landscape, and bumped into the most stunning man I'd ever seen at a beautiful waterfall.

His silver wings were tucked against his back, but his long, dark hair whipped wildly in the light, spring breeze.

The water cascaded down his strong shoulders in silvery ribbons. He dove off the edge of the rocks and into the pool of fresh water below without so much as a splash to mark his entrance. For hours, he swam back and forth, diving and swimming underwater for remarkable lengths of time like some kind of creature from a fairytale. And to me, he really was. I'd only known about the fae in Castanea.

For hours, I watched him scale the rocky face and dive off, never revealing myself to him. It wasn't until later he admitted he'd known I was there the whole time. Merfae have a fae-like appearance as well as silver wings and gills at will. Rows of razor-sharp teeth appear when he's fighting. Eyes the color of a stormy sea, he stripped me bare before I stood a chance.

"What happened to your sight?" He caresses my brow. Merfae can see in the dark just as well as in the light thanks to a preternatural form of echolocation that works on both land and in the water.

I can't make out his features, but I can tell it's pitch dark down here. The power must've gone out. A steady drip of water in the space tells me he's at least got access to some form of way to release his magic.

"My eyes were seared by a malfunctioning scanner, and then I tripped down a hole and ended up here."

"I'm sorry," he whispers. "Though I can't say I'm upset you found your way back to me. I've missed you."

"I still carry your shell."

"After all this time?"

"Always." I lift my wrist, waving my hand over the dark, heart-shaped glass, lighting it up so he can see the exquisite shell inside. He'd given it to me the day we met.

I've never met another merfae on the mainland aside from Wilder's parents. The rest of his order prefer to live deep in the Triune Sea. Every fourth Sunday, though, I visit his mom and dad. Without him around, they get lonely.

They spend most of their time in their merfae form, living beneath a shipwreck at the North end of Convectus. All I have to do is park my toes in the sand and wait. Within an hour, they're joining me at shore, their merfae forms shifting into fae while we catch up. I like to drop off a type of syrup I make from the sap of a tree near the water-fall in Castanea in exchange for their company. A small sliver of famil-iarity to get me by.

Wilder hoists me up, cradling me in his massive arms and carries me closer to the sound of trickling water. "Here, Little Bird." He nestles me closer to his chest as we're plunged into water.

I gasp from the cold, clawing at his arms to draw heat to me. He chuckles.

"I'm going to heal you now."

Nodding, I cling to him as he presses a kiss to each of my eyes, his saliva always having had a healing effect on me. His faint outline becomes clearer until I'm met with his steely grey irises, and I begin to weep, the sight of him almost too much to bear. Long, dark hair falls in damp waves over his shoulders and down his back, past the waistband of his soaking wet prison-issued uniform. High cheekbones and a sharply angled jaw give him a harsh, unforgiving beauty I know all too well. I want to run my fingers over his features, trace the arrow of his eyebrows, caress the angular lines of his chin. I want to kiss him but settle for squeezing him harder and placing my head against his chest as silent tears spill down my cheeks.

His lips meet my neck, heat searing me as he whispers against my skin. "Don't cry, Little Bird."

By the Gods, do I cry. For the man I love more than life. For my best friend. For the years that have separated us.

When he'd been sentenced, they had to sedate me for a month. And when I woke, all I could do was shriek and tear into anyone who got in my way when I tried to get him out. I'd spent fifteen years suspended in a cryochamber as a result. There, I underwent mandatory intensive rehabilitation, therapy, and mental health counseling to help repro-gram me. When I got out, I began my attempts to peacefully see him. I'd come a long way from being that broken girl, watching as they slap his magic suppressant bracelet on him as they haul him out of the room.

And in mere hours, I'm back to being that blubbering mess again.

Wilder continues healing my injuries with his kiss, the warmth doing more than just restoring my health. Merfae have something in their saliva that helps, even without using magic. By the time he reaches the gash on my leg, we're both panting.

Our whole lives, stolen glances, tense exchanges, and heated make-out sessions were the extent of our adventures in sexual frustration together.

And because Wilder's likelihood of meeting his anchor while cordoned off in a prison basement is next to nothing, he'll remain a virgin.

I'm a terrible person because the thought of that isn't as unsettling as it should be.

Even now, I curl around him, tightening my hold at the thought anyone else would lay claim to someone I've spent my entire life loving.

Wilder rocks me, shushing the sobs that wrack my body. I'm selfish, knowing what's likely taking place a hundred stories above us. I should be busy tracking down the escaped inmate, not holed up in a cell, nursing my wounds. But being in his arms is a sanctuary I can't stop seeking.

Loving him is my truth, even if it comes with a world of hurt and sorrow. There's never been another for me. His friendship, for all the years I had it, seems so fleeting in comparison to the painful longing I feel now.

I cursed the gods every night for not giving me to him. How can they look at what we have and not think it destined? That our two hearts beat in harmony, echoing the same melody? I feel his own deep-seated grief like it were my own.

Because it is.

"I made a friend down here," he whispers against my cheek.

A pang of agony takes my breath. "A friend?"

"He's a seer named Mordecai." His voice rumbles from his chest.

"Is he more than a friend?" I'm afraid to ask, but I must know. My heart can't take it.

"No." He cups my cheek, using his body heat to warm me in the freezing water. "I've never desired another. Ever, Little Bird."

The vice around my chest eases as I draw in a ragged breath and release it. "Okay." I breathe. "Did he see something?"

His hands thread through my hair, gripping me tight to him. "He's the one who told me you'd be here today. I didn't believe him."

26

"Did he say anything else?" I crane my neck to see him.

Grief mars his features. "A lot of stuff, actually." He sighs. "He was raving mad by the time he finished."

"Like?"

Wilder carries me out of the water and over to his stone cot. He unfolds his wings and tucks me into his side while we lie down.

"He said today would be the best and the worst day of our lives."

Silence stretches between us, and I inhale his scent deep into my lungs. "I think I can agree with that," I whisper. My hand rests on his chest, and I feel the steady thrum of his heart and the softness of his feathers at my side.

It's the best day because I'm back in his arms, and the worst day, knowing it won't last. Wilder says nothing, but his body tenses when I offer no more words. He knows I'm referring to the truth neither of us wants to say out loud.

His head lifts from its cradle on the arch of his wings and he stares at me with a desolate gaze. His strong hands grip my arms, his voice gruff. "Little Bird, I have something to tell you, and you're probably going to hate me for it."

My heart thrashes in my chest, though I go preternaturally still.

"But please know, I only found out moments before my sentencing, and I didn't tell you because I wanted to spare you the agony."

He's found his mate. Oh gods. "Wilder, you're scaring me," I breathe. Nausea roils through me, traveling up my throat and I have to bite my fist to keep it in. A choked sob escapes between my fingers.

The sound of my heartbreak echoes through the space so loud, it startles him. I'm so lost in my grief, it takes me a moment to realize through the roar in my head that it isn't me, but something else.

Screeching metal and explosive crashes come from the hallway, and it's only then I realize Wilder is on his feet, dragging me towards the water. He snaps his wings open wide, blocking me from whatever's coming through.

"Close your eyes and hold onto me," he whispers fiercely. His arms wrap around me and shield me with the enormous plumage.

"No, Wilder! I can't die!" I shriek, trying to hurl myself over his shoulders to see who, or what's coming. Though, I have a feeling I already know.

He squeezes me tight, my body shuddering as his wings collide and encircle me in darkness.

Inhuman wails of agony meet our ears just before the hydra barrels through the cell, taking out the four-foot-thick door and almost the entire hallway-facing wall. Before one of its giant heads can reach us, Wilder takes flight with a furious roar, arms banded around me, leaving the carnage below.

One of the hydra's heads snaps through the air and bites down onto Wilder's leg before we're too far away, and another slices into my torso. Agony cuts through me, carving deep at the heart of me. With the last of his energy, Wilder hurls me towards the pool and away from the bloodbath so he can grapple with the hydra. I can't correct myself in time, and I scream as I plummet into the water, watching as the beast tears into Wilder with its razor-sharp teeth.

I fight my way to the surface, lungs burning, straining towards him. Bleeding from the gash in my abdomen, my pain leaves me, and only the knowledge that Wilder is caught in the hydra's crushing maw keeps me company.

I scream, trying to surface but choke with water and blood. If I can just make it a little further, I can try to save him. I'm wailing, calling out through the water as he's dragged away. Grief and fear smother me, sawing me in two as I kick through the water blindly. It's so murky with blood, I can't see.

My only thought as darkness creeps along the edges of my vision is thank the gods I gave him my feather. Because a world without Wilder isn't a world I want to live in.

CHAPTER THREE

MORTE

The heat.

It overwhelms me. For millennia, fire had been my constant companion, but now I feel the lick of its kiss, the scald of its power against my skin. I can hear the crackle of it, smell the sickening stink of burning flesh and bone.

For the first time in my life, smoke chokes me, and my cry comes out as more of a bark and less of a plea. Tears roll down my cheeks as I fight for air, for life, for something so foreign to me.

Here I am on all fours, gasping in the dark, with no idea where I am or how I got here. The acrid haze burns my nose and throat and causes my eyes to water. Sucking in a deep breath causes me to cough. Hard.

This place that smells of sulfur and ash and slowly building rot—a death smell that builds as I struggle to rake in another breath. My hands claw at the rough stone beneath me, seeking help for something, anything that will get me out of this dark place.

Through the acrid haze, I drag myself forward, calling out Wilder's name. The clang of metal-on-metal jars me, and that's when I notice that someone—something—has caught me. I kick out, trying to free myself, but they cleave tight to my flesh, their touch blistering.

Reaching down to pry them off me, my nails meet steel.

A manacle?!

"Wilder!" I croak, ending on a cough.

The darkness presses closer, further consuming every inch of me. There's no answer. No late-arriving hero to save me from where I am. No respite from the burning, blistering heat and smoke.

"Will you shut up already?" A voice like iced honey slips into the space. Despite his poisoned words, they wrap around me, as though tasting the fear from my cries. The air displaces as though someone's approaching. "My, my. This is a first. He's going to love this. A noisy goose!"

Oh, my gods. The hydra is keeping me prisoner.

Slowly, I twist my gaze up. In the haze, a figure crouches before me, pale and muscled and nude but for a pair of heavy, leathery wings tipped with blood red talons.

"No one's coming for you, pigeon, so accept it, and move on."

I still. This isn't the hydra. Who the fuck is this? Another inmate? Maybe the seer? The creature who spoke draws me closer, though I can't make out any more of his details.

His laugh, cold and cruel, echoes through the chamber.

"Who are you?" I croak. "What have you done with Wilder?"

"Oh, he was a fine specimen of a male, but alas, it was not meant to be." My captor pouts. "Pity that."

A vice squeezes my chest, cutting off my air supply. "Was?" Tears prick at my eyes. "No. No. No. Where is he?!" I lunge for him, catching a brief flash of iced irises in a face illuminated by the fires behind us.

He ducks out of the way as though he expected it.

"Tsk tsk," he runs a talon down the side of my face. "If you want me, you've got to earn it, little goose."

The cold of his nail sears into my bare skin, granting me a tiny reprieve from the miserable heat.

Unbidden, I chase his touch, desperate for more cooling relief. "Please," I breathe. "Where is Wilder?"

"He died."

I fully expected this but suspecting it and hearing it confirmed are two very different experiences. Tears brim in my eyes, a soundless sob the only other indication of my grief. "My feather." I reach for the male's ankle. "He has a feather."

A taloned hand grips my chin, bringing me close enough to see the malicious glee in the male's glittering eyes. A bare whisper of a smile touches his full, bowed lips, as though savoring the taste of my misery. "That he does, pet."

What I thought was pale skin isn't. It's more translucent, almost blue, with a luminescent sheen, so at odds with the flames licking at his body. His touch eases, though the fierceness of it remains. Runes dance and swirl across his cheeks, forehead, and chest. He's a peculiar creature, one that I haven't seen before.

Fae, I think, but his order? No clue.

Dark blue hair falls into his eyes, and he peers at me through a fringe of black lashes. He gives me a devilish grin, as if he knows something that I don't. He toys with my desperation, a cruel game for his own amusement.

"Where are you keeping him?" I glare.

If he died, then my feather revived him. *So where the fuck is he?*

"Oh, he isn't here, little gull." He rakes a talon across my bottom lip, and I recoil back.

"Stop calling me bird names," I growl. "And tell me where they're keeping him."

He throws his head back and laughs, a deep guttural chuckle that sends chills down my spine. Releasing me, he steps back, rising to his full height. As a female fae, I'm average height at six foot six inches. But this male? He's almost got an entire foot on me.

"It's time you and I deal, little grouse. I tell you where Wilder is, and I get something in return." He licks his lips, desire for something more than knowledge and power burning in his eyes.

"What do you want?" I narrow my tear-stained eyes. With him this close to me, the smoke seems to have dissipated some.

His gaze trails over me, from the top of my head to the tips of my toes before he grins and moves back to capture my stare. "Your loyalty. You will help me in whatever way I require, for as long as I require it."

"What? No. I owe nothing to no one."

"Very well." He turns, his giant wings caressing me as he turns away.

"Wait!" I shout. "Aren't we negotiating?"

He pauses his retreat, and a tail I hadn't noticed before flicks with intrigue. The male spins around, and I get a full view of his very naked body. Most of it, anyway. All the good parts hidden by the smoke.

Lean muscle cords ripple beneath pale blue skin and his wings stretch out, black and iridescent like a raven's feathers. When his gaze catches mine again, it has changed from devious to something more animalistic.

"Negotiate?" He watches me take him in and smiles, a slow, lazy smirk that spells trouble. "As soon as you stop ogling me, we may begin."

My cheeks burn, but I don't look away. Not this time. Looking directly into his eyes, I say, "What *else* do you want in return for telling me where they're keeping Wilder?"

He assesses me again, his attention on my form like a caress. "Oh," he purrs, moving in quickly. "You have something I most desire indeed."

"What?"

His tail strikes out fast but slows its ascent as soon as it meets my skin, a careful, sensual brush. It sweeps up my hip before dipping down to my center.

I rear back, scuffing my palms on the rough stone beneath me. "Get that thing away from me."

It wraps its way around my bicep, yanking me closer. "Tell me, little sparrow, how old are you?"

I grunt as I try to escape his hold, but I don't answer him. Because honestly, I don't know. For a long time, I restarted counting with each rebirth. I'm way over a couple thousand years.

He eyes me, curiosity brewing in his gaze. "Interesting," he murmurs, his voice low. He leans closer and I feel the coolness of his skin in the tiny distance between us. How is he so cold down here? His nostrils flare, and he inhales. "How?"

"How what?"

"No one has bedded you?"

I recoil. "What?"

"You're intact. How?"

How in the gods does he know that? I can feel my cheeks flush. "None of your gods damned business," I hiss, yanking myself out of his hold.

"Pretty bird," he purrs, kneeling next to me.

I scramble back until the chain pulls taught and I can't go any further. The male crawls towards me, his hand branding my skin. It trails up my calf, over the tops of my knees, before he grips both of my thighs and pries them open. Attempting to kick away is futile.

He drops his head, pressing his nose to my center, and inhaling. Thank the gods someone thought to dress me before shackling me here. Wherever here is.

"What the fuck is wrong with you?" I shriek, trying to twist away.

"Yes, yes." He pulls back, kneeling before me. His eyes have taken on a glazed quality. "I think we'll keep you."

"What? No. No one is *keeping* me." Though if I'm being honest, the coolness of his body has made me less miserable down here. "I demand you take me to General Risç, now."

He cocks his head. "Who now?"

"General Risç, head of the royal guard?" My brows bunch.

"I know no such General," he scoffs. "I'm the head of the royal guard."

My pulse quickens. "What happened to him?" Am I living in an alternate universe?

"Don't know who you're talking about, pet, but you can forget about him. I guarantee I'm much prettier to look at." He preens.

"You're insane," I blurt.

"Perhaps so," he murmurs, lifting my arm to inspect me. His eyes spark with mischief. "You've got to be to lead his army."

His army?

Before I can ask, he continues, "Why are you looking for a General Risç when you're in love with someone else?"

"The general is my boss, nothing more. Please have someone get him for me."

"You're boring me." He heaves a great sigh before he perks up. "You should remove your clothes."

"What is your problem?" I hiss. "If you can't help me, then get me your boss!"

He throws his head back and laughs; the sound echoing through the chamber. "He answers to no one, least of all you."

I shake my head. I've personally met both the high king and queen, and while they're not fae you want to mess with, they're generally fair and willing to listen to their people. "If you tell High Queen Lana that Morte needs to speak with her, I'm certain she can make herself available."

His attention snaps back to me. "Who did you say?"

"Well, if Lana isn't available, you could ask for High King Finian?"

He blinks. "Why would they be here? I'm the first to know about all arrivals, even those merely passing through." He curses under his breath something that sounds like, *fucking feathers.*

"Well, I don't expect the king and queen to be at the penitentiary, not with the escaped inmate on the loose, but you could get me an audience and we'll have this all cleared up. I'd hate for you to get in trouble for keeping me prisoner."

"Who escaped?" His wings ruffle behind him and his spine goes rigid.

"Noah Tackwater?"

"Have you gone mad? There's no prisoner by that name here."

My brows furrow, and I rack my brain. Am I getting his name wrong? Oh, wait— "Sometimes they call him No-No? He's a hydra?"

"Just where do you think you are?"

"The prison?"

"Which prison?"

What is this guys' deal? "Bedlam Penitentiary?"

34

A look of pity settles over his features. "You, my naive little bird, aren't in Bedlam."

"Where in the gods name am I?"

A grin crosses his face. "That'll cost you."

I let out a frustrated shriek. "I don't have anything to bargain with!"

His eyes flash dangerously. "Oh, but you do," he purrs, rolling back until he's seated on the ground, knees supporting his forearms. "I'll tell you what. You want to know where Wilder is?"

"Of course!"

"And you want to know where you are?"

"We've established that already."

"I'll tell you both in exchange for your virginity."

My eyes widen. "You're joking," I barely manage to choke out. "I'm not bargaining what's between my thighs."

"No? How about what's between mine?" He grins, fluffing his wings and dropping his knees so he's bared to me.

I shutter my eyes and turn my head quickly. I've seen plenty of naked people—mostly during battle, or when one of my phoenix sisters regenerate. But I've never seen an erect male before.

"That's quite enough," I snap. "You can keep whatever you have between your legs. You'll tell me what I want to know, and no more."

He maneuvers himself so he's lying on his side, one knee up, still showing off all his goods. "Do they not negotiate where you're from?"

"Do they not wear clothes where you're from?"

"They do. I just find I look better without them; wouldn't you agree?"

I don't deign to give him a response to that. "Here's what I'm willing to give you in exchange for information about where Wilder is and where I am. A kiss on the hand is all you'll get."

He huffs a laugh. "You're going to have to do better than that, dodo."

"Did you just call me a dodo?"

"Peculiar creatures. I'd visited the Earth realm eons ago and found them rather delicious."

My mouth hangs open. "Those are extinct."

"Yes, yes. I was quite sad when I'd ran out."

"Is that what you plan to do with me?"

He favors me a hooded gaze. "Eat you? Why, you offering?" He runs a claw up the seam of my leg. "Savor the finest this plump little morsel has to offer?" He cups me between my thighs. "Let me sample you?"

I squirm out of his grasp. "No!" I shout at him.

He assumes a softer demeanor and pulls back from me. "Alright, I won't touch you there ever again. Only when I've got you on your knees, begging for it."

I frown at him.

He reaches up and runs a finger along my jawline. "If you're going to win this game, Morte, you'll have to learn to negotiate a better deal. You won't get much in exchange for a kiss on the hand."

I roll my eyes at his bravado. "What else do you want?"

"Your loyalty, my little loon. That's all I need." He takes my hand and brushes a gentle kiss against it, the simple act sending a shiver through my entire body. Goosebumps line my arm, and he grins. "Promise me you'll let no one else take your virginity but me."

"I'm not promising you that."

He sighs. "How about this. If you choose to give someone *else* your virginity, you'll let me watch."

My eyebrows shoot up and I pull my hand away. I hadn't realized he was still holding it. "You must think I'm a fool if you think I'd agree to something like that."

He grins lopsidedly, his eyes heavy with desire. "Here's my final offer: If you choose not to give me your virginity, and you want to give it to someone else while here, you will let me watch. Fair enough?"

My desire to stay away from him wars with my curiosity. "Only while here?"

"Only while here." He splays his hand, gesturing to the area.

I place mine in his. "You have yourself a deal."

He tsks. "That's not how we make deals here."

"How do you make deals here ... wherever here is?"

"We seal it with a kiss."

"You're full of shit."

"Not likely. I have a date in the king's chamber soon."

I open and close my mouth several times, gaping like a fish, but nothing comes out.

"You've got to actually press those lips to mine for a kiss, love bird. It has to be a real kiss, with tongue, and must last a minimum of twenty seconds to activate our deal."

"That's absurd."

"Never been kissed?"

"Of course, I have."

"Good, then you know how it works. Now come here," he purrs.

My heart races and I know I'm going to regret this, but I lean in and place my lips to his, feeling the coolness beneath me. He wraps his arm around my waist and hoists me into his lap, deepening the kiss. My head spins in a mix of pleasure and panic. Every nerve ending sparks and ignites, and I can't breathe, can't think. His tongue slips into my mouth, and I forget where we are and why I'm here, and I moan before realizing what I'm doing.

His length nudges at the seam of my pants, and before I can do anything embarrassing like press closer, he breaks from the kiss, dragging my bottom lip between his teeth before letting it go.

"Deal sealed," he whispers against my lips.

Magic tingles between us and my breath comes out in short, strangled pants. Heat rises in my cheeks as I scramble off his lap.

"Now where the hell is Wilder?" I use the back of my ash-coated hand to wipe my mouth.

"He's at Bedlam Penitentiary. Your feather brought him back to life."

All the air escapes my lungs. I'd already known it should've, but hearing confirmation of my feather saving him gives me immense relief. I brace a hand against the wall, tilting my head to the ceiling to survey my surroundings.

"And where in the gods am I?"

"Aggonid's realm."

The underworld?

A terrified shriek rips from my throat as my stomach lurches and I stumble backwards, the heavy metal manacle around my ankle clanging noisily. The fire and ash in this realm seem to come alive, closing in on me like a suffocating blanket of smoke. The heat sears my skin, singeing every inch of me where the flames brush against my body. I'm paralyzed by fear and dread, unable to escape this consuming inferno.

38

CHAPTER FOUR

MORTE

From far away, I hear a woman screaming. Screams in human movies are always shrieks and yells—and everyone can recognize them. But mine is different. It's deeper, hoarser, and rougher, as though my throat is being torn out of my body. It echoes around the cavern walls, bouncing off the hard surfaces. My vision becomes a blur, and I stumble forward where everything turns to night.

My stomach twists in knots of nausea, and I fall to my knees. Hands clammy, I slide on the rough stone beneath me, but then I clutch onto something soft and scented.

A flower.

Not just any flower, but one that tugs at my memory. *I was given one of these before.*

And suddenly, I'm standing in the middle of a meadow filled with flowers, right on the ledge of the sea as one of the sweetest sounds calls for me from below. Like pure notes flowing from a flute in an orchestra. It calms me, soothing my worry and fear like a comforting blanket. Is that a Sea Serenade? Those plants are native to Bedlam. The air in front of me ripples, and flashes of memories fill my head: *Wilder and the Hydra. My Feather.*

The deal.

The air turns sour then—the sweet scent of flowers becoming the coppery tang of blood.

I wake on a scream. It's the kind that forces out against your will, sends you crashing to your knees, and has your mind racing in circles, trying to make sense of why it's happening.

And I do understand.

I'm in Aggonid's Realm.

Hell.

Nausea climbs my throat, and I wretch giant heaving sobs that have me shrieking to the cavern above. The stone walls, like the color of coal, rise toward a towering ceiling. Gashes streak the rock with orange and ruby, and smoke billows from the fissures. A massive lava river carves through the center of the cave, glistering saffron where it flows over an island of broken white marble.

My wings deploy on a quiet whoosh, and they ache as though confused at their own mortality.

Mortality.

Now that's a word I understand all too well. I'm not supposed to stay dead. Phoenix fae come back from their ashes. But here, there's no promise of resurrection, only an unknown abyss of darkness and fear.

And right now, fear wins.

The blood on my feathers is thick and sticky as my wings flutter weakly, gathering the ash of the fire below and stitching it together like a tapestry of pain and regret. Fear is a heavy weight; it takes all my strength I have to move at all.

But it's the guilt that consumes me.

I didn't get my prison in life, so now, I'm getting it afterwards. It's no less than what I deserve. But Wilder is still stuck inside his because of me, so I'll do what I can to make things right.

Slowly, I rise on unsteady feet, my body trembling with the searing pain that burns its way through my veins and the marks of death on my body. But it's not really death, is it?

It's anti-life. It's terror and nightmares and everything I knew but can never be again.

And Wilder? He's not here.

It fills me with as much sorrow as it does joy.

From that thought, tears cascade down my face in a bittersweet and desperate mix of remorse and relief. I stand here, terror-stricken, and uncertain, my wings spread wide as the darkness consumes me.

Through the haze in front of me, a figure appears, but they're too obscured by smoke to make out.

"Hello?" I call out.

"I wanted to see what the fuss was all about," a feminine voice replies. "You've sure got my brother worked up."

"Who are you?"

She steps into the light of a flame, and I can make out her features —a face like a porcelain doll, with the same shimmery blue skin as the man I made a deal with. Her gilded runes glow brightly against her skin, just like her brother's. Only she wears clothes: a simple tunic, and matching trousers with little silver filigreed swirls along the edging.

"Irid." She props herself against the wall, the flames dancing over her sleek form. They do nothing to harm her, just as they wouldn't hurt me.

"Are you here to release me?"

Her laughter titters the air like a symphony of bells. "Release you? No, sweetheart, I'm here to make sure you stay. My brother has the habit of breaking pretty things, and through a cruel twist of fate, it wouldn't work out in my favor this time. I'm here to make sure you stay here, no matter what."

Yeah, that won't be happening. I take a deep breath, desperate for the courage to face this unknown future.

"What do you want from me?"

"Well, Morte," she says slowly, her eyes surveying me in an appraising manner. "First, I'm going to need you to get cleaned up."

A wave of her hand and suddenly, I'm in a steaming bath of hot water.

"Then," she continues, her lips curling into a smile, "we talk business."

I'm too shocked to have the sense to cover myself from her searing gaze. She inclines her head just as a bar of soap drops into the tub.

"Why can't I use my magic, but you can?"

She raises a brow. "I'm not a prisoner. You are."

My teeth clench as I scrub the blood from under my fingernails, trying to ease the tension in my body.

"You and I both know I don't belong here," I hiss. "I'm a phoenix fae."

When she doesn't respond, I dunk my head under the water, bubbles spilling out from the sides of my mouth.

"Ah," she says when I resurface, her voice laced with amusement. "That's a good point. You had a tether to the world, didn't you?"

I pause soaping up my arm to look at her. "Tether?"

"If you happened to die when that tether was severed," she shrugs, "well, it makes sense why you'd find a one-way ticket to the underworld."

I frown, the implications of her words sinking in. "So, you're saying I'm actually dead? For good?" Part of me hoped I'd been dreaming this entire time, or that someone was playing a cruel trick on me. The longer I'm here, the more that notion slips through my fingers.

And if my soul is here, and I feel the bite of flames against my skin, does this mean my body is here, too?

"Dead, dead, dead." She nods, her expression a little unhinged as she braids her waist-length hair while sitting on the edge of the tub.

For millennia, I worried the gods would call me home. Maybe the myths aren't just legends after all.

"Who dressed me when I arrived?" I never regenerate with clothes.

"One of the minions, I'm sure."

Irid pokes a finger into the water, swirling it around, and I watch as it creates a little tornado. All the soot, grime, and blood get caught in it, funnel into the air, and evaporate on a puff. She reaches into a

42

tiny pouch at her belt line, pulling out a vial, uncorks it, and pours the contents into the water.

Before I can ask what the hell she just put in there, she volunteers, "You stink. This will make you smell pretty."

I narrow my eyes at her. "For what? I'll just smell nasty as soon as I get chained back to the ground."

"You're not going back there." She rises. "I'm moving you into a nicer place."

"What will this cost me?"

She grins. "You're learning."

With a snap of her fingers, the tub disappears along with the water, and I spill onto the ground, sopping wet, naked, and sputtering. She tosses a bundle at my feet.

"Dry off and put these on."

Irid leans against the stone wall, watching as I dress. My cheeks heat under her perusal, her attention less clinical and more curious.

"Tell me, why is your hair straight and the thatch between your thighs curly?"

"What?" I yank the skirt on, cheeks burning.

"Well?" She raises an eyebrow. "I'm not asking out of prying. It's a viable question. Most fae have the same hair texture between the two, but you have ... variations."

"Ask the gods," I mutter. Her tail trails up my leg, and I kick it away, smacking her with a vicious glare. "You do that again, and I'll cut it off."

She raises her hands, her eyes dancing with glee. "And the kitten has claws. Who knew? You'll need them here," she sing-songs.

I pull the tank top over my bare breasts, not missing the way her eyes rove over them. They're bigger than hers, though I'm not proud of that. These just get in my way.

"No underthings?" I hiss.

She hums. "Mmm, no. I quite like you like this." Her hand reaches for my hair, and I slap it away.

"Keep your paws off me."

She laughs. "No wonder he likes you so much."

My eyes narrow. "What's that supposed to mean?"

"Well, you're obviously not like the other fae. He likes your spirit, your wildness—your refusal to be tamed."

"Or what's between my thighs," I mutter as I follow her out of the cavern.

Our footsteps sound down the passage, echoing off the stone walls until we reach another intersection. The exit opens into a vast, dark forest. A chill runs through me at the thought of what could be hiding in the trees. These aren't like the ones in Castanea, where gentle fae put their sleeping babies to bed inside treehouses and curl up to read a book by the fae flies dancing amongst the canopies.

"Where are all the other inmates?" I ask, my whisper a frightened hush on the air.

"It's not like the other realms, Morte. This one is for the truly terrible—the ones who have committed such heinous crimes that even the gods won't forgive." Her icy eyes gleam in the moonlight as she looks me up and down. "The others are out there—" She nods towards the forest. "It's difficult to find your way through the woods without a guide."

Grief nearly saws me in half. I *am* a monster. Part of me always knew it, that I was capable of terrible things, but having done them and facing the repercussions almost has me crashing to my knees.

"Where are you taking me?"

She smiles. "Your room."

My steps falter. "You haven't told me what it'll cost me yet."

The woman turns around, her mouth set in a grim line. "Come with me, and let's see what we can agree upon?"

I follow her into a decrepit shack at the edge of the forest and she ushers me into a small room. Nails are missing from the walls, which are made from weathered wood, and a single cot rests in the corner. I can smell that someone spent a long time chained there recently, and I'm troubled by both the stench and the implications.

I'm about to ask what she wants from me when the familiar weight of the manacle latches onto my ankle once again.

A groan rumbles in my chest, and I plop onto the bed, the mattress lumpy and riddled with claw marks. Better than a cave floor, I suppose. But it's still unbearably warm.

Each cold link in my shackles digs into my skin as I shift on my knees. "Will I always have to be chained up?"

Irid runs her fingers along the braid that hangs down her back. Five red ribbons are woven into the braid, and each one has a different jewel set in it. The light from a single fire-lit bulb swings from the ceiling and bathes the room in an uneven glow. Iris stares at the light. "No." She sighs, bored. "You can earn privileges, like the ability to settle in other parts of Aggonid's Realm, or you could even earn weapons and armor."

"Why would I need weapons?" I ask, tensing at her implication.

She meets my eyes, fingers paused on the ends of her hair. "For the Forsaken Hunt, of course."

"I have no idea what that is," I whisper, my voice reflecting the confusion I feel.

"It's a tradition here in the underworld," Irid explains. "Once every two months, the denizens of hell are allowed to participate in a hunt. Whoever catches and kills the most prey is granted a single favor from Aggonid."

My mouth goes dry. "And the prey are—"

She grins. "You. And anyone else with enough gall to foolishly enter the hunt."

"Why every two months? And what happens when they're killed here?"

"When you die here, you simply cease to exist. Lights out."

The idea is unsettling. She crouches so she's at my level, and I have to lean back as her breath fans my cheeks. Her solid frame nearly blocks out the light in the room, her piercing eyes exuding a fierce intensity. I can smell the sweat from her skin, though it isn't unpleasant.

"It's for population control, and to keep those who can't use their magic from going insane," she sing-songs. "And during even months, we hunt."

"We?"

"Demon fae."

"That hardly seems fair. I'll sit that one out. I'm without magic and—"

"The Wild Pursuit isn't something you can bow out of. You don't get a prize, we do." She cuts me off. "No one is safe."

"Why hunt us?"

"We go feral for twenty-four hours every two months. It's the only time we can be the demons we truly are. To hunt, to feel."

I shrink back from her in horror as my mind flashes with the implications. "Feel?" That can't mean what I think it does.

Her finger traces my collar bone, and I'm paralyzed with fear as my breath locks in my lungs. "Fuck or fight, it makes no difference to us. We hunt for pleasure, Morte. We want to feel alive."

"Wha-what?" I can't even form words as nausea swims in my gut. Bracing myself on the bed frame, I meet her eyes. "How many of you are there?"

"Hundreds," she gloats from her throne. "Though only a handful of us in the court."

I slump farther into my crouch. "For pleasure." I hunker down, arms crossed over my knees. Even the back of my fingers throb. "When?"

She waves me away with an absent gesture. "Three weeks' time." Her voice holds a note of cheer, as if she's given me excellent news. "Which brings me to our bargain."

Her light eyes flick to mine with something like pity. I watch her, the way she moves and the language her body displays. She is wary, like a wild animal, though cunning. I blink back frustrated tears. Whatever I choose, I'm doomed.

I unclench my jaw. "Go on," I whisper, my throat tight.

Her lips curl into a smirk and after a moment, she speaks, fingers tapping on her arm. "In exchange for these fine accommodations," she gestures to the squat room, "you will wear this." Irid slips a silver necklace from her pocket and drops it into my hand. "For the entire pursuit, or for however long you choose."

The cool metal presses into my skin and a shiver runs down my spine. It's smooth, like heavy chainmail or a wedding ring. "What does it do?"

"It will ensure Caius can't hurt you."

"Who's that?"

Her gaze bores into me for a moment before she replies. "My brother." She considers her words for a moment. "Only you can remove it once it's on."

My mouth goes dry. I swallow hard. "Why would he hurt me?" I was under the impression he was infatuated with me.

"We need you to survive him. When he's feral, there's no doubt he'll come straight for you." She chuckles. "There's a reason my brother's only lover is Aggonid. He's too powerful. And when feral?" She shakes her head. "No one has survived him yet."

I clutch the necklace tighter. "And this will ensure I do?"

She nods. "It will protect you from his worst. Without this, it would be too dangerous."

"And what's in it for you? Why do you care what happens to me?"

Her gaze is serious. "Your survival benefits us both. I need the Wild Pursuit to end. And you are my only chance of making sure it does."

"But why?"

She laughs bitterly. "You ask too many questions. I promise you'll know soon enough."

I stare at the necklace in my hand. "Fine. I'll do it." My voice echoes in the small room, a tiny spark of rebellion kindling in my chest. I look up and she smiles, a strange glint in her eyes. If I can wear this necklace, I won't be harmed, and I'll be able to fight back when Caius tries to bed me.

"Good." She steps back. "Now stand, and let's make this official."

I'd forgotten about how they seal their promises here.

She places her hands on either side of my face, her eyes closing in concentration. She starts mouthing strange words, and a sudden warmth wraps around me. Her cool lips press to mine, and a wave of power crashes into me, almost knocking me off my feet.

When she pulls away, I can taste her power on my lips.

"Don't let him know you have that." She gestures towards the glowing necklace.

"Why?"

"He doesn't like me meddling in his affairs."

"That'll cost you."

"And here, I was beginning to like you," she purrs. After studying me for a moment, she sighs. "What'll it be?"

I reach down and hold up the chain at my ankle. "Get this off of me."

She grins. "No can do. The only one who can take it off is the one who put it on. I'd only made it seem like you didn't have it on when you bathed."

"I'm assuming that was Caius." I frown.

"Correct. Although, I can lengthen it so you can leave the hut? Only twenty yards or so." She inspects it. "Deal?"

"Deal." I sigh, pressing my lips to hers.

This time, her hand cups my neck, holding me in place as she deepens the kiss. When she pulls away, her eyes twinkle with something akin to appreciation.

"Until we meet again," she says softly, stepping back and turning away.

I stay where I am until the door closes behind her, and then I reach up to touch my lips. Plopping back onto the bed, I shove the necklace into one of the slashes in the mattress for safekeeping.

CHAPTER FIVE

MORTE

*H*oisting the heavy chain into my arms, I bring it with me out the door, letting it drop link by link as I venture outside. Glancing up at the star-speckled sky, I count three moons hidden behind clouds. Smoke no longer obscures the land.

My stomach growls, and I rub it. Do I get meals here, or do I have to forage for food? And will I continue to be hungry even if I eat? Eternal damnation and all that. What happens if I don't eat? Do I cease to be?

I decide I don't ever want to find out.

The plants around the perimeter of the building are unfamiliar to me. Going without proper nutrition has never been an issue before. Now I'm worried that if I eat something that doesn't agree with me, it could be fatal. Where do I turn to get sustenance in the underworld?

I crouch down, fingers grazing the soft leaves of an unknown plant. Its dense foliage forms a canopy overhead, prompting me to recoil instinctively. Despite this, my gaze fixates on a small vine clinging to a nearby tree trunk. Clusters of vibrant magenta berries hang from its end, and the prospect of satiating my hunger overcomes my apprehension. I reach out to pluck a single fruit and place it in my mouth. The taste is sweet and refreshing, urging me to eat more. I consume the entire vine without noticing, only to be startled by a deep voice that pierces the darkness.

"You're in for a miserable night after eating those."

I yelp, stumbling backwards as a figure emerges from the trees. His wings are huge and leathery like a bat's, gleaming in the moonlight. More ethereal than physical, they appear to be made of mist. When he moves, they ripple like silk flowing in the wind, and when he stops, they vanish into the shadows. Sharp spikes adorn his livery, and his face is punctured with multiple piercings, intensifying his intimidating presence. Black hair lies in loose strands around his face, cascading down his back in perfect waves like liquid night. Eyes the color of the darkest blue flames meet mine, and they root me to the spot. Skin like spun gold makes him look like a god, and he might be.

The godlike creature stops in front of me, and I crane my neck, staring up at him. His wingspan is wider than I am tall. The edges of each feather are serrated, like talons, and the tips of them glow a brilliant white. Smoke curls from his nostrils, and it rolls around my feet and laps at my toes. I'm immediately intimidated by his size and fierceness, yet I stay rooted to the ground.

A flash of lightning pierces the sky, followed by crashing thunder. Forked lightning fills the sky, creating a storm unlike any I had seen before.

"Who are you?" I utter nervously.

He stretches out his wings with a slight arch of his back. "Azazel. First night?"

I nod and slowly get to my feet, brushing dirt from my clothes. He takes a step closer, and I take an involuntary step back as my heart makes a racket in my chest. Then he breaks into a breathtaking boyish grin. "I'm sorry. I just wanted to make sure you were alone."

He motions over his shoulder with his chin. "A tavern sits up that way. People go there for a bit of company." I suspected debauchery, but not something as normal as a bar. His gaze drops to the ground, then returns to meet mine. "Or we could hang out here." He gestures to my little hut.

"Uhh." I clutch the chain to my chest as if to use it as a shield, but then I hold it up, jingling it for him to see. "Not going much of anywhere with this."

"Who put it on you?"

"Caius."

His wings arc dramatically. "Figures. A pretty little thing like you?" He shakes his head. "He doesn't want you commingling with anyone else before he's sampled the goods."

I roll my eyes. "Shocker," I mutter.

"Can I come in?" He motions to my hut. He watches me hesitate before he points to the bag slung around his shoulder. "I've got food and drink. You're also going to need medicine," he glances at the moons, "in about sixteen more seconds."

"Huh?"

"You'll see." He steps back, making a gesture of invitation toward my hut.

My heart pounds as I hesitate, but then I step aside and let him enter. He sets the bag down, pulling out a clay jar full of herbs and a mortar and pestle.

Just as I enter the threshold, a searing pain rips through my stomach. I double over in agony, clutching the chains as I grunt and groan, cursing myself for eating the berries.

Azazel kneels beside me, pushing back my clothes to reveal a wide black mark on my stomach. He hisses. "Inferno's Kiss."

He pulls the mortar and pestle towards him and grinds the herbs with a little bit of water. He spreads the paste over the mark, wrapping my stomach with a strip of cloth.

"It'll help keep the pain at bay." He helps me sit up, handing me the jar. "You'll want to reapply this every few hours. Wait until the pain is gone before you eat or drink anything else."

"How long do you think it'll take?"

He shakes his head. "A day or two, unless you can get Caius to take pity on you."

I groan, my insides churning. "I don't belong here."

He grins. "They all say that."

"You don't understand." I shake my head. "I'm a phoenix."

He cocks his head. "The longer you stay here, the easier it gets. Well, maybe that's the wrong choice of words." He considers his thoughts for a moment. "You get used to it." He shrugs.

"How long have you been here?"

He sinks to the mattress next to me. "Long enough. I've seen a lot of souls come and go. It's like a revolving door." He holds up the jar. "I guess this is just part of the job."

"Job?" I furrow my brow. "Wait. You're a demon fae?" I try to sit up, but the movement sends me into another bout of pain.

Azazel smiles sadly. "Sure, if you want to call it that. I don't have any real authority here. I just do what the demon court asks of me. It's not ideal, but it's all I can do to make the best of a bad situation."

"What do I owe you?"

He drags his gaze up and down my torso, seeming to remember he helped me. "When you're feeling better, I'd like to buy you a drink."

Arching a brow, I study him. "A drink?" I assume at the tavern. "I should mention I'm not interested in dating anyone." He's all muscled and has a wild edge to his beauty, but all my thoughts are on Wilder. I've never let another man get close to me. In fact, Caius is the only other man I've kissed. And now I've kissed his sister, too.

He grins. "Yet." He stretches out his long form and begins to saunter away. "I'll check on you in the morning. Don't open that door after midnight," he adds before pausing in the doorway.

"What happens after midnight?"

Azazel chuckles. "That's when most of the more dangerous fae shift into their beasts. It's not quite the Forsaken Hunt, as they have some sentience, but you must remember we're in the underworld for a reason. You can't trust anyone here."

"Even you?"

"Least of all me." He bows mockingly before making his exit with a wink.

The door latches behind him, and I hold my stomach as I curl into a ball on the mattress.

Just what have I gotten myself into?

AFTER SPENDING half the night heaving nothing but bile and tears, I slip into a fitful sleep. No strange dreams haunt my slumber, and when I feel my body again, it's more like an echo of the pain before. Whatever Azazel did to heal me has worked.

I'm just cleaning the sleep out of my eyes when a shadow falls over the small crack in the wooden wall.

"Oh good, you're awake."

My head whips to the door as Caius strolls in. "Wow, you've got clothes on." My eyes trail over his pectorals and down past his rippling abs to his taut stomach before reaching his loincloth. The scrap of muslin hangs from one hip and is knotted loosely around his waist, leaving little to the imagination. The thick muscles of his body, resembling sculpted marble, draw my gaze until I look away, flushed. I look back when he undoes the knot and clear my throat.

"Oh, sorry, I can take this off." He snaps his fingers, and the thin fabric falls away to reveal him in all his glory.

"Caius!" I hiss as I train my attention on the wall. The scorching heat causes the air to ripple in front of me. A bead of sweat rolls down my temple, and it's definitely not from what I think I just saw.

Was he ... pierced? *Down there?* Why didn't I see that before?

My attention falls back to his penis. A long silver ring glints at the base of his shaft, with two more strung together to make a heavy chain that rings the base of his cock, with a final one dangling on either side. He swishes it from side to side, and I jerk my head to his face, where he smirks.

"Ooh, how I love hearing my name on your lips. Say it again." He smiles so wide that the fullness of his face transforms.

I can feel heat rising to my cheeks. "What do you want?"

He hums as he strides around the room. "Oh, I just came by to check on you and to tell you that I have something precise planned for us today." He teases one corner of his mouth up in a half smile and begins strolling around the room.

"Afraid I can't go anywhere on account of this." I toss the slack length of chain at him. "Take this off me."

He falls to his knees at my side. "I thought you'd never ask." He reaches for my shirt, and I roll out of his way.

"Not my clothes!" I screech.

Caius lets out a deep belly laugh, and his eyes sparkle with amusement. "Morte," he scolds. "I was going to give you a hug."

"Liar," I grumble, but my protest dies on my lips when he gently wraps his arms around me.

"Maybe," he whispers. "But your protests are really cute."

My body trembles against his embrace and I'm not sure if it is because of fear or something else entirely. Caius moves away too soon, leaving me with a million questions.

"So," he purrs as he leans back and clears his throat, "how about we take these off?"

"The chains." I gesture towards the heavy shackles and the giant ball that sits at the end of them.

He grins and fiddles with the ends of my hair. "What'll you give me?"

I narrow my eyes. "What do you want?"

"Your trust."

My conversation with Azazel comes back to me. *You can't trust anyone here.*

I shake my head. "I can't do that. Not in this place."

Caius's blue eyes become stormy, so much like Wilder's, but his voice is even when he speaks. "You don't have to trust me all the way, but you'd be surprised how far a little trust can go in this realm."

I study him for a moment. This might be my opportunity to get answers. "How do I eat around here?" I'm testing him. He probably has no idea I'd ingested poisonous berries last night, or that Azazel helped me.

"Don't touch any of the plants around this place," he warns, and my eyebrows shoot up. Huh. Didn't expect honesty. "There's a tavern, but I'd stay out of it if you care about maintaining your innocence."

"Why do you say that?"

"How else would you pay? They trade in favors."

"Favors?"

"Promises, secrets, favors, even debt." He grins. "Plenty of the sexual kind."

"How else do I feed myself?" I brush my hair out of my face. "Do I get a job?"

"There are a few demons whose sole job is to pillage resources from other realms, and we use those to supply the underworld with what it needs. There are far too many prisoners to feed and clothe." He leans forward, resting his elbows on his knees. "Steal it, grow it, barter for it, hunt for it, or, as I mentioned before, you can pay with favors." He pauses, his eyes twinkling with amusement. "Or I could feed you."

"Your sister let me use the bathroom in what I assume was a dungeon. Where am I supposed to go to the bathroom here?"

He pauses again and shrugs. "The woods, I suppose." He appears deep in thought before looking at me with a faint smile. "And you could bathe with me."

I shake my head and sit up, tucking my legs under me. The manacle bites into my thigh and I hiss, pulling it around to the front. "No," I reply flatly. "How do I earn my magic back?" If I can get my magic back, I may be able to find a way back to Bedlam.

"Only Aggonid grants that."

"Can you take me to him?"

He chuckles. "He'll eat you alive, sweet bird."

Here we go again with the bird names. "If there was a way around that ..." I prompt, raising my eyebrow.

"Mmmm," he purrs, leaning close. His breath fans my lips. "Now you're talking."

"How might one convince him to give me my magic?"

His hand cups my cheek. "That'll cost you."

"Argh!" I shove him back. "You know what? What if trust was *earned* instead of bargained for? You can't just demand I trust you without *giving me a reason to trust you!*"

He grabs my hand, and I make to yank it back, but his claws dig into my wrist. I let out a cry as crimson wells up in the grooves, and it drips down my forearm before wicking into my clothes. Ice forms in its place for a brief moment before melting into my blood.

"I—" I begin to protest, but before I can get any more words out, he speaks a strange language. A jolt of energy courses through me, rushing towards every cell. The heat of the realm no longer suffocates me, and I can breathe properly for the first time in the underworld.

"What did you just do?" I gasp, staring at him wide-eyed. The sweltering effects of this entire place no longer harms me.

"Earned your trust," he croons before his tongue darts out, licking the blood from my wrist, trailing along my arm and up to my elbow.

I shiver, my skin tingling where his mouth touched me.

"Trust, Morte." He pulls away, eyes hooded, and I see the sincerity in them. "In this realm, we work on a balance system. Everyone has something of value, whatever it is, and I just gave you a part of mine."

"I'm not saying I agree with it, but I understand it." I swallow. "Will you please tell me how I can earn a favor from Aggonid?"

"And you will trust me in exchange?"

A sigh passes my lips, and I hesitate. "I will trust you more than I do now. Fair enough?"

He grins at me with his crooked smile, a roguish twinkle in his eyes. "For now," he says, cupping my cheeks and pulling me towards him.

I feel my body responding to this man before I can think twice. My blood warms, a hot blush spreading across my face. What is happening to me?

He leans in, and I close my eyes. His lips are warm and soft, like a spring day, tender in their movement against mine. Sparks flare up inside of me, searing and sudden. I can feel the energy zinging between us as he pulls away, his eyes a brilliant shade of blue that somehow keeps me captivated.

"Deal sealed."

"What?" I mutter, transfixed by the glowing orbs in front of me.

"You may use my name to earn a favor from Aggonid after you've won the hunt."

I blink, rage blinding me. "But winning the hunt already grants me a favor!"

"Yes, but this will give you one more." He grins. "But use it wisely. He'll do anything for me, but even he has his limits."

"Thank you, Caius."

The air seems to thicken as he hears his name on my lips, each syllable traveling through his body like electricity. His muscles tense as he stares. "Say that again," he murmurs.

I hesitate. "Caius?"

Goosebumps line his arms as he closes his eyes. "One more time, please."

My voice is a whisper, spoken so softly. "Caius."

This time, it's me who shudders with a full-body shiver.

His hooded eyes meet mine, and his features soften. "I knew it."

"Knew what?"

His hand grips the manacle at my ankle, and he avoids answering my question. I'm about to call him on it when he speaks.

"Do you want to deal for this?" He produces a key out of thin air. It's tiny and gold and attached to a small chain. "This key will remove your manacle, and you can keep it, or use it as a weapon if you must."

Blinking, I try to make sense of the abrupt change in him, but then I consider his words for a moment. Technically, he's offering two favors. Removing my chains *and* giving me a way to defend myself. "And I'm the only one who can remove those chains once I place them?"

"So long as you have the key, yes."

"And you're doing this to earn my trust?"

He nods.

"Alright."

He crawls onto the bed, naked as the day he was born, and pulls me onto his lap. His hand cups my neck as he brings his mouth to mine. My lips part, and his tongue sweeps against mine as he slides his fingers through my hair. He crushes me against his chest. Our kiss is long and passionate and hungry, and despite knowing this has nothing to do with sealing the deal, I let it all go and just enjoy the moment. It's a little slice of pleasure in a realm full of pain.

When we finally pull apart, his stiff length juts against me as his lips hover close to mine. He speaks two words.

"Deal sealed." He remains there, our breath mingling. "Please tell me you have more favors to ask of me." His voice is low and rough.

I can only nod, my words forgotten. I thought of them, though, of telling him to finish what he started. But I can't bring myself to ask. For some reason, it's too intimate. Most of my life, I'd pined for one man I couldn't have. But even now, with realms between us, my thoughts turn back to him.

"Tell me how I can get back to Bedlam."

This demand breaks the spell woven between us, and Caius shrinks back, scowling.

"There is no way," he says coldly, storm clouds in his eyes. "You're stuck here."

I exhale, stunned by the finality of his sentence. I'm here for good. A tear spills down my cheek, and the sight of it enrages him.

He tosses the key into my lap before storming out, the door slamming so hard it swings off its hinge. I sink into the bed, my thoughts a jumbled mess. My gaze falls on little glimmer of metal and an idea sparks in my mind.

I slot the key into the lock in my manacle, feeling the resistance of the pins inside, and I twist. It clicks, the sound reverberating throughout my bones, and the lock pops open. I pull the cuffs apart and sigh in relief. My ankle, streaked with a raw red mark, is finally free.

I coil the chain, my hands working in a familiar rhythm as I pry apart a floorboard, shoving the restraints in the hole. I've always used the floorboards to hide things from prying eyes. Replacing the board, I marvel at the perfect fit.

While I'd been hoping for a way back to Bedlam, it might be enough—for now—to just be freed from my restraints. No longer bound by that tiny bit of metal and whatever Caius's actual intentions were, I feel in control once more.

When I win the Forsaken Hunt, I know *exactly* what favor I'm asking for. But first I've just got to survive the Underworld.

CHAPTER SIX

AGGONID

"Kill them," my voice thunders across my throne room. The throne I sit on is fashioned from every manner of bone you can imagine. The very ones my enemies had to offer. The back of the throne is made of tangled branches from the wildest forests, woven together with thorns so that none may escape once they are caught.

A river of blood flows beneath our feet, coming from the countless denizens of hell who've met their fate before me. Their bones weave a footpath above it, the shrieks of their souls caught in limbo echoing through the chamber.

I'll get to theirs eventually.

Flames separate the courtiers from my throne, encasing them in a ring of heat that they dare not cross. They remain along the edges of the gothic room, its walls adorned with frescoes depicting the most torturous agony imaginable. The screams of those depicted in the paintings meld with the cacophony of tormented souls.

Caius and Irid stalk down the dais stairs, approaching the trembling demons who dared to defy me. Smoke fills the chamber, billowing in thick plumes as the fire licks at their heels.

Their shrieks cut off as Caius swings his scythe in a wide arc, and a spray of blood paints the walls. He steps over the pile of corpses, heading towards me in a confident stride while Irid drags their bodies away.

"Any more orders, love?" He grins, flipping his hood back to reveal his handsome features, now stained crimson.

He's the only one who can speak to me with such familiarity. I'd eaten the last person to overstep their boundary with me.

"Come here," I purr.

He saunters closer, eyes full of hunger. I can feel his desire radiating off him in waves, making my skin prickle with anticipation. His gaze falls to my lips, and I know he hungers for more than just a kiss.

I reach out and grasp his chin, tilting his head up as he kneels before me. Inhaling, I catch an unfamiliar scent on him, and it sends my hackles up. My nostrils flare as I try to place the smell. Cocking my head, I study him.

"Who have you made a deal with?" I demand, my voice a dangerous whisper. Him making deals isn't the problem, but I taste blood in the air that doesn't belong to him. *He's tasted another?*

My lips twist into a tight line as he hesitates. I can feel the tension in the air thickening as he struggles with how to answer.

Finally, taking a deep breath, he speaks. "There is a phoenix fae. Her name is Morte."

A searing heat of envy swirls in my chest, and my grip tightens on his chin, spilling crimson liquid dripping down my fingertips and to the ground. His pupils dilate as he swallows hard, eyes wide with fear. The vulnerability reflected in his gaze is like a dagger piercing my heart, and I'm reminded of how much time has passed since I'd last seen him in this state of fear. Fear of *me*.

It's been hundreds of years.

My entire being aches with a sadness I can't explain.

Blinking, I release him and bring my fingers to my mouth. "Morte," I murmur, tasting his blood on my tongue.

And someone else's.

The name stirs something inside me, something primal and

60

untamed. A searing bitterness coats my tongue as I demand of him, "What has she bargained for?"

Caius swallows again, and he doesn't meet my eyes, but the guilt is written all over his face. He shifts uneasily, and I hate her with everything I am. Who is this creature who's taken my most loyal demon from me? My lover. My mate. My reason for being.

I don't care who he kisses or flirts with. Or if his feral beast stalks another during the Wild Pursuit. But to taste someone else's blood?

He only drinks when he's making love to me.

To feed from someone else ... I shake my head.

"Morte," I whisper again, the name filling me with rage. I glance at Irid, her gaze locked on me, waiting for her next command.

"Find her," I spit. "Bring her to me."

She takes off without another word, and I turn back to Caius. He rises from his kneeling position, his features heavy with remorse and pain, but also determination.

"Leave," I boom.

The rest of the room clears, leaving the two of us to face off against each other.

The silent anguish etched on his face mirrors my own shattered heart, as the full weight of his betrayal crashes down upon me.

Is he conspiring with the very one who's to doom us all?

How could he do this to me, to us? How could he shatter everything we had with a single, thoughtless act of infidelity? The questions swirl within me, a tempest of agony and betrayal.

"I'll hang her from the rafters and rip her apart," I snarl. "Flay her and strip the meat from her bones. You belong to me, Caius. That creature has no power here. Tell me, when you were fucking her, did you think of me?"

"I didn't sleep with her." His nostrils flare. "She loves another."

"So, she rejected you?" I spit. "Is that all my love is worth to you?" My heartbreak is palpable, as though you could puncture it with a knife, and it'd spill its remains at his feet. I've never been so blindsided by betrayal.

A tear spills down his cheek, and in all our years together, I've never seen him cry. "Answer me!" I shout, the words fall from my mouth like shattered glass. I don't know what to do with him in this state.

"I made several deals with her," he whispers. "She wanted answers, and I gave them to her. Where she was, how she can get home, what's happened with the man she loves, and she begged me to remove her chains." By the time he finishes, his eyes plead with me to understand. "She is untouched."

"Unbelievable," I hiss. "No one who comes here is." I don't *want* to believe it's her.

"She is."

I collapse onto my throne, shock and despair clouding my mind. "What do you want with her?" I know the answer, but I need to hear it all the same.

"You already know."

I nod once. "You won't be the only one coming for her." My words tumble out of my mouth like the trappings of a defeated soul. Taking someone's virginity almost grants you as much power one would gain from having multiple mates. It's rare and coveted.

He sinks into my lap, wrapping his arm around my neck. "Do you doubt me?"

"Forgive me." I take a shuddering breath, my voice thick with emotion. For not trusting him, *and for what I'll be forced to do.*

Agony bleeds into my chest. I grip his face, and we meet in a clash of teeth and tongues, desperation radiating out of us both. He kisses me long and deep, as if it's the last time, and he weeps into my embrace, knowing exactly what he's asking of me.

And for the first time in my life, it's me who will need to earn his redemption, even if it destroys us both in the end.

THE SOFT ROSE glow of the setting sun casts long, even shadows across the tiled floor. The sharp smell of metal and dying flower petals drift through our windows, carried on a slow breeze.

I lift my head from the pillow and yawn, bracing my weight on an elbow as Caius stirs in his sleep, his dark, silky hair flopping into his eyes. His breathing is steady and deep, a soft snore sawing through the night as he slips deeper into dreamland.

I slide out of the covers and pad my way to my desk, a piece of furniture I crafted myself from the old timber on the North end of the island. The heavy table lamp, with its hand-painted shade, bathes the room with a warmth over everything it touches.

The second drawer from the bottom creaks as I ease it open, the smooth wood whispering with each turn. Buried at the very back is an old parchment with a name written in script I'd recognize everywhere, in any language.

Morte.

The long-burned wax seal cracks and flakes away as I carefully read the scroll, my last hope to re-interpret the words. A mercy, I pray, but my stiff heart won't allow me the luxury of such an emotion.

When a virgin phoenix falls,
Her blood does hold a hidden call,
To those who taste its flaming hue,
Their bond forever true.
But not all who taste her flame,
Will feel this bond and take its name,
Only the chosen few will see,
The bond that's meant to be.
Loathing consumes one lover whole,
And he plots to take control,
He schemes to end her fate,
With a wicked, malevolent hate.
As he's distracted by this strife,
His enemies plot to take his life,
Leaving him to face the fight,
All on his own, with all his might.

I never believed in what was written here; it sounds too far-fetched, but the implications of the words horrify me. Here I am, ready to betray the one person I love. The dark truth of what must be done sends a chill through my bones, my chest hollow, and my soul, dry and brittle.

I grip the edge of the desk with my hand, sinking under the strain of my grief. Each of my sobs rises like a tempest and I can barely breathe. I can do it; for I must do it. Such is the way of life in the underworld, where everything comes with a price.

Not even I am immune.

A tear streaks down my face and splatters on the page. I choke back more tears and try to breathe, but it's no use. Between my fingers, I ignite the paper and watch as it turns to ash. The note is gone now, along with all its secrets. I can't allow anything or anyone to take my throne, nor my mate. No distractions.

When a knock sounds at my door, I wipe my eyes and pull on my robe.

"Yes?" I say, my voice ragged as I pull it open. It sounds like a blade made from sandpaper, rough and gravelly. Irid stands there, her cheeks red and wet with tears, but she's alone. "Where is she?"

"My lord." She bows. Her eyes flicker up to meet mine for a moment before she bows her head again. "Morte is in one of the wooden cottages at the edge of the forest."

I blink. "You do know I asked you to bring her to me hours ago, right?" Am I remembering it correctly?

"That's the thing, my lord. She's chained herself to the bed and refuses to unlock it."

Rage becomes a choking ball of fire, burning through me as I slam the door. I can barely contain my anger long enough to get dressed, hopping about in an attempt to pull on my leather cord tunic and pants, working my feet into my boots. Feeling at my throat for my necklaces, I leave my quarters and head out into the night.

The trees loom around me, darkness hiding the forest floor. A thousand eyes watch me as I storm to Morte's cottage. My heart makes a racket in my chest and my palms sweat as I prepare myself for what lies ahead.

I stalk towards the little hut and throw the door open, taking with me the fury of a thousand fires. Morte stands before me, her face pale, but determined. She looks so brave, so beautiful in her defiance, and my heart cracks. Her crimson tresses, like fire, spill down her back, her eyes smoldering with a strength and fight rarely seen here.

"Why did you defy me?"

"I didn't feel like dying today."

I hear the fear underlining her brave words, but her gaze never wavers from mine.

"You don't have the luxury of picking your fate, Morte." My words are harsh, even to my own ears.

She's the one who will take everything from me. Caius. My throne. The entire realm.

I can't let that happen.

Morte

THE AIR around me thickens like tar as I stand in the presence of the devil. Every fiber of my being screams at me to turn and run, but I know that if I do, there's no chance of saving Wilder.

Aggonid's intensity draws me in, and I can feel it swimming around inside me like a vengeful spirit. His power enters my veins like venom, a phantom hand gripping my bones until they crumble to dust. I may be in the devil's domain, but no matter how hard he tries, he can't take away my will to survive.

A molten rage boils in his eyes, and I feel my heart shatter at the sight. Is he angry because Caius wants to fuck me?

His silver hair is tightly woven to his scalp on one side, revealing a pointed ear that mirrors my own. His burnished pewter skin shimmers in the flickering torchlight, and for a minute, I'm mesmerized by his beauty. But in that same moment, I feel the force of his hatred and my knees buckle beneath me.

"Send me back, and I swear you'll never have to deal with me again." I keep my voice level, betraying none of my inner tumult.

"I can't. The only other place one goes from here is nowhere. This is the last stop before oblivion." He takes slow, calculated steps towards me, more predator than male.

My heart rate skyrockets, a frantic beat hammering against my ribcage. Agony flashes across his features as he strikes, his fingernails turning to razor-sharp claws. In a sudden rage-fueled burst, he grabs me by the throat and slams me hard against the wall. His lips part as his breath, like fire on my skin, reaches my cheeks. His grip is vice-like iron, the crushing force draining me of everything I have.

My mouth gapes open, but no words come out. My heart thrashes in my chest, and I can't break free from his grasp. His rage is tangible, and his possessiveness is suffocating, but within his eyes there's something more—a torment so deep and widespread that it pierces me like an arrow. An unbearable despair envelopes me, making it almost impossible to breathe. My fingers dig into his wrist, shredding his bracers as I desperately cling onto him.

I bare my teeth in a snarl as I unleash a storm of fury from deep within me. My hand whips out, connecting with the cold metal of my manacle. Seizing the opportunity, I wrap it around his wrist, chaining us together. He staggers back as my foot slams into his gut, pushing him away from me and giving me the opportunity to claw air into my lungs.

I dive for my bed, ripping into the mattress like a caged animal, desperate to find my salvation. I snatch the necklace from its hiding spot, securing its safekeeping around my bruised neck. An immense power radiates through me as I feel the dark magic it holds bound to my soul. The metal links dig into my skin, but with each breath I take, I sense my strength continuing to grow.

I'm dragged backward by my ankle. I'm dangled upside down for a moment before Aggonid releases me, dropping me to the ground. Under the bed, I spy a glint of light and I surge for it, slapping my palm on top of it.

Without thinking, I open my mouth and shove it down my throat, swallowing as I scramble onto my backside.

Flames lick the walls, and the devil snarls, taking a step back, his expression bewildered. He holds his hand, an oily substance dripping from between his fingers.

His eyes bulge with rage as he lets out an earth-shaking roar. "WHAT HAVE YOU DONE?!"

My heart pounds against my ribs as I clasp my throat, hoping desperately that I'm right and he can't hurt me. I grip the medallion, feeling its energy coursing through my veins as I try to calm my ragged breathing. My voice is hoarse and broken as I respond, "Nothing that can't be undone. You can't hurt me." With a renewed determination I rise to my feet and stand tall against him.

He reaches for the chain and yanks on it, nearly sending me back to the floor. He lassos it around me, wrenching me towards him.

"Unlock this fucking thing or I'll tear out your throat," he seethes, his sweet breath a cruel contrast to his sinister words.

"You can't," I hiss. I hold my ground as he stares me down, my chest rising and falling against his with rage. He can't attack me, not while I wear this necklace. And like the chain binding us, he can't take that off, either. Only I can do that.

Except, I swallowed the key.

His arms band around me and he hauls me outside, my feet dragging on the ground as I try to get out from his grip. His wings spread wide, giant, leathery things blotting out the moons. He shoots into the air with a burst of power, leaving the trees in his wake as tiny dots.

With a cruel snicker, he hurls me into the air, and I free fall into oblivion until the manacle cuff clamps down hard on my wrist, jolting me to a sudden stop. I cry out in pain as my bones scream in agony.

He soars above the clouds, taking his sweet time as I dangle helplessly beneath him. I begin swinging, causing him to teeter in the air as he struggles to keep control. He grunts before giving a feral growl, veering off course as his wings shift direction, so fast that I am swung around in a wide circle and go head over heels in the turbulence of his wake.

With a burst of adrenaline, I launch myself up the iron chain, each link beneath my fingers as if clenched in a vise-grip. He's oblivious to my presence until I'm within reach of his vital organs. I gather every ounce of strength within me and unleash a furious blow, aiming right for his groin with a power that can only be drawn from the depths of my soul.

I connect right with his balls.

He howls as his wings snap tight, and we plummet to the ground in a free fall. I release my wings, screaming from the strain it puts on my muscles to carry the two of us to a slower descent. We make an impact that shakes the forest floor, tumbling into a heap of limbs. He cries out as my fist connects again, this time with his face. I vault off the ground and gain my feet, running as fast as my legs will carry me.

I hear him cursing behind me as we zig-zag through the underbrush, dodging branches and leaping over logs.

Suddenly, a figure appears in front of me, blocking my path. I skid to a stop and look up into the ice blue eyes of Caius, his body shimmering in the silver moonlight. My heart stumbles in my chest as he steps closer, and I recoil.

He holds up his hands in a sign of peace, eyes darting between Aggonid and I just as I'm tackled from behind. My mouth fills with dirt as the air jets out of my lungs.

Aggonid presses his body against mine, hands stretching to capture my wrists tightly between his.

Caius stands there silently, watching as Aggonid drags me backwards. He stalks after us, running to keep up beside the bastard.

"Good call chaining her to you. Now she can't get away from us." Caius smirks.

CHAPTER SEVEN

MORTE

*M*aybe I've made a mistake chaining myself to a monster.
My wrist protests in agony as Aggonid drags me across the unforgiving terrain of the forest floor. Each jagged rock digs into my flesh, and my bones grind against one another from the sheer force of the manacle's grip. A gasp of misery falls from my lips as I stumble forward and a stick jams into my shoulder.

Remember who you're doing this for.

Caius pauses and turns back to me, worry etched across his face. "Perhaps, love, we should let her walk?" He tugs on Aggonid's sleeve. "I can smell her blood. Would be a pity to waste it."

Aggonid snarls, his steps faltering. His dark eyes survey me from where he stands, cataloging my every wound, a cruel smirk tugging at the corners of his lips as his malicious intent radiates from him.

He turns to Caius, tracing a finger along his cheekbone and leaning in to whisper. "Let the servants prepare another bed next to ours. I've got some stuff to discuss with Morte. You go on ahead."

"You want to sift back to the castle tonight? Or where do you want to stay?"

"Sorrow's Manor, I think we could use a little quiet after today."

Caius grins, pressing his mouth to the devils before nipping at his

70

bottom lip, earning him a growl. "Just look at her." Caius's voice is low and husky as he grips Aggonid's chin and turns his face towards me. "She'll look so beautiful between us. Isn't it fitting that she sleeps with us tonight?"

But before Aggonid can respond, I cut in with a firm "No." Pulling myself to my knees, I wipe the dirt from my mouth and rip the stick out of my shoulder, sending an electric wave of pain through my veins. I'll go with them—but only because they're my greatest chance at finding a way home.

Caius's eyes find mine, and the startled expression on his face tells me he wasn't expecting me to say no. His mouth twitches like he's struggling to compose himself.

"You heard her." Aggonid winds his hand around the chain, bringing me closer. "She doesn't want this."

His voice is stern, but there's something in it I can't quite make out. It almost seems ... regretful. As he's speaking, his eyes drop to my lips, and there's a flicker of something before he slowly turns away.

My heart hammers against my rib cage, a soundtrack of terror that seems to amplify in the stillness of the forest. I slowly lift my eyes to meet Caius's, their icy depths clouded with dejection.

"I'll meet you at Sorrow's Manor then." He sighs before leaving without another word to either of us. Caius launches himself into the air with his massive leathery wings, slicing through the sky with such force that the air crackles around him.

Aggonid sprints ahead, and I'm momentarily dazed before I break into a sprint, dodging trees and logs as I try to keep up with his lightning pace. My breaths come in short bursts as my feet pound against the ground faster and faster; it's like trying to catch a spirit fish. Caius ascends rapidly, leaving Aggonid and me in a cloud of dust. Despite the intense effort I must put in, I manage to stay on the devil's heels as we dodge obstacles in our path.

My voice cracks as I plead for him to slow down, but his cruel laughter mocks me instead. His feet beat against the earth with increasing speed, striving to outpace the wind, until my sight becomes a streak of color. He moves between trees with uncanny accuracy, weaving through the branches and obstacles in his path. I stumble and tumble blindly, hitting every trunk along the way before I trip, impaling myself on a sharp branch. Without magic, I can't heal myself, and because he isn't directly causing injury to me, my necklace allows it.

He pauses at a clearing, a moment of reprieve before I realize he has no intention of helping me. I whimper, my hands shaking as I grip the gnarled stick embedded in my abdomen. As hot agony courses through me, I pull and blood gushes from the wound, cascading down my legs. I collapse to my knees, breath ragged and trembling from pain and fear, but Aggonid does not so much as glance back at me.

I beg for mercy as I see him take a turn towards the grassy shoulder, hoping for a reprieve from this harsh punishment. Yet what I find there is far more torturous. Like a million razor-sharp knives, the blades of grass tear through my body. Every wound feels like a billion glass shards, slicing and shredding my flesh and causing unbridled agony to rip through me. My cries rent the air, desperate, pitiful whimpers of a broken soul. My will to survive fades with each passing second as my lifeblood soaks into the ground.

Darkness edges in from the corners of my vision, and I know that this is it, like thousands of times before. We've stopped moving, and I witness Aggonid's face crumpled in grief as the flames catch me. My eyes lose their focus as I greet an old friend.

Hello, I whisper to the fire. *Have you come to carry me away?*

∼

Aggonid

THE CHAIN DROPS LIKE A STONE, clanging loudly as Morte's body disintegrates into a pile of ash. An unbearable agony seizes my being, ripping through me like hot pokers. I knew her death was coming, yet I still can't fathom the magnitude of my loss, the pain so acute it numbs my senses. My body collapses to the ground and an animal-like sob escapes from me.

It had to be this way.

Oh, how I wish it didn't.

Caius will be devastated, never understanding why I had to do this and how much love I have for him, for my realm. But he will never truly comprehend the sacrifice I made for us.

Because he can never know what I've done. This secret will remain with me, hidden in the depths of my agony. I'll just have to say she bled out from the stick, and I was unable to heal her.

As I lay there, despairing in my grief, a flicker of light catches my eye. Surrounded by the ashes, a glowing ember pulses rhythmically, as if alive and breathing. I blink back the tears, unable to believe what I'm seeing as I rise to my knees.

For a moment, the world comes to a halt. Then a tiny flame begins to dance in the air, swirling and twisting until the ember has transformed into a phoenix, just as Morte had been in life.

The creature swells in size, its wings shining a deep, glossy red like freshly spilled blood against snow. They glitter like a million flaming, red-hot campfires, each one burning with an intense, pulsating heat. As it nears, the air trembles with its heat and intensity, a beacon of danger that warns all those who cross its path.

Cuffed to its wing is the manacle, tethering the two of us together. I'm equal parts relieved and terrified as the bird transforms into its fae form.

Naked.

Morte's furious eyes, like molten honey, search my soul as she stares at me, her angelic face a picture of shock and rage. I can taste her fury in the air.

"You killed me," she whispers, her voice growing more affronted as she speaks. "Caius is the one who keeps coming on to me. If you don't want your man poking his dick where it doesn't belong, take that up with him!"

She can't die here either, I guess.

She launches at me with a feral growl, her rabid claws scratching and tearing at my clothes. Her nails dig into my skin, slicing through my flesh like a sharpened blade. A fiery pain fills my body as I grapple

KATHY HAAN

with her, trying to stop her from ripping off the necklace around my throat.

"Enough!" I manage to push her away from me and am met with a shrill shriek as she collapses hard into the vorpal blades.

In a fit of rage, she grabs something from the grass and shoves it into her mouth. That's when I see the gilded key to the chains clutched between her teeth. Before I can make a move, she swallows it whole.

I snatch her up, my fingers sinking into her delicate skin as I drag her towards the gravel path. "I will have a guard gut you," I snarl.

"Just send me back!" she screams through her sobs. "I don't belong here!"

"I already told you there is no way back once you arrive!" I roar, my voice like thunder that echoes through the forest. "The only place to go is *gone*. Blinked out of existence. Is that what you want?"

But even as I say that a memory itches at the back of my mind. I'd had a vampire not too long ago that went back. Someone came for him, and I let him go, earning a boon from the high king. My gaze hardens as I turn away from her, my thoughts racing with the possibility I may not have to kill her to get her to leave.

I may just need to call in a boon.

CHAPTER EIGHT

MORTE

The devil and I forge ahead through the twisted darkness of the underworld forest, the air saturated with the noxious aroma of death and smoldering embers. A blanket of writhing, serpentine vines drapes over the towering trees that line the path, which is made treacherous by the jagged rubble beneath our feet.

I keep a safe distance from Aggonid, still wary of his intentions as we make our way towards Sorrow's Manor. He's lost in thought, and movement in the bushes doesn't seem to bother him. Blinking red eyes appear from behind the brush, watching us, and they seem to fade into the shadows as quickly as they appear. We continue in silence, but my thoughts are still tangling in knots. Though I'm alive and whole, my fate is still unknown.

Why didn't Azazel stop by like he said he would? Did my unit ever eliminate the hydra? Was Wilder going to tell me who his anchor is before we'd been killed? Are they worried I've gone AWOL, and if so, have they figured out my connection to him?

Fear slithers into my chest at the thought. Would they hurt him to get answers? I hope not.

If I can get back to Bedlam, with my position as commander, I may still be able to get Wilder out of prison. No one has ever escaped before, though the hydra came close.

I don't notice Aggonid has stopped in his tracks, and I barrel into him, sending us sprawling to the ground in a heap of limbs.

He's pinned me beneath him, and for a moment I'm caught in his gaze—crimson eyes burning into me like liquid fire.

"Morte," he murmurs, then immediately withdraws from me, his expression a mix of confusion and anger. "Watch where you're going," he hisses.

He jumps up as though he's been burned. Flustered, I climb to my feet, keeping my eyes trained on the large, glowering gatehouse we've stopped in front of.

This must be Sorrow's Manor.

Trees loom overhead like skeletal sentinels, guarding the entrance. The manor itself is a gothic beauty—its walls a deep tourmaline, like it's been carved out of a mountain, and its windows give off a faint glow.

Aggonid hauls himself up the crumbling stone steps, every movement in silhouette against the slivered moonlight that seeps out of a single sconce on the veranda. Cobwebs and ragged shutters thicken the air like murky memories, seeming to grab at us as we approach. With a single push, the door groans open, and we enter, each step into the unknown sending a chill up my spine.

The night is as black as ink, and I stand still, holding my breath. My eyes gradually adjust to the dim light, and I take in the eerie sight before me—walls adorned with spectral images of strange creatures both familiar and foreign, illuminated portraits of fae, demons, and other unknown monsters from distant realms. Massive murals depicting scenes of great battles and overpowering triumph cascade across the arched ceiling.

Caius's larger-than-life presence looms over my shoulder. "Welcome to Sorrow's Manor," he whispers in my ear, causing goosebumps to skirt my body. His eyes trail down my naked form, eyebrow lifted as he casts Aggonid a concerned glance.

We're in a living room of sorts, with ancient furniture draped in blankets and fur. The only noise comes from a large marble fireplace in the corner, where fire crackles and pops, flickering dancing shadows across the room.

Aggonid sits just a few feet away, his hands on each arm of his chair, regal, like a king surveying his kingdom.

"Are the beds prepared?" the devil asks, his voice rippling through my core like silken bedsheets against smooth skin.

"About that." Caius steps around me and approaches his lover. "It appears I accidentally broke the spare. Pity that." He pouts with a measure of glee in his eyes as he tosses what appears to be a bed post into the overfilled hearth.

I glance down at the glide of coolness against my skin. Shadows hug my curves, wrapping around my body to hide the delicate parts. Scowling Aggonid's way, I don't say anything because I'd rather be clothed than not, I suppose.

Caius is a mountain of muscle, looming large and strong like a titan, while Aggonid is mean and lean like a coiled viper. But when the devil rises, the air thickens with his oppressive power and the walls bend inward, until he consumes the entire room with dread, a reminder of his lethal reputation.

Aggonid's gaze slides over to me, and a smirk curves his lips. I feel like a butterfly pinned to a board. "The floor it is, I suppose."

"You're joking." Caius laughs. "She can share with us, can't you? Or you could shorten the chain, so she *has* to share." He glances at Aggonid.

He doesn't know. He thinks Aggonid chained us, but it was me. Why doesn't Aggonid want Caius to know?

The devil nods, and the atmosphere shifts, becoming heavy with the kind of heat that raises torrents of vivid memories in my mind. His attention locks with mine, a challenge in his stare.

My throat tightens and the fire behind us seems to die down, as though it, too, is waiting on bated breath.

"If you give me my magic back, I can repair the other bed." I steel my voice, pumping as much bravado into it as I can.

"Denizens of hell do not get magic back for at least the first hundred years they're here. You've been here days, and you've already managed to annoy me. Not happening," he clips. "And besides, there are limits to the magic prisoners earn back. Whatever you hope to do with it, I'm certain you won't be able to."

My chin dips and I fight the urge to look away from his intense scowl. Can I befriend the devil and convince him to find a way for me to return to Wilder?

Perhaps this is my chance.

"Well, then, I suppose I'm sharing with you two."

Caius claps, the gesture surprisingly genuine. "Then it's settled."

Aggonid merely narrows his eyes, as though daring me to fuck this up. An unspoken challenge to be obedient, lest I face the consequences.

A servant, a small troll-like creature, scurries in with a plate of food and sets it on the table in the adjacent dining room. The scent of roasted vegetables and delicious sauces wafts through the room.

My stomach roars with hunger, demanding satisfaction, and I try to ignore the tantalizing aroma, focusing on my goal. I can make this work. Aggonid doesn't have to be an obstacle—he can be an ally.

For now, I'll eat and plan my next move.

Caius holds out a chair for me, and paired with the white button-up shirt and dress slacks he has on, I'd almost think he's a gentleman.

Almost.

The devil watches us with a smirk, and as I sit, I can feel the heat of his gaze on my neck. He's willing to see what I do now and whether I truly wither in his presence or not.

My lungs strain as I struggle to take a deep breath, my gaze glued to the putrid slop that lies on the plate in front of us. The food squirms and squeals, still alive. Shock makes my eyes bulge with horror, and I spin around to Caius, demanding an answer. "What the hell is this?" I hiss, rage and terror mingling in my voice.

He chuckles, an amused glint in his eyes. "Silly bird, it's ground gnomes."

A horrified cry escapes me. No. No way.

I jump out of my chair and back away from the table, my heart thrashing in my chest. "Ground gnomes? But—that's just cruel!"

We have ground gnomes in Bedlam, and they're little helpers that live in the dirt. If you bury worn clothing, they'll repair the garments in seconds in exchange for something shiny. They are innocent creatures. Harmless.

My stomach churns and I push away from the table, backing away until I feel Caius's breath on my neck. I freeze and turn to look up into his face.

"It's alright," he says softly. His voice is like honey, reassuring and gentle. He places a hand on my shoulder, turning me away while he calls for a servant to bring something else.

With his hand still on me, he leads me away from the table and back to the sofa. I sit there, my fingers wringing and fear coursing through me.

Aggonid says nothing as Caius and I sit together, but I can feel the weight of his stare.

"You can't eat those anymore, Caius," I choke as I turn to him, and I'm surprised when I feel a tear track down my cheek. "Please."

His hand moves to my cheek, his fingers quivering as he brushes away the tear. His thumb moves with an almost reverent slowness as he erases the pain from my face. His eyes appear to crawl deep into my soul, and I shudder from the intensity of his understanding and tenderness.

"It'll cost you, though." Aggonid's voice is heavy, and it sends a shiver through me. He stands, slowly, looming over us like a dark angel.

"What do you mean?" I stammer, my nerves coiled tight.

He smiles coldly and gestures to the new food on the table. "You want us to stop eating ground gnomes? Fine. But you need to give up something in exchange."

Caius winces, knowing how I feel about deals, but doesn't intervene.

I take a deep breath. "What do you want?"

"Something shiny," he purrs. And if he didn't hate me, I'd think he was suggesting something else entirely.

I hold open my hands, gesturing wildly. "I have nothing!"

His attention draws on the shadows coiled across me, and I cross my arms over my chest.

"You swallowed it, and I intend on getting it back."

My mouth hangs open, horrified, and find that I can't speak. Aggonid steps closer and I instinctively shrink away.

"You will stay here with us," he continues, his voice deep. "Until you can find a way to return that which you have taken."

The key to the manacles.

He stares down at me, a wicked smile on his face. His slightly elongated canines gleam in the firelight, and chills run down my spine.

"How do you anticipate I return it to you?" I squeak.

A grin takes over his entire face, and Caius shifts uncomfortably next to me, his knee brushing mine.

"I'll have a guard cut it out of—"

"No!" Caius interjects, his voice hard.

Aggonid spins on his heal and strides back to the table, calling over his shoulder for the servant to bring him an extra helping of ground gnomes.

I shriek, vaulting myself over the back of the couch, my nails extended. Just as I make to rake them across his face, he catches my wrist, and I fall into his lap. He digs his claws into me, drawing blood.

He hisses, yanking his hand back at the contact. "And you'll take off that fucking necklace!" He holds his hand, which oozes that sinister black oil that bleeds from him whenever he tries to injure me.

I snarl, pressing my free hand to the pendant around my neck. "Never."

He roars like an enraged beast, shoving me off him.

I tumble to the floor, scrambling away on all fours.

His eyes harden, and he moves towards me like a predator, the oil dripping to the floor from his wound as his shadows work to repair it.

I back away, shaking my head. "Please," I plead, tears spilling from my eyes. "Don't hurt me." Visions of my flesh tearing on the sharp grass assaults my mind. Drops of crimson, staining my clothes.

He stops, staring at me with a mix of pain and anguish in his eyes. His hand comes up as if to touch me, but then he draws it back, clenching his jaw.

Caius helps me up, turning my chin towards him. "Don't be silly, he's not going to hurt you. Here," he threads his fingers through my hair. "In exchange for a kiss, a real one, I'll stop eating the ground gnomes. Alright?"

I hesitate, my gaze flicking between the two of them. Aggonid's no longer oozing that acidic oil, but his face looks guarded. I turn back to Caius and nod.

"Okay," I whisper.

I cower as Aggonid launches the platter across the room in an angry rage. It shatters into a thousand pieces, showering the room in a stream of gravy, meat, and bone. The servants stop and stare, unable to process the sudden outburst, until Aggonid storms out of the room, slamming a door with such force that the chain rattles and echoes through the hallway like a gunshot.

He can't have gone far because the chain is still slack, and I can feel his wrath linger in the air.

As soon as he's gone, Caius turns to me, his gaze smoldering with something primal. Heat radiates from his skin as his hand cups my face, and I succumb to the allure of his touch, desperate for the comfort it provides. He pulls me closer until our bodies are so close, I can feel his breath against my skin.

"Everything will be alright. Don't you worry." His words promise safety, yet there's an underlying urgency in his voice that promises something far more than security. It promises something magical.

He crashes into me, his hands gripping my waist while his lips touch mine. His kiss is filled with passion, charged with electricity that spreads through my veins like wildfire. His grip tightens and his kiss deepens, and I can feel the weight of the walls I've built around my heart crumbling away. An emotional torrent overwhelms me, something that I never knew was still alive and hidden away in the corners of my soul. His kiss unlocks ancient parts of me, and I'm filled with a warmth that I thought was long gone.

My body slams into the wall, my back aching with the force of impact, and I'm suddenly aware of Caius's rough hand in my hair. I part my lips and surrender to the whirlwind of heat and desire that is Caius. I revel in his touch as he twists my locks in his fist, his tongue tasting me and sending shivers down my spine. I can't help but grind against him, seeking more of his heat. With a gasp I rip free of him, embarrassed by my own blind passion.

Wilder. I'm doing this for Wilder.

"Deal sealed." He grins, his chest heaving. "You okay, Morte?"

I back away from him, overwhelmed by the intensity of the moment. My cheeks heat, and I press a hand to my mouth, feeling the lingering echo of his kiss. Caius smirks, his eyes twinkling as he leans against the wall, crossing his arms over his chest. "Now that you've accepted my deal, I'll collect it at a later time."

"Wait, what?" I sputter. "But we ... we just kissed." More than kissed. It was like a storm had broken loose, and our bodies were the eye of the hurricane, intense and focused on only one thing: consumption.

"Ah, that we did, little bird." He stalks towards me. "That was us sealing the deal. I still have to collect it. I can't help you got a little carried away." He shrugs, his tail tracing the curve of my thigh.

I take a step back, willing my heart to settle in my chest. "Fine."

"Perfect," he grins. "Now, let's eat some ... vegetables?"

I nod, and he brings me back to the table, now free of any spilled food. The servants bring us a variety of fruits, nuts, vegetables, and greens, arranging them neatly on the silken tablecloth. As we eat, I can still feel the heat of his lips on mine. No matter how many times I try to push it away, it's always there. I tell myself that no good will come from entertaining his advances.

But sometimes, my lady parts want to just throw everything to the floor like Aggonid did, and let Caius lay me on the table, becoming his willing feast.

His eyes linger on me longer than they should. Each glance sends shivers through my body that I can't deny, and I know I'm in trouble.

Aggonid might be the devil, but Caius is the one who will tempt me all the way to hell. Planting ideas in my head that maybe this place isn't so bad after all. And that is a very dangerous thought indeed.

When we're sated, Caius pushes his chair back and offers me his hand. "Come, my darling starling. Let's see what our Aggonid is up to."

I reluctantly take his hand, and we follow my chain to an adjoining room. As soon as I get a full view, I recoil, spinning on my heel after having gotten an eyeful of Aggonid submerged up to his neck in a steaming pool of water.

But with Caius still holding my hand, he spins me right back around, capturing me in his arms to make sure I stay to watch Aggonid bathe.

He languidly dunks his head under the water and then resurfaces with a satisfied sigh, a slight smirk on his face as if he knows I'm watching.

I blush, embarrassed and flustered, and try to squirm out of Caius' grasp. He holds me tight, whispering in my ear, "Let him know you don't fear him."

My breath hitches, and I can't help but feel a ripple of desire course through me. For a moment, I forget everything—the chains, the darkness of the underworld, Bedlam, and my mission—and focus on Caius' breath against my neck.

I can no longer deny he holds sway over me, especially as his lips meet the base of my throat, his tongue grazing against my skin. Before a moan escapes me, the moment is broken when Aggonid stands from the tub, a glint in his eye as if he knew exactly what he was interrupting.

I breathe in deeply, feeling the balance of power shift back to him. Willing my eyes to remain above his waist, I focus on the necklaces dangling from Aggonid. It appears to be made from giant talons, or teeth. Or perhaps they're bones?

He strides toward us, a fierce possessiveness in his gaze, and I go preternaturally still, though my heart thunders against its cage. I flinch when he reaches his hand up, relaxing a measure when I realize it isn't me he's reaching for, but Caius.

Aggonid leans in, locking lips with his lover, and I'm caught between the heat of their bodies and the cooling water dripping off his naked form.

Caius keeps me plastered to his front, and I combust in his embrace as their kiss deepens. A groan rumbles in Aggonid's chest, and I feel it all the way to my toes from the intimacy of it all.

My breathing quickens as they close in, the space between us melting away until it's as though the only thing that exists is the three of us in this moment.

Caius's tail wraps around my leg, tugging me harder against him, and I'm overwhelmed by the intensity of their attraction.

When they finally break apart, I can only stare in shock at the raw, primal connection that had just passed between all of us.

I'm royally fucked.

CHAPTER NINE

CAIUS

*M*orte might be a virgin, but arousal pours off her so thick, I nearly choke on it. Her pupils dilate, her skin flushes, and her breathing quickens. So when I lead her to the bedroom, she doesn't protest. As though caught in a trance, she follows me up the stairs, Aggonid not far behind her.

I open the door to the bedroom, and she's clearly awestruck by the sheer decadence of the room, a regal setting befitting Aggonid's status.

The walls are adorned with deep purples, blacks, and blues, and the four-poster bed is draped with garnet silk and strewn with fluffy pillows. A few candles light the room, casting a gentle glow. Though, not enough light to scare her away.

She'd bolt from the room if she saw the straps on the side of the bed, the leather cuffs and chains, the whip and flogger resting on a table nearby. For now, these things remain hidden from her view.

When she turns to me, I'm enraptured by her beauty. Her curves are perfect, enveloped in Aggonid's shadows, and her eyes are wide with an innocence I want to consume. Like a fresh daisy resting high upon a hilltop, ready to be plucked and admired.

Morte tugs at her top made of shadows, shifting on her feet. "I don't have pajamas," she whispers.

Oh, this sweet little bird. In a single motion, I brush the hair away from her eyes, like scarlet satin contrasting with the roughness of my fingertips. "We don't wear those here."

Leaning in closer, I can smell her fear, and it only makes my need for her sharper. I clasp my hands around her waist, sliding them over her hips, caressing her curves.

"Then what do we wear?" Her voice trembles slightly, her breath coming faster by the second.

I want to answer that she will wear my marks on her body, but the words form a knot in my throat. "Nothing." I step back, reaching behind me to pull my shirt over my head.

She swallows, eyes trained on my hips, and where they dip below my waistband. With one hand, I undo the buckle on my belt, then tug it free of my pants. She watches, transfixed as I unbutton them, and drag down the zipper with agonizing slowness.

Aggonid's form presses behind me, enveloping me in a sea of heat and seduction. His fingertips trace the soft dip of my shoulder blades, right where my wings sit when I have them out. They trail down to my hips, before circling towards the front to tug my pants off.

Morte stares, entranced, her breath caught in her chest. Her throat bobs as my desire springs free, and her own blooms in response; her eyes take on a glazed quality, and her heat perfumes the air.

"This is how we dress." My voice is a purr as I tilt my head, allowing Aggonid access to my neck. His teeth graze my skin as his hands move around my waist, pulling me tight against him. "Do you like it?" I whisper.

She swallows, her cheeks a bright pink. "Yes," she breathes.

My hand follows the curve of my thigh before I grasp my cock, giving it a firm stroke as the rings clink together at the base.

"Get undressed," I breathe, the tension draining out of me with each pull.

With achingly slow movements, she wrenches her shirt off, allowing Aggonid's shadows to fall away and revealing the smooth contours of her flesh.

Morte's nipples are tight and hard, pale skin dusted with a faint blush. My breath catches as her skirt follows, and my gaze is drawn to the graceful line of her hips, down to the creamy skin at the juncture of her thighs. Nestled between them is a small patch of hair. I'd love to spend hours worshipping her with my tongue, drinking in her arousal. It's all I can think about as the fire in my veins ignites while I marvel at the sight before me. She's a vision; a stunningly beautiful creature I can't wait to get my mouth on. But there will be time for that later.

"Come here," I growl, my voice thick with need.

She remains frozen, transfixed on the movement of my hand.

"She's no phoenix, Caius, she's just a chicken." Aggonid chuckles in my ear. "And chickens can peck in their own yard."

He drags me over to the bed, tossing me onto the mattress. Gaze heavy, he tackles me and rolls me over, pinning me down with one hand on either side of my head. His face is inches from my own, his breath fanning across my skin.

"And this is my yard," he growls.

My eyes remain trained on Morte, who stands sentinel at the side of the bed while Aggonid sucks on my neck. Desire has me trembling even as my body relaxes beneath his hold. He takes his time, exploring my bulk with his tongue and teeth.

I reach a hand toward Morte, begging her to join us. As soon as her palm touches mine, a knock sounds at the door, and she yanks it back.

Morte

WHAT THE FUCK was I thinking, about to join the devil in his bed? I take several steps back, plastering myself to the wall opposite them, clutching it as though it can keep me from doing something stupid. Like beg them to let me join.

I love Wilder. I may never have sex with him, especially seeing how he's probably found his anchor—I never did find out what he was trying to tell me before the hydra came—but shame and guilt still war with my lust for these strangers I feel a strange pull to.

Aggonid rumbles in warning, yet he flops onto his haunches and bellows for whoever is outside the door to enter. Before I can even make an attempt at covering myself, the knob twists and the door creaks ajar, allowing a flood of light to engulf the room, fully revealing me in a twisted heap on the floor trying to collect Caius' shirt to steal. Though it's too dark to make out their exact features— not that I recognize anyone around here anyway—I can tell by their large stature that this figure is a male.

He glances at the bed, candlelight flickering over his face like liquid silver, and I suck in a breath, immobile to the spot. He whips his head in my direction, and then his eyes trail back to the bed for a moment before settling back on me. Fire licks around his pupils, sending my heart into a frenzy.

Azazel.

Azazel clears his throat, speaking to Aggonid though his eyes don't leave mine. "High King Finian Drake will meet with you during the next Bedlam Moon."

My heart pounds in my chest and I struggle to hold my chain steady in my hands. "Finn? You talked to Finn?" I approach him, my chain dragging on the ground behind me.

He swallows and looks away from me, jaw clenching with the effort of not devouring me with his gaze. He shakes his head and opens his mouth to speak, but no words come out.

"Did he find a way to get me home? Does he know I'm here?" I search his face for answers, my heart beating like a drum in my chest. From here, I hear his pulse skyrocket. "Azazel?"

The spell is broken when Caius wraps a possessive arm around my waist and tugs me against his side.

Azazel blinks, meeting my eyes. "Huh?"

"Does Finn know I'm here?" I cling to the shirt in my hand, holding my breath.

"Oh, uh. No, I didn't talk to their king, just relayed a message that Aggonid needs to speak with him."

His throat dips, and as he turns to face Aggonid, I survey Azazel's form. Tall, broad shouldered, and oh. *Oh my.* Erect. *Very erect.* I swallow and quickly break my gaze. The thought of him so aroused for me turns my insides to jelly.

I clear my throat, despite Caius' arm squeezing my waist—a warning, I'm sure—and direct my attention back to Aggonid.

"Do you think he'll be able to bring me home?" Had I been wrong about him? Maybe he's really going to ask him to help me get back to Bedlam.

Aggonid barks out a laugh. "Doubtful. It's only ever happened once before."

My chest deflates, and I slink out of Caius's hold, retreating to the shadows to steal another one of their clothes.

Once I'm dressed, I bring my eyes back to the group, the sudden need to escape nagging at me like a persistent itch.

"Was that all?" Aggonid asks.

"Yes, my lord." Azazel bows.

"Then you are dismissed."

Azazel pauses, then looks to me once more. He smiles, a flicker of something strange in his expression. And then he's gone.

I stand frozen in his wake, my heart hammering against my ribcage. Before I can process what just happened, Caius drags me to the bed, throwing the covers back for me to climb in. He's naked and in a sour mood.

Curling up, I try to keep my distance from him, though as soon as he crawls in next to me, he pulls me into his chest without a word. His magical aura engulfs me in warmth and comfort, and the bed dips on his other side as Aggonid joins us.

"How do you know Azazel?" Caius whispers against my ear, sending a chill through me, despite its heat.

"He healed me."

He stiffens behind me. "When?"

"My first night. I'd eaten some berries near my hut. He called them Inferno's Kiss?"

89

Caius curses, tugging me closer. "I'll feed you, little bird. No ground gnomes, and no Inferno's Kiss berries, either."

I adjust so my wrist is on top of Caius's enormous bulk and the chain isn't between us but draw my hand back when I meet Aggonid's.

Tucked into his embrace, I allow my thoughts to wander. If anyone can find me a way home, it's Finn. His mother is the Luna goddess, who holds dominion over fates. She controls all magic, and if you're a good fae when you die, you join her beyond the veil. If she can't restore me to Bedlam, maybe I can go with her. I haven't been a good fae, but I'm trying to make it right, to fix what I broke.

My intentions were good.

It was the execution that I royally fucked up. Is that enough to convince the Luna goddess to take me with her, after I get Wilder out of prison?

If I could just do that, I'll gladly go wherever she thinks I deserve.

Even if it means I'm stuck in the underworld.

Aggonid

I ALMOST GAVE IN. The call of her soul is almost too much to take, begging for me to hold it, to love it.

Is that what caused her to chain herself to me? Does she feel it, too?

My mate is cruel, but I am crueler. I won't give Morte a chance to break the bond between Caius and me; the bond I cherish above all else. Morte will be safe in his arms until I can get rid of her for good. Once she's back where she belongs, I'll stop pining for her; the distance between worlds too great to feel the pull.

I need to stop imagining what it'd be like to slide between her thighs and make her mine. To sate this ache inside of me, demanding I claim her. Like a siren, she tempts me with every lashing, every heated gaze thrown my way when she thinks I'm not looking. It calls to the beast in me.

But no, I can't let her win. She'll take everything from me.

My heart twists painfully as I watch Morte pressed against Caius's chest, his steady breaths lulling her to sleep in his arms. I can feel the warmth radiating from her body and my cock twitches with longing, desperate to bury itself inside her. So much so, I use my magic to eviscerate the clothes she came to bed with. She knew the rules, but chose to ignore them.

I clench my fists until my nails dig deep into my palms, controlling my urges to rip her away from him and make her mine. I can't help but slide my hand downwards, imagining it's her curves that I'm caressing, her body that trembles in anticipation of my touch. Morte may be off limits, but I can still dream.

With my head thrown back and eyes tightly shut, I picture her in my arms and my skin tingles in anticipation of the forbidden pleasure. Fisting myself, I pretend she's ours, and I'm buried in her.

It's a dangerous game to play, the metal clanking together from where the manacle is cuffed at my wrist, but I can't seem to help myself. I beat a steady rhythm against the mattress and let my thoughts will me away, thrusting against my palm's tight grip as I picture her curves. I'm so close to coming, so close to being lost to the pleasure of it all.

But then a quiet moan from Caius reminds me of my limits. He rolls to his back, still sound asleep, but lying on his chest is the one woman who can ruin this all for us.

She breathes deeply, her crimson tresses splayed over his abs. Her bowed lips part, and a soft, quiet wind blows from them with each exhale. I can't help but stare, mesmerized by the beauty in front of me. The blanket is pulled tight against her, her breasts nearly spilling out the top of it. All it would take is a little tug and I'd reveal those perfect little rosebuds I'm dying to close my mouth around.

Desire climbs inside me, the heat slicking my skin with sweat, so I throw the covers off me, continuing to stroke my cock. I watch the rise and fall of her chest, unable to turn away from the sight. My own breathing becomes shallow, the urge to pull her onto my lap growing ever stronger.

A tiny gasp escapes her, and my eyes snap to her face, meeting her wide-eyed stare. My gaze never wavers, as if daring her to look away. Her hand slowly inches up Caius's chest, her fingers curling around his shoulder. I can feel the pull between us even though we're not touching. Her leg hitches over him, and she rocks her hips against his in time to my stroke.

I can't take much more of this and with a groan of pleasure, I let go, thick ropes jetting out and spilling my seed on my abdomen. Morte's eyes widen and a whisper of pleasure escapes her lips. I've never wanted anyone more in my life than I want her now, *but I can't have her.*

Still strung high despite my orgasm, I roll to my side, drawing myself closer to Caius. She watches as I gather my release from my stomach, then I pull the blanket down and strain my neck to reach Caius's ear.

"I need you," I whisper.

He stirs, eyes fluttering open. A gasp escapes Morte and she makes to shrink away from him, but his hand flies out, clasping tight to keep her in place.

I reach between us, tugging on Caius's cock, feeling the metal bars against my palm. A groan escapes him, and he rocks his hips against my lubricated fist.

Morte watches us intently, her cheeks pink, eyes glazed and heavy. But I see where Caius has her pinned to him, and with every piston of his hips, he's creating friction for her, right where she needs it.

Voice laced with desire, Caius calls her name. Her eyes snap to his.

"I'm redeeming that kiss."

"Now?" she squeaks.

"Now."

Morte

92

IF I WEREN'T ALREADY in hell, I'd know exactly where I'd be headed. While I was too chicken to be more than a spectator, Caius made the decision for me, forcing my hand.

I lunge for his face, my fingers dragging along his rough skin as my eyes lock onto his. I press my lips against his with a hunger that could devour worlds, feeling my heart race and my soul tremble as I succumb to the kiss. His gaze pierces me, seeing all my secrets and desires without ever uttering a word. It's too much, so I shutter my eyes.

Caius groans, the sound vibrating between our mouths, tongue dancing with mine. The feel of him, the smell of him, and the warmth of his body merely feed the flames of my desire and my hands explore his muscled shoulders and chest as our tongues tangle in a slow dance. His fingers wrap around my thigh, and he pulls me closer until I'm straddling him, right above where Aggonid stokes him. Where my clothes went, I don't know, but I don't care right now.

My breath catches as he maneuvers me lower, exposing me to Aggonid. Caius swallows my gasp, just as Aggonid grips my hips, sliding me against Caius's length, skin against skin.

The cool bite of metal hits the small bundle of nerves hidden between my folds, and I glide over the bars, back and forth in a steady rhythm, the pleasure building, punching me with sharp need. My lips hum against his as my head falls back in utter surrender, and Caius kisses the column of my exposed throat. If I were to adjust the angle just right, he'd spear me, but I'm not ready for that leap.

Instead, his canines drag against me, and my hips buck as the bliss that floods through me is too much, and I come undone. I'm too raddled with lust to feel any shame or guilt.

I slump against him, the pleasure, and our combined scents, a drugging mix that leaves me languid and groggy.

The heat of Aggonid retreats, but he doesn't go far because the slack remains in our chain. Caius holds me close, face in my hair. After a few long moments, he pulls away, and I open my eyes to find him watching me with a smoldering hunger, his hand twined in mine.

"I'm going to keep this," he murmurs, his eyes bright with emotion.

"What?" I ask dumbly.

"You." His fingers tighten around mine. "Your heart, your soul, my eternal flame." His accent rolls through each word like a prayer.

I swallow, unable to deny the thrill his words send through me. My beast purrs and preens inside of me, rolling over, desperate to be taken care of by him.

Then reality comes crashing in as my thoughts turn to what Wilder would think, and I scramble off his lap, already missing the fire between us. Shame creeps in my chest.

Aggonid watches us with a knowing smirk, lounging lazily against the headboard, but I don't care.

I turn back to Caius, determined to make him see sense. "Caius," I urge him, willing him to understand. "You and I can never be together. I don't belong here."

He shakes his head, the intensity in his gaze growing until it almost burns me. "You belong here with us more than you could ever imagine."

I force myself away, but Caius catches my arm and pulls me close once more. Angrily, I wrench myself away, pushing back until I meet the wall, and I slump down, folding my arms over my knees and hanging my head.

Like a whirlpool spinning out of control, my thoughts drown me.

Wilder is in *prison* because of me, and I'm in bed with the devil and his lover. The same devil who killed me without a thought or care. He didn't know I'd regenerate here, but he killed me anyway, all because Caius wants to fuck me.

And why the hell was I about to give in? To them both?

Holding tight, I try hard to suppress the tears that threaten to overcome me. But no matter how much I fight it, the pleas for me to return to bed push me over the edge. By the time they roll down my cheeks, I'm burying my face against my thighs, heaving quiet, quaking sobs.

CHAPTER TEN

CAIUS

*M*y chest aches, the beast clawing desperately to take over, to tend to her needs. Hour after hour, my pleas for her to come to bed remained unanswered as she lay broken on the floor, despair wracking her body in fits and convulsions of silent sobs. Finally, when exhaustion had taken hold of her and lulled her into a deep sleep, I carefully picked her up and brought her back to my side of the bed.

A pale light streams in through the curtains, though she doesn't stir. Not even when Aggonid speaks to me.

"I need to prepare for the hunt, so I'll need Azazel to remove the key from her stomach."

My beast rears its head inside of me, knowing what this signifies. Morte will no longer be chained to Aggonid, so I won't be able to keep a close eye on her. And with the hunt coming up, she'll be at risk. He prowls at the back of my mind, daring anyone to come close, so he can sate his growing hunger to protect her.

"When were you planning on telling me it wasn't you who chained her?"

He swallows, and I run my fingers through Morte's hair, desperate for touch.

"I think it was her beast who did it."

I nod. Sometimes, they have a will of their own, though I'm not mad. I'm glad she tethered herself to him. She can't get away.

"She would've, you know."

"Would've what?" he asks.

"Let us both take her." I sigh. "But she loves another."

Agony rips through me at the thought. My only comfort is knowing she'll never get to go back to him. The only chance she has at reuniting with him is if he dies and is sent here. Considering she's so innocent and pure, he probably is, too, and he will end up beyond the veil. It gives me some measure of comfort, knowing I won't have to share her with any more males. Though ... if he's keeping her from being with us, maybe I'll drag him to hell.

Aggonid is so determined to deny what he feels for her, but I see it in his face. Feel it in his heart. Just as my own beats for them both, his beats for us.

A knock sounds at the door before Aggonid can respond to me, and he shouts for them to come in. The smell of sizzling eggs and buttery pastries permeates the room as servants push the door open, carting in a full meal and setting it on the table across the room.

"Would you like us to serve you in bed, my lord?"

"No, but I need you to get me Azazel."

The servants bob their heads and scurry away, pulling the door shut behind them.

Morte stirs, and once she realizes where she's at—in my arms—she scrambles back. I hate when she does that. Doesn't she know I just want to hold her?

"What was that about Azazel?" she asks, her voice still groggy with sleep, and it's the cutest fucking thing I've ever heard.

"Say that again," I whisper.

"What?"

"Enough," Aggonid clips. "The food is getting cold."

Morte snaps her attention to him, looking wary.

"No ground gnomes," I whisper to reassure her.

She crawls out of bed, approaching the table with tentative steps, and I follow her. She mutters something under her breath before sitting down and reaching for the food, but I stop her.

"Let me." I place my hand on hers, my warmth seeping into hers.

Aggonid stares us down, his features twisted with a storm of emotions, from rage to sorrow. He violently turns away, smacking his temples with the heels of his hands and grinding his teeth so hard his jaw clicks. Every inch of him screams with seething anger.

I make her a plate and set it in front of her. She takes a hesitant bite before letting out a groan that goes straight to my dick.

A smile spreads across my face as I make myself a plate and join them. Morte hums happily, scarfing down the food as though she'd been starved for days. I watch her, unable to take my eyes off the gentle sweep of her lashes and the soft fullness of her lips as she eats. The same lips I'd devoured last night.

When she finishes, I slide my plate over to her and she takes it gladly.

I might've spelled it to put her in a good disposition, but she doesn't have to know that. Resting my chin in my palm, I watch her eat with a kind of satisfaction, knowing it's me who made her happy. So what if I had a little help from my magic. I should've done this weeks ago.

From the scowl Aggonid sends me, he's probably figured it out, too. Oh well.

He should've thought of it first.

Morte leans back, sighing in contentment. "I'm stuffed."

"You could be," I purr, earning me a grin from her.

Aggonid clears his throat, drawing our attention to him.

"Yes, love?"

He turns towards Morte. "I'm going to need you to unlock the chains once we've retrieved the key," he smiles sweetly at her. He's using my spell to make her more agreeable.

"Mmm," she hums. "I don't think so."

My posture relaxes, watching the two volley back and forth.

"You don't have a choice," Aggonid says darkly. "Unlock the chains or else."

She stares at him, and his face turns hard. She takes a deep breath and stands, pushing her chair back. Planting her hands on her hips, she narrows her gaze. "Or else what?"

Morte meanders towards the bedroom door, and I scramble after her. Where in the blazes is she going?

Aggonid has no choice but to follow, lest he want to be dragged behind her. She trots down the hallway, taking the stairs to the main level where the giant bathroom is. By the time Aggonid slips inside, she's stripping out of her clothes, revealing her slender curves.

He stares at her in shock, then spins to face me. "What is she doing?"

"Bathing." I smirk, already following in her wake. "You going to join us, or are you just a spectator now?" There's more than enough room for a small army in this.

Morte steps into the bathtub, and the warm water envelopes her body. Steam rises from the surface, creating a thin, impenetrable fog that swirls around us as I climb in with her.

Aggonid stops just outside the tub, a torn expression on his face. "Morte," he hisses.

She brings her hand to the amulet around her throat, playing with it between her fingers before dipping them between her breasts. "Yes?" she purrs, a smirk playing on her lips.

His jaw tightens, and he slams his fist on the edge of the tub. "You will unlock those chains after I pry the key from your body," he growls.

I wade over to her, pulling her away from his wrath. "Let's be civil, shall we?"

She only lifts her chin and regards him with stoic resolve. "You can try."

I band my arm around her waist, loving the hold she has over the both of us, even if Aggonid won't admit it. My little phoenix is less of a sparrow and more like an earth-like cassowary.

Pressing a kiss to the junction where her shoulder meets her neck, I keep my eyes trained on Aggonid, who's still shirtless and looking just as tempting as our little morsel. "You could make a deal," I offer.

His scowl deepens. He's not used to people bargaining with him because they fear him too much to ever tell him no.

Morte seems okay letting me hold her, so I back away to the little ledge along the far wall and keep her on my lap. All it would take it for her to tell me yes, she wants this, and I'd spear her right here. But instead, I'm content to feel her heat against mine.

"How about this, Aggie," she purrs. Oh, he hates that name. "If you promise to give Finn a message to pass along to Wilder, I'll unchain us as soon as I get hold of the key."

His eyes turn stormy, and he considers her proposal for a moment. Finally, he grunts. "If I must."

A grin spreads across my face. Perfect. "Come on in here, love, and make it official."

He levels me with a look that says I'll pay for that later. My tongue darts out to wet my lips, and a shiver of excitement runs up my spine in anticipation of it.

His fingers move with purpose as he undoes the knot around his waist, letting his pants puddle around his feet. He's full and erect, and I can taste the desire pouring off Morte as she drinks him in.

Me, too, little dove, me too.

He saunters into the tub, steam billowing around him as he takes his seat. Using his free hand, Aggonid takes hold of the chain and pulls us both in with a tug. My cock twitches at the contact, eager for what comes next.

We settle into the water, our feet just barely touching the bottom as we face each other. He grasps Morte's chin and drags his thumb over her bottom lip, eliciting a soft moan from her.

Morte

Aggonid gazes into my eyes, his lips soft and inviting. I know he won't kiss me—not yet—so I lean forward and trace my own lips along his jawline until I reach the hollow of his ear. His breath catches as I whisper my offer.

"I vow to free us from these chains, but will you want me to?"

Where that comes from, I don't know. Ever since breakfast, I've felt braver, more willing to take risks without fear. Almost as though the little hussy of a beast inside me has taken over, fallen to her back, and is begging them to sate her.

His knuckles graze over my cheek, and his hand gently cards through my hair. Behind me, I feel Caius's hard erection pressing into my back.

Aggonid pulls back, his eyes dark with desire yet tinged with sadness. I see my own longing reflected in his face, and the combination is both beautiful and heartbreaking. He opens his mouth to speak before he closes it, seeming to change his mind about what he's going to say. Instead, he says, "And I vow to ask High King Finian to bring your message to this Wilder."

And then he takes hold of my face and draws my lips to his own, and I surrender. This isn't like kissing Caius. This is like falling into a starry night sky, surrounded by more beauty than I can comprehend, and the only thing I can do is keep falling. It's a kiss of possession, a scorching, passionate claiming that promises far more than we bargained for.

His hands grasp the back of my neck, and his mouth moves with mine, not exploring, but knowing, exactly where to caress, exactly what pressure to use in order to tease a moan from the depths of my throat. It conquers me, and I know that if I let him, he could consume my soul as easily as he consumes my body in this single kiss.

His taste is molten honey, a mingling of heaven and hell, and I cling to him as though I could drown in it. He draws my legs around his waist, hoisting me as though I were weightless. He presses me against Caius's chest, and I revel in the feel of two hearts beating in perfect harmony with my own. Pinned between two demon fae, I'm overcome by an ache so exquisite I can scarcely breathe.

Aggonid rips himself away, dropping me as though I'd burned him, and I feel as though I've been deprived of something essential. Caius utters words that sound both like a prayer and a curse as he scoops me up to go after him. I catch two glowing red orbs in Aggonid's gaze before he storms away.

The moment is gone, and I'm bereft, my body and my heart transformed by the power of his kiss. I feel as though I've just seen a glimpse of something I'm not meant to understand. Something I'm not sure I will ever experience again.

Why does it feel as though I've been cleaved in two?

CHAPTER ELEVEN

MORTE

*I*t's pitch dark, and I feel trapped. I've locked myself in a closet, overcome with a grief I can't understand. Aggonid is somewhere on the other side of the room, and Caius pleads for me to open the door, but I ignore him.

Surrounded by linens and towels, I remain huddled in a corner, trying to make sense of how I got here. Confusing emotions run through me: longing, guilt, rejection, feelings of inadequacy. As hard as I try, I can't seem to get a grip on any of it.

Being in here reminds me of my small treehouse in Castanea, where after a long mission, I'd seek solace in the quiet. But the softness of the cotton linens and the warmth of the closet doesn't offer me the same peace this time. Instead, all it does is remind me that I'm trapped in a place I don't belong.

I can hear the voices on the other side of the door, deep and authoritative—Aggonid and Caius engaging in a fierce debate that I can't make out. A third joins them, and the ferocity of the argument builds until it is suddenly silenced. My heart races as I wait for the approaching footsteps to reach my door.

"Morte?" There's a soft tap on the wood.

It isn't Aggonid and it isn't Caius, either.

"What?" I croak, mortified that I now have yet another person witnessing my petulant-child act.

The phoenix who can enter the most dangerous missions Bedlam has to offer but hides when her feelings get too strong.

"Can I come in?"

I feel around in the dark, and after determining I might be able to fit one more in here, I say, "Okay."

The door opens, catching on my chain. Light spills in, and a giant hulking shadow fills the doorway. He squeezes in, joining me on the floor after he maneuvers the chain so he can shut the closet door.

"You okay?" Azazel asks, his voice a deep rumble.

A tear-riddled laugh escapes me. "Yeah."

"You want to talk about it?" His scent invades my nostrils, a warm, spiced aroma.

"No."

"Alright."

We sit in the darkness for what seems like an eternity before he speaks again.

"Looks like you're eating and sleeping better than the night I found you. I worried something happened to you when you weren't there the next day."

"You said you were going to stop by in the morning." I shift to face him, though I can barely see him in the dark. Fae have pretty good eyesight, but the shadows are different here.

"I did."

"Really?"

"You were sound asleep, so I refilled your canteen at the river and left you a basket of bread and butter just outside your door. Didn't you see it?"

"Oh." I deflate. "I'm sorry, I didn't leave my hut until Aggonid dragged me out of it that night."

He hums in response. "You ready to untether yourself from the devil?" Amusement coats his voice.

"Will it hurt to get the key?"

He's quiet for a moment. "It doesn't have to."

103

I'm taken aback by his softness and compassion once again. It's something I don't expect from a demon, but his warning not to trust him still hangs in the back of my mind. "What do you mean?"

"I'm a master of elements, but I need to feed from you to coax the key up your throat."

My breath catches. "You need to ... feed from me. Like a vampire?"

He chuckles. "Kind of."

"What will it feel like?" I swallow hard.

"If I make it hurt, you'll feel like I'm pouring molten metal through your veins."

I flinch. "But you won't, right?" I've had more than my fair share of agonizing torture. It comes with being a phoenix.

"I could make it feel good."

"Well, of course I'd want—"

"It'll feel like the best, most drawn-out orgasm of your life," he interrupts, "and you will climax."

"Oh ... that sounds ... nice." My face heats.

He laughs and I swear there's a hint of tenderness in it this time. "You'll try to get us both naked."

"What?" I sit up straighter.

"It's an intimate process, and that's why Caius is against it." His voice drops an octave.

"What other alternative is there?"

"Cutting it out of you, or hoping it passes, though it's unlikely on account of its shape."

"You've done this before?"

"Once. It was during war, and the enemy had swallowed the key to Aggonid's chains. I made it hurt."

My heart squeezes. Someone chained him? Suddenly, the fact that I put my own chain on him eats at me.

I want to get him out of them now more than ever.

"Let's do this."

He chuckles. "In here?"

"Where else would we do it? I don't want them watching." On the other hand, maybe I should, since he already established, he can't be trusted.

"The bed would be better. More room." To emphasize his point, he shifts in the cramped space.

"Okay," I whisper, dreading seeing Caius and Aggonid.

Azazel slips his hand in mine, helping me up before turning the knob and pushing the door open. Blinding light penetrates my eyes, and I'm forced to squint until someone quickly shuts the heavy curtains.

Caius lunges towards me, crushing me in his embrace. As comforting as it is, I can't succumb to the temptation and push him away. I can't allow myself to get further attached since I have no status here and am just a disposable prisoner they can use for their own entertainment. His grip tightens, before he reluctantly lets go of me.

My eyes find Aggonid, lounging on the bed like a spoiled cat. His gaze moves from my nervous face to Azazel's, then to our intertwined hands. He raises an eyebrow, but doesn't comment, though his jaw ticks.

"Well, well," he drawls. "She lives. Let's get this over with."

I hesitate, squeezing Azazel's hand. "You're not staying on the bed."

He smiles, but there's no warmth in it. "I'll be here to make sure he doesn't take too much."

I whip my head towards Azazel. "Is that possible?"

He pauses, the air tense. "Theoretically, yes. Likely? No."

We stand in silence for a moment before Caius clears his throat. "Let's get this done."

I force my trembling legs to take me closer to the bed, my chest tightening with anticipation. I can barely breathe as I lie down, my gaze fixed on the canopy above me. Then, with a tug of the chain, Aggonid adjusts it, so it isn't too tight against my skin.

An inferno of heat radiates around me as Azazel's body envelopes mine and Caius joins us on the bed. The warmth pooling in my stomach is almost painful as Azazel's breath caresses my cheek. Despite my fear that has me frozen in place, he chuckles in my ear and whispers, "Relax, this is going to be the best night of your life."

Gritting my teeth, I try to keep my breathing even. Azazel's fingertips trace my collarbone, and I can't help the way goosebumps raise on my skin. I feel the shadows in the room converge, as if watchful of what we're about to do, keeping vigil over my terror. He leans in closer, and I can feel the fire of his essence melting away the chill of my panic.

His hand moves to grip my throat, his thumb pushing my chin back as my heart thrashes against its prison of bone, a wild surge of adrenaline coursing through my veins. My beast paces in the depths of my mind, hungry for whatever he's about to offer.

Desperate for it.

He closes in, his body pressing heavily against mine, engulfing me in his heat. His lips press against my pulse, igniting a passion like I've never felt before. Just below my ear, his fangs pierce my skin.

Pain blooms into pleasure, an exquisite flame that has my body thrumming with a bliss I've never experienced before. My breath catches as the power swirls around us, and I claw at his back, pulling him closer until he's nestled between my thighs.

His fangs draw my essence from my veins, and a need so deep has me tearing at his shirt. I don't know who he is anymore, nor who I am, or where we are. I've shredded his shirt, hooking my legs around him, driving his pelvis against mine. His bare chest meets mine when I slice a nail down the front of my top.

As he feasts, his power courses through me. He works his mouth, tasting me as I gasp and moan, dragging my hips against his, but it isn't enough. I hike my skirt up, bunching it around my waist, desperate for more friction as he laps at my neck. There's still too much separating us, and while his erection presses where I need it, it isn't enough.

"More," I beg. "I need you."

"Who?" someone asks.

"All of you," I moan.

His teeth sink further into my flesh and he—whoever he is— groans at my neck.

"Fuck, I need to be in her," someone grits out next to me. "Come on, Az, let me in."

The man at my neck shifts, but a growl from the other side has him remaining in place.

"You can't fuck her, Caius," they snarl. "She's not in her right mind—"

"Someone better get me off," I whine as pleasure climbs.

The man's tongue slides over my neck, and I cry out at the pleasure. He rises between my hips, pushing against me and adjusting his position at the same time, better angling himself as he drives into me.

"Take your gods damned pants off," I beg, but he just chuckles.

His fangs pull deeper, and the pressure builds low in my core. I'm struggling to think, my body rules my mind, caught in a wave of pleasure as he moves against me. I arch into him, floating and soaring as he claims me with his bite and thrusts.

I throw my head back, ecstasy crashing over me as I reach a deafening peak and moments later cry out my release. My nails dig into his back, shuddering as pleasure radiates through me in waves. It's so intense that my consciousness fades in and out—one second, I'm aware, the next I'm gone, lost in the sensation.

When I come to, he's still between my thighs, his fangs embedded in my neck as aftershocks rip through me.

Sometime later, I'm aware of voices and movement around me, but I'm too weak to open my eyes, and I'm still locked in a lust-induced haze. There's pressure at my neck before cool air rushes in, my body still humming with pleasure.

"Fuck," someone curses.

"Did you get enough?" another asks.

"I think so."

"Well, get on with it then."

"She needs to rest. Maybe get some clothes back on her," the man says, his voice thick. "She's going to be a bit out of it for a while."

"Mmm," I groan, rolling onto my front, capturing someone as I do so. He's warm. So warm. "No clothes."

Whoever's under me stiffens in my hold.

"I think Morte wants some more orgasms," the other man chuckles.

"Yes." I reach between my thighs. "More. I like those."

The man under me shifts, his heat seeping into me as he stills. I nuzzle my face into his neck, breathing in his scent as I press my body closer to him.

"You," I murmur in his ear. "You'll give me orgasms?"

He doesn't respond, but his breathing deepens, so I take matters into my own hands. My fingers slide between my folds, finding the spot that still throbs. I circle it slowly, seeking out my pleasure with his body beneath mine. Moaning, I arch into him, desperate for more. His arousal presses against me, and he readjusts, rumbling low as he wraps an arm around my waist. His other hand moves up my back, to thread through my hair and tilt my head back.

I'm just finding my release as he lifts my head and my eyes fly open, and as my vision clears, meeting his molten gaze, his burning with an intensity I can almost feel.

And that's when I know who's beneath me—the devil himself.

I scramble off him, my cheeks burning as I curl into a ball, my eyes wide and unblinking. Aggonid stares at me for a long moment before he finally speaks.

"Well, that was unexpected," he says, his voice low and a little rough.

I swallow, unable to find the words I need. Staring, I try to make sense of the last however many hours, as though the devil holds all the answers, I just have to find the right questions.

"Did we have sex?" I whisper, my voice barely audible.

The corner of Aggonid's mouth quirks and he pushes himself up, settling into a sitting position. He's bare-chested and wears only a pair of low-slung black silk boxers. "Make no mistake, Morte, if we had sex, you'd know."

Gulping, I swivel my head to the other side of the bed where Caius lounges.

He's naked.

"Did you ... did we ...?" My eyes trail to the metal bars ringing his rigid erection. Is that what felt so good? Oh gods.

I gave him my virginity.

Caius smirks. "No."

I move to a seated position. "I wasn't dreaming," I mutter, searching my thoughts for all the fragments of my memories.

He laughs, his eyes twinkling. "No, you weren't."

I glance behind me and startle to find Azazel there, his lip piercing glinting in the candlelight. This man is fine as hell. "I had sex with *you?*"

"Don't sound so put out," he growls, running a hand through his hair.

Oh, that did sound bad. "No, I didn't mean it like that." I brush a strand of hair behind my ear, heat crawling up my neck. "It was just ... *wow.*"

Azazel grins, revealing sharp white fangs. "We didn't have sex, Morte. I only bit you."

My brow furrows. "B-bit me?"

He nods and steps closer, his eyes burning with an intensity that sends a shiver down my spine. "It gave you the best orgasm of your life, didn't it?"

I nod, my cheeks flushing at the memory.

"Do you remember swallowing the key?" Aggonid asks, and when I turn towards him, his eyes are heated.

"The key ..." I look away, searching my memory. I glance down at my arm, suddenly aware of the cold metal of the manacle. "Oh. Did you get it?" I whip towards Azazel.

"Not yet." He grins, and my eyes dip to where an erection strains against his pants.

He notices me staring, and adjusts himself, though it does little good: he's *packing.* Good gods.

"You may want to get some clothes on." He clears his throat.

"Huh? Oh!" I stammer, realizing I'm naked. Quickly, I scramble to wrap the comforter around myself.

Caius takes me in with a hooded gaze, his voice low and suggestive. "Next time, Morte."

Clutching the blanket to my chest, I turn back to Azazel. "Did you get what you needed from me?

The intensity of his gaze scorches me, and images of him crushed against my naked body have me pressing my thighs together.

"No, Morte." He grins. "But I got what we need to get the key."

I swallow, heat pooling low in my stomach.

Azazel steps closer, and his hand brushes mine, sending a jolt of pleasure through me. "Ready to get the key out?"

"Will it hurt?" I gulp, my pulse racing.

Azazel reaches up and touches my chin, lifting it until my gaze meets his. He leans closer and speaks softly. "No, Morte. I can promise you that it won't hurt. You're wearing your necklace of protection, remember? It'll feel good, for the most part."

I nod, barely able to think straight, and Azazel takes my hand. He lays me down, cradling me against his chest.

He places his lips against my neck, breath igniting a flame of desire deep within me.

I shouldn't be feeling this way.

His teeth scrape lightly against my flesh, and he rests his hand low on my stomach. A tingling sensation radiates outward, and I close my eyes, lost in the intimacy of it.

"This is only the beginning, Morte," Azazel whispers in my ear.

I nod, barely even aware of what's happening as his hand moves in slow circles against my stomach. My body relaxes, and a pulsing warmth builds inside me until I feel a surge of pleasure.

Azazel speaks a single word in an ancient language, and the feeling intensifies. My body throbs, and I cling to his shoulder, doing my best to keep my whimpers and moans to myself. It's as though he's stroking every nerve ending, and I throw my head back to rest in the crux between his neck and shoulder, panting like an animal in heat. My hand cups the nape of his hair, and I hold on as the sensation grows.

He continues working his magic on me, rubbing and massaging in an upward motion. Each caress of his fingers is as though he's stoking the flame between my thighs, and I moan, helpless against his power. I writhe in his lap, the pressure building until I shatter. Arching my back, I cry out.

Azazel presses between my breastbone, and something shifts inside of me. My eyes fly open as an impression of heat passes from my navel to my throat, and something hard settles against my tongue. I cough, struggling to breathe as the key falls from my lips with a clatter.

I stare down at it in shock, my hand still clenched in Azazel's hair.

"Fuck," I swear.

Caius appears in my field of vision with a jealous look on his face. "You can let go, little dove."

I blink, arching into Azazel and releasing my grip.

"I'm going to need you to stop wiggling," he purrs in my ear, and I suck in a deep breath.

"That was ... intense," I murmur, my voice barely a whisper.

Azazel chuckles, helping me adjust the comforter around me, though he doesn't remove me from his lap. Caius peers at the key on the ground, and Aggonid steps forward to snatch it away.

He holds it up, along with his manacle. "Release me, *now*."

I snatch the key from his outstretched hand and force it into the keyhole, the metal scraping against the lock with a shrill whine. I turn it and a loud click reverberates through the air, followed by a clank as the metal band restraining him snaps and falls away. He wastes no time in rubbing his wounded wrist, hatred glaring from his eyes.

Crossing to the dresser, he pulls on some clothes before pressing a searing kiss to Caius' lips.

His voice is rough as he growls, "See to it that the prisoner is taken back to her hut, will you?"

The cavalier, impersonal way he says it sends a stab of agony through my chest. I am a prisoner. Nothing more. Nothing less. Tears come to my eyes, and I turn away, not wanting them to see my pain as I scramble out of Azazel's lap and towards the dresser to grab some clothes.

A small part of me was hoping things were different, that someone wanted me. Needed me as much as I needed them. But it's just history repeating itself.

Morte, loved by one, but not enough to convince the gods I deserve it.

In the corner, I unlock my manacle, wincing at the raw wound beneath it. Pulling clothes on, I stow the key in the pocket of my over-sized pants before scooping my chain up to bring back to my hut.

I take one last glance at the devil and his lover, feeling a heavy sadness settle over me before I turn and stumble towards the door, Azazel right behind me.

Never again.

CHAPTER TWELVE

AZAZEL

*M*orte strides through life with a steely confidence, but I now know her vulnerability. Aggonid's rejection cut her deeply, and I felt the same pain as if it had been my own. Even now as we soar together in the sky, her movements are stiff, mechanical, almost like she's desperately trying to suppress the fear she feels.

As we soar over the Lake of Souls, her anxieties radiate like a beacon. The dark depths of the pond mirror the sorrow in her eyes, and a sharp ache pierces my chest at the sight of it.

"Hey," I shout across the chasm, willing her to look at me. "What's wrong?"

She meets my gaze, her eyes glistening, and then looks away in an attempt to hide the single tear spilling down her cheek. Her crimson wings flare brighter as she ascends higher.

I cast a sideways glance at Caius, who shrugs his shoulders. I want to reach out and comfort her, to tell her that everything will be alright. But I know better than to push it. Nothing about the underworld is alright. Instead, I focus my gaze ahead and fall in line beside her—a silent vigil, ready to hold her hand should she need it.

We carry on in silence until we reach the other side of the forest where her hut is. Caius remains in the sky, scanning the area for threats, and I decide I hate him a little less. Morte lands first and I follow, only to find her leaning against a tree, sobbing.

I grapple her close to my chest, my heart pounding in my ears as her tears spill down her face. I whisper fiercely against her hair, desperate for her to hear me. "It'll be alright," I insist, feeling the urgency of my plea course through me as I pull her even closer.

Morte turns to me, her eyes awash with tears, and smiles weakly. Her body still shaking, she buries her head in my chest. I hug her closer, feeling a surge of protectiveness that I never thought I could feel for anyone.

Caius lands on quiet feet, coming to our side. "Little dove?" he murmurs.

He looks down at Morte, and his gentle expression makes me feel even more protective of her. Caius nods subtly, understanding the battle she's fighting in her heart.

"There you three are!" someone calls. "I was worried something had happened."

Morte pulls from my embrace, blinking the tears out of her eyes.

"Irid," I greet Caius' sister. She looks less menacing than usual. She's had a chip on her shoulder ever since her mate was killed. Not that I blame her any.

Caius steps protectively in front of Morte, as if to shield her.

"Oh, brother. I won't harm the girl." She chuckles. "I'm here to see if she's ready for the upcoming hunt?"

Morte rises to her full height, standing stoic. "As I'll ever be, I suppose."

"Good." Irid smiles, her gaze turning almost indulgent. "I come bearing gifts." She reaches into a satchel over her shoulder and takes out a dagger.

Morte stares at the offer for a beat and then she reaches out and takes it. She turns it over, almost in awe, running her fingers over the intricate engravings along its hilt.

Irid points to the blade. "You'll need something to defend yourself with. Word has gotten out that you're close with Aggonid and my brother, so you're a prime target. Keep it close, and strike first." She unsnaps her breastplate and hands it to Morte. "Wear this during battle. You may have that necklace, but it only protects you if they aren't willing to die to hurt you. If you die, they die."

Morte nods and tucks the dagger in her pocket. "Thank you," she says softly as she slides the plate under her arm.

Irid bows, then turns to Caius. "Come, brother. We have a hunt to plan for."

Caius gives Morte one last lingering look before turning back and following his sister.

"Hey." I give Morte's shoulder a squeeze. "I'll treat you to some dinner at the tavern. You were busy getting off during lunch, and I'm sure you're starving."

Her head snaps up, eyes narrowed. "What do you want for it?"

I smirk, amused. This fae. "Your company is payment enough."

Morte hesitates. "You told me I can't trust you."

I sigh. "Fine, if you would like to repay me by allowing me to feed from you, consider us even." The idea sends a jolt straight to my cock.

"F-feed from me?" Her eyes widen. "Isn't that kind of already giving me something?"

"What do you mean?" I keep my face stoic.

"You know ..." She gestures vaguely.

"Ohh," I smirk. "The orgasms. Yes, I suppose you're getting those, too."

A deep flush spreads over her porcelain skin, from her cheeks to her neck and down to the valley between her breasts. A wave of desire radiates from her, making my heart pound and my cock twitch. Her lips part slightly, and a tantalizing scent wafts up to me, my nostrils flaring to breathe her arousal in deep. Fuck. It has me wanting to haul her over my shoulder, drag her through the door, and ravage her until she's screaming my name. I need to feel her tight little pussy around me as I make her mine.

A rumble of desire escapes my throat as I draw near to Morte and suggest, "You could let me feed from you somewhere else." I let my smoldering gaze drift across her body, before settling between her thighs and raising a brow. My tongue flicking against my tongue ring, and I purr, "Has anyone ever made you come with their tongue?"

A pink blush spreads across her cheeks as a breathy whisper escapes her lips. "No."

I step even closer and growl, "That's a shame." My hand slides slowly down her stomach, settling to cup the mound between her thighs. With a shuddering hiss I beg, "Let me feed from you here."

She inhales sharply, her breath hitching in her throat. I can feel her trembling beneath my touch, her body warring with her mind. She stares at me for a long moment before finally nodding and allowing herself to succumb to desire.

"Excellent," I murmur. I hook her arm around mine and lead her to her hut. "Get changed into some clothes that fit you, and we'll head out." *I really just want her out of Aggonid's clothes.*

"I don't have anything else."

"You sure about that?" I raise a brow and glance over her shoulder.

She follows my line of sight to a small trunk at the foot of her bed I'd had delivered while she was recovering earlier.

"Who in the … I didn't earn anyone's favor," she mumbles as she kneels in front of it. After lifting the lid, she pulls out a few simple pieces of combat gear. I could've got her something lacy and frilly, but she's going to need something to fight in if she wants to survive here.

"This will do." She slips the leather corset on, cinching it tight against her torso. She grabs a pair of pants and slides them up her legs.

"Good." I smile approvingly. "Now let's eat."

She gulps, looking nervous.

"Ay, at the tavern. We'll save my meal for later." I wink.

Morte and I stride solemnly down the winding path, surrounded by a dense forest that looms taller with each step. She gazes up at the sky, her face awash in wonder at the lofty spires that penetrate the clouds, and the menacing gargoyles that guard the treetops and shield these ancient woods from intruders.

My grip tightens on her shoulder as a monstrous beast lumbers across our path. I sharply turn us away so it can't spot us, heart pounding in my chest and an icy chill running up my spine. Night stalker. I hate those little fuckers.

My hands grip hers as I drag her through the winding passageway, lit only by a single torch. We descend a steep staircase, worn into the rocky wall, and arrive at a seedy tavern nestled in the nook of an old village. Patrons cease their conversations and watch us cautiously as we stride forward, no delicate steps but powerful strides, until I spot an empty table near the back. Their hostile glares follow Morte. No doubt they've heard of the phoenix with bright red hair.

A loud, boisterous laugh explodes from the bar as Victoria de Feu saunters over. Her eyes, as black and deep as the far side of the moons, are locked on Morte.

"My, my," she purrs, fluttering her eyelashes. "Who do we have here?"

She's an incubus fae from the realm of Bedlam, and she's as rotten as they come. Her presence is like a menacing cloud, cloaked in black velvet and bedazzled with glittering jewels. She reeks of enchanted glamour that clouds the senses, luring unsuspecting victims with her lust magic. Thank the gods I'm immune to her charm, and to others like her.

"Morte, this is Vic," I grumble. "She's not your friend."

Victoria laughs, not offended in the least.

"No," she agrees. "But I can be very accommodating." Her eyes rake over Morte's body, and I have to suppress a growl. "What can I get you, sweetheart?"

Morte's eyes heat, but she turns to me. "What are we having?"

"Get her the nectar wine and chargrilled bat wings smothered in a sticky black sauce with a side of hellbeast hearts. I'll have the same."

Victoria turns to Morte, whose eyes glaze and she leans in closer. "Why don't you come pay for this now, sugar, and I'll return you to your little friend after?" She trails a nail down the side of Morte's face, and I snatch her arm away before she can do more.

A whimper escapes Morte's lips, no doubt the lust rolling off Vic in waves. "I'm paying," I snap, and I slam a bag of coins into her hand. "Now fuck off."

Victoria hesitates and looks back over her shoulder with a smirk, her eyes burning with a dark power. The air around her is thick like tar, smothering all in its presence with a heavy veil of her sorcery, yet I remain untouched by its hold. A rancid stench of bitterness lingers on my tongue, like an indelible mark of her spell.

I turn to Morte, taking her hands in mine. "Are you okay? She didn't hurt you, did she?"

Morte shakes her head and takes in a deep breath. "She smells good. Who is that?" She tries to get a better look.

"She's an incubus fae," I snarl, my lips curling back in revulsion.

"Oh, no." Her eyes widen, and fear and panic spread across her face. "The lust. I'm drowning in it." She gasps, her body trembling as she fights against her own desires.

"Best way is to expel it," I purr, a sly smirk on my lips. "But seeing how we're in the middle of a crowded tavern, you'll just have to wait. Unless," I lower my voice, leaning close enough that my breath tickles the side of her ear, "you want me to take you out back."

Morte's eyes go hooded and her lips part, her tongue brushing against her lips. She leans against me like a hellcat in heat before she manages to pull away.

Someone bumps into me from behind and I spin around with a snarl before my eyes settle on a familiar sight.

Emeric.

I launch to my feet, my arms wrapping tightly around him in a crushing hug. His chest rumbles with laughter before he slides into the chair across from Morte and me. His black hair falls in disarray and his dark skin glistens with sweat. His eyes sparkle with an icy brilliance; when his gaze falls onto Morte, an unmistakable craving flashes across his face. He smirks, his sharp fangs glimmering in the light.

"Who's the beauty?" His eyes dance with interest.

"Morte." I gesture to my friend. "Meet Emeric. He's a pain in my ass, but one of the only people you can trust around here."

I give him a pointed look.

"Nice to meet you." Emeric smirks and offers his hand.

Morte takes it gingerly and glances over at me with a nervous smile. "It's nice to meet you, too."

Emeric raises a brow. "What are you doing running around with a guy like him?"

Her face reddens, still caught in the crosshairs of Vic's potent magic as she squirms in her seat. My fingers curl around her thigh, seeking to reassure her.

Morte's desperate eyes lock on mine. The hunger radiating from her is palpable, and my heart thuds wildly in my chest. She wraps her lips around her bottom teeth, trembling from the intensity of her desire as she stares at me, unable to look away.

Emeric's amused chuckle pierces the silence and I feel his eyes on me. "Ah, I see what's happening here," he says. "Are you going to help her out or do you need me to step in?"

Emeric catches my eye and a smirk tugs at his lips as he watches the incubus set up a table beside us. I feel an invisible force radiating off him, his eyes full of knowledge and silent understanding. Emeric eyes Morte hungrily, licking his lips as if tasting her already.

She glances at me nervously and I give her a nod of encouragement. "Phoenix fae from Bedlam," she says, and Emeric takes a sharp intake of breath.

"Can't say I've ever encountered one of you before," he says, taking a longer swig of his nectar wine. His eyes never leave Morte's face as she inches away from him, her gaze wary.

"Emeric is a hellhound," I add, trying to lighten the mood. "He bites."

Morte's mouth forms an O of shock and Emeric barks out a laugh, leaning in close to her.

"Don't worry," he drawls, his voice low and dangerous. "I only bite if you ask nicely." He winks at her and takes another sip of nectar wine.

"You on a mission?" I brace my hand against Morte's thigh, letting her know I'm still thinking of her, even though my attention isn't on her.

He nods. "Irid has me helping out during a meeting for the hunt.

Says Aggonid's got a guest during it and I'm not to let anyone in or out without his say-so. Something about the upcoming Bedlam Moon." He thumbs through the napkins before pulling one out, scribbling something on it with a pen he had tucked in his leather jacket.

My eyebrows pinch as I absently trace a finger around the rim of my glass. "Aggonid's guest? Who?"

"Don't know. He didn't say, but I figure it's someone important if Irid doesn't want him getting disturbed." He frowns and takes another swig of his drink. "Sounds like trouble brewing."

Emeric turns back to Morte. "You be careful out there, okay?" He gives her a wicked look. "Especially with that stunning face of yours." He slides the napkin across the table towards her.

She glances at me before grabbing it, her cheeks turning a deep shade of pink as she turns it over. I peek over her shoulder and read the words with her:

He might have a big cock, but I've got two.

At the bottom, he's drawn a small map of how to get to his place.

Her head snaps up, her eyes wide with shock, but he's already disappeared. If it weren't so funny seeing that look on her face, I'd be pissed.

"Is it true?" she whispers, leaning in.

I snort and nod. "I'm surprised he didn't whip them out right here. Always showing off his prehensile appendages."

"Wait ... you mean he can control them?" Her face is twisted in horror. "W-what does he do with the other while one is in use?"

A half-smile curls my lips before I give her thigh a gentle squeeze. "Don't you worry, he never does anything with either one without consent." I lean back and take another sip of my drink, the alcohol buzzing through my veins. "Food's here." I nod to where Vic balances a tray on her hip.

The woman prowls towards our table, her lips curled back in a wicked smile as a malevolent stench of dark magic assails my nostrils. My stomach lurches and an invisible force crashes over us like an ocean wave, and I can feel Morte's hand trembling in mine beneath the table.

Vic sets our plates down slowly before us, allowing us time to suffer under the oppressive force of the woman's lust magic.

Morte ducks her head, refusing to make eye contact with the predator, her entire being focused on the plates before her. A whimper escapes her lips, and Vic's maniacal laughter fills the space before vanishing as suddenly as she appeared.

Taking a deep breath, Morte's eyes lift to find mine. "That was ... intense."

"Once you get your magic back, you'll be better prepared to resist." I reach for a fork to give to her.

"What kinds of magic can you do ... besides ..." She clears her throat.

"My specialty is in metals, a lot like dragon fae, except I don't hoard treasure. The easiest way to fuel my magic is to feed, where I get access to concentrated metals and energies. I can then use the magic to form, shape, and manipulate metal in whatever way I want." I pause, drawing in a breath as I turn towards her. "As a phoenix, you obviously can regenerate ... or could until recently, I assume?"

She nods, her gaze hardening as she stares at her plate. "For thousands of years, until one day I didn't come back." I strain to hear her words over the clamor of the tavern, so I lean in closer. "But while here, I died after being dragged across some type of metal grass."

Vorpal blades. My breath whooshes from my lungs and I numbly sit back, my mind reeling. If she weren't a phoenix, she would have been gone. Forever. An emotion like broken glass slices through my heart, leaving me with painfully shallow breath. Terror engulfs me in a vice-like grip, a desperate need to never let Morte out of my sight. To protect her no matter what.

When I finally speak my voice is raw with emotion. "Who did that to you?"

The tenderness in Morte's gaze tells me all I need to know; she offers me a melancholy smile and whispers a single word. "Aggonid."

As though her pain were my own, a surge of rage and sorrow explodes within me, my hands clenching and releasing in an attempt to contain it. My mind screams for vengeance, thoughts of retribution clouding my judgment. I thought they'd been getting along great. More than once I'd caught them naked together, though maybe it wasn't what it looked like. Is that why she'd been hiding in the closet? To get away from him?

Pushing my plate aside, I cup her chin, my thumb brushing the line of her jaw. "I'll never let anyone hurt you again," I vow.

I'll make sure of it.

CHAPTER THIRTEEN

MORTE

*A*zazel reminds me so much of Wilder, but with a much darker edge. His protective streak manifests in violent threats toward anyone who dares to cast a glance in my direction. His intimidating aura is like a menacing forcefield, shielding me from harm and the jeers of people in the underworld.

Aggonid's rejection stung hard, but it's a comfort to be taken care of by someone who understands what I've been through and wants to keep me safe. Leading a legion of the fiercest warriors in Bedlam might give me an edge to others brand new to the underworld, but it'd be a mistake not to find allies in this place.

With a full belly, Azazel and I make our way back to my hut, the lust having worn off as soon as we left the tavern.

"Where do you live?" I glance at him, noticing the way his eyes keep darting to the sky.

He gestures towards the path to the left of my hovel. "About a two-minute flight that way. I'm your nearest neighbor, unless you count the animals that prowl these woods. I'll show it to you sometime."

"Azazel, why are you being so nice to me?" I pause, bracing my hand against my doorway, the wood and metal worn. It's got deep gouges, as though someone raked their claws across it. A chilling reminder I'm not in Bedlam anymore.

Which brings me back to my suspicions. He told me I can't trust him.

"I don't know." He cups the back of his neck, his eyes averted from mine. "Maybe we could help each other."

Narrowing my eyes at him, I cross my arms over my chest. "In what way?"

He grins, his shoulder propped against the outside wall of my shack. "I told you how I fuel my magic, right?"

I blink. "You want me to be your food source."

"And in return, I'd be yours." He shoves off the wall, stooping to pinch a berry off a plant at our feet. "See this? It'll kill you." He gestures to the rest of the plants. "You have no food source. No water. The underworld isn't meant to be an easy place to survive in, Morte. It's designed for torture and suffering. If you had someone who could supply you with what you need, you'd have a fighting chance to stay alive."

He hurls the fruit at the trees and I'm about to respond when something swoops in and grabs it, snarling a throaty growl. The creature is as big as a house cat, with wings of fire and teeth like jagged daggers. I stumble back in horror.

"What was that?!" I gasp.

He pulls me inside and slams the door shut. "Cinderwings," he says gravely. "It's midnight. The beasts of the woods begin their hunt for prey. If you see one, run for cover."

"What do they do?" I peer through the window as another shadow passes by.

He takes a step closer and speaks in a whisper, his voice tight with dread. "They'll tear the flesh from your bones, but first they'll pin you down with their talons. Cinderwings might seem small, but their weight is almost as much as yours and if you're trapped beneath one, there's no getting out." He yanks the curtains shut, showering us with a thick blanket of dust that makes me double over in fits of sneezes.

An ear-splitting screech pierces the night, and terror freezes me.

"What the fuck was that?" I whisper hoarsely before Azazel grabs me in his iron hold, his hand slamming over my mouth.

He drags us away from the window as it shakes violently from the force of something lurking outside. A wave of panic surges through me and my heart thrashes like a wild animal. Not even Azazel's protective embrace can quell the terror flooding my veins.

The haunting sound of claws scratching against the hut walls causes my skin to crawl with alarm. My grip on his arm tightens as I stare at the menacing shadow passing through the small gaps in the wood. Every nerve in my body screams that this flimsy structure won't be enough to keep the creature out.

A muffled shriek escapes between my fingers clamped over my mouth when the beast slams against the door, causing it to vibrate and groan under its weight. I frantically try to undo the buckle of my belt loop, until I'm able to produce Irid's dagger, firmly held in front of me with a trembling hand. The beast circles around and around the building, snarling with menace and all I can do is stand there, unable to move, and pray that we'll survive.

My heart thunders as the vibration shakes the floor beneath my feet and I can feel it digging to get in. With a firm grip, Azazel tightens his hold on me and pulls me further away from the window, without ever taking his eyes off it. He releases me, standing to face me with a finger pressed to his lips, his eyes blazing in warning. I nod in understanding, and he drops to one knee, reaching under the bed to grab the metal chest plate Irid had given me earlier.

He holds up three fingers for me, his dark blue eyes stern in their intensity, and it takes me a moment to realize he wants me to do something on the count of three. He inclines his head towards the window, and I approach on wobbly legs. Gesturing for me to move the drapes on the count of three, he mouths the words:

Three!

Two!

One!

I yank the drapes open as the beast comes charging at the glass, its giant maw gaping open as it slams into the window just as Azazel uses his magic to seal the metal plate to it. The creature screams in agonizing pain as it crashes to the ground, yet it quickly recovers and skitters away into the night.

Azazel wraps me in his embrace, crushing me to his chest as my limbs tremble with fear.

"Will it come back?" I whisper, and my voice doesn't sound like my own. It's terrified.

He pulls back to look me in the eye, holding my face between his hands as he brushes a crimson strand from my cheek. "Not tonight. But others might."

"What was that thing?"

"A soulstealer. They can't get through metal—it burns them—but there's no telling where it will find a way in next time." He takes a deep breath, his eyes softening. It's so at odds with his hardened exterior. "You're not safe in this dilapidated shack."

"But where will I go?".

"I'll build you a metal fortress," he pauses. "I won't leave you unprotected."

Gripping his shirt, I shake my head. "I don't have any more metal."

"I'll get some."

"You can't go out there!" I shriek, clinging to him.

He chuckles. "In the morning."

"You'll stay with me tonight?" I peer into his eyes, lost in the deep blues.

"Yeah, I'll stay." He presses his forehead to mine and places a tender kiss on my brow when he releases me.

Azazel uses magic to light the torch on the wall. It fills the room with a soft glow as he reaches into his bag he has near the door, pulling out a canteen and taking a swig before passing it to me. The bottle is metal, with a warm, silver-plated finish. Bringing it to my lips, the water is cool and refreshing, settling my panic for a moment. Sharing a bottle with him feels intimate, and I can't say I hate it.

He gestures to the trunk near my bed. "There are some pajamas in there."

"How do you know that?"

"I sent them."

"You're the one who sent me the trunk full of clothes and supplies?" I ask, feeling a little choked up. "When I was ... recovering?"

Why did he tell me not to trust him when all he's done is given me reason to trust him?

Azazel nods before he pulls his shirt over his head, revealing his tanned skin and tattooed chest. Swirls of ink coil in patterns that seem to move, like the lake full of souls I flew over. The sight is breathtaking, and I can't help but stare.

"Azazel..." I whisper.

His gaze never leaves mine as he reaches for his belt, undoing it with one hand and throws it aside. "Yes?"

It's all I can do not to run my fingers along his chest and back. "Thank you for taking care of me."

He smiles, and it's so at odds with his hardened exterior. He takes the canteen from my hands and sets it aside before he wraps me in his arms. "You're welcome, Morte. I think it's time you call me Az. It's what my friends call me."

Heat envelopes me, and I let out a strangled sound, feeling as lust-ridden as I'd been at the tavern. Only this isn't manufactured lust. It's the real deal. Or at least, it's an adrenaline-fueled breakdown after fearing for his life.

As though he knows the effect he's having on me, he pulls back, motioning towards the trunk. "See if there's anything in there you like."

His voice is low and though not tender, it's kind.

I obey, knees shaking as I make my way to the trunk and rummage through the clothing until I find a loose-fitting silk button-down shirt. It's azure, the fabric so dark it's nearly black. The cuffs are frayed, though the rest of it is pristine. Feeling shy, I wait until he's turned around and slip it over my head. It falls mid-thigh, and the distinct scent of spice curls around me.

He turns around and surveys me, eyes trailing to my bare thighs. "It suits you," he says huskily.

My heart flutters as those words linger in my mind, echoing over and over. I take a shaky breath, forcing my mind to stop relishing in the closeness of him. He grins, slowly dragging his gaze up and down my body and I feel the heat pooling between my legs. Gesturing to the bed, he suggests what's to come and my mouth goes dry. I slowly stand, feeling a tug toward the bed as I approach it. Sitting on the mattress I cross my ankles, trying to block out the anticipation that's climbing up my spine.

"We don't have to do this." He joins me, intertwining our hands as electricity buzzes between us. His touch sends waves of pleasure through me, making it harder and harder to resist. "But if you choose to, I won't stop you."

I gaze up at him warily, my eyes darting over every inch of his face, trying to uncover whatever secrets lie hidden within. Somehow the closeness of him is soothing, but I'm still guarded. "I don't even know you—"

A feral cry from outside pierces the air and I jerk backward, the moment broken by the beast's looming presence.

"Will it get us?" I curl up into a ball and tuck myself further back onto the bed, making sure every part of me is safely tucked away.

"I won't let anything hurt you," he murmurs as he wraps his arms around me, pulling me tight against him.

I take a deep breath, trying to calm myself. His heart thumps steadily in my ear and I can feel its power both reassuring and terrifying me to my core.

I grip his shirt tightly in my fist as the ravenous cries of what sounds like wolves claw at my door, desperate to claim me. I shudder, my body trembling with fear, and yet I find comfort in his tender touch as his hand moves through my hair. My finger follows the lines of his chest, learning the hard dips and curves that form the armor of this mysterious man.

I know next to nothing about this man who came to save me. All I know is he works for the court.

"Where are you from?" I ask, still unnerved by the sounds just outside.

"Here," he murmurs.

"You were born in the underworld?" I prod.

He hums. "More or less. Two hundred more years until my servitude is over." He speaks solemnly, as if a heavy weight sits on his shoulders.

"Then what?" I press him further.

"Then I'll be free to go wherever I wish in the abyss of the underworld."

"Why do you have to serve Aggonid?" I ask, dreading the answer.

"Punishment for being an acquaintance to someone who wronged him. Mine was a thousand years of servitude to the court."

"But that's not fair." I look up at him, my eyebrows furrowing. A pang of sorrow reverberates through me. "I'm sorry," I whisper. "You shouldn't be forced to pay for someone else's sins."

All the more reason for me to get Wilder out of prison.

Az drops his head in resignation. "It is what it is. That's how life works in hell, Morte."

"Have you tried winning the hunt to get out of it?"

He sneers, mocking himself. "I've won the last thirty hunts. But I can never wish away my servitude."

"Why not?"

"I pissed Aggonid off. So, he cursed me to stay put, even if I win the hunt every time. Caius is the only one who can break the curse."

I gape at him in shock. "Caius?"

"Yep," he clips.

"Oh." I consider Caius for a moment. "Why him?"

"He's the Lord of the Hunt and head of the Royal Guard."

He shifts to face me. "Why do you care?" he asks, searching my face.

I shrug. "No reason," I mumble and look away, my heart fluttering.

"Really?" he prods, his voice low.

The way he looks at me makes me feel exposed. I bite my lip and sigh. "I guess I just wanted to know more about you," I admit softly.

A smile slowly spreads across his face, and something in the air shifts. "I'm flattered." He takes my chin in his hand, forcing me to meet his gaze. "What else do you want to know?"

My breath catches in my throat and adrenaline rushes through my veins. I'm not sure what to say. I opened Pandora's box and now I'm not sure what to do with it.

"Everything," I blurt out eventually, steeling myself for whatever may come next. "I want to know everything."

He chuckles, his eyes flashing with amusement. "My favorite color is black," he declares, his voice low and passionate, capturing me in its thrall. "But not black like the shadows that haunt us in our sleep, but black like the color the night sky turns when the sun retreats into nothingness. I love the smell just before it storms, because it's like all the bad is being washed away by a cleansing rain, and the sound of darksteeds taking flight. That's my favorite thing about being here." His words drift away, his gaze distant, as though searching the room for something long forgotten. "I used to have parents, and I'm still getting used to being alone." He releases my chin. "Do you have any more questions?"

I shake my head, overwhelmed by the vulnerability in his words. We sit in silence for a few moments, both of us lost in our own thoughts. Then I reach out and take his hand in mine. He looks at me with surprise but doesn't pull away. He intertwines our fingers and gives my palm a kiss.

My secrets are what caused so much pain to the man I love. I don't want to hold them alone anymore.

My vision blurs with tears as I choke out, "My best friend is in prison because of me." I committed an abominable crime, yet he had taken sole responsibility for it. Nothing I said could convince them otherwise, and he had stayed true to his decision to protect me at all costs.

"He must love you very much," he murmurs, rubbing his thumb across my hand.

The unbridled love on Wilder's face that day on the beach cleaves my chest in two as the memories resurface. He was always protecting me.

I might not be his anchor, but he's mine in all the ways that matter.

"And I love him too," I whisper, my voice cracking with grief.

"How long is he in for?"

"Forever," I reply, feeling the weight of the sentence crash down on me.

He nods and pulls me close, and we lay together, holding each other tightly as the screeching and howling outside picks up. There are no words to convey the depth of my sorrow, nor can he offer me respite from the guilt I feel. All we can do is hold each other and accept that in this place, injustice and heartache are the only constants.

Sometime in the middle of the night, sleep claims us both, and I wake in his arms, content to stay in that moment. I'm safe here, in the arms of this man who no longer feels like a stranger, and for now, that's enough.

CHAPTER FOURTEEN

MORTE

*A*z works ferociously, transforming my wooden shack into a metal fortress, where I'm safe from the monsters and beasts of hell. With each clank of metal and deafening bang of a hammer, I feel more at ease. As he works, I pepper him with questions about the cruel reality of the underworld, Aggonid's malicious reign, and the ways in which everyone must obey his rules or else. He answers diligently, but his tone changes with each passing remark about Aggonid —it's clear he despises the ruler of this realm. His hatred intensifies with every rivet and bolt he places, until the shack is a fortress that only he can breach.

He speaks of Caius, and I'm completely taken aback to learn that Caius and Aggonid are actually mates and not just lovers, sending a wave of jealousy through me.

The idea feels foreign and out of place. I examine the feeling, and decide it's because they get to have each other, and I'm stuck on the outskirts, watching them being happy.

"What's Irid's deal?" I ask, my curiosity piqued.

"She loves Caius, but things between Aggonid and her are complicated, and that causes contention with her brother."

Dark images of a shared past flash through my mind. "How so?" I press on, dreading the answer.

"Aggonid forced her to execute her mate, Vayne," comes the chilling reply. The shock of it knocks me back and I drop the canteen I'd been about to take a sip from. Water soaks into the ground as I scramble to pick it up, my heart racing wildly as I try to comprehend the agony Irid must have gone through. "He makes her work for him, but she hates every minute of it."

"Why would he do such a cruel thing?" I whisper to myself in disbelief.

Az, who hammers away at a sheet of metal, stops and looks up at me. "Vayne was supposed to be next to rule," he says gravely. "But Aggonid had other plans, so he made sure his own brother would never take the throne."

"Aggonid's brother was Irid's mate?"

He hums. My heart sinks as I slowly understand what he means. So that is why Aggonid rules the underworld—not because he's actually supposed to, but because he'd forced his way into power by killing his own brother. It's no wonder Irid despises him so much.

"Oh my gods." I throw a hand over my mouth. Aggonid had his own brother killed by his mate. "What does Caius see in him?!"

"They were mates long before he took the throne." He sighs, pulling a poisonous plant and tossing it into the woods to make room for a few metal spikes. "Thousands of years in the making." He shrugs.

"Love," I supply, and he nods somberly.

"Who ruled before Aggonid?"

"His parents. Someone slipped into their room in the dead of night and silenced them with the slash of an enchanted blade—designed to kill gods."

The realization crashes into my mind with the force of a tidal wave, freezing me in place. "What? No!" I manage to gasp, my voice barely audible as I try to comprehend the thought. How could such a coldhearted act be committed, and by whom?

He stands, turning to face me with a solemn expression, his words confirming what I already know. "It's true," he says.

Dread fills me as I ask him the question on my mind. "Do you think it was Aggonid who killed them?" My voice trembles, and I feel horror at the thought that this being who shows so much love to Caius could commit such an atrocity. But then again, he killed me with zero hesitation.

His unwavering gaze tells me everything I need to know. "No doubt in my mind."

"Did you know his parents?"

"Not well, but enough. Before they were killed, Aggonid and Vayne were in charge of both hunts, as well as doling out favors. Vayne was my mentor, and I, his protege."

Realization sinks in. This is another reason why he doesn't like Aggonid. "I'm sorry." I place my hand on his arm, feeling the weight of his pain and sorrow.

He nods, looking away as if he can't bear to show emotion. We stand in the silence, connected by grief and the unspoken truth that the world isn't always fair. Then, something in his posture shifts, radiating with a brave, burning courage that forces his gaze to mine. "Someone has to hold him accountable."

My breath catches and I yank him inside, glancing around before slamming the door. "He's a god. You can't plot against him, Az, it's suicide!"

"Who said anything about that?"

I open my mouth to reply, but he continues before I can speak.

"Besides," he says, his expression softening a bit. "If I thought it would make a difference, I'd do it. But I'm not foolish enough to try and take Aggonid on my own." He moves closer, backing me into a wall. "Then I'd miss out on this pretty little face and redeeming my payment for dinner."

He winks, and a burning heat spreads across my cheeks, sending a tingle of anticipation through my body. His promise of what lies ahead sends the conversation into a feverish frenzy and I can no longer contain the anticipation. I wrap my arms around his neck, pressing my body hard against his as I whisper in his ear, "Well, you'd better not forget your promise, then."

"No one could forget the promise of spreading wide your thighs and tasting the sweet nectar that lies between." His lips crash down onto mine, tasting the metal bar against his tongue as ours dual, forgetting the darkness of reality for just one moment.

He hitches my leg over his hip, deepening the kiss and sending lightning bolts of pleasure straight through me. The heat between us intensifies, engulfing every inch of our skin with an insatiable craving. Aggonid's name is quickly forgotten as we give in to our desires.

The promise of a night of passion pulls us further away from the darkness, spinning us into a world separate from our reality, where we're prisoners to a cruel god.

Hoisting me up, he pins me to the wall, rolling his hips against mine. His mouth trails along my neck as he unbuttons my top, pressing his lips against the exposed skin.

The sudden jolt of a knock sounding against the door acts as a bucket of ice water poured over us. My heart races in my chest and I catch my breath, my body tingling with lingering desire. I briefly consider pushing him away and pretending nothing happened, but something stops me, an invisible force keeping me in his arms.

I clear my throat. "Who is it?"

"Caius and Irid." A familiar feminine voice chuckles. "Who've you got in there?"

Az looks at me for a moment before releasing me, stepping away and taking a deep breath. His eyes fill with frustration as he storms to the door, yanking it open enough to stick his head out.

"We're a little busy." He wedges himself in the door so they can't see beyond it.

"What in the gods name are you doing here?" Caius bellows, wrenching Az by his shirt collar.

"We were ... just talking," he responds, his voice cool, eyes blazing with fury.

Irid slides her body around Caius's shoulder, her eyes blazing with hungry intensity, like a wild animal ready to pounce. She inhales deeply, and I can see the understanding in her eyes—she knows what we were doing.

"I'll say," she purrs, prowling towards me. "I want a taste, too."

Just before she reaches me, Caius blocks her path with an outstretched arm and says in a low voice filled with warning. "This one is mine."

She freezes, her mouth twisting into a frustrated pout before she turns to look at him. "You're a spoilsport. She smells so delicious."

Caius's icy gaze strikes me like a lightning bolt, and my heart jolts in my chest. He looks at me with an intensity that is unmistakable, his voice deep and dark. "Morte."

My breath catches in my throat as my name rolls off his lips like thick velvet.

"You made me a promise," he croons, each step closer to me as if stalking his prey.

"What promise?" Az challenges, his arms crossed in defiance.

Caius whips around with a snarl, his countenance that of a ravenous wolf. "If she gives anyone her virginity while she's here, it's mine."

My heart thunders, my breathing erratic. Az stares at me, mouth gaping and brows furrowed.

Caius steps closer, his gaze hot and blazing as he lifts a hand to my cheek. My skin prickles with electricity, desire pounding through my veins like an unstoppable river. His thumb grazes my bottom lip, and I know I'm moments away from surrendering. My skin pebbles at the feel of his fingertips brushing against my cheek.

Until I remember—he's Aggonid's mate. My head jerks back, pulling away with effort, and I level him with a fierce glare. "No! You forget my other stipulation," I snap, the words tasting like ashes in my mouth.

He steps closer but doesn't try to touch me again. His gaze is tender now, and it's doing more damage than his hungry one.

"And what's that?"

"You could take my virginity or watch." I stand tall, forcing as much bravado into my words as I can.

Irid barks a laugh. "Gods, I love this girl." With a grace that belies her size, she saunters over to my bed, ominously making it her own.

Her gaze is heated, like a blazing fire, as if she could devour me whole with a mere glance. "I'll rock your world, phoenix." A smirk curves her lips into a devilish grin. "Just say the word."

"I am not watching my sister have sex." Caius whirls on her.

Irid rolls her eyes and shrugs, unfazed by his incredulity. "You've done worse." She flops onto her back, tucking her hands behind her head for a pillow since my bed lacks one.

"Like what?" He runs a hand through his dark blue hair.

"Oh, I don't know." She sits up, leveling him with a look. "Letting your mate order me to kill mine?"

The room grows suddenly still, the air thick with tension. I swallow hard. Caius stares at her, his face stretched tight with anger and grief.

"That was different," he growls, his fists clenched at his sides.

Irid snorts and shakes her head, though a flicker of agony crosses her features as she turns her attention to the ceiling. A wave of grief radiates from her, pummeling me so hard, it steals the breath from my lungs.

I can't speak. Can't do anything but blink away tears as I try to wrangle my feelings.

She's the first to break the silence. "You did something different to this place."

I raise a brow. "Uh, it's all metal now?" It's not quite Bedlam Penitentiary, but it'll keep the monsters out.

"No, there's something else. Like a feeling. Something I've never felt before." Her eyes narrow, her voice a rich whisper, as though if she speaks too loud, someone will overhear us. "What did you do?"

I shake my head, glancing at Az, who sulks against the wall. He shrugs. "All we did was reinforce the place and would've christened it had you two not shown up." The sweat of our labors still clings to our bodies, even now, making the scent permeate the air. No doubt, lust, too.

Caius growls. "It's a good thing we did, then, otherwise you would've killed her."

I sink to the trunk at the foot of my bed, no longer able to stand. He's right. I'd forgotten all about it.

"Fae promises work the same here as they do in Bedlam." He crosses his arms. "If you break one, you're dead." He spins on me. "And you're the one telling me I'm not trustworthy? Did you really plan to break the promise you made to me?" Hurt flashes across his features.

"I'm sorry," I whisper. "Please ... I wasn't thinking." We'd been caught up in the moment.

"No, no one ever does." He shakes his head, crouching next to me and burying his head in his hands. "Get out."

No one moves, unsure who he's telling to get out. He looks up, a pained expression in his eyes. "Both of you, get out," he turns towards Irid before glancing at Az.

"But—" Az starts to protest.

"GET OUT!" Caius roars, his fury rippling through the room.

I squeeze my eyes shut, waiting for the explosion, but it never comes. After a moment, I open them again to find both Irid and Az gone. Caius doesn't look up, and his shoulders are shaking. Is he crying?

Slowly, I move over to him and place a hesitant hand on his shoulder, expecting him to pull away. He doesn't. Instead, he leans into my touch and wraps his arms around my legs, burying his face against me.

"I'm sorry," he whispers, his breath hot on my skin.

"For what?"

"I didn't ..." he shakes his head. "I didn't expect you'd try to break it."

I sink to a crouch, crushing him to my chest. "No, Caius. I'm the one who's sorry." My throat is tight, and the words barely escape me.

He lifts his head, and tears streak his handsome face. They leave tracks of glittering silver, like tiny stars in the night sky. "Do you love him?"

"What?" I sputter. "Azazel?"

He hangs his head, the anguish in his eyes visible. I've never seen this broken version of him before, and it's so at odds from his role in this realm.

I shake my head in disbelief. "Caius," I murmur, "I barely know him."

"So, you don't love him?"

Gently, I wipe away the wet streaks on his cheeks with the back of my hand. "No," I smile, my voice barely above a whisper. "I don't love him." But I could.

He inhales sharply and brings a shaking hand up to his face to wipe away the remaining tears. Then he grabs my hand, pulling me up towards him before dragging me to the bed. Before sitting down, he wraps his other arm around me, tugging me along with him.

"Please," he begs quietly, his voice shaking, "let me just hold you."

I wrap my arms tightly around him as I bury my face into his shoulder. His tears are still warm against my skin, and the thought fills me with an immense tenderness.

We lay there for what feels like hours, Caius running his hand over my back in soothing circles while I cling to him.

"Why did Azazel turn your place metal?" His breath fans across my cheek.

"We'd gone out to dinner at the tavern—"

"He brought you to the tavern?!" He stiffens, his voice hard. "With that wretched incubus working there? Gods. What if she'd seduced you? You'd be dead, Morte!"

"It's okay, I kept it under control, and if I die, I would've come back to life. Az kept an eye on me, and his friend was there, too."

"Who?"

"Um." I scour my mind for an answer. "I can't recall his name. But he's got two cocks?"

"What the actual fuck?" He sits upright, facing me. "Emeric showed you?"

"No!" I laugh nervously. "But he did draw me a map showing me how to get to his house."

Caius scowls. "Burn it."

"I'm not going over there." I chuckle.

"Good." His shoulders relax. He leans back against the wall, pulling me with him. "Finish your story. Sorry, baby bird."

"Far from it, old man." I grin, resting the back of my head against his chest and he kisses the crown of my hair. Despite my reservations, there's something soothing about being in his arms. Maybe I can use him as a buffer from Aggonid. "After we'd gotten back, it was right at midnight—"

"You shouldn't be out after midnight!" He tenses under me. "Have you any idea the types of beasts that roam these woods? The dangers?"

"Time got away from us," I grit out, swallowing hard.

"What happened?" he demands, voice ragged now.

"Well, the first thing we saw was a cinderwing? Then a soulstealer, and something that sounded like a wolf?"

"Shadow wolf," he says, haunted. "You're not safe by yourself, Morte."

I hum. "I am now I've got all this metal." I give the wall a pat.

He growls. "You should come stay with us."

"Who?"

"Aggonid and me."

I let out a bitter laugh. "No." So he can kill me again? Humiliate me? My heart clenches in agony, as I relieve the memory of his cruel rejection.

"You wound me." He entwines our fingers.

"I don't like Aggonid." I shrug.

"He's an acquired taste." He presses a kiss to my temple.

Caius is wrong about one thing: Aggonid is a taste I'm already addicted to. I've had a sip of its sweet poison, and I still feel the searing heat of his lips on mine, and the brush of his tongue against my own.

He's a magic all his own, and for some reason, I'm drawn to it. Which is exactly why I have to stay as far away from him as I can.

Caius's chest swells with a deep inhale as his hot breath scorches my skin. His iron grip clamps around my throat, not hard enough to choke me, but firm enough to trap me in place. A low, rumbling growl escapes his lips as he speaks in my ear. "Morte, why do I smell your arousal?" His words are laced with a dark desire that sends a wave of pleasure rippling through my body.

I mutter under my breath, "I should've known better than to make a deal with him."

"So, you don't like the god." His grip tightens around my throat and his thumb trails up to my bottom lip. "But love his touch?"

I whimper, "Something like that."

He tilts my head back to face him, and his lips crash down onto mine. His kiss is demanding and possessive, like he wants to reclaim my soul from Aggonid and lock it away in himself. My heart races madly as lust floods my veins and my body craves more of his touch.

Caius pulls away, the warmth lingering on our lips and the longing etched in his gaze. His thumb sweeps across my cheek as his icy eyes search mine. "Be careful, Morte," he murmurs softly. "He may have given you a taste of his power, but there's so much more to him than that. The Aggonid I know is just as likely to capture your heart as he is to enslave your soul. He's already got one, but will you give him the other?"

"No," I blurt out, trying to break the tension. "Never. He's a monster." My words hang heavy in the air, cooling the fire between us.

"I think you'll find that over time," he continues calmly, "there's a reason for everything he does. Even if we don't like it."

My blood runs cold as Caius speaks. His smooth words, his calm demeanor—they only serve to heighten my dread. I slowly sit up and shove myself away from him.

"Caius," I demand, my voice trembling despite my best efforts. "Why are you here?"

He locks his dark gaze on me and the intensity of it takes my breath away. My heart races as he speaks, the words striking fear into my soul.

"This Forsaken Hunt is in twenty-nine hours," he murmurs. "It's optional, but that necklace won't protect you from everything. Do you really want to go through with this?"

I hesitate, teetering on the edge of determination and terror. I know what I'm asking for if I do win ... but can I really pull it off? For Caius's extra favor?

Though, the longer I'm here, the sadder the idea of leaving the life I'm building. Or at least the people in it.

But I owe it to Wilder, to get him out of prison. Finally, I meet Caius' gaze and nod. "Yes."

"Then you'll need this," he sighs, rising to his feet and crossing to the door. He heaves it open and steps outside before dragging a mammoth trunk behind him.

"What's this?" I ask as I approach him, eyeing the chest warily.

He grins devilishly as he crouches and lifts the lid to reveal an assortment of weapons and armor that I'd never be able to find anywhere else. From a sleek black bow and a quiver full of arrows to small knives for close combat and even a full suit of armor that gleams in the early evening light pouring in from the window.

"This." He smiles. "Is your ticket to a successful Hunt."

My eyes narrow as I sense a catch. There has to be one. "Isn't this cheating? You're the Lord of the Hunt, Caius."

"Cheating?" He scowls before breaking into a smirk. "It isn't free."

I glare at him, my voice dripping with disdain. "What do you want from me this time?"

"Stay the night with me at the castle," he says in a tone that belies his confidence.

"When?"

"Tonight."

His answer catches me off guard, my breath hitched as desperation hangs in the air. "Will Aggonid be there?"

He avoids my gaze, spinning around to examine a wall with an almost absent expression. "He might be," he says nonchalantly. Before I can respond, he adds, "Before you say—"

"No," I snap, cutting him off.

"The Bedlam Moon is in four days' time, so if you want Aggonid to relay your message to your little friend, you'd better get it to him tonight."

"What?!" I drop the arrow I'd picked up to inspect. "I thought I had more time."

He grins. "Guess we've got ourselves a deal?" He approaches me.

"For fucks' sake." I rise to my feet, grab him by the back of the neck and yank him in for a bruising kiss.

The kiss is wild and desperate, as if I am trying to prove something to both of us. When I pull away, Caius looks at me with a mixture of surprise and admiration, and I can't help but feel a spark of pride.

We lock eyes for a few moments before he breaks the silence. "Deal sealed," he grins.

CHAPTER FIFTEEN

MORTE

Dearest Wilder,

Gods, do I miss you. My heart aches to be with you once more, yet I fear we don't get forever after all. I want you to know I didn't abandon you, and if it's in my power, I'll do everything I can to make it back to you.

After I died, the devil reaped my soul, dragging me down into the abyss that is the underworld. Claimed at last.

I'm here, but I'm not alone. I've made some odd acquaintances, one of which put some kind of spell on me so I can't feel the heat. This makes being here less miserable. Silver linings and all that.

One of the demons explained how my soul works; I had a tether in Bedlam that kept me coming back. Until I didn't.

At night, I lie awake wondering ... maybe that tether is you. If it is, my dying makes sense. I watched the light bleed out of your eyes, a death so much worse than my own. The agony of it stole my breath away and crippled my spirit.

My soul had nothing more to live for in that moment, so I assume I died when my heart broke. This is all speculation, but if it's true, I have some measure of comfort knowing I gave you a feather. I only wish I'd been able to leave you with more before I left.

Someday, I'll see you again. Whether in Bedlam, or in the afterlife, I don't know. While the penitentiary kept me from you, I have a confession to make. Each night, I'd sift to the shores of Penn Island just so I could feel close to you. It eased the ache in my chest knowing you weren't far, even if I couldn't see you.

I only wish I could do that now.

There's an event coming up called the Forsaken Hunt. If I win, I get a favor from Aggonid. I've got a plan that'll hopefully bring me home. And just maybe we can be together again. Now that I know the security protocol at the prison, I think I'll be able to get in without being under their watch.

We'll run away together.

Whether we go to Earth, Romarie, or some other realm, wherever I'm with you, I'm home.

Missing you like crazy,

Morte

I slam open the desk drawer and rifle through it, scooping out handfuls of wax and tossing them onto the desk. Arranging a cluster, I grab an iron sigil, and press it hard into the wax. Watching it pool and spread, it seals the letter with a searing flame.

Caius watches me from across the imposing room, leaning leisurely against a deep-seated couch. The walls are made of cold stone and the floors are hard marble, radiating the power of the god that resides here. Every corner of Hellwing Castle speaks of the grandeur of a royal figure who commands absolute obedience. Where the manor was all homey and cozy, perfect for family, this place is meant to intimidate and exude power. Every inch of the looming edifice demands authority, from the granite walls to the windows that glare like the eyes of a predator. Its regal archways reach for the vaulted ceiling, daring anyone to challenge its primacy; a silent reminder this place was built solely for force.

"All finished," I call out, my voice ringing off the walls as I stride towards him. "Can you take me to Aggonid?"

I feel the oppressive weight of his magic before I see or hear him. "What do you need with me?" His voice is like a cold blade, barbed with venom.

I spin around on my heel, my gaze meeting the devil's ruby eyes, and I try not to tremble. He normally wears his hair braided close to his scalp on one side, but he looks freshly washed. I lift my chin, determined. "This is my letter for Wilder." I clutch the wax-sealed letter close to my chest for a beat, then extend it out to him. "Please ensure he gets it."

He clicks his tongue in disapproval. "That wasn't our agreement. I vowed to ask High King Finian to bring your message to him. Whether or not he delivers is no longer in my hands."

"He'll do it. I'm friends with the high king and queen."

"Are you now?" he sneers, eyes narrowing and jaw tightening. "Look at you, reaching above your station. Nasty habit."

Scowling, I choose to ignore the jab, straightening my shoulders and glaring at him. "Are you going to make sure Finn takes the letter, or should I?" The weight of his stare presses down on me, but I don't back down.

He barks an amused laugh. "I may rarely grant deals, but make no mistake," he toys with the suppression necklace at my throat before his hand retreats, taking his warmth with it, "I always hold up my end of the bargain. I'll make sure the high king receives your letter."

It takes a moment for the words to sink in, but I don't bother to thank him. Instead, I turn my back on the devil and approach his closet, flinging the door open.

"What the fuck are you doing?" He grabs my arm, spinning me around to face him.

"Get your hand off me," I hiss, yanking out of his grip. "I'm getting pajamas."

His nostrils flare. "You do not get to enter my closet without permission."

"I'm not stealing anything. I'm getting clothes for the night," I say flatly, reaching for a hanger. "Do you treat all of Caius' guests this way?"

He pauses for a moment, considering. "Caius never has guests. Just you."

Caius appears next to Aggonid, looping an arm around his waist and pressing a kiss to his temple before leveling me with a look. "Did you forget already?"

"What?" I hiss.

He grins, unbuttoning the billowy white shirt he wears. "We sleep naked."

My face burns. "I think I preferred sleeping with Azazel," I mutter, striding past them both.

"You slept with Azazel?" Aggonid roars, his voice like thunder as it shakes the castle walls.

Though they can't see it, a wicked smile curves across my lips as I tear off my clothing and dive into the golden silk sheets. They glide across my skin like a whisper, and I can't help but admire the devil's taste as I sink into the pillow with a purr of pleasure. I might never have expected to be welcomed into Aggonid's bed again, but I can't deny that the experience is good. It might even make the upcoming hunt a little more bearable.

"We shared a bed, yes." I turn my head to respond, and startle to see him looming over me.

Aggonid's nostrils flare, and the heat of his anger seeps from his pores as his body trembles with restrained anger. The room fills with his shadows, and they climb the walls, blotting out almost all of the light. His pupils are slits as a red-hot fire burns in his eyes, making him look every bit the god of the underworld. "Did you fuck him?" he snarls, and Caius opens his mouth to speak, but quickly clamps it shut when he catches my anxious glance.

Aggonid's claws lengthen, and he hammers them into the bedding with ferocity, leaving eight angry punctures on the bedspread as though he were only cutting butter with a hot knife. The air feels heavy with tension as I stretch, allowing the sheets to slide down until they rest seductively at the tops of my breasts. I watch as both of their attentions gravitate to my chest and a primal hunger darkens their eyes.

"What if I did?" I raise a challenging brow and Aggonid's head snaps up, his lips curling into an animalistic snarl.

His chest heaves as a dark rage takes over him. His mouth contorts into a devilish scowl as he grits his teeth and growls, "Did you?" He scrutinizes me as if he could rip the truth from me with his gaze alone. Caius seemed to know I was a virgin ... could Aggonid tell too?

I smirk at him, challenging him to answer. "I may have had someone to keep me company last night. Did you know Emeric has two cocks?"

My words hit Aggonid like a burning arrow and his expression blackens as his fists clench together in anger.

Caius smirks, shaking his head, his eyes conveying a warning that I'm playing with fire.

I arch a brow and meet his gaze with a defiant glint and a grin.

My heart is thundering in my chest as Aggonid slowly climbs onto the bed, prowling towards me like a vicious predator. He hovers over me, looming with a splayed hand that clasps my chin firmly. His grip presses me back against the bed, forcing my neck to the side. I'm rooted to the spot with fear, yet I can't help but experience a meandering thrill as he breathes deeply around me. His powerful hands are gentle and guarded as he moves them around my neck, careful not to anger the powerful protection of my necklace.

The fire of his touch scorches the length of my body, leaving a trail of heat that dances like flames upon me. I'm exposed to him as he rips the blanket away, baring my skin to his gaze.

My breath catches as he brings his face to my most intimate spot and I'm left frozen in shock, suspended between desire and fear. He's more beast than man right now.

He presses his face against me, and I shiver, all too aware that should he decide it so—I am completely his to take. He draws a deep breath, and the whimper that escapes me brings a smirk to his lips. "You lie." Then, slowly, he rises and steps away.

The air between us is thick, heavy with the unspoken understanding that the game has changed. He retreats a few paces and looks to Caius.

"Lucky for them." Aggonid's voice is a deep purr, a sharp contrast to the heated atmosphere. His hand slides from Caius' chest and trails leisurely over his hip and low-slung pants. His nails slice through the belt and with a sudden release, Caius' pants fall to the floor.

Caius shifts, a hand twining in Aggonid's hair and the other resting on his hip. His voice is tight, but there is something in it that hadn't been there before. "Don't you want to play with the little gift I brought you?"

Aggonid peers up at Caius. "I'd rather have you," he croons.

Caius' answering smile is sultry. "Then take me."

Slowly, Aggonid undresses, pulling Caius close. He turns them to face me, and I'm pinned by their combined heat. Aggonid's gaze slides over me as he seizes Caius' neck in a passionate, almost savage kiss, as if he's claiming him as his own.

Point taken.

Caius sighs and closes his eyes, tipping his head to the side to grant

Aggonid access. My stomach tightens as I watch, mesmerized by their intensity and undeniable desire for each other.

A twinge of something stirs inside me and I desperately try to control my racing thoughts.

I swallow hard, willing my body to stay rooted beneath me as my mind reels in confusion. Did Caius really bring me here so they could share me? He has to know Aggonid doesn't want anything to do with me. His rejection still stings.

Aggonid drags him over to the bed, and I scramble to the opposite end, my back facing the couple.

I squeeze my eyes shut and press my fists against my eyelids, trying desperately to block out the scene. But even that is not enough to muffle their passionate moans and the heat radiating from their intertwined bodies. Tears stream down my cheeks as I feel my chest tighten, a deep longing for affection coursing through me.

Back when it was just Wilder and me, before everything went terribly wrong, he'd hold me almost every weekend until I fell asleep. I long for the intimacy Aggonid and Caius share.

Eventually, their moans die down, and I can feel the bed shift as they find their own space. I don't dare move, and I remain motionless until I'm sure they're asleep.

I let out a staggered breath and force my eyes to open, my vision coming into focus on the two of them. Aggonid's arm is like a steel band around Caius' waist, trapping him in an embrace that borders on possessiveness. They lie quiet, and I take in the picture of them together with a heavy heart and a painful twist in my gut. It's clear how content they are in each other's arms, something that I can never have.

When I wake the next morning, sunlight blanches my puffy eyelids and I glance over my shoulder to find Caius and Aggonid still asleep.

I slide out of bed, my feet touching the cold marble floor as I make my way to the closet door. Carefully, I pull it open, and my eyes widen at the sight of a trove of weapons tucked at the back behind the rack of clothes.

I run my fingers over the various blades, swords, and spears that line the walls, my eyes dance around the blades, my fingers trembling as they touch the metal hilts. Warily, I stretch out and grab a long katana before pulling it out of its sheath.

The weight of the weapon feels strange in my hand, almost alien, and yet I find comfort in its familiarity. We don't have any metal like this in Bedlam. I can almost feel a spark of energy radiating from the weapon, a reminder that I am a warrior, and yet I'm aware that I'm still far from prepared for what lies ahead. Thoughts of the Forsaken Hunt rumble in my mind as my muscles tense, and determination runs through my veins like fire.

I hold the katana up to the light and take a deep breath, pushing back the fear that threatens to consume me. I've got to win this.

I sheath the blade and pull a long dress shirt off its hanger, shrugging it over my head before moving to the large window that dominates the far wall of the room. Pulling back the drapes, I take in the sights of Hell as the morning sun casts its orange light over the landscape.

Winged beasts soar in the skies, the rumble of their cries echoing across the ash-covered land. Smoke and fire fill the horizon, a stark contrast to the peace of Aggonid and Caius' chambers.

I yelp, jumping when a hand lands on my shoulder, and I whirl around to find Caius, naked. He grins cockily, his gaze locked on my face.

"You look good in my shirt," he purrs, eyes raking down my body. "Though if I'm being honest, you look much better naked."

"Caius!" I hiss, swatting his arm.

Aggonid

THE SOUND of Morte shrieking tears me from sleep, and I sit up, ready to come to her aid when I see Caius only startled her.

Plopping back down onto my pillow, I watch from the shadows where they flirt by the window. A deep sense of longing rises inside me as I take in Morte's beauty, seeing for the first time just how perfect she is for us.

For several moments, I lay still and silent, aching for the closeness I know I can never have from her.

Caius cups her cheek. "Were you trying to make him jealous?"

"What do you mean?" she whispers.

"I knew you'd had died if you gave them your virginity instead of giving it to me, but even I got jealous hearing you lie about fucking someone else."

My breathing stills as I strain to listen. She made a deal with Caius to give him her virginity?

A dark thought worms its way through my mind, and I shiver. If I can't return her to Bedlam, there is another way I can make sure she's out of our lives forever.

No one will take my throne.

CHAPTER SIXTEEN

MORTE

*S*itting at the foot of my bed, I use a rock to sharpen one of the blades Caius had given me. My belly is full, on account of Aggonid making sure I was well-fed. He'd been acting strange all day, allowing his attention to linger on me, the heat in his gaze unmistakable.

I've only just returned with a small map Caius drew me of all the huts across the forest with participants in tonight's hunt. For twenty-four hours, it's kill or be killed.

Once all my blades are sharpened, I pull on my cuirass, securing it with a few leather straps. Sliding the glowing red gemstone into the breastplate, designating me as a participant, I cross to the door when a knock sounds.

"Who is it?" I call through it. The hunt can't have started already.

"Az," a gruff voice responds.

I unlock it, yanking it open. My breath catches as I take him in. His hair is braided close to his scalp, and ash covers every inch of exposed skin. His smile gleams at me from beneath the layer of soot and dirt.

"What in the gods did you roll in?" I yank him inside, checking behind him to make sure he's alone.

He raises his arms, smirking. "It's camouflage." My attention draws to the little pot in his hand. "I brought some for you."

"Oh." I close the door and turn back to him, crossing my arms over my chest. "What is it?"

"Powdered wolfshade and ash," he explains. "It'll help you hide in the shadows." He hands me the container, and my fingers tremble as I take it. His eyes flick to the gemstone in my breastplate and then back to my face. "Are you ready?"

I nod, though in the weeks since I've been here, I've only grown weaker. And without magic, I'm at a major disadvantage. My warrior training and skills with a blade might be all that saves me.

And the necklace.

One glance at it, and others will be more hesitant to attack me, unless they've got a death wish.

The lid screeches as I wrench it open, unleashing a lengthy hiss that fills the air around me. I take a deep breath of the dusty fumes and scoop a handful of the ashen substance, smearing it into my skin with a deliberate ferocity. The ash clings to me with a thick and heavy weight, as if I'm coated in dark paint. Its particles course through my veins, clinging to my face and arms like a second skin.

"You missed some," Az notes, pulling at the fabric of my shirt and tracing the outline of my neck where I hadn't applied it. His fingers linger on my flesh, sending a shiver through me that has nothing to do with the cold.

"Thanks," I mumble, more heat in my voice than I intended.

He steps away, but not quickly enough that I can't see the smirk on his face. We both know what just passed between us and neither of us say anything.

You don't need to, his gaze whispers.

I swallow and look away, my cheeks hot.

"You know, only one of us can win." He plops onto my bed, body splayed as though it's his own. "But even though we're competing, we should still look out for each other. So you make it back in one piece."

The muscles in his biceps flex where he's got an arm slung behind his head, and I can't help but remember the way he held me. I clear my throat and force my eyes to the floor. "You could let me win."

He throws his head back with a deep throated laugh that burrows straight into my core. "And why would I do that?" he croons, the heat in his voice setting my heart racing. "Maybe I want to win and earn *you* a favor?"

Instead of meeting his gaze, I lock eyes with the red gemstone at his chest. I will beg, steal, lie, and cheat to win this hunt. If I do, I'll earn two favors instead of one.

I approach the bed, my intent predatory as I sink to my knees. Az swallows, his throat bobbing as he adjusts himself.

"There's something I want," I whisper, my fingertips tracing a path around the gemstone. "Let me have it." His eyes close, a sigh escaping his lips as my hands continue to explore.

"And what's that?" His voice is husky.

Tracing the lines of his armor with my fingers, I follow them until I meet the soft flesh of his hip bone. My grip tightens.

"I want to win," I whisper.

At any cost. It's probably why I ended up dead. The gods were tired of me being a terrible person, capable of grievous sins, regenerating time after time. This is my hell.

He groans and his eyes fly open, an emotion that looks a lot like admiration flashing through his gaze. He cups my chin in one hand and looks into my eyes. "Why should I let you?"

"Because I can ask for something you can't."

He stills. "What are you talking about?"

"If I win, I earn two favors. I'll use one to ask Caius to release you from your curse," I whisper.

He sucks in a breath, and I can see how much it hurts him to even contemplate the possibility of freedom from being at Aggonid's every whim. He could live wherever he wants in the underworld, away from court.

His hand drops from my chin, and he turns his head away, his shoulders slumping. "Don't toy with me like that."

I crawl onto his lap, settling myself in the cradle of his legs. Tilting his chin to meet my gaze, I whisper, "Let me win and I will."

Adjusting myself, his hands fly to my hips to still me as he grunts. "You keep moving like that and you're going to get yourself killed, little devil. Assuming you're still a virgin?" His brow rises.

I give him a curt nod.

He bites his lip, the ring glinting in the light. He opens his mouth to speak but I cut him off.

"I'll make a promise to you, that when I win, I will use one of my favors to ask for your freedom from your servitude."

Closing his eyes and leaning his head against my shoulder, he lets out a shuddering breath.

"You don't have to do this." His tone is soft but there is something fierce in his words. "You could ask for anything. Anything at all to make life so much easier for you."

I meet his eyes. "I won't let anyone else I care about rot in a prison when I have the power to help them within my reach."

My heart seizes in my chest at the reminder of Wilder. He stares into my eyes for what feels like an eternity, so many emotions flitting across his features, then he finally nods.

I cup the back of his neck as my lips crash to his, savoring his taste as I swallow his moan, like a long-deprived man finally getting a drink of cold water. His kiss becomes desperate, as his hands haul my hips closer, feeling the evidence of his desire right at my core. My mouth parts, and his tongue sweeps in, exploring mine.

The kiss deepens, and his hands travel up my sides as our hips start to move in a gentle rhythm. The clank of our armor and our heavy breathing echo around the room, amplifying the intensity of this moment.

A bright red light flashes behind my eyelids, and we break apart, glancing down at our flashing red gemstones adorning our chest pieces.

His eyes meet mine. "Deal sealed," he croaks. "The hunt starts now."

I scramble off his lap, pulling him to a seated position. Before I can turn away, he clamps a hand on the back of my thigh, pulling me so I'm between his legs.

"After you win, I'm cashing in the favor you owe me," he says, his voice thick with desire. "And I'll need to feed."

A grin tugs at my lips. "Of course."

I step away, the hum of anticipation coursing through my veins as we both turn to face the door. We are going to fight for our freedom … and we're not going to lose.

Az and I haunt the woods, the air charged with something dangerous. It's after midnight, and the beasts we encountered the other night are no comparison to what stalks these woods now. Flashes of red light catch our vision through the trees, and before we can turn in that direction, a twig snaps on the other side of me.

I whirl around, readying my bow and arrow. A creature with the body of a man and the head of a wolf stares back at me, its golden eyes twinkling in the moonlight. It snarls, baring its fangs. Before it can charge, I've loosed the arrow and it flies through the air and straight into its gemstone affixed to its chest piece. The man staggers and roars in pain before it collapses to the ground.

The mangled body turns to ash, and I watch as it sends a firework into the sky, illuminating my name with a one beside it. One kill.

Other fireworks sound in the periphery, but we can't see them through the canopy. They go off so often, it sounds like the bass of music.

I'm too distracted by a crimson light bobbing through the trees to notice someone sneaking up behind the trees until an arm wraps around my throat. My necklace activates, and the person drops to their knees, roaring as I whip around and drive my dagger into her skull.

One more kill.

Tangerine-colored light blinds me as I take in the sight of the fallen corpse, her face morphing from beautiful to monstrous in a matter of seconds.

Az slams his hand hard against my shoulder, turning me to face the giant line of crimson lights looming towards us in the darkness. They blink in and out like a warning beacon, snaking through the trees.

"How am I supposed to take out all of them?" I frantically search for a target and loose an arrow, but it splinters against the trees when one of the fae ducks.

"You let me handle this," Az growls in my ear, "and you take 'em out, one by one." His words vibrate with intensity and my fingers itch around a bowstring.

"What?" I hiss.

I can do this. All of us are here because we're monsters. Not the kind that lurk under beds, but the kind who whisper honeyed words with our barbs of poison, leaching into everything we touch. Hurting good people who don't deserve it.

He doesn't respond, and instead rushes straight at the wave of combatants weaving through the woods.

Terror constricts my throat as I watch him disappear into the shadows. Fifteen. I count fifteen glowing orbs. My fingers tremble as I release arrow after arrow, some slicing through their flesh, others thudding into dead tree trunks. The lights bob and weave in the night air like fae flies, mocking my glaring attempts to take them out.

Suddenly, the lights stop bobbing, each of them standing in place as though they've been frozen. With my last arrow plucked, I hurl throwing knives at the dark forms, desperate to bring down my enemies before they come for me. As soon as a spark flickers in the sky, a force slams into me from behind with enough power to knock me off balance. I try to turn around, but there's no time—it hooks into the shoulder straps of my cuirass and lifts me up into the air.

I howl my war cry as I'm snatched from the epic battle below and catapulted into the sky. My lungs gasp for air as I'm swept away by the giant flying beast, its powerful talons digging into me and its wings pounding against the air. I drift higher and higher as the wind rushes past me, carrying with it my fate.

CHAPTER SEVENTEEN

MORTE

I struggle against the heavy straps but I'm unable to release them or unfurl my wings with my armor encasing me. A firework explodes in front of us, and I lose my grip on my knife, watching helplessly as it plunges into the trees below.

Fuck!

My body thrashes and writhes with every ounce of strength I can muster, shaking the creature off-balance. Its wings pitch and yaw as I keep rocking, my limbs flailing in a blind fury. Its talons cling to my armor, but I twist and turn out of their grasp. I thrust forward again and again until the beast finally releases me on one side.

The night sky erupts above us with firecrackers of different colors, leaving a trail of scorched embers in their wake that expand like a spider web of glowing brilliance. The creature that holds me tight decides I'm not a threat and releases its grip, hurling me towards the tree line with dizzying speed. I can hear the thunderous flap of its wings as it rushes to battle another adversary, leaving me to my fate of the darkened forest.

I plummet, reaching for the giant sword at my back just as a dragon catches me in its giant maw. Its slimy tongue pushes me down its throat with the force of a hurricane, threatening to drown me in its depths. With an iron grip I cling to the sword, defying death with each passing second as I slide back down its throat. I roar with rage as I scramble to keep upright in its mouth, sword still tight in my fist. After readying myself to do battle within the belly of a monster, I shout with a feral defiance as I plunge the sword through the hatch and into the monster's gullet, tearing through its rancid flesh like a hot knife through butter.

The creature bellows in pain, only to be met by my ceaseless onslaught. Blood spatters from its wounds, raining down upon me like a crimson shower.

A deafening roar rattles my bones, my eardrums wailing in pain at the sound. I cling to the hilt of my sword, each muscle screaming with effort and strain as the dragon chokes and gargles in an attempt to dislodge me. I draw on a deep reserve of strength, and with a fierce shove of my feet, I thrust off from its tongue whilst digging in the blade deeper.

The screeching whine of metal against soft tissue echoes through my ears as I dig the blade in further, the dragon's throat compressing around me with its death throes. A hot blast of air sears my face as I am suddenly weightless, a realization dawning that I have killed this ancient beast and we are both falling fast.

We crash to the ground with a cacophonous bang, my body shaking violently from the force, sweat, saliva, and blood lifting off me as the vessel around me turns to ash and floats along on the wind. I push myself to my knees through the pain, each breath feeling like a thousand needles piercing my lungs as my limbs scream in agony against the weight of the impact. I raise my head, fear coursing through me as I see a figure rise before me, shrouded in shadows against the twilight sky.

My heart pounding, I frantically back away, desperate for a way out. When I don't see a glinting gemstone on his chest, I let out a shaky breath of relief. He approaches me cautiously, extending a hand to help me stand.

The minute my feet touch the ground, a searing pain shoots through my leg and I wince in agony. He notices it immediately and scoops me in his arms. I look up and meet his eyes, recognition blazing in them.

"Emeric?" I rasp, my throat dry and cracked. Fear and confusion mingle on the air.

His mouth moves, but I can't hear his words. Blinking, I shake my head, trying to clear it. My eardrums have ruptured, and I can hardly hear him. I point to my ears, but it takes him a moment to catch on.

He carries me inside a large home, kicking the door shut behind him. As he places me on a long, pewter-colored couch, I wince at the pain radiating down my leg and the blood pouring like a river from a deep gash in my thigh.

"Is Az here?" I try to crane my neck, but I'm so stiff, I can't move.

Emeric shakes his head. My chest deflates. I hope he's okay.

With quick hands, Emeric unbuttons my pants and carefully slides them down my legs so he can get to work on healing my injury. Bruises mottle my legs, ribbons of blood snaking their way down from the wound.

His lips move as though he's reciting something, and he presses a hand to the gash. I suck in a breath, screwing my eyes shut at the pain. The sting doesn't lessen, and my eyes fly open as Emeric casts me a worried glance before he mouths, "trust me."

Az's words echo back to me: *He's a pain in my ass, but one of the only people you can trust around here.*

I give him a curt nod.

His head moves towards my thigh, his tongue swiping once at the injury. What the fuck?

Ohh. Oh. The pain lessens. He laps at my thigh, his eyes taking on a glazed quality as I groan, my head lolling to the side as he works. Each swipe of his tongue diminishes the hurt. My heart hammers in my chest, his touch both soothing and thrilling at the same time. His tongue moves faster, lapping and licking at my wound. The cut vanishes almost as though it were never there, like a drop of ink in the ocean. The layers of flesh that had been cut fall away like petals of a flower to the cushion beneath me.

Emeric leans into my hair, the silky feel of his black curls brushing my face. My heart catches in my throat as his warm hands cup my ears and begin to heal the damaged eardrums. Almost as once, I feel the insistent throbbing at one ear disappear, and then the other. His lips hover against my ear as he whispers to me and the delicate touch of his breath fans my skin.

"Thank fuck." I sigh.

"You want to give me a thank fuck?" He grins down at me, my head still cradled in his hands.

I lean closer, letting his touch linger as I whisper, "You know damn well what I meant." Electricity crackles between us before I wrench myself away, his warmth like molten honey.

"Does this mean you're done with the hunt?" His eyes are hooded and intense, a stark reminder of the power that lies beneath his exterior. He sits back on his heels, his attention over my bare lower half, lips tight.

I shake my head. "No, I need to win." For Wilder. And Az. I swing my legs off the couch and stand, realizing my mistake as soon as I do it.

His nostrils flare as he takes in my scent before his gaze moves up my body with deliberate slowness. His darkened eyes finally meet mine, and the air around us is thick and heady, as though I'm a teacup and he is an endless, churning ocean. His voice becomes low and husky as he asks the question I'm dreading, because I'm tempted to give in. "Sure I can't convince you to stay?"

I swallow down a strangled whimper and pivot around him. "Sorry, this is too important."

"Why?" He stands, handing me my ripped pants, his hold on them lingering. "They hold these all the time."

"I'm going to free Azazel."

His eyes widen, realization donning on him. "Holy fuck."

"Yeah," I mutter, struggling to yank my pants up where I need them.

"What the hell did he do to earn that?" He cards a trembling hand through his hair, mussing the curls.

My lips curl into a satisfied smirk as I think back to our passionate night. Sure, it was him drinking my blood, but I'd never come so hard in my life. "He certainly gave me the best orgasm I'd ever experienced," I purr, feeling my cheeks flush with heat.

"Just think: two times the cock, two times the pleasure, baby," he whispers huskily, pressing his lips to my temple as his fingertips caress the nape of my neck. I shudder in delight, feeling an electric current course through my veins.

His hooded gaze sears through me, and while his offer is tempting, I shake my head. Nothing will happen if I break my promise, except it'll hurt a whole hell of a lot when it kills me. And though nothing bad happens if I lose, Az and Wilder deserve to be free. My tongue is like lead when I try to form the words, "I can't—"

"They vibrate." His sultry response swirls around me like a dark fog, threatening to consume me.

"What?" I manage to breathe, my heart in my throat.

"And I knot," he adds, heat pooling low in my belly.

A choked sound escapes my throat. "Help me win and I'll let you show me," I gasp, wanting to snatch the words back as soon as they tumble out. "I mean, if you help me win, I'll let you show me, but we're not having sex." He doesn't need to know about my deal with Caius.

Emeric pauses thoughtfully before me, his eyes piercing through me like a dagger. "So no sex ..." His gaze drops, and a smirk forms on his lips. "... but are other things on the table?" His suggestive eyebrows waggle mischievously, and it feels as though he's parsing through every naughty thought in my head.

"Maybe," I concede with a sly grin, fully aware that I'm playing with fire. "When I get to know you better."

He steps closer and cups my face, his eyes hooded. "You've got yourself a deal. I'll help you win this, and in return, I'll show you how my cocks work."

EMERIC'S BODY burns against mine, the sealing kiss of our deal sending shockwave after shockwave of pleasure through my veins. He grasps my hips, pressing me closer until I can feel every inch of him, his cocks rising in response to my warmth.

The kiss turns frantic as he explores the softness of my lips, tasting me as though he's a starving man. His tongue writhes with mine, sending sparks of electric energy down my body, and I can feel his desire unraveling, his whole being throbbing with need.

I rip myself away, lust heavy in his eyes as I unbuckle my breastplate and discard it on the floor.

"Deal sealed." He groans as he watches me.

My chest heaves as I peel out of my top, tossing it behind me. In seconds, I'm out of my pants, but I struggle with my belt, which has a lone knife tucked at the back, so I abandon the effort.

My bare skin, creamy white, nearly has Emeric crashing to his knees, begging at my altar as he takes me in. Taught nipples beg for his fingers.

"There's something so hot about a woman wearing a combat belt," his voice croons. "And only a belt." He looks up at me, his eyes hot with desire and an invitation.

I don't hesitate.

He cups my face and I crash my mouth onto his, allowing him to devour every inch of me. I cling to him, my hands fisting in his soft hair, and I can feel the aching need building within me. His hands leave my face to trace along my curves, caressing me until my body trembles and I moan against his mouth. I wrap my arms around him, digging my fingers into his sides as the kiss intensifies, our hands finding forgotten places before I reach for his belt.

He sucks in a breath, relishing the sharp pleasure of my touch as I release him from his pants. Emeric presses into me, our kisses becoming desperate as we both lose ourselves in the sensation coursing through us.

Kicking the coffee table away, he lowers me to the floor, having enough cognizance to know the couch is covered in blood. He reaches behind his head to pull his shirt off and throw it to the side.

I smile, my eyes half-lidded and heavy with need. He presses my body against his, a ragged sigh escaping my lips as he kisses his way down my neck.

"You're fucking perfect," he breathes. "One little taste of you is all it took."

He captures one of my nipples in his mouth, and my body arches into his touch, my moans of pleasure feeding his desire.

"Emeric, I need you," I whimper, hips bucking under him. "It hurts." I squeeze my thighs together, trying to get some friction.

I ache for him. He smells of the sweetest fruit, drizzled in caramel.

"I know, baby." He pauses at the apex of my heat. "I'll make you feel good."

My head thrashes. "No," I whine. "I need you to fuck me. You smell so good."

"But you said—"

"Now, Emeric. Please."

"Are you sure?"

I rise to my elbows, glancing between us. "Show me how those work," I pant.

A grin curls his lips. As though it were a reflex, he turns the vibration on, settling between my legs, running his upper cock between my folds, nudging at my clit.

"Ohh," I groan, my eyes rolling back in my head. "Holy shit. Yes, yes..."

He passes the vibration over my clit, and I dig my nails into his back, my entire body trembling.

"More," I beg. "Put the other one in me."

"Morte," he hesitates, slowly pistoning his hips as his cock glides through my folds.

"So help me I will march out that door and find the next man willing to fuck me right now, Emeric," I hiss. "Where's Azazel?" I grumble.

A possessive growl rises in his throat. "Mine," he whispers, pressing a hard kiss against my thirsty lips.

"Az!" I call out, and Emeric takes the bait.

He positions himself at my entrance, about to press in when he pauses. His head whips up, his gaze locking over my shoulder. Crashing against me, Emeric grips the couch and flips it over to act as a shield.

"What the fuck!" I shout.

"Get down!" he growls, reaching for the weapons abandoned amongst my things.

My spine turns rigid, fear a wild beast in my chest. "I'm not into knife play," I choke out.

"What?" He moves for the dagger as I scramble out from under him, jumping to my feet.

"I said I'm not—"

The unmistakable sound of an arrow loosing through the air cuts me off mid-sentence as he lunges for me. His arms wrap around my body, shielding me as he crashes us both to the ground. Shards of stone rain down from the arrow lodged in the wall just inches above us.

My attention snaps to where it vibrates and realization dawns on me that another hunt participant has found me. "Who's here?"

"Vic."

I shake my head. "No, I can't withstand her magic," I whisper, eyes wide.

"If you kill her, the magic disappears." He cups my cheeks fiercely, forcing me to meet his eyes. "You can do this."

I swallow, a whimper escaping me.

Victoria's voice calls out like a siren from the darkness outside the window, her words filling the night with a sinful promise. "Come on out, love," she coaxes, "let me give you the ride of your life." Her voice lingers in the air, offering a temptation too enticing to resist.

"I'm not afraid of you," I shout, my chin jutting out just as a second arrow shoots through the window and slams into the couch Emeric had knocked down to protect us.

"Oh, no?" Vic laughs. "I beg to differ. Your precious Azazel isn't here to protect you now."

I stiffen, hand inches from where I reach for another dagger to add to my belt. "What did you do to him?" My voice breaks as panic claws at me.

"Nothing yet, but as soon as we're done here, I'll rip him apart." She cackles. "Saw him snooping around the woods. Was it you he's looking for? Pity that. You're off fucking his best friend."

I bolt to my feet, hands held up as though cornering a wild animal.

"You want a taste of me?" I cock my head, and Emeric lunges for a larger blade tucked under the pile of discarded clothes. I give him a barely perceptible shake of my head as I slowly advance towards the window.

Vic huffs. "You offering, sugar?"

"Put the weapon down and we'll talk," I say calmly.

"And why the fuck would I do that?" she sneers, leaning closer to the barred window.

"I have something you want."

"I'm listening," Vic growls, her hand still on her bow.

I can sense the moment Emeric uses an invisibility cloak; the heat of his body is right next to mine as we approach the window.

"You want my virginity?"

I feel him freeze, displaced air moving as he whips his head in my direction.

"Bullshit," Vic hisses, raising her bow.

I grin. "Why do you think Caius and Aggonid are so close to me? They want it, too. It's yours if you want it." I pause right within arms' reach of Vic.

I steady my quaking body, my fingers digging into the wooden frame out of sight of Vic, the strain of resisting the magic becoming almost too much. I feel Emeric extract the dagger from my belt loop, placing it delicately in my hand. I wrap my trembling digits around the cold steel, the sound of my heart thrashing in my ears.

"I wasn't born yesterday, girl." Vic narrows her eyes, pushing a wave of carnal desire at me. Fucking incubus. "Make a deal with me that I can have your virginity and I'll surrender the game."

My smile widens, my eyes still hazy with desire. "Okay."

Vic reaches her hand through the bars, yanking my face to hers. "If this is some kind of trick, I'll gut you," she sneers, but just before she crashes her lips to mine, I sink the blade into her neck.

The energy of the room is almost overwhelming, desire pouring from the walls and seeping into our veins like a poison. Vic's agonized scream rips through the air, and she stumbles back, her lips dripping with a stream of crimson. Her hands grasp desperately at the blade wedged into her neck, and her fingers tremble as she staggers backward.

No longer hidden, Emeric bolts towards the window, throwing his body against the ledge to peer out into the darkness. In a heartbeat, Vic crumples to the ground, her blood staining the stones beneath her feet like roses in snow. As her red light flickers out and rockets into the night sky, a flash of orange illuminating the stars, followed by a crack as the embers shoot in a brilliant display above.

His attention snaps back to the wretched soul beneath the window. The grim number six flashes in a trance-like state above her body, signaling the end of her reign of terror.

He whips his head back to me, watching as I lick my lips with a savage grin, my eyes wild as I use the back of my hand to wipe my mouth of Vic's blood.

CHAPTER EIGHTEEN

MORTE

"I'm sorry," Emeric spins around, yanking his clothes back on.

"It wasn't your fault," I call out as I slip my shirt over my head.

"I should've known something was up. One minute you weren't interested, and the next you were begging me to fuck you."

Turning to face him, I still my hand on his shoulder. "I never said I wasn't interested. What I said was that I had a game to win, and I need to get to know you better."

"Yeah?" He grins, raking a hand through his hair. "I can accept that."

We stand there and stare at each other for a moment. The air is charged with electricity, and I'm not sure what will happen next. I'm still shaking from the adrenaline of taking down another fae, but I know I have to keep my focus if I want to win.

My breath catches in my throat as his eyes bore into me and I can feel the intensity of his gaze on every inch of my skin. As I reach for my cuirass, an ominous knock echoes throughout the room like the toll of a bell, sending a chill down my spine. For a moment, time stands still as I wait for whatever's coming next.

He motions for me to get behind him, and I shake my head at him, making a flapping motion with my wings, mouthing *phoenix* to him. My death wouldn't be as permanent as his.

Emeric rolls his eyes before peering through the peep hole. "Shit," he curses, throwing the door open.

Azazel grips the door frame, his free hand clutching at his neck as a fountain of blood gushes from a gruesome injury. His skin is deathly pale, and his eyes are glassy and filled with fear. His gaze locks on to me; his shoulders momentarily relaxing before his eyes slip shut, and he collapses backwards off the steps and into a crumpled heap on the ground.

A desperate scream escapes my lips as I throw myself down the steps. With trembling hands I grasp at the gaping wound on Az's neck, desperately attempting to stem the tide of blood. My eyes dart to Emeric, pleading for his help. "Please," I beg, my voice broken with desperation, "I don't have magic. You have to save him!"

His fangs extend like twin blades, shredding through his wrist and he thrusts it against Az's lips, demanding he drink. His other hand presses against the rip in Az's neck, glowing a brilliant scarlet, its luminescent light highlighting the thick crimson liquid that pools underneath, gradually saturating the dirt.

I crouch on my knees, trembling as every nerve of my body is set on high alert, scanning the darkness of the woods for any sign of a ruby light. I know that if I see one, I have mere seconds to react.

Emeric throws his head back and roars in anger. "He's fading away!" His face contorts in agony, lines of ancient grief washing over his features like an unstoppable tide. His eyes close and a single tear trickles down his face, as if it was a river of sorrow unleashed from deep within his soul.

"FEATHERS!" I shriek, my voice rising to a fever pitch. "Do you have one?"

Emeric's glassy eyes meet mine. "We're demon fae, Morte. Ours don't work like that."

A roar erupts from my throat as my wings unfurl with a furious flourish. Scarlet flames lick the air, illuminating the area with an otherworldly light. I stretch out a hand to pluck a feather, just as an intense agony sears through my chest, rending me speechless. My gaze shifts downward, focusing on the arrow that penetrates my ribcage, embedding itself deep within my flesh.

I lock eyes with Emeric, my vision tunneling until I see only his handsome face, his mouth forming words I can't distinguish over the wild pulse of my heart. A veil of shadows creeps up my vision, the world tilting on its axis as scorching flames engulf me in their familiar, smothering embrace.

THE MOMENT I REGENERATE, I barrel towards Emeric's house, fear a living thing inside me at the thought I might lose Az. I burst through the door, unencumbered by armor and clothing. I drop my gear on the ground and rush to Emeric's side, my guttural cry filling the air as I kneel beside Azazel's limp body.

"Hold on, big guy," he whispers with determination, aware that time is slipping away. "Let's put him on this giant hunk of metal."

It takes me a bewildered beat before I connect the dots. We maneuver him across the floor and towards the oven, pinning our hopes on a force he can control—ferrokinesis—to save him.

I take his ankles, helping Emeric heave Az onto the surface barely big enough to cook on, let alone hold a massive beast of a demon fae. His head lolls at an awkward position.

I sprint to the door, snatching my armor and rushing back to them.

"You're gonna kill yourself, you've given him too much." I yank his wrists away from Az's mouth.

He shakes his head, his body swaying with the movement. "No," he croaks. "Demon fae don't have souls. A feather isn't going to bring him back."

"What?!" I shriek, lunging for his face but he's too stunned to move out of the way.

Before he can fully comprehend what's happening, I've used his fangs to slice open both my wrists, my blood spilling down my arms and onto the floor.

I shove one in Az's mouth, and the other in Emeric's. "Drink!" I roar. "Take it all!"

He tries to mumble a protest, but with my hand right next to his hair, I take a tight hold of it, eyes wild as I get in his face.

"I said take. It. All." I punctuate each word. "I'll regenerate. You won't, gods dammit!"

My eyes dart over to Az, desperate to see if his injury has improved in the slightest. Gripping Emeric's hand, I force it against his gushing wound. "Now, use your magic. Quickly!"

A faint glow illuminates where they're joined. But it's not enough, not fast enough. He forces more vitality into him, the room heating with the energy of it as I plead with the gods to heal him.

Azazel's body trembles beneath Emeric's hand and he lets out a low groan. I watch, amazed as his fingers dig into the meat of my arm, trapping it beneath his own hand. I have to close my eyes for a moment, preparing for another burst of pain.

Instead, a whimper escapes me. With Az's feeding, he can either make it extremely painful or extremely pleasurable—there is no in-between. He lives to the extreme. His lids flutter open, and he immediately zeros in on me.

My eyes lock on his face, burning with a frenzied passion. Fear, desire and anticipation all simmer beneath my skin, begging him to take me. My entire body trembles with arousal. Pleasure fuels my veins, my lips part and my tongue darts out, as if begging for him to satisfy the raging fire within me.

Pure, unbridled need takes over me as Az digs his fingers into my flesh, holding me as he takes what he needs. I gasp, moaning and arching back as his fangs sink deeper into my veins. His grip is primal and possessive, driven by instinct and wild craving, as though claiming me for himself.

And in that moment, he is. But when I start to sway, Emeric releases his bite and heals it, confident he has enough to mend him the rest of the way.

When Az sits up, still gripping my wrist, he slides to the ground, back pressed against the stove. He pulls me into his lap, and I curl into him with a sigh as Emeric is forced to follow to keep healing him. Crouching beside us, he watches as Az's free hand wanders along my curves, exploring my body as if coming back to a familiar form. I'm trembling in his arms, head thrown back in blissful abandon.

This isn't just him saving my life, or him giving me pleasure through his bite. It's an intimate moment between three people who are growing closer by the minute.

Az

SLIDING my fangs out of Morte's wrist, I lap at the puncture wounds to close them. My hand tangles in her hair as I take in her glazed eyes.

"Thanks for saving me," I whisper. "I'm sorry I couldn't save you, but I'm glad you found Emeric."

Considering she's naked, she must've died between my passing out and her reviving me. Unease stirs in my gut at the idea of it.

A blissful smile crosses her lips just before she presses them to mine. She nips at them before pulling back and scrambling out of my lap. "I have a hunt to win." She helps me up and we both sway a little.

"Let's go find where Emeric ran off to."

"I'm going to have a bowl of this soup really quick, be there in ninety seconds." She grabs a ladle, and I turn towards the bedroom to find where Emeric snuck off to while I finished healing.

I find him sitting on the bed, head hung.

"Hey, man, you alright?" I sit beside him.

"Nah." He grips his hair. "I'm fucked. So fucked."

"What—"

"You're in love with her, aren't you?" Emeric interrupts me.

I hang my head in my hands, too. "Is it that obvious?"

"In the end, all of us demon fae are searching for something. It's good to see that even you have found a little slice of heaven in the form of a fiery redhead."

This fierce little phoenix, with all her fire and strength, is loyal and brave, and has captivated me in ways I never could've imagined. But something stirs in me as I turn to face Emeric, the longing in his voice registers a moment later.

"You, too?" I croak.

"Like I need air to breathe."

Just then, Morte comes bouncing into the room, a hunk of bread hanging from between her teeth. She pulls up short when she sees us. "Guys?"

The two of us stand quickly, rushing to hunt for a change of clothes.

"Is everything okay?" she calls from the door.

I turn from where I'm grabbing a shirt off a hanger and flash her a grin. "Yeah, we're alright."

"My clothes have been incinerated." She winces, glancing down at her naked form. Her cheeks flush a deep crimson as she stands there, exposed.

Emeric pulls himself to his feet. "Come on, I've got a shirt and some drawstring pants you can cinch tight under your armor."

The idea of a hunt again makes me bristle, after having spent more than an hour searching for her before I'd been overrun and attacked, but we have no other choice. After dressing, Emeric, Morte, and I link hands and walk towards the living room, three battle-worn warriors in search of more bloodshed.

I glance from the corner of my eye at the woman beside me, trying to remember the last time I felt contentment like this.

We pause in front of the upturned couch, and I take in the state of the living room. Blood covers the couch cushions, there's an arrow embedded in the wall, and a trail of blood is smeared across the floor.

Letting go of Morte's hand, I stand at the center of the room and close my eyes, my arms outstretched as I call to the metals in the blood all over the room. It sparks and shifts, gathering around me in a shimmering aura I can feel behind my eyelids. A gasp next to me has my lips curling into a satisfied smirk before I open my eyes and turn to Morte.

"Let's go get your victory." I hold out a hand to her.

"Oh, wait! I need boots." She glances down at her adorable bare feet.

"Come on." Emeric chuckles, taking off towards the back room.

Morte shoots me a grateful glance before scurrying after him down the hall, leaving me alone in the living room. I take a few moments to myself, gathering the power around me into a small blade before sheathing it in my pocket.

A crescendo of joyous laughter drifts down the hallway, stirring me from my daze. I force my feet forward, propping myself up in the doorway, my breath held in awe as I take in the scene. Morte stands in the center of the room, her body engulfed in a pair of boots that are eight sizes too large. Emeric isn't as big as me, but he's still tall, like most demons, and has thick thighs and a solid waist. He sits at the foot of his bed, his face splitting into a deranged smile as he watches Morte with an unshakable fascination. Light from the morning sun filters through the window, illuminating her hair as though it were a brilliant fire.

They don't notice me standing here, and she stomps around the room, her laughter ringing out as she wraps her hands around the drawstring around her waist and clomps the enormous boots on her feet. The pants billow as she spins, her movements full of all the grace I'd expect from a phoenix fae, despite the too-big attire, but it's her smile that steals my breath. The sight takes me back to the days when I was a boy, back when I would play in the gardens of the palace with my brother and sister. That same unrestrained joy is there in Morte's laugh, and I'm suddenly filled with intense yearning.

A wave of longing grips my chest, tugging me towards the warmth of home and her laughter. I hunger to be engulfed in it, to bask in the brilliance of her joy that radiates like a blinding sun. But before my dreamlike trance can take me any further, Emeric's voice jolts me back to reality—a painful reminder of what I can never be.

"Morte."

She stops twirling and turns to face him, her laughter dying down as she takes in his expression. Her eyes dance between the two of us, and for a brief moment, I sense something in the air. If there was more time. If she hadn't made a promise to Caius.

Fucking Caius.

Emeric gestures to the door. "How about you give us a dance once we secure you a victory?"

"Good idea." Her cheeks ignite with color as she crouches to lace the boots, and I use my magic to bolt metal to them to cinch them tighter.

I retreat to grab her armor from the other room and return with it in hand. After helping her buckle it around her slim waist, I step back and try to ignore the rapid pounding of my heart.

"I was thinking," Emeric approaches us, arms folded across his chest, "we've got about sixteen hours left of the hunt, and Morte is behind." He turns his attention to me. "Let's head to the Crimson Trail, and she'll be caught up in no time."

"And how do you propose we avoid her getting slaughtered at every turn? That's the busiest path through these woods, and it's teeming with deathwings, night stalkers, soulstealers, and shadow stalkers at night. And then you've got all the wraiths."

"If we can hide in the trees near the Charred Glade, you can handle the beasts, while I use my shadow magic to create a trap. It'll just be a matter of getting enough arrows together."

"A trap?" Morte furrows her brows.

Emeric grins. "Everyone wants to get their hands on Caius' favorite pet—their words, not mine—so let them think you're wounded, then pick them off from the trees."

"And how the hell am I supposed to be in two places at once?"

I clap my hand on Emeric' shoulder. "You're a genius," I bellow, my face split into a maniacal grin.

CHAPTER NINETEEN

MORTE

*E*meric's hands roam around my body, tracing every curve, cataloging each and every mark and divot that makes me who I am. His hands card through my hair, sending goosebumps along my flesh.

I'm panting by the time he finishes, a smirk adorning his face as he steps back from me. His throat bobs as he draws his attention to his hands, where shadows form between them. He pulls them apart, and I watch in morbid fascination as another *me* begins to take shape right in front of us.

The shadows dance around my fake form, spinning and caressing the body as though they'd always meant to be a part of me. It solidifies, dropping to the forest floor before stalking towards the mission Emeric sends it on.

Unease pulses through my veins as I watch my doppelgänger writhe and moan on the dirt path below. Even though it's made of shadows, it looks identical to me. The same flaming hair, the glowing gem on my chest, and even the tiny crease between my brows.

We're perched in a nightfire oak, Emeric behind me, and I'm settled between his thighs for support as I ready my bow. A few branches above us sits Az, keeping vigilant watch for beasts. It's daylight, so his duties are light until the sun goes down. Four hours is how long it took to get here, and I'd racked up twenty-three more easy kills during that time.

In the distance is a bridge they call the Ember Gateway. It has a shimmering archway made from black marble, wrought iron, and gold. The stone is carved with ancient runes that glow red as they reflect the setting sun. It towers higher than the trees and spans the wide river that separates the forest and Duskvale. On either side of the bridge stand two huge statues of demons, their eyes glowing a bright orange like fire. Their wingspans stretch out over fifteen feet across, and they each hold a giant mace in one clawed hand and a flaming staff in the other.

The faint odor of sulfur lingers in the air, mixed with hints of burning wood and brimstone. The bridge creaks and groans as if it's alive, and every thirty seconds the sound of a firework cracks in the distance.

My heart stops as I catch a glimpse of movement in my periphery. The figure moves with a grace that could only belong to a wolf shifter, its fur a sleek blanket of black and orange patches, illuminated by a gleaming ruby above its shoulder blades. In a flash, it lunges towards my shadow self, its eyes blazing with an animalistic hunger.

I loose the arrow with a fierce determination, watching as it pierces through the creature's hide and sinks deep into its side. The creature howls in agony, its enraged bellowing echoing through the forest, yet it continues its relentless charge. I draw another arrow and release it, the shaft finding its mark in the beast's left shoulder. The creature immediately stops in its tracks, hanging in the air like a marionette whose strings have suddenly been cut. It slowly slides to the ground, its heavy body illuminated by the fiery rays of the setting sun. Its lifeless body twitches once before slipping into an eternal slumber.

The faintest glimmer of light shimmers above the lifeless body before a sudden eruption of energy sends the kill count soaring up into the sky with a deafening crack. The majestic beams of light pierce through the air like blades and the thunderous boom that follows sends shockwaves trembling through the trees.

"Hey, Az," Emeric calls up to Azazel. He leans down, raising a brow. "I'm not sure which is sexier, the Forsaken Hunt or the Wild Pursuit."

"Why's that?" I ask him, and Az must have guessed the punchline because he's grinning.

"Seeing you take down competitor after competitor has me all hot and bothered."

Heat creeps up my cheeks, but I just shake my head. "You two are insufferable."

"That's where you're wrong, Morte. I think I speak for us both when I say we'd gladly suffer under the weight of your aim if it meant you'd pin us in the end," Az teases.

"Uh huh," I muse.

For hours, we use my phantom apparition to lure contestants in before I finish them off with an arrow.

With no way of knowing how well other hunt participants are doing unless I see their kill number, we just have to keep killing. If this were Bedlam, I'd probably feel bad, but in the underworld? There's a reason we're all here.

A crackling in the trees behind us signals that another creature has entered the fray. This time, from the canopy.

Already nocking an arrow, I glance nervously at Emeric when I see the beast. Its fur is pitch black and its eyes are an unnatural yellow, intense in their warmth, though its giant maw full of razor-sharp teeth is anything but welcoming.

With a quick nod, I launch the arrow, only for the monster to extend arms three times as long as its body. It reaches for a limb above its head and swoops over the top of us, its claws rending the branches to nothing in its wake.

This isn't a contestant, but some hideous creature reminiscent of a gorilla, but more terrifying. Its fangs protrude from its upper lip, dripping with a putrid green saliva that smells of death and decay when it splatters on the limb next to me. With every breath it takes, it unleashes an agonizing rumble like a storm brewing in the distance.

Azazel hisses, "Move!" and we scatter in opposite directions. I land on my feet and spin around just in time to see the monster demolish a thicket of trees, splitting boulders and branches into fragments. Including the ancient nightfire oak we'd kept sentry in.

It notices Azazel and takes off towards him, moving faster than I thought possible with its size. Shaking, I bring up my bow again with trembling fingers and aim. I let loose an arrow in desperation and thank the gods when it lodges in the monster's shoulder. But it barely slows its charge.

Az rolls out of the way as it lunges, and its giant paw crashes into the ground instead. It doesn't stop, though. It roars and turns towards me, snarling and slobbering as it runs closer.

"Get behind the tree!" Emeric shouts.

I circle the enormous willow just as my shadow doppelgänger takes off in the opposite direction, drawing the beast's attention away from me. I breathe a sigh of relief, but my heart stops when I see that Emeric is still standing close by the monster.

Without a thought, I take off towards them. Az sees my intent and leaps towards the lumbering monstrosity, but I'm faster. I grab Emeric and heave him out of the way just in time, tumbling onto the ground as the creature passes by us with a thunderous roar.

The fight is on. Az engages it, dodging and swiping with his claws and teeth, while I take aim and shoot blindly at the massive body. It's a large target, but it moves faster than it should for its size.

The monster takes a swipe at Azazel, and I scream in terror as a contestant rushes me from my other side. It's in its fae form, wielding a large sword.

"When I'm through with you, I'm going to gut your little boyfriends," he sneers. He has a deep voice that is edged with malice, taunting and threatening as he moves closer. The swish of his sword slicing through the air echoes around us, and each step he takes is marked by the rhythmic clanking of his armor. "Might have a taste first."

He is tall and slender, wearing a suit of armor that's stained in patches of old blood. His eyes are narrow slits of gold, his face marred with scars. He bares his teeth when he speaks and draws back his lips to reveal sharp teeth, as though he's chiseled them to points. His sword has an intricate design carved into its steel blade and an emerald stone embedded in its hilt.

"Kill the monkey and you can," I shoot back, my voice dripping with venom.

He throws his head back in a harsh, mocking laugh, the sound a cruel echo that raises the hairs on my arms. "You want me to kill the rampager for your little boy toys? Give up the hunt, give me a taste, and then I'll bring you its head," he grins, the sight of his sharpened teeth almost enough to make me sick.

Rather than voice the string of curses that spring to my lips, I wave him off with a lazy shrug. "Might be worth it," I sigh, my voice dripping with nonchalance.

The fae's aid comes at a price, and I'm willing to pretend he'll earn it. Together, we unleash a blaze of steel, slicing through the creature's flesh. A spray of crimson flies through the air. With a snarl, the beast falls limp in death, and I let out a savage cry as I watch its demise. Mixed with the ash on his skin, Az is covered in its blood.

Az's voice cracks like lightning, "Go home Pantatel, or suffer the consequences."

The fae who helped us snarls in response, eyes narrowed, and a wicked grin painted on his lips. He steps closer and towers over me, waiting for my compliance. "Nah, I think I'll collect my prize now," he drawls. "Get behind the hollow."

Just as I make eye contact with Emeric to tell them to trust me, Pantatel is upon me and his arm clamps around my waist like a steel shackle. His aggression radiates through him. I try to squirm away, but he's too strong.

So I let him take me a few paces away to a dip in the ground, hidden amongst the tree roots.

"Right," he growls, his hot breath tickling my neck. "You made a deal with me, and I intend to collect." He leans closer and presses a kiss against my cheek, his lips lingering for a moment too long.

"But did I?" I grin. He doesn't see the blade I grip in my hand, but he feels it when I slash it across his neck. A spray of hot blood arcs across my face, and his grip slackens. A mix of fury and agony flashes in his eyes before he staggers back, a soft thud as he hits the ground.

"Remind me never to get on your bad side," Emeric croons from where he's propped against a tree.

A grin tugs at my lips as I watch the kill count dance above Pantatel's body and explode into the sky. "How much longer do we have?" Having died and regenerated, I'm not nearly as tired as Az and Emeric must be.

Az rubs a hand over his face and sighs. "Two more hours."

I climb out of the hole and take in the sight of the two demon fae. They're filthy, covered in a mixture of dirt, blood, ash, and sweat. Heavy bags hang under their eyes, a testament to their fatigue. But even in their exhausted state, I can see the wild determination on their faces—they want me to win this as badly as I do.

I turn to Az with a challenge in my voice. "How many did you have to take down to win the last few times?"

"Forty," Az replies without hesitation, "sixty at the most."

I look down at my count of thirty-eight and sigh. "We need more." I must win this. It's my only chance at going home and freeing Wilder and Az.

Emeric's voice interrupts my thoughts. "What if instead of making your shadow doppelgänger writhe and whine, I make it scream and wail? It'll seem like you're on your death bed, and they'll swoop in to try for an easy kill." He slides away from the tree, landing beside us. "That'll bring more people out here to try and take advantage of you."

Az returns with a thoughtful expression on his face. "That could work."

THE SKY ROILS WITH THUNDERCLAPS, and fat raindrops pummel our skin as we scramble up the giant oak on the other side of the trail. My fingernails scrape and dig footing into its ancient bark, but soon I reach the apex. Through the veil of rain I see them, a pack of eight demon fae, their eyes glinting menacingly as they move along the path. It's a group of contestants who've banded together, their strength multiplied by eight to swarm and take down their kills.

"Now," I whisper.

Emeric gestures, and a ghastly figure bursts out of the woods and into the clearing. It's an exact replica of me, screaming in agony as a glowing hatchet slices through its chest. The howls of its pain draw the demons near, luring them closer and closer to their fate.

I take a deep inhale, notch my arrow, and on the exhale, release it. The arrow lands with a faint thud, piercing through one of the fae's hearts, sending a firework into the sky. Even with the rain pelting down, I can still smell the acrid stench of gunpowder drift our way.

Her friends whip around, searching for the source of the attack. But the idea of getting an easy kill with my shrieking doppelgänger is too good for them to pass up, so instead of hunting us down, they stalk towards my shadow.

With a trembling hand, I furiously nock arrow after arrow, letting each one fly with pinpoint accuracy. Four of the demon fae fall, their blood matting the grass and dirt beneath them before the remaining three vanish into the shadowy depths of the woods.

I look to Az, my breath held in anticipation. He surveys the area before finally nodding in agreement. "They'll come after us if we don't take the fight to them," he growls.

Looping my bow through my arm, I make the climb down, landing on soft feet as I prowl forward. Az is close behind me, his indigo eyes surveying the area for any signs of the remaining demons.

We spot them on the winding trail, and I raise my bow, the thick string tensing between my fingers. With a steady force I stretch the bow to its full strength, feeling the heat of exhaustion as my muscles fight against me. I'm determined not to miss.

Luck is not on my side, because they hear the arrow whistling through the trees and duck.

My heart roars in my chest, but I remain still, waiting for the perfect moment to strike, but it appears they're circling around. When they near the giant willow, Az and Emeric use a combination of their shadow and metal magic to bind them, folding the trees into an inescapable cage.

Finally, I fire an arrow, hitting my mark and striking one of the fae in the chest. He lets out a scream of agony before crumpling to the ground.

The man and woman are almost exact replicas of each other. They have pale, glowing skin and sharp features with icy eyes that shine like moonlit diamonds. Their movements are graceful and precise, as if they were performing some kind of unheard-of dance.

Az and Emeric unleash a flurry of their own magic, a storm of purple and pink energy that clashes against the ice magic of the captives. The ice shatters, fragments of frozen power cascading onto the forest floor, but still the cage refuses to unlock. No matter how hard they try, they remain trapped and isolated, unable to break free from the iron grip of Az and Emeric's powerful combined magic. Is it fair? No.

Do I care?

Also no. That's probably why I ended up here in the first place.

Clenching my teeth, I draw back the bowstring to its full extension, the quivering arrowhead seeking retribution. Two successive shots fly through the air towards my foes, their screams a mortal plea as each arrow pierces their flesh. The creatures crash to the ground, dissolving into a cloud of vapor, colorful fireworks bursting into the night sky as an ear-piercing siren reverberates throughout the forest.

My head jerks around to Az, eyes wide with anticipation. "Is it finished?" I demand.

"It's done," Az replies with finality as thunder crashes in the background, rolling through my bones with the weight of a deadening finality. My heart misses a beat, and my body stands still, daring to hope.

It's over.

"How do I know if I won?"

"Aggonid will steal you from your sleep, and you'll spend the next thirty days in his company," Az growls.

CHAPTER TWENTY

MORTE

*I*rip off my blood-soaked garments, leaving shredded cloth and pieces of armor in its wake. The damp stickiness seeps into my skin, an inescapable reminder of what I've endured. Though I can't say I have remorse for killing. Whatever it takes, I'll find my way back to him. I don't know if its exhaustion or the adrenaline from all the killing, but I'm finding it harder than ever to push away the memories.

To push away *that* memory.

The judge's sentence rings through the courtroom, as I hold Wilder's parent's hands in a death grip. "Wilder Nereus, guilty of eight counts of murder, you are sentenced vita damnationem."

When Wilder had seen what I'd done, there was zero hesitation. A split-second decision to follow me into the dark has kept him in it for hundreds of years.

I've been fighting for a way to drag him into the light ever since.

The putrid stench of death and sweat clings to my body like an evil omen. I'm both looking forward to and dreading winning.

After the hunt, we flew to Emeric's place so we could avoid the beasts that come out after midnight. We'd encountered a dozen flying monsters, but none we couldn't handle with the three of us, and still managed to make it back here in under two hours.

"Please tell me you have a shower." I poke my head out of the bedroom door, shouting down the hallway. The scent of warm spices drifts my way, so at odds with the filth and grime coating me. I want to scrub it all away.

"There's a tub and shower in the en suite," Emeric calls. "But the handle is tricky. You've got to jiggle it to get it to work."

Before I can shut the door, Az appears in the hallway. "Need any help?"

"I think I can figure it out." I bite my lip to keep from smiling, the coppery tang of someone else's blood filling my mouth.

Az's eyes smolder as they drift across me, a dare. "If we shower together, we could save water," he murmurs in a low voice. He brings up the prize I owe him, and my heart thumps loudly in my chest.

I glance behind him, spying Emeric tidying up the living room, and I swallow hard. "What about Emeric? I owe him one, too," I ask meekly.

Az's lips curve into a devious grin as he looks over his shoulder and purrs, "Imagine that."

Emeric feels our gaze and he straightens, his eyes meeting ours. He drops the pillow he was holding and strides towards us. "What are we conspiring about?" An easy smile plays across his lips.

"Orgasms." Az shrugs, and heat shoots to my cheeks.

"Az!" I hiss.

"Am I wrong?" He swings his attention back to me, humor dancing in his eyes.

With a resigned sigh, I step away from the door, allowing it to swing open as I saunter to the attached bathroom. The sound of shuffling feet follows close behind.

Once inside, Emeric shuts the door and leans against it while Az parks himself on the lip of the tub.

The scent of fresh herbs lingers in the air—delicate notes of moondew and firethorn—while a faint sweetness lingers like glazed starseed cake. The bathroom is much nicer than I expected for a bachelor living by himself. A sleek onyx countertop curves around the basin, glittering in the light of the overhead fixtures. A porcelain tub stands tall in the corner, gleaming with its hammered metallic accents and built-in shower system. Black towels hang on a rack and the walls are painted a calming azure.

I spin on my heel to face Emeric, fixing him with a piercing gaze. "Are you mated?"

His eyes widen, startled by my inquiry. "No?"

I sweep my hand in an arc around the room, my voice carrying an accusatory note. "This is practically as lavish as Aggonid and Caius' bathroom!"

Emeric offers a slight, satisfied smirk. "Just because we're stuck in the depths of the underworld doesn't mean I can't spoil myself with luxuries. I've been victorious in numerous hunts," he holds out his hands in a flourish, showcasing the room, "allowing myself to enjoy the finer things down here." His attention drops to my naked form and his throat bobs. "Feel free to enjoy it as often as you'd like."

He pushes off the door, sauntering towards Az and me, his gaze never leaving me. The scent of plants grows stronger as the room warms with his proximity, and I can feel the electric charges of heat between us.

"Morte," he says in a low whisper, "allow me." He leans over me to reach for the faucet, his arm brushing my shoulder. My skin buzzes in response, and I shiver as a cool droplet of water descends from the showerhead and lands on my chest.

Emeric chuckles and continues to adjust the flow of water, creating a soothing rhythm. "There you go," he murmurs, turning to face me again. His gaze is tender as he takes in my expression.

"Thank you," I reply, appreciative of both his gesture and his restraint.

He nods and steps away, motioning for me to get in. "Endless hot water, so take your time."

I dip my foot in the stream and immediately sigh in pleasure. It's like stepping into a cloud; it's been so long since I've been able to indulge myself.

Submerging myself under the spray, I close my eyes, tilting my head back and allowing the water to wash away the dirt and grime of the hunt. As it cascades down my body, tension seeps out of me, leaving me lighter and more at ease. The sound of Azazel's laughter is distant under the roar of the shower, and the beginnings of a smile tugs at my lips.

Opening my eyes, I'm met with a different sort of pleasure. Az joins me in the shower, and his gaze is fixed on the spot where I'm swiping my hands down my body to remove caked-on blood.

My attention dips to the tapered V of his waist, and I can feel the heat of his skin before I reach out to touch him. He shudders under my fingertips and brings his hand to the back of my neck, claiming my lips with a hunger that leaves me breathless.

Our kiss deepens, tongue and teeth tangling as I explore him, feeling every ridge and plane of his body. His hands grip the sides of my waist, pulling me closer until our hips are flush and I can feel just how aroused he is.

I cast a mischievous glance at Emeric. "You plan on joining us?" I purr.

With the showerhead above us, he can join behind me and still get just as much water as Az does.

"I don't think Az likes to share." He grins, but there's a hint of melancholy in his eyes.

I turn back to Az, placing a bar of soap in his hand before bringing it to my skin. "You don't mind sharing, do you?"

He takes the soap and starts to lather my body, eyes fixed on mine. His touch is gentle, yet thorough, and I find myself arching my back in pleasure as he draws circles around my nipples, then follows them down my stomach.

Az pauses for a moment before offering the soap to Emeric. They exchange no words as Emeric strips and presses in behind me.

I look over my shoulder and see his hands on my hips, pulling me back until our bodies mesh together. His lips press against the nape of my neck and his breath is hot against my skin.

My heart rate picks up as I'm sandwiched between two of the most handsome men I've ever seen. The three of us slip into an easy rhythm as we take turns washing each other, exploring every curve and hidden crevice. It's sensual, tantalizing, and before I know it, I'm caught up in something that feels bigger than myself. With each touch I become more and more lost in the pleasure of it all.

It's just our hands and our mouths, but when the time finally comes for us to step out of the shower, I feel as if my body has been marked by Az and Emeric in some way that I can't even begin to explain.

We barely make it to Emeric's bed, our trembling hands interlocking tightly. Something passes between the three of us, the exhaustion of our journey and the thrill of the hunt binding us even closer.

Az wraps an arm around my waist possessively, while Emeric laces his fingers through mine and our legs intertwine in a desperate embrace.

Az trails a line of kisses up my neck until his lips reach my ear and he asks, "Can I feed from you?"

I wrap my fingers around his, guiding it along my curves, feeling the heat radiating from his skin. My stomach quivers as his palm moves inch by inch closer to my core, until my body trembles with anticipation. His fingers trace circles around my hips before finally resting at the apex of my thighs. A guttural moan escapes my lips as I whisper, "Here?" in a needy, wanton voice.

"Fuck," Emeric swears. "You do that and none of us are getting sleep tonight." He groans.

Az rolls me to my back, trailing his fingers over my hip as he settles between my legs. His lips press to my inner thigh before he moves higher. I arch my back, crying out softly as his tongue meets my sensitive flesh.

Emeric takes my hand, twining our fingers together just when Az sinks his fangs into me. A low keening fills the room as pleasure radiates through my body, making me dizzy and lightheaded.

It washes over me in waves, each one a higher crest, and I find myself lost in it. Lost in them.

Turning my head towards Emeric, I grip the nape of his hair and pull his lips to mine, our tongues sliding and tasting each other in unison.

When I come up for air, I meet Emeric's pale blue eyes. "Show me again how this works." I grip him below, feeling the vibration a second later as he grins.

My other hand cards through Az's silky hair, and I ride his face as though my life—

"Entertaining as this may be, might I have a word, Morte?"

Each of us freezes, my blood runs like ice through my veins, each beat of my heart a reminder of the power radiating from his body. It wraps us up in a blanket of horror and dread, so strong that every breath I take is a challenge.

A strangled gasp escapes my lips as his name slips past them. The devil stands before us, pure hatred and malice wafting off him. His eyes, like two burning rubies, bore into my soul, scorching me with the intensity of his gaze. He advances closer, looming above us like a colossus of dark power. His confidence is palpable in the air, a smothering weight of fear that claws down my throat and burrows into my chest.

Yanking the blanket pooled at my feet, Az covers me, shielding me from Aggonid's roving stare.

"I assume you know why I'm here." His voice fills the room, a sibilant whisper that echoes around us like a storm.

"Ah, I've earned your favor after all." I grin, pumping as much false bravado into my tone as I can.

Aggonid's eyes narrow, a malicious smirk playing on his lips. "Indeed, you have," he drawls, the tone husky and laden with promise. His gaze flicks between me and my two almost-lovers before settling back on me. "No doubt these two had everything to do with it."

Az places a protective arm around me, a low growl slipping from his throat.

Aggonid holds up his hands in a mocking gesture of peace. "There's no need for violence here. After all, I'm simply here to collect my due." His eyes flare with a faint glint of triumph as they flick between the three of us.

"If I'd had any inkling that I'd be cursed with the sight of your repulsive face for a full month, I would've stayed home," I snarl. My words may not be completely honest, but if he believes he can come here and insult me without me biting back, he has no idea who I am.

Aggonid claps his hands together in a show of mock delight. "Ah, such spirit!" His tone is partly scoffing, but it's clear he's impressed by my courage. He steps closer, looming over me like a dark specter. "But I'm afraid it is I who must endure the likes of you." He pivots on his heel, striding towards the door. "Come now, I don't want to stay in this hovel any longer than I must."

Az and Emeric exit the bed and help me to my feet. Emeric is the first to embrace me, his hand threading through my hair as he places a firm kiss on my lips. I lean into him, savoring his touch before Az clears his throat. Heat fills my cheeks when I take a step back.

"Here are some clothes that might fit you." Az holds up a pair of drawstring pants and a button-up shirt.

I take them from him, and the three of us dress in silence.

"You've got thirty seconds to get out here before I revoke your favor," Aggonid calls from the hallway, and I curse him under my breath with every evil name I can think of.

Once dressed, I launch myself at Az, and our lips crash together in a heated kiss. I don't care that Aggonid is watching, and when we break apart, I tuck my head into the crook of his neck. "I'm going to miss you."

It's only thirty days. Get ahold of yourself.

"You'd better be careful there," Az whispers in my ear.

"Please come visit as often as you can," I plead, meeting his dark blue eyes.

His thumb traces my bottom lip. "He can try to keep me away." He grins.

Emeric takes my hand as I reluctantly release Az, leading me to the door, where Aggonid awaits.

"You won the Forsaken Hunt," Aggonid says, turning away from us and stepping out into the night. "But be warned—if you fail to use that favor wisely, you may very well regret it."

~

Aggonid

WATCHING those two demons have their way with Morte makes me want to claw my eyes out and shred them limb from limb. Even now, the scent of them wafts from her skin, and it's taking every ounce of strength I have not to bury myself in her so I can erase her memory of anyone but me.

But I've got to play the long game so I can rid myself of this little phoenix before she destroys my kingdom. I can't allow my emotions to control me, and I must tread carefully.

My plan will work. It has to.

Glancing at the fiery redhead, I catch a scowl on her face. Normally victors of the Forsaken Hunt are thrilled to win a favor, but not Morte. *Is my company so bad?*

Sure, I might've killed her. But she's a phoenix. She's used to that, and I had to see if she'd actually die.

"Have you given any consideration into what you want?" I train my eyes in front of us, focusing on the soft tread of her bare feet on the worn path back to Hellwing. Did she lose her shoes during the hunt?

"I have," she clips.

"Think long and hard about what you want bec—"

"I told you I already know what I want. I don't need to think about it any more than I already have." Her snarl is like daggers slicing through the air.

If I don't turn her opinion of me around, my plan won't work. Fuck. Caius will know something is up if I can't get her on my side by the time we get to the castle. It's another half-hour walk through the forest, even if we walk slow.

"Morte, I'm sorry." Her steps falter, and I swallow my pride. "You didn't deserve half of what I put you through."

Her eyes flare in anger. "Isn't that your thing, though? You're Aggonid. The most feared creature in all the realms."

I can't help the grin tugging at my lips if I tried. "You flatter me."

"That isn't a compliment."

"I rule the underworld. To us, it is." I shrug. "In any case, I let my jealousy get the better of me."

"Your mate came onto me; I had nothing to do with his behavior."

"Yes, he does seem quite fond of you. I can learn to share."

She huffs a laugh. "Nah, I'm good."

"You didn't seem to mind when we shared a bed, and I helped him get you off." I glance at her, catching the crimson staining her cheeks.

She truly is a breathtaking beauty with her cascading locks, finely sculpted nose, soft lips, and alabaster skin in stark contrast to my ashen complexion. Only she and Caius stir my blood like this.

Just imagining her between us again, but with more contact, makes my cock twitch. I'd love nothing more than to make her writhe in pleasure until she screams.

Her gaze darts to mine, and the hunger in it is enough to make a man kneel in worship. She takes a step, her mouth opening as if to speak, but no words emerge.

"I can see I've unnerved you." I bring her out of her trance as I continue our path.

The air stands still around us, as not even the wind dares to disturb the silence of the night. Not a single being can be seen, as if all of nature cowers in fear of me. The mere thought of coming close is enough to make any living creature freeze in terror, ceding whatever claim they might have to this place. I am the sole master of this night, and every day and night, and I will not rest until my will is done.

She fixes me with a piercing look and spits, "You have a way of doing that, yes," she muses. "So when I say it's not you, it's me, know that I'm lying through my teeth." Her words drip with an edge of venom and contempt, slicing through the air like a sharpened blade. "Know that it's all you—every last bit of it."

Fuck.

I need to build trust. But how can I do that in the next fifteen minutes? My heart makes a racket in my chest as I try to stall for time.

"I think I've figured out why you were able to die." I slow my steps until we stop under a giant spawn willow, its vines draping all over the path at our feet.

A real sense of vulnerability crosses her features now, her face framed by the stars above us. "Why did I die?"

No doubt she dies all the time, but I've figured out what keeps her here.

"Make me a deal, and I'll tell you," I challenge her.

Her face contorts with rage, her eyes blazing with fury.

Fuck, she's perfect.

A frustrated sound escapes her lips, and she spins around on her heel, fists clenched as she brings her leg back to kick the tree in anger.

I snag her around the waist to haul her back before she shreds her foot on the razor-sharp bark.

"You," she shrieks, "are a monster!"

My arms band around her, dragging her to the center of the path, holding her tight as she tries to flail. "Morte," I whisper in her ear.

I release her, and she steps away from me, keeping her eyes trained on the tree line.

Tucking my hands in my pocket, I saunter down the path, a smirk playing across my lips as the patter of her feet follow behind quickly.

"Wait!"

"You've got ten seconds to make a decision." I keep the humor out of my voice. "What'll it be? Do you want to know why you died and ended up here?"

She makes another indignant shriek of frustration. "Fine!"

Relief seeps into my shoulders, and I can't help the smile that plasters my face as I stop on the trail.

Turning around to face her, I hold out my hands in supplication. "You know how this works," I purr.

Her eyes narrow. "You're psychotic."

"Quite." I grin.

She hesitates, taking a few steps closer to me and my nose flares, breathing in her intoxicating scent. Below the stench of the other two she spent her night with is the sweet scent of her desire, anger, and curiosity.

194

Her lips press to mine for half a second before she rears back, and I raise my brow.

"Well, now you've got to kiss me twice. It's got to be much longer to count as a deal." I smirk. "And if you want to double down on that, I'll even let you share our bed the next thirty days."

Her face screws in revulsion. "Why the hell would I want to do that?!"

I shrug, turning to continue the path. "The alternative is the dungeon," I call behind me.

"But I'm your victor!" she shouts, her hand clamping down on my shoulder in an attempt to spin me back around, but I'm too strong.

Instead, I turn around at my own pace. "Even my guests stay in the hot dungeons." I chuckle. "Who do you think I am?"

"You're a monster," she whispers.

"Yes, yes, we've established that. What'll it be?" I glance at the position of the stars in the sky. "My patience is wearing thin."

"Double down?" she questions.

"Five minutes," I grin.

"FIVE? But that's way more than double!"

"I did give you ten seconds to come to an agreement, and I think we can both agree it's been a lot longer than that. So now, you must give me a proper kiss for at least five minutes to seal our deal, and in return, I'll tell you why I think you ended up here, and you can share our bed." *Please say yes, please say yes.*

"And what the hell are you going to do when I throw up in your mouth?"

An unbidden laugh barrels out of my chest. *This woman.*

"You and I both know the reason you don't want to kiss me is because you're afraid to get carried away." I give her a smug grin. "Tick-tock, five seconds, Morte, or the offer is off the table."

Her face turns a delicious shade of scarlet as she clenches her teeth. "Fine," she grits.

Thank fuck.

We slowly approach one another, not quite touching yet. I delicately brush my fingertips across her cheek, and she gasps softly, her eyes fluttering closed. The sensation of her hot breath on my face sends tingles through my body, and I can feel the intense longing radiating from her.

My lips meet hers, and I take my time, my arms slowly wrapping around her waist. I savor every second, every detail of this moment. I know that this kiss will be the one thing I remember for a very long time.

There's warmth and sweetness in her kiss, and our tongues meet, exploring one another in an obsessive embrace. Every nerve in my body is alive and firing, demanding me to take her and lay claim to her.

Fire ignites in my veins, my shadows unfurling from my body and wrapping around her, bringing her tighter against my form. My feet walk her back until she's pressed against a tree, my shadows cushioning her as I bring her legs up to wrap around my waist.

A gasp escapes her lips as I press my hips against hers, eliciting a shudder from her as I grind against her heat, wishing these scraps of fabric weren't between us. But I can't take her now.

Not yet.

But I can give her a taste of what it'll be like. I drag my hips against hers as her legs tighten around me, her warmth searing through my veins as her hands claw through my hair, desperate to crawl inside of me, if only to sate her hunger.

She wants this as much as I do.

Five minutes has come and gone, so I tear myself away from her mouth and press my lips against her jaw, her neck. "Deal sealed," I breathe against her skin, sending shivers down her spine. "This is only the beginning."

She murmurs something incoherent in response, the sound thick with lust. My chest heaves against hers, and I close my eyes, savoring the feeling of having her in my arms.

Reluctantly, I take a step back, allowing her legs to unwrap from around me. The heat in her eyes shutters as she realizes how carried away we got.

"Why did I die?" she whispers, and it's a rare show of vulnerability in her eyes that causes me to keep the ire out of my voice.

"You're in love with someone in Bedlam, aren't you?" I mask the jealous rage coursing through my body.

She averts her eyes. "What does that have to do with anything?"

"He, or she, was your tether."

"Irid already told me as much!" Her sibilant tone claws at my skin.

"Did he die?"

She stills. "Yes." She furrows her brows, but I see the gears turning in her mind as she mulls over what I'm getting at.

"Your tether severed, then you died." A breeze ruffles her crimson locks, pasting it to her forehead. Before I can brush it back for her, she swipes at her skin until it's tucked behind her.

"But I gave him a feather, so he should've come right back, so why didn't I?"

Of course she gave him a stupid feather.

"You must've died before he regenerated."

"Then who was my tether before him? I died a hundred times before I ever met him!"

I shrug. "Your parents, probably."

"If my tether is in Bedlam, why am I stuck here?!"

That's the real question, isn't it? I think I know, but I can't tell her. Instead, I give her another shrug. "We'd better head back. The ceremony is early tomorrow morning."

"Ceremony?"

I tuck my hands in my pockets, leisurely making my way towards the castle. "Where you ask for your favor, of course."

Morte

THE CASTLE IS quiet when we arrive, not a soul in sight. Not even Caius awaits our arrival, something that strikes me as odd. Instead,

Irid stands sentry in the grand entrance, ready to escort me to the dungeon.

"She comes with me." Aggonid doesn't so much as glance at Irid as he ushers me down the hall.

I walk beside him, a million questions coursing through my mind. But I can't utter a word; I'm too choked with emotion knowing I'm so close to my goal. Before I know it, the hall changes from one of sheer darkness and despair to beautiful tapestries and velvet drapes.

We stand outside a door, twice as tall as Aggonid, with hand-carved demons spanning the entire face of it. He takes a deep breath before pushing it open, revealing a grand bedroom with a marble floor with veins of onyx. It's different than the one I stayed in before. The walls are adorned with frescos of fire and wings, all depicting some kind of epic battles. And in the middle of it all, lays a bed grander than the other one, draped in various shades of inky silk.

The sound of a running bath draws my attention to a door at the far side of the room and Aggonid motions me forward before nodding, a gesture of silent understanding. I walk cautiously towards the room and find myself in a grand bathroom with a walk-in pool-like tub full of hot steamy water.

My eyes scan the room and take in the lush décor. The walls are lined with marble panels, creating a sort of elegant mosaic with several alcoves. In one of the recesses sits a golden goblet with a drop of something in it. I take the glass in my hand and bring it to my nose to smell its contents.

My head whips around, my eyes locking with Aggonid. "How did you get this here?"

He grins. "Oh, please." He stalks towards me. "Where do you think the humans get it from?"

He takes the chalice and brings it to his lips, indulging in a sip of the glowing green liquid.

A spicy aroma fills the air as he swallows and his eyes meet mine, the pupils glowing red. "Only the finest absinthe for you." He tilts the cup towards me.

198

I take a sip and feel the fire travel down my throat. I gulp it down and almost choke as my body starts to shiver.

"Surprised?" He laughs.

I sputter and try to hand him back the cup. "That was ... that was strong."

He grins, taking the goblet back and setting it in the nook. Something passes between us. Something unspoken and silent, but I can't put my finger on it.

Aggonid steps back, gesturing towards the bath. "Join me?"

I eye it warily. "I've already bathed tonight."

"That was before you'd allowed those two mongrels to—"

Red hot fury swirls in my gut and I cannot contain it. In a single, violent motion, I barrel myself forward and shove the devil into the pool, watching in satisfaction as the water rises to greet him.

He splutters as he emerges, water dripping from his hair and down his face.

I sneer, crossing my arms. "Who's the mongrel now?"

Aggonid takes a deep breath, composing himself. A slow, lazy smile creeps up his face, the anger replaced with admiration.

Before I can even process what's happening, he lunges forward, snatching me by the ankle and yanking me towards the giant, recessed tub. I scream in terror as I'm dragged, feeling the warm water engulf me and fill my lungs.

I propel myself to the surface, ready to let Aggonid have it for his hurtful words and for almost drowning me. But as soon as I break through the water, my anger dissolves into confusion. There's the devil, drenched and grinning from ear to ear, his features softened by the breathtaking smile on his face.

For a moment, I'm caught off guard by the sight of him. I've seen him smile plenty, mostly smug grins, but never like this. Here he is, looking like he's having the time of his life.

As I watch him, a new feeling creeps over me, replacing my rage with something else. It's hard to put my finger on it, but there's something about the way he's looking at me that makes my heart race and my skin tingle. Suddenly, I'm acutely aware of the fact that we're both soaking wet, and our clothes are near-translucent now. What might happen next?

The buzz of absinthe steels my nerves, and I can't help but grin back as I sink until just my chin juts out of the water. "And here I thought you only had eyes for your mate," I murmur.

He chuckles as he moves closer, his gaze never leaving mine. "Some things are worth a closer look."

I'm so fascinated by his words and the intensity in his eyes that I almost miss it when one arm reaches around my waist, and he pulls me flush against him. His free hand cups my face, thumb brushing against my cheek. We're so close now, I can feel the heat radiating off of his breath, the feel of it not an unwelcome one.

"Caius won't mind?"

His lips press against my jaw before pausing below my ear. "Mind?" He chuckles. "He'll beg to join."

"He's right," the voice like velvet calls from behind me and I shove Aggonid back, spinning to face Caius.

Heat flames my cheeks as I haul myself out of the water, dripping it everywhere before grabbing a towel from the edge and wrapping it around my trembling body. I try to keep my cool, but my words still come out a little shaky. "You two are something else."

He laughs, the same way Aggonid did. Like he's toying with me, instead of being genuinely interested. "Come to bed, little dove." His countenance softens.

I storm into the bedroom, scanning it for a closet. Tucked around the corner is a giant walk-in, and I move towards it before Caius' voice stops me.

"What are the rules?"

I roll my eyes before dropping the towel and peeling off my sopping wet clothes and tossing them onto the tile floor. I feel the heat of their gazes as I saunter to the bed and climb in, naked, and turn to face the opposite side.

Pulling the silk comforter around me, I settle down, trying to imagine I'm with Wilder. Or Az. Emeric? Maybe all three. That I'm safe; that they're the ones crawling into the bed with me, and Aggonid and Caius are just figments of my imagination.

Aggonid

"Do you want me to come with you?" Caius places a kiss on my forehead, his lips lingering there while he waits for my answer.

I consider his offer, but ultimately shake my head. "No, I need you to stay and keep an eye on Morte. Your sister has been acting strangely and I don't trust her intentions. Who knows what kind of poison she'll feed Morte."

Caius furrows his brow. "What do you mean?"

"Irid keeps trying to get me alone. If she weren't still upset about her mate, I'd say she was making advances," I explain with a hint of annoyance. "But I can't risk it. Someone needs to watch her."

Caius quirks an eyebrow. "She knows I'd gut her before I'd let her lay a finger on you. Blood or not."

He glances to the bedroom door where Morte is still sleeping, and then back to me where I'm brushing my teeth.

"Better go wake the little heathen so I can be on my way," I garble before spitting. "See you in a bit."

I give him a wink and then head for the throne room, nodding to Vorcan and Riven as they stand guard outside the door. I enter the opulent room, with its high domed ceiling and stony grey walls, and see the banquet table across the room, where staff ready the dishes for after the ceremony.

I stride to the throne and take my place, feeling the weight of authority settle on my shoulders. I'm ready to get this over with. If there weren't so many evil fae arriving from Romarie, we wouldn't have to constantly purge our denizens in these games.

I cast a glance to the portaled window where the sky can be seen beyond and notice a storm brewing in the distance. I wonder if it's a sign of worse things to come.

The courtiers and attendants soon assemble, having been summoned to witness the ceremony and await my judgment. But first, I have to hear their requests, and it takes hours.

A loud crash of thunder echoes through the hall and rain begins to pour outside just as Caius escorts Morte into the room.

A smile curves my face when I see what she has on. Is this a power play?

She wears my black and gold armor, something I never let anyone wear unless they are of my blood, and I haven't had a blood relative around for years. It's the purest symbol of my rule, and here she stands, bold as day wearing it. Caius must've used magic to make it fit her slight form.

The courtiers whisper to each other in surprise and dismay. Morte looks directly at me, her gaze steady and unaffected.

I chuckle and break the tension. "You always did have a flair for the dramatic," I say, a hint of amusement in my voice. "But I trust there's a reason for this bold fashion statement?"

Morte steps forward, confident in her stride. "I come to honor you, my lord." The grin she gives me is pure malice despite her honeyed words.

Raising my voice, I call out to the rest of the room for silence. Their words hush, and the only sound is the rain and the quiet shuffle of wings until I speak.

"Morte of Bedlam, you've won the Forsaken Hunt, and now you get a favor. What shall it be?"

Morte's smirk fades into a solemn expression. "I'm here to collect two favors."

I raise an eyebrow, considering her words carefully and my laughter joins the rest of the audiences. "Two? The game is for one."

Caius' steps falter where he's climbing the dais to be at my side. He, too, wears armor, but instead of black and gold, it's his usual black and silver. The metal clinks as he takes his place next to me.

Morte bows deeply, a gesture of respect and submission if it weren't for the mocking glint in her eye. She stands, turning her attention to Caius.

"I'm here to collect yours, too." She grins.

I turn to face him, leaning in to whisper, "What the fuck is she talking about?"

He winces. "It's the deal I made with her when she first got here."

I grit my teeth and silence the room once more. "Go on." I sigh.

Morte glances behind her, seeking someone in the throng of attendees. When she can't find who she's looking for, she leaves the plinth and makes her way through the crowd.

Morte

SHOCKED FACES of fae and demons greet me as I barge through the revelers. My wings snap out, sending a gust of wind at such angles that they create an open path, and Aggonid's gaze burns against my back, but I don't dare turn around. When I spot his handsome face along the far wall, his wide eyes meet mine and he hisses, "Morte, what are you doing?"

"Trust me." I grab his hand and drag him through the outraged chatter, pushing my way back to the footpace.

Caius' uncertain gaze lingers on me as I approach the throne, and as I take my place before it, his lips part as if to speak, but he remains silent. Azazel stands rigid beside me, his nervous glances darting between us.

"The favor I ask of you, Caius, is to release Azazel from his servitude," I declare, my voice ringing through the throne room.

Incensed cries mix with the booming thunder outside, but beneath the commotion, I hear Azazel suck in a shocked breath before he drops to his knees in front of me, shaking his head. "Morte, you can use your magic to do anything," he pleads. "I was going to let you win anyway."

I silence him with a gentle touch on his cheek, savoring the roughness of his stubble against my skin. "Az, you deserve this," I say with a soft smile.

"She's lost her mind!" someone shouts from the crowd, but I pay them no heed.

I have never agreed to be sane, not in this lifetime, nor the next.

"Morte?" Caius calls out, his voice drawing my attention.

I turn to face him, my eyes meeting his. "Yes?"

"Is this what you really want?" he asks, his expression creased with concern.

I meet his gaze, unwavering. "Yes."

"Very well," he sighs, making his way down the steps towards Azazel. "Rise."

Azazel pulls himself to his feet, shellshocked as he stands before us.

With practiced ease, Caius unclips the harness that stretches across Azazel's chest, and rips his shirt open, revealing the taught, tan skin beneath. He places his hands, one on either side of his shoulders, and begins mumbling words, too low for me to make out. The room becomes deathly quiet as a soft light radiates from Caius' fingertips, wrapping around Azazel in a cocoon of warmth, matching the glowing runes on his skin.

A single word appears tattooed on Az's abdomen.

Minion.

With a gesture of one hand, Caius banishes the script in a puff of pitch-black smoke, and it disappears, only leaving his standard tattoos.

Azazel stares down at his chest, overawed by what he has been freed from. When he looks up again, his eyes rest on mine.

"Thank you," he whispers, his voice ragged with emotion.

I'm too caught up in Az's eyes to notice Caius retreat back to the throne until Aggonid speaks.

The courtiers and attendants murmur amongst themselves, still taken aback by my audacity.

A booming roar reverberates from Aggonid, startling everyone into quiet.

"Enough!" he bellows, his voice ringing out. "Morte has earned a favor by winning the Forsaken Hunt. She will be granted whatever it is she wishes to ask for."

My eyebrows climb up in surprise, not expecting the devil to be so quick to disparage his courtiers for me. I won, yes, but he also hates me, so there's that.

"Take me with you tonight when you visit with Finn."

Aggonid barks a laugh, and the rest of the room joins in, but I stand my ground.

"You said anything."

"Finn can't bring you home with him, Morte." He smirks. "Trust me, it would've been the first thing I asked for," he spits.

I shrug. "That's fine. I'd still like to go with."

"You realize the meeting isn't taking place in Bedlam, but in Romarie?"

"Changes nothing," I reply, holding his gaze and crossing my arms.

He reclines in his throne, like a cat lounging lazily atop a hill. "You know going to Romarie is only temporary, right? Denizens of the underworld can only visit other realms briefly. The realm will reject you and send you right back where you belong if you stay too long."

The devil stares at me for a moment, then waves his hand in exasperation when I just roll my eyes at him. "Granted. Be prepared to leave in an hour."

The courtiers whisper as I walk away, feeling a sense of accomplishment as I step out of the throne room.

I make it just outside the doors when they open again, and Azazel bursts through them.

He closes the space between us, hauling me into his arms and squeezing me to his chest. "No one has ever done anything like this for me before." Emotion clogs his voice. "Fuck, Morte." He threads a hand through my hair, crashing his lips to mine.

The sound of people filtering into the hallway interrupts our kiss, so I drag him around the corner and lean back against the wall, catching my breath.

"What can I do for you? Just name it." Azazel leans down, pressing his forehead to mine and grinning. "All the orgasms you want," he murmurs into my neck, his hands running up and down my sides. "Forever."

I shake my head, taking his face in my hands. "You don't have to do anything," I say, then hesitate once I consider his words. "Okay, maybe you can give me an orgasm again and I'll consider it a fair trade."

"Morte," Azazel breathes, still holding me close. He smiles at me, then shakes his head. "I'm not even sure I remember what it's like to not beholden to Aggonid."

"More time for orgasms?" I grin, leaning into his touch.

"Mm," he agrees, nuzzling my neck.

"Time to go, Morte," Aggonid growls, startling me.

I turn to see him standing there, scowling. "Go on, I'll find you when I get back," I prompt, and Az presses his lips to mine.

"Please, be safe," he reminds me before heading off down the hallway.

I take a deep breath, then prepare myself to face the devil.

"You told me I had an hour," I grumble.

"I changed my mind."

CHAPTER TWENTY-ONE

MORTE

Romarie

I've never been to the realm of Romarie, mostly on account of it being almost as terrifying as the underworld. Not a single fae from this whole realm is a good person. They lie, cheat, steal, and kill without a second thought. Only sheer power holds the balance in Romarie, and King Valtorious has it.

Irid dresses me in a hurry, her hands shaking. "King Valtorious is a shrewd and cunning king," she says, her voice faltering slightly. "He believes that by forming an alliance with Finn, he can gain an ally who will help him bring down Aggonid and take control of the underworld. Valtorious knows that he can't do this alone, and he needs the support of other powerful fae rulers to achieve his goal."

I nod, but I can't help but feel suspicious of Irid's words. They don't quite match the worry etched onto her face. "And Finn is considering the offer?" I ask, hoping to gain some insight into the situation.

Irid hesitates for a moment before answering. "He's considering it," she says finally, avoiding my gaze.

I can't help but feel uneasy about the whole situation, and Irid's words only add to my apprehension. Something about the way she speaks of Valtorious doesn't quite sit right with me, and I can't shake the feeling that there's more to this than what Irid is telling me. Finn would never align himself with a power-hungry king, and even if he didn't like Aggonid, he knows we need the underworld.

I stay silent as she helps me into a long black gown, complete with a floor-length, hooded cloak. Its plunging necklace is far more revealing than anything I wore on Bedlam, but I understand the power dynamic at play. With the gold filigree, I look more like a consort than a prisoner.

Aggonid wants to show off what King Valtorious cannot have. But if I can face the fae devil, Romarie's king should be easy.

Irid pauses in front of me, grabbing my face in her hands. "Here." She swipes them across my eyelids, my cheeks, and then my lips.

"What did you do?"

"Just a little makeup." She grins.

I step around her to check out her work in the mirror, and hardly recognize myself. The protection necklace still sits at my throat, but it's the makeup that draws my attention. It accents my features in a subtle gilded glow, though my lips are as gold as the sun, and Aggonid's crest is painted across my forehead.

I still, studying it. Seeing something so foreign on my skin should be jarring, but instead, it settles something in my chest. My fingers trace the gold lines around the crest, my chin tilting in reverence.

"Ready?" Irid's voice snaps me out of my trance.

"Ready," I agree.

We make our way through the castle and back down the path towards the draw bridge, the sun warming on my face. Irid strides ahead of me, eyes scanning the guard posts even though she can't see their faces on account of the metal helmets with a mohawk of spikes atop them.

Taking a deep breath, I steel myself for what I'm about to face. As we approach the gates, they open without a word, and I'm led across the narrow suspension bridge where Aggonid waits under an arch of thorns and flames. He stands with his hands clasped behind his back, looking regal despite the simple finery of black and gold adorning him. His eyes flick over me as Irid steps away, taking up a post at the base of the arch.

"Morte," Aggonid purrs, and I feel a shiver run down my spine. "You look beautiful." His fingers trace his emblem on my forehead, his touch searing me with its tenderness. "I really, really like this on you."

It startles me to hear his voice without contempt in it. He seems to realize it, too, because the corner of his mouth twists up ever so slightly. I force myself to school my expression and bow my head. "Thank you," I reply.

"Come," he says, before gesturing for me to follow him.

We walk in silence through the arch and down a long granite path lined with gnarled oaks and towering pines. A retinue of guards follows several yards behind, the clack of their boots against the stones echoing in the otherwise still air. Winged fae soar in the sky above, scouting the surroundings.

At last, we come to a set of tall silver doors set at the base of a giant hawthorn, set with in frame of gold. As we approach, I can see that the hawthorn tree is like none I have ever seen before. Its twisted branches are thick with thorns, some as fine as a hair and others as thick as a finger. The trunk is knotted and gnarled, and the bark is rough and grey, marked with deep grooves and fissures. The leaves are small and oval-shaped, with a waxy texture and a deep, rich green color. The blooms are clusters of small, white flowers tinged with a pale, ghostly blue, and their scent is sweet and heady.

Aggonid steps forward and places his palm against it, and the door swings open. I gasp when I see what's inside—it reaches up into the darkness, tall and golden, glowing with an eerie light. This is unlike any portal in Bedlam. There, our portals are enormous, windy, and just as likely to take you out as it is to strip the clothes from your body. How did something like this end up *here* of all places?

The walls of the chamber are lined with marble statues, intricately carved, and painted in vibrant hues. Along one wall, a massive mural stretches from floor to ceiling, depicting dozens of scenes from the Underworld.

We climb the stairs—odd, because from the outside it seems as though we'd be climbing inside the tree—until we reach an imposing door made of solid bronze. Aggonid pauses, as if considering his next move, before pushing the door open with a wave of his hand.

Behind it lies an open courtyard, bathed in the soft light of the setting sun. At the center is a fountain shaped like a pair of hands cupping water, and all around it are lush gardens filled with exotic plants and vibrant wildflowers.

A red carpet leads from the fountain to a set of golden gates guarded by two enormous demons. Aggonid strides forward, not pausing for a moment as he passes between them and into the palace.

As I step through the portal, I feel a chill run down my spine. The air is thick with the scent of perfumed flowers, and I can't help but wonder what kind of place we've entered. Looking around, I see that we've arrived in a grand, open air entrance hall, the likes of which I've never seen before. The ceiling is lined with rich tapestries, depicting scenes of war and seduction. Gleaming marble statues of twisted fae creatures loom from the corners of the hall, their eyes seeming to follow our every move. The furniture is equally lavish, with ornate chairs and tables crafted from dark, twisted wood.

"This is Romarie?" I whisper, my eyes wide as I take in the opulent surroundings.

"Don't let it fool you," Aggonid says, tucking my arm around his and bringing me close to his side. "He hides the ugly beneath a façade of beauty. Look closer."

Studying our surroundings with a new lens, I see that Aggonid is right. The grandeur of the entrance hall belies the true nature of this realm. The tapestries, once beautiful, are now stained and frayed at the edges, as if they've been through countless battles. The marble statues are grotesque, their features contorted in pain and agony. The furniture, while ornate, is also battered and worn.

As we make our way through the entrance hall, I can't shake the feeling that someone is watching us. I look up, expecting to see one of the twisted fae creatures staring down at us, but the hall is empty. The only sound is the echo of our footsteps against the carpet covered marble floors, and the soft rustle of the tapestries in the breeze.

As we make our way deeper into Romarie, the chill in the air grows more pronounced. I can feel the weight of the realm's malevolent energy bearing down on me, suffocating and oppressive.

Keep your eyes on the prize: we're one step closer to getting back to Wilder.

"Why isn't anyone greeting us?" I ask, glancing around in search of any sign of life.

"It's a power play," Aggonid grumbles, his brow furrowed in frustration.

Golden cords are threaded through his braided hair, adorned with small glass beads that clack together with every step. It's a stark contrast to the darkness that seems to permeate every inch of this realm despite the sun warming my cheeks.

Without any attendants to guide us, we're left to wander the entrance hall alone. A chill runs through me as I realize that this is just one of the many games of deception and manipulation that the King of Romarie plays. No one is immune from his schemes.

As we approach the castle, I'm struck by its sheer size and imposing presence. The structure towers above us, its walls seemingly stretching up into the very clouds above. The doors are more than twice as tall as a man and are made of thick, dark wood, reinforced with iron bands that gleam dully in the dim light. I can't help but wonder what kind of beings might call this fortress home.

As we move closer, I see that the walls are covered in intricate carvings and designs, etched into the very stone itself. The carvings depict scenes of war and conquest, of battles fought and won by the inhabitants of this castle. It's a testament to the power and might of the ruler.

"Do you know where we're going?" I whisper to Aggonid, my eyes darting around nervously.

He doesn't answer, but instead leads me towards the doors. Intricate runes and sigils are etched into them with a precision that speaks of great skill and magic.

As my eyes adjust to the darkness, I can make out an imposing, tan figure standing in front of us. He's dressed in dark, regal clothing, and a heavy crown rests upon his head, waves of jet-black hair styled to his shoulders. He exudes an air of power and authority, and my heart makes a racket in my chest as he strides towards us.

"Welcome," he booms, his voice echoing off the walls. "I am Ollin Valtorious, King of Romarie." He approaches me, taking my hand in his and pressing a kiss to it. I feel a shiver run down my spine at his touch, and I pull away instinctively.

Wrong. He feels wrong.

This man is familiar to me, but I can't put my finger on it. Shadows pour off him, curling around my legs.

"You shouldn't have, Aggie, but I accept," he continues, his predatory, indigo eyes flicking towards me. I feel a sudden surge of panic as I realize that he thinks I'm a gift for him. He's handsome, but not for me.

Aggonid growls, his hand tightening around mine. "She's not for you," he snarls, his eyes flashing with anger.

Valtorious raises an eyebrow but doesn't seem surprised by Aggonid's reaction. "We'll see about that," he grins. "Well then, what brings you to my realm, Aggie?"

Aggonid's grip on my hand doesn't falter, and I can feel the tension in his body as he glares at Valtorious. "Where is King Finian?" he asks through gritted teeth.

Ollin smiles, but there's a dangerous glint in his eyes. "Oh, I told him you've postponed the visit," he says, before turning and gesturing for us to follow him deeper into the castle.

"What!" I rage as fury pours off Aggonid, suffocating the room. "You had no right to do that!"

Valtorious stops and turns around, his eyes dark with amusement. "I'm afraid I did, pet," he says, his voice condescending. "My rules are absolute here in Romarie." He smirks before continuing down the corridor.

My heart bellows in my chest as Aggonid lunges for the king, grabbing him around the neck and lifting him off his feet as though he weighs no more than a rag doll.

Panic wages a war inside of me, all because this prick thought he could rip everything out from under me.

"How dare you," Aggonid snarls, fury radiating from his body. His shadows curl around them, nearly blocking them out completely. "Give me one good reason I shouldn't pluck your eyeballs from your skull for daring to look at what isn't yours and sever your tongue from your mouth for having the audacity to speak to me this way."

The king's red face is one of surprise and fear. "Let go of me!" he gasps, clawing at Aggonid's arm in a futile attempt to free himself. "He'll be here in a couple days!"

I rest a hand on Aggonid's shoulder, and his entire body is vibrating with rage. "If you kill him now, his people will never let us see Finn," I reason with him. "Besides, if he ruins this for me, I want to be the one to string him up by his balls while I feast on his entrails." I cross my arms over my chest. "We'll just go back now and meet him in two days."

Still maintaining his hold on Ollin, Aggonid's head swivels to look my way, his face displaying a mixture of equal parts horror and … arousal? His mouth tips up in a smirk. "Fuck. Say that again."

I roll my eyes at him. "Let's go."

I can't jeopardize my meeting with Finn. We need this asshole of a king so I can see mine, and maybe find a way home.

The devil narrows his eyes, returning his attention to the king. "We can't, though, can we?" Aggonid squeezes tighter, inches from Ollin's face.

"Maybe let him breathe so he can answer our questions," I offer.

Aggonid lets go, and the king crumples to the floor, sucking in deep, gasping breaths.

"You fucking asshole," he growls before climbing to his feet.

"Guess you should've worn one of your stupid protection amulets, huh?" Aggonid folds his arms across his chest, smug.

I'd forgotten that all the protection jewelry is made here. This realm specializes in all sorts of metals not found elsewhere, imbued with magical properties like protection, invisibility, and luck.

The king sputters in rage, but Aggonid's shadow magic looms threateningly. "Tell us what you know," he commands.

He sighs and wipes the sweat dripping from his forehead before finally relenting. "Finn should be here in two days, but you won't be able to leave for the portal to the underworld."

"For how long?" Aggonid growls.

The king visibly pales and mutters something under his breath neither of us catch.

"Speak up." I step closer, and his eyes snap to mine.

"A month."

"What?!" I charge him, hands already balling into fists, but Aggonid steps between us. He knows how important this is for us, and he's purposefully trying to delay us?

He shrinks from me and shakes his head. "It'll take a month for the required energy to be focused around the portal."

"Can't we do anything to speed up the process?" I ask, my frustration mounting.

Valtorious shakes his head. "The process cannot be rushed. It requires a delicate balance of energies to be properly aligned, or the portal could become unstable and unpredictable."

A sense of defeat washes over me. A whole month trapped in Romarie feels like an eternity, and the weight of this news presses down on me.

"Then how is Finn planning to return home once he arrives here in two days?" I ask the king.

He considers my words, cocking his head to study me intently, and suddenly I realize my mistake. Using such a familiar name gives away the fact that I'm on friendly terms with the high king of the fae, and I curse myself for being so careless.

"His mother built his portal." He narrows his eyes, taking too much interest in me now. "Only he can travel through it."

His mother, the Luna goddess. She's who the good fae go to when they die, and she lives beyond the veil, supplying magic to all fae, no matter your realm.

I feel Aggonid's hand on my shoulder as he steps protectively in front of me. I've said too much, and he's determined to protect me.

"You will get your portal back to the underworld, but it won't be ready for another month," Valtorious says gruffly, effectively closing the conversation.

He snaps his fingers, and all manner of staff step out of concealed doors. They begin to usher us through the halls, and Valtorious turns to me. "You will be our guest for the next month. I hope you find the hospitality of Romarie satisfactory."

I swallow hard, trying to keep my emotions in check.

"Show us to our chamber and we'll be out of your hair," Aggonid growls.

"Apologies, I wasn't expecting more than one of you. I've got you on the West wing, and your little friend here will have to stay in the tower with me. We've got a celebration tomorrow night, so we're quite full." He raises a brow, gesturing towards a stairwell, and my steps falter.

"The fuck you will." Aggonid moves in between us. "She'll stay with me."

Valtorious holds his hands up in surrender. "Doing business with you always comes with complications," he mutters, frustration clear in his voice. Then, he turns to a slight woman standing nearby. She is dressed in a light green gown that shimmers like the sea, and her hair matches the color perfectly. The woman's ankles are bound tightly together with a rope, preventing her from taking large steps, and the sight of it unsettles me. She reminds me so much of Wilder's mother. Is she a merfae?

"Bring them to the West wing and have someone ready their chambers. We've got a big day tomorrow."

"Yes, my Lord." The fae obediently bows and leads us down a winding corridor.

We arrive at our chamber, a lavish room adorned with rich red tapestries, a large bed, and a massive fireplace. Aggonid sinks down onto the bed without ceremony, and I hesitate in the doorway.

"Well, I suppose this is our home for the next month," he says, forcing a small smile.

I hesitate as I shut the door behind me. "Why are you being nice to me?"

He sighs, flopping back so his legs still touch the floor, but the rest of his body lays on the bed. "You're my only ally here."

I climb onto the soft mattress and lean my back against the headboard. "Maybe I'm planning on seeking refuge here and finding my way back to Bedlam," I deadpan.

"Then you'd be a fool."

"Why?"

"King Valtorious is cruel, and only pretends to be a civilized host. People rarely make it out of Romarie alive, and you'd probably end up back in his care one way or another." He frowns slightly, then meets my eyes. "And I couldn't protect you if that happened."

"I don't know, Aggie." I grin at the nickname the king gave him. "You had me in chains, tortured me, and killed me in the short time I've known you. At least Ollin treats me with a modicum of respect."

"By ogling you?" His shadows curl around my form, the feel of them cool against my skin.

"You noticed that did you?"

He grumbles and throws an arm over his eyes.

"What was that?" I lean closer.

"I said," he sighs, "better the devil you know than the devil you don't. That's what they say, right?"

"You're giving me whiplash."

He tucks his legs up so he can roll further onto the bed and face me. "What do you want to talk to King Finian Drake about?"

"It'll be nice just to have a conversation with a familiar face," I hedge, but think better of it. "I think you know why I'm going to talk to him."

A shadow falls over his features. "Do you love him?"

"Uhh." I furrow my brows. "No. We're friendly, and he has a soul bonded mate who is also my friend."

"Why did you save Azazel?" His voice is low and his gaze distant.

I pause, taken aback. He's talking like he's some kind of jealous lover, and it's jarring to think of him in that light.

"Because he, too, is a friend."

"Lover."

"I'm a virgin."

"I know, but you don't have to have intercourse to be someone's lover."

He stares at the vaulted ceiling for a few moments, then sighs and scoots so he's lying next to me.

"What makes someone a lover, then?" My voice is barely a whisper and comes out more of a squeak than anything.

"Soul bonds may be preordained by fate, but what constitutes a lover is something we craft with another. It can be a union of flesh and desire, but it can also flourish from shared conversations and time spent together." He tucks his arm behind his head, a far off look on his face. "A lover possesses the ability to dismantle and rebuild us anew, and the depth of that connection transcends mere physicality." He turns to me, his gaze intense. "For love is a journey, not a destination, and the truest bonds are forged by the strength of the heart, not just the passion of the flesh."

Wilder is my lover, too. "What is Caius to you? Is he your soul bond?" I trace the stitching on the bedspread beneath me.

"No, he was my lover before our mating bond."

"And it doesn't bother you that he hits on other people?" I ask him.

"He doesn't."

I scoff. "But he hits on me all the—"

"You're different," he says, cutting me off and turning me to face him now.

"Why?"

His face hardens, and the air in the room shifts. He sits up and stares at me with a burning intensity.

"You just are." He climbs off the bed and strides out of the room without another word.

CHAPTER TWENTY-TWO

AGGONID

$\mathcal{G}$uests cower away from me in fear as I stalk the halls, my shadows licking the walls and snaking around their ankles. They can feel the power radiating from me and keep their distance. I've spent the last two hours trying to stay away from Morte, afraid she'll know the depths of my feelings for her. That moment in our shared room, when she asked what Caius was to me, I could feel something coming alive in me. Things would be different if I'd never received that parchment from Mordecai, the seer who'd told me my fate. I'd almost killed him for it, but he'd gotten away.

I take a deep breath and push away my feelings. I have more important things to deal with right now, like figuring out why the hell Romarie's power has weakened so much since my last visit here. Ollin used to flex he could come and go as he pleased with his portals, so why the change now?

I make my way to the throne room and enter without knocking, as is my right. Inside, King Valtorious is seated on his throne with his advisor beside him. My steps resound throughout the chamber as I approach.

"Aggonid." His advisor greets me with a slight bow. "Good to see you." Finally, someone who respects the power thrumming through my veins. This is how you regard a god, though his use of my first name is a little familiar for my tastes.

"Lorcan," I reply coolly. "Why is Romarie low on power?"

He furrows his brow. "We're no—"

"What do you need, Aggonid?" King Valtorious interrupts, gesturing to the room. "Can't you see we're busy?"

I'm in no mood to be belittled by someone whose power is wholly insignificant compared to mine.

"I was just inquiring about the source of Romarie's weakening power."

The king leans back in his throne and sighs as Lorcan shifts uncomfortably. "Our mines are drying up," the king says, and his advisor stiffens. "The sanguimetal ores are becoming rarer and the magical energy they produce is being depleted." He places a hand on his forehead as if to ward off a headache.

I study Lorcan's minuscule reactions to what Ollin says, and it doesn't take a genius to figure out he's not being entirely truthful.

"My Lord, are you feeling alright?" Lorcan leans over his king. "I can have supper brought to your room."

"Perhaps that would be best." The king rises from his throne and pauses to glance my way. "Have food brought to their chamber as well, we won't be having a big meal tonight."

He and Lorcan scurry out of the room, leaving me standing in the center of the grand hall. I look around, taking in the intricately carved walls and glittering chandeliers that adorn this imposing place.

But it's all a façade. And beneath the surface, something sinister is taking place in Romarie. I'm going to get to the bottom of it, and soon.

I return to the room to find Morte soaking in a claw-foot tub, her arms outstretched, and her face tilted up to the ceiling. She's a beautiful sight, her curves framed by the rising steam. I approach without a sound and kneel beside the tub. It kills me to do it, but I've got to get her to let her guard down if my plan is going to work.

"Beauty is a dangerous gift, bestowed upon the lucky few," I whisper, running my finger along her arm. She starts in surprise, her eyes flashing to mine. "But with you, my dear Morte, it's more than just a gift, it's a weapon."

"A weapon?" she squeaks, her chest heaving, the swell of her breasts peaking above the water.

"A weapon that can ensnare even the wariest of hearts, leaving them at your mercy. And yet, in your presence, I find myself willingly surrendering to its power. You are a vision of divine grace, a master-piece crafted by the gods themselves. And in this moment, as I trace the lines of your delicate form, I'm struck by the thought that you are more than just beautiful. You are exquisite, a rare and precious jewel in a world of ordinary stones."

She bursts out laughing, causing ripples in the water. "You're so full of shit, Aggonid. I can't believe you actually thought that would work on me. Nice try though." She swallows, looking more vulnerable than she's trying to let on.

All the words I speak are true. "I may be a villain, but even villains have eyes. And in my eyes, you are the fairest of them all."

"You shouldn't be here," she says, lifting a hand to cover her body instinctively.

I reach out and brush a wet lock of hair away from her face. "It's just us," I say softly. "No one else."

She looks at me for a moment, her face unreadable, before finally sighing and leaning back in the tub. "What do you want?"

I move closer and lean in, so close our lips are almost touching. My heart beats faster as I feel the heat of her skin against mine and hear the labored breath coming from her lips.

"I came to ask you something," I whisper, my gaze never leaving hers.

"What?"

"Can we have a clean slate? Put our past behind us?"

She laughs, and the short bursts of air hit my cheeks. I sit back on my haunches. "You want me to forget how you tortured me, and then killed me?"

I wince. "I'll make it up to you."

"How the fuck do you plan on doing that? Just because I'm a phoenix doesn't mean it doesn't hurt to *die*, Aggie."

I grit my teeth at the nickname but allow her this small measure of control. "I'm sorry. Let me show you what kind of man I can be," I murmur, gripping her hand in mine.

"And what's that?" She looks at me skeptically.

"A powerful ally, a loyal friend, and someone who gets you," I say, my tone earnest.

"You're insane."

"Probably." I smirk. "A clean slate isn't easy to come by." My grip on her hand tightens. "I am the devil, Morte. I do not ask for forgiveness, but I am sorry. I've tried to keep away, but I can't. You are the spark that ignites my desires, the flame that consumes my thoughts. I am the lord of fire and ash, and between you, Caius, and me, no one can stand in our way."

"They literally have nursery rhymes meant to scare children about you," she warns, and it warms my heart to hear it.

Before I can respond, she starts singing it, quite off-key, but it still brings a smile to my face.

> Aggonid, Aggonid, in the underworld,
> A devil so fearsome, a power to behold,
> With eyes that gleam and a fiery gaze,
> Beware his tricks, for he loves to play.
> He dances with demons and drinks with the dead,
> His laughter echoes through the caverns ahead,
> For those who cross him, a terrible fate,
> Beware Aggonid, the devil so great.
> So if you venture down to the underworld,
> Be sure to tread lightly, be sure to be bold,
> And never forget, in the land of the dead,
> Aggonid, the devil, is always ahead.

"Well, they're not wrong." I grin. "But I'm willing to prove that I can be more than that. That I can be an ally and a friend, and hopefully even more."

Morte still looks skeptical, but she nods slowly. "Alright, I'll give you that chance. But no tricks or games."

"No tricks." I chuckle, lifting her hand to my lips and placing a gentle kiss on her knuckles.

She smiles sadly. "It's going to take some time, Aggonid."

"I'll wait," I say softly. The words taste like ash on my tongue. "For however long it takes."

I leave her to her bath and explore the room we're in. My suspicions are confirmed when I locate sixteen different spying devices and crush each one in my fist. I enchant the room so only Morte or me can enter, just in case Ollin sends anyone in to replace these.

"Aggonid?" Morte calls from the bathroom, and I head back to her, my steps quiet.

"Yes?"

"Um," she hesitates. "You didn't happen to find any tampons when you were poking around the bedroom?"

"Oh." I rifle through the cabinets and drawers until I locate a box. "Here," I say, handing her one.

She nods her thanks before sinking back into the tub.

"Is there anything else I can do for you?" I ask as I turn towards the door.

"Yes," she murmurs, her cheeks flushing. "Stay."

I pause, and then smile softly before making my way back to the edge of the tub. *How I wish things could be different.* We stay like that for a while, not speaking, but sharing a comfortable silence until someone knocks at the bedroom door.

I cross the room and use magic to sense who is on the other side of it.

Dinner.

I take it from the terrified servant, shutting the door and locking it behind me. I turn back to Morte and set the tray of food down on the vanity.

"Can I stay and eat with you? Or do you want me to leave?" I ask, hesitating in the doorway.

Morte considers the offer before finally nodding.

"I'd like that," she says, her voice small. "But I'm going to eat in here, my cramps are killing me."

I smile and pour us both a glass of wine before sitting next to her in the tub. We eat in silence, but as the meal progresses, there's so much I want to know about her, but the questions die on my tongue.

It's better this way.

After supper, we crawl into bed, but I don't make a fuss about the not-wearing-clothes rule, knowing she wants comfort.

We lie next to each other under the covers, and a whimper escapes Morte.

"What's wrong?" I prop myself on my elbow and face her.

In the dim light of the fireplace, I can see her shake her head. "Just a cramp."

"Let me help," I offer. "You can't use your magic, but I can."

"Please," she breathes.

I pull her into my arms, savoring her warmth as I breathe her in. I can feel it, like a stirring in my core, and I guide it towards her, surrounding her with magic. My hands slide down her body, massaging away the pain.

Morte lets out a deep sigh as the magic takes hold, but rather than stopping, I keep going, molding her like putty in my hands. It's less clinical now, and much more intimate, as I work to smooth away the tension. My fingertips skim her soft skin until she's soothed and relaxed.

Eventually, the moments of silence are filled with whispers and touches, a subtle shift in the air between us as something new kindles within. I can feel it growing already, this bond, a bridge between us I'm reluctant to give up, but I don't push her any further. Not when I've got to get her to let her guard down.

When my hands still, she doesn't pull away, and we stay like that until she eventually drifts off to sleep. Her breathing evens out and I press my lips to her crown, feeling a little piece of me die inside.

~

Morte

SOFT PUFFS of air stir against my cheek, and a hint of vetiver and tobacco reaches my nose. I slowly open my eyes to find Aggonid gazing at me, a smile dancing across his lips. His eyes are warmer than I've ever seen, as if they're reflecting the flickering flames of the fireplace rather than his usual maelstrom of a volcano.

"Do you know why I make your perfect villain?" he whispers, brushing his thumb across my cheek.

"Impart me with your wisdom, oh great one," I tease.

He grins. "Now you're getting it! Now more of that, please, and less of the 'Aggie this, Aggie that.'" He grips my chin between his fingers, his canines on full display. "I'm your perfect villain because you are the phoenix rising from the ashes, and I am the fire that brings about destruction. Together, we can burn the realms to ashes and rebuild them anew."

"Who said I want a villain?" I retort, but his hand tightens around my chin, and I gasp as his other hand slides across my throat, the touch sending shivers through my body.

"You need a villain," he murmurs, pressing his lips to my ear. "Someone who can handle the heat of your flames and the weight of your immortality. Someone who understands the chaos that burns within you and embraces it. And who better than me, the God of the Underworld, to be your partner in this dance of destruction and rebirth?"

A sense of trepidation and wonder overwhelms me. My heart beats so fast I can hear it roaring against my eardrums, and my skin prickles in anticipation when his hands roam over me. His deep chuckle is like thunder, and he pulls me closer. His lips are like the most exquisite velvet upon mine, expressing an intensity of emotion that robs me of breath. I can feel his desire searing through me as his hands wander down my body, setting fire to every inch of my being. I arch into him as if my soul is calling for his.

He nips at my bottom lip before pulling away, a smirk adorning his face as he surveys me. "You're mine, Morte. You always have been," he growls, trailing his fingers down my spine. "Let me show you just how good we can be together."

I give him a coy smile before leaning up to whisper in his ear. "In time."

His eyes flash with something dangerous, and I can see my words have sparked something inside of him. But he doesn't push the issue, instead pulling me close once more for a fierce, possessive kiss. It's as if he's trying to stake his claim on me, and I can't help but reel from the intensity of it. Every touch electrifies me, and I find myself wanting more.

After a few seconds, he pulls away, his eyes dark with desire. "As you wish, love," he says with a chuckle. He falls onto his back, taking his heat with him. "I don't think it's safe for us to leave the room. Things aren't what they seem here, and I'd rather not risk you getting hurt."

"Don't you want to find out what's going on?" I sit up, tucking my legs under me and he mirrors me. The thought of staying cooped up in this room is too much temptation for me.

I have one mission, and until I free Wilder, I can't let anyone side-track me.

Aggonid's eyes flicker with annoyance. "In the grand scheme of things, none of it matters. After you meet with Finian, we'll find a way out of here."

"You're not worried about what he said? A month, Agg—"

"Pfft. I'm a *god*, Morte." He chuckles, and it reverberates throughout the room. When he speaks like this, the nursery rhymes children tell on playgrounds and in mirrors before bed at slumber parties hold a lot more weight. I've seen his cruelty, been a victim of it first-hand. "He can try to keep us here, but he won't succeed."

I bite my lip, tugging it between my teeth in a nervous gesture.

Aggonid takes my hand in his, his eyes flashing with a dangerous glint. "Let them try to hurt what's mine," he growls, his voice low and menacing. "Anyone who dares to harm you will face my wrath. I'm a god, and I will not hesitate to rain down fire and brimstone upon those who dare to cross us. No one will take you from me. I will protect you, and together we will watch as our enemies fall at our feet, consumed by the flames of our power." He pulls me close, his lips brushing against my ear. "Trust me, love. With me by your side, no one can touch you."

His words hold no evidence of lies, and I feel the full power of his conviction behind them. Whether or not he's lying to himself, though, is another question.

One I intend to find out the answer to. *After I free Wilder.*

I LEARN the servant with hobbled legs *is* a merfae, and her name is Oceana. The ache in my chest at Wilder's absence intensifies as I watch her take a few pieces of clothing out of a closet I hadn't noticed before.

Is he still in a cell by himself? Does he think of me?

Oceana had tried to enter the room earlier, but Aggonid blocked anyone from coming into it, so I had to wake him up to let her in.

It's late morning and we missed them knocking for breakfast.

"Sorry," I mumble as she sets the folded pile of clothing onto the bed.

"It's alright." Oceana grins, her eyes crinkling with warmth.

"My best friend is merfae," I whisper, and her mouth drops open. "In Bedlam."

"Really?" she asks, her voice hushed.

I nod, and she grins wider.

"Why does he hobble you like that?" I point to the binds around her ankles.

Her face shutters. "So I can't shift."

Bile rises in my throat as memories of Wilder in chains he can't undo flood my mind. I couldn't even fit enough pieces of fabric around his wrists without them cutting into his skin.

Wilder is strong, but he's not that strong.

Oceana's gaze slides away in the sudden silence, like she knows exactly what I'm thinking.

"It's okay," she says softly. "It's just how things are around here."

My guilt overwhelms me, and I can't say anything, so instead I just nod, and she sets about gathering jewelry from a pouch at her waist.

She hands me a simple metal bracelet with a pearl adorning the center. "King Valtorious asks that you wear this as his guest tonight." She winces.

"His guest?" I ask, glancing behind me to where Aggonid inspects the bookshelf. What is he looking for? I thought he'd gotten all the spy devices.

"There's a ball—"

"No." Aggonid booms, and the room shakes from the power of it, causing Oceana to cower.

I place my hand on her forearm to steady her as I glare behind me. She trembles under my touch.

"Stop scaring her," I hiss.

He blinks, glancing at Oceana. "Sorry." He turns his attention back to me. "Ollin is not your friend. He would sooner kidnap you and make you his concubine than he would treat you with a modicum of respect. We're staying in tonight, waiting for the meeting with King Finian tomorrow, then we're finding a way out of here."

His gaze is hard, but I can see a hint of vulnerability in his features. He's worried.

"I understand." I nod. "We'll stay in."

He turns away before I can get a read on his expression, but I can tell he's happy with my agreement.

"Thank you, Oceana." I smile at the merfae, and she hops up, curtsying.

"You're most welcome, milady," she says as she scurries away out the door.

Aggonid is already back at the bookcase, but I'm still standing there, the pearl bracelet in my hand.

If I can't convince Finn to bring me home to Bedlam, maybe I can hide out here and find a portal home. I'll miss Az, Emeric, and maybe even Caius, but I'm a prisoner before I'm a friend or lover.

And I don't like being caged, even if it comes with carefully constructed freedoms.

Lowering myself into a thick, cushioned chair by the hearth, I sit in front of the fire and tuck my legs under me. The heat warms my skin from the chill of the morning. "Are we really staying in here until Finn arrives?"

"Yes," Aggonid doesn't hesitate to answer.

I take the pearl bracelet and slip it over my wrist, rubbing it lightly as I ponder my next move.

"Did you bring the letter I wrote?"

"It's in my bag by the bed."

I glance back at him, and he gestures to the leather satchel leaning against the nightstand on his side.

I nod, not trusting myself to speak. I'm so close to potentially going home after all this time.

The afternoon comes and goes, and the drone of music and chatter drifts up from the lawn below my window. I can't help but wonder what I'm missing—the bright colors and joyous laughter of a celebration.

It's a sharp contrast to the quiet, still atmosphere of our chamber.

I unlock the window and slide it open, and music floods the room. I can hear people clapping and cheering for something or someone, but I can't quite make out the words.

Suddenly, a burst of flames shoots up into the air, illuminating the night sky in a dazzling display of fireworks. The spectacle draws me from my thoughts, and I find myself smiling as I watch the sparks dance and die out in the night.

The fireworks eventually fade away, replaced by a sudden cheer that sounds like it's coming right from below me. I lean out the window to get a better view of what's happening.

Dignitaries from all over Romarie mingle and exchange pleasantries. Women in elegant gowns adorned with jewels and intricate embroidery, men in tailored suits and crisp dress shirts, the air electric with the anticipation of a grand celebration. More arrive in exquisite carriages, drawn by elaborately dressed horses and driven by matching liveried coachmen.

Hundreds more buzz with excitement on the lawn and Ollin's right in the center, crowned in a regal robe of crimson and gold, speaking to a woman wearing feathers for a dress and her breasts spilling over the bodice.

Aromas of roast meat, baked cheese, garlic seafood, and other savory dishes drift from the giant buffet table. Wafts of floral perfumes mix with cologne from the guests. It's a feast for the eyes and the nose—I've never been to a ball before. They have plenty of them in Bedlam, but I've never felt much like celebrating when my best friend is stuck in prison.

Aggonid is but a breath away from me, until he notices Ollin's eye lingering on me. In a flurry, he grabs me around the waist and yanks us away from the window, crashing to the floor. His magic slams the glass shut, and he holds me in his arms, his heart beating ferociously against mine.

"Why are we hiding?" I chastise him in a whisper, my lips mere inches from his.

His deep gaze holds mine as he breathes, "Because if he catches those wistful glances you keep giving the party, he'll demand you to come downstairs. And I'm not sharing you tonight."

"You know." My chest heaves against him as I press closer. "If I had magic, he'd be much less of a threat."

Aggonid's smile is like sunlight, brightening up my world. "What will you give me for it?"

My heart races as I look up at him. "Seriously? You'd bargain for it?"

He raises a sultry eyebrow and murmurs against my skin. "Depends on what you're offering."

I whisper, "I can't give you what you want."

His lips curl into a seductive grin and he dips his head, brushing his nose against mine. His deep voice rumbles in my ear as he murmurs, "What makes you so sure?"

My breath catches in my throat as his lips press firmly against mine. Every part of my body ignites with pleasure, and just as he settles between my thighs, I place a hand on his chest.

I can't forget what this god did to me. No matter how tempting he is. And though my deal with Caius only pertains to losing my virginity in the Underworld, I can't forget my mission.

I can't get sidetracked by lust.

"No."

He settles back, regret lining his features as he twines his hand with mine. "You're right, I'm sorry."

Why is he acting so ... nice? Yeah, he said he wants a clean slate, but he's Aggonid.

Feared God of the underworld.

The fact that he had Irid kill her mate proves to me his cruelty towards me isn't unusual. He's not a good person, and I've got to guard my head and my heart.

"Let's just go to bed," I whisper. "The sooner we do, the sooner we can see Finn and find a way out of here."

THE RAIN HAMMERS my skin like a thousand tiny bullets, and the wind assaults me with such force I can barely keep my footing. Aggonid's face is whipped by my hair as we huddle in the thick evergreen forest near the portal to Bedlam. My dress clings to me like a second skin, soaking up the rain and stained with mud, but I don't care. This will be my first sighting of a familiar face in months, and it's all that matters.

Aggonid notices the goosebumps peppering my skin when I shiver, and he pulls me into his embrace as he uses his magic to create a barrier around us.

"Sorry, I wasn't thinking about the rain—"

"It's alright."

The night sky roils and churns as the ominous black portal pulses with menacing intensity. I eye it warily, desperate for any sign of movement within. After an eternity of waiting, a figure emerges, cloaked in a suit of dark armor that gleams in the starlight. I draw in a sharp breath as I recognize the features of the warrior; his straight white hair tied in a bun, and his presence radiating with the same formidable air as Aggonid's.

This is no ordinary king. He's high king of the fae, son of a goddess, and ruler of Bedlam.

"Finn!" I shout, racing towards him.

He startles when he sees me. "Morte?"

I crash into his arms, nearly knocking him off balance. I don't move as he places his hands on either side of my face and studies me in disbelief.

"It is you. I can't believe it," he breathes. "We've been looking everywhere for you!"

He snatches his sword from its scabbard and steps in front of me. "How did she end up in your clutches?"

"He's with me, it's okay." I place my hand gently on his shoulder, causing him to turn towards me.

"What?" He stares at me, confusion and horror etched into his features.

"I died, Finn." I say softly.

His grip slackens on the hilt of his sword as he takes in my words, but still he keeps his wary gaze trained on Aggonid, never turning away from his ancient adversary. A shield of courage and devotion protecting me from the god's wrath. His bright blue eyes radiate with an ethereal quality as he studies me. My words seem to register as he expels air from his lungs and brings his attention back to Aggonid. "What did you do to her?"

Aggonid smirks, putting on an air of arrogance. "Nothing she didn't want."

"Aggie!" I shout louder, emphasizing the nickname he detests.

He rolls his eyes. "She died and ended up in the underworld." He shrugs. "I have no control over where *your* fae are sent, Finian."

"I'm the one who asked for you to come here." I steady a hand on Finn's arm. "Aggonid is going to give us a few minutes to chat."

He regards Aggonid warily, and I raise a brow at the devil as if to say, *well?*

After he found listening devices in the castle, we don't want to risk our meeting being overheard by Ollin.

"Can you give us a few minutes of privacy, please?"

Aggonid grins. "That wasn't part of the agreement."

I grit my teeth. "Fine."

Aggonid

I OBSERVE FINN AND MORTE, careful to look for any sign they're on friendlier terms than she let on. Finn owed me a boon after he reclaimed the life of a vampire he calls Gideon. Thankfully, I only sense a platonic friendship from the two of them.

Finn places a silencing bubble around the three of us as I hand Morte the letter she wrote.

She passes it to Finn. "This is for inmate Wilder Nereus at Bedlam Penitentiary, can you make sure he gets it?"

He furrows his brow and takes it with a weary hand. "This won't get me into any trouble, will it?"

She shakes her head. "No, just a love letter."

"A love letter?" He tucks it into his pocket. "Do I even want to know?"

She grins. "Nope," emphasizing the 'p.'

My jaw clenches so hard, my teeth strain under the force of it.

"I'll make sure he gets it." He pats his pocket.

"Thank you," she whispers before she blurts, "Can you bring me back to Bedlam? I'm not supposed to be dead."

And there it is. I stiffen beside them, and she ignores this, too. Finn doesn't. Though it's what I need, it doesn't make me feel any less ill at the thought of her leaving me.

"Morte." the high king sighs. "I don't have that kind of magic, not when it's been so long. If I'd known within a few hours where you were, I might've been able to resurrect you, but not now."

She bites her lip. "You can't, but you know someone who can."

He sucks in a breath. "I haven't seen my mother in years, and it's not like I can just call her." He cups the back of his neck.

"I know." Morte toes a small stone with her foot. "You know I'd never ask you to make a promise you might not be able to keep. I'm just asking for you to try."

"You know I will."

"That's all I ask." She gives him a small smile. "Did they ever contain Noah Tackwater?"

Finn nods. "It took another two days after you disappeared. Your entire unit is on sabbatical right now, mourning your disappearance. My family and I had to go in and contain him."

Morte apologizes, her eyes filling with tears. Finn shakes his head, his voice soft and comforting, "Don't even think about it."

The portal rumbles like a thunderstorm, threatening to tear through the sky at any moment. "Time's up, Finian," I say, taking a step back uneasily.

He steps closer to the portal, his face bathed in its pulsing light. A look of determination flashes in his eyes as he wraps Morte in an embrace, whispering, "I'll do what I can." Then he turns away and leaps through the portal, vanishing just as it slams shut behind him.

"That should've lasted way longer than that, right?" Morte glances at me before we turn out attention back to where the portal was.

"Yeah," I grumble, unable to chase the unease settling in my chest. "We need to get out of here. C'mon."

I SEIZE Morte by the hand and focus my energy on the destination, teleporting us to our room in the castle. My heart is pounding, and my vision blurs as we swirl through a portal of light and land with a thud. I barely register the heat of Morte's hand against mine as we rush to change into dry clothes.

My attention weighs thick on her naked form as she pulls the dress over her head, exposing her pale skin. The air is still heavy, and I don't think she notices the way my gaze lingers on her curves instead of the conversation.

She glances up at me after she pulls on a pair of pants, her hands still on the button. Her breasts hang heavy against her chest, and her voice is husky when she finds my focus there.

"You go on without me." She grabs a shirt from the closet, and when she emerges, she slips it over her head. "I'm going to try and get home from here."

"No." I close the distance between us, stopping in front of her and placing my hands on each of her shoulders. "What part of me telling you that *King Ollin Valtorious is a monster* isn't computing for you?"

She yanks herself out of my hold, face screwed up in fury. "He hasn't bothered me once while I've been here!"

"That's what he wants you to think!" I roar before having the wisdom to place a sound barrier up. "He tortures, maims, and kills people, Morte!"

"So do you!" She shoves my chest, but I stand firm.

"Only people who deserve it!"

"And did I, Aggonid?" Hurt flashes across her face. "What did I do that was so heinous in the devil's eyes that he thought to extinguish the light from mine?" By the time she finishes, fat tears pour down her cheeks and her voice breaks. "Forever?"

Agony cleaves my chest. Telling her will only make it worse, but I can assuage her pain a little. "You didn't."

"And did your brother?" Anger flares in her eyes. "Huh? I know you to be cruel, Aggonid, but I never thought you'd make your mate's sister kill her own!"

"It was a punishment for them both!" I roar, picking up a glass vase and hurling it at the wall. It shatters, raining shards onto the floor.

"There is nothing that can justify making someone kill their mate." She wipes angry tears off her cheeks, her voice shaking with rage.

How wrong she is.

My shadows coil in anger, bathing the room in inky blackness.

The only color in the room are the glowing rubies of my eyes and the crimson locks of her hair. "Do not lecture me on justice, Morte," I hiss, my fangs elongating as I stalk closer to her.

But she doesn't back away. Instead, she faces me down with a fierce defiance, her eyes blazing with fury. "I've known a lot of monsters in my thousands of years of eradicating them from the realms, but none eviler than you," she hisses, her voice dripping with venom.

"Oh?" I smirk, delighted by her fervor.

"Yes!" She steps closer, her face inches from mine. Heat radiates from her body, and it sends a thrill coursing through my veins. "You take away what people love, destroy families, and rip out hope from their hearts like a cruel puppeteer," she seethes.

"And yet, here you are." I chuckle. I grab her wrists, holding them between us. "You let me. You let me do all these things and still you're here, in my arms."

She looks away, her breaths coming out harsh and ragged. A hint of vulnerability swims in her eyes as she trains them on the fire flickering in the hearth. No woman has the power to destroy me like her.

Love is like that, though. It has great capacity to burn. Fitting for a phoenix and the devil.

"You speak of my cruelty, yet it is your love that has captured me in its merciless embrace." I cup her cheek, and her eyes shutter against my palm as a tear tracks down her face. "You say I'm a puppeteer, but it's you who pulls at the strings of my heart with every tear. Don't cry."

My words, though true, taste like glass. If things could just be different, our love could burn brighter than the sun. Add Caius to this mix and we could be unstoppable.

If she weren't destined to destroy us all.

"You say that like it's a bad thing," she whispers, leaning into my touch. "You act like you're the only one who's been burned by love, or the idea of it."

"I am the devil," I remind her, but my voice is gentle.

"And I am a phoenix," she counters, her voice strong despite the tears. "Together, we can rise from the ashes, even if it's not in the way we expected."

Her words stir something in my chest, something dangerous and wild. Love may burn, but it can also ignite, lighting the way to something new and uncharted. I press my forehead to hers, willing her to feel the intensity of my love, the depth of my need for her.

Those thoughts turn to ashes when she speaks next.

"But I can never think to warm your bed or hold court with you because I'm cursed with the knowledge that one day, your cruelty will push me too far, and my flames will consume me, and I will be reborn into something I don't recognize. I'm not naive enough to know why I ended up here rather than beyond the veil, but I'm not Caius, and there's no way I could ever condone the brutal way you treat others."

Her words are like a cold bucket of water over my head, bringing me back to reality. I know what she says is true, but it doesn't make the ache in my chest any less painful.

"I know," I say, my voice low and heavy with regret. Who would want to be with the devil? Caius is my mate, so he has no choice but to love me. "Come back with me to the underworld, and I'll give you your magic back."

"What?"

"I want you to trust me. As soon as we get back, I'll release the bind on your magic."

A woosh of air escapes between her parted lips as she studies me. "Okay." She nods, and I release her wrists, pulling her into a tight embrace. In this moment, nothing else matters but her, her warmth, her scent, the sound of her heartbeat. I will hold onto this moment, this fragile connection between us, for as long as I can.

Before I have to ruin it all.

CHAPTER TWENTY-THREE

MORTE

*I*f the king is as cruel as Aggonid says he is, I'd be stupid to stay here without magic. Just because I can resurrect, doesn't mean he can't keep me in a cage, torturing me as soon as I come back to life.

So back to the underworld it is.

I'm filled with a strange sort of relief. I'm grateful for a chance to be free of the unknown situation in Romarie, where I'm so vulnerable and helpless—stuck between Aggonid's dick measuring contest with Ollin and my own survival. I never thought I'd hear Aggonid claim someone else is crueler.

"Strip the metal from that mantel." Aggonid inclines his head.

"And how exactly is this going to get us out of here?"

"Romarie's magic comes from the Luna goddess just like all the other fae realms, but they've learned how to amplify it using certain metals only found here. If we can get enough of it, we should be able to generate enough to get us back home."

I raise a brow his way at the use of the word 'home', but I don't comment on it. "And you can't just magic one into existence wherever you're at?"

It's his turn to level me with a look. "And that's the million-dollar question, isn't it? I should be able to do it from anywhere. But while you were bathing, I practiced for an hour, and nothing happens. Something, or someone, is blocking it."

I pry at the sanguimetal with a chisel I fashioned from the fireplace poker. The metal is tough and has a strange electric tingle, like when you plug in a computer or phone with an outlet that has a short in it.

"It could be the power of the king," Aggonid muses as he watches me work, while his shadows strip the room of its metal furnishings. "I've heard stories about him—that he can draw energy from others and use it to fuel his own magic. Maybe he's exerting enough energy to block my own."

"You're a god," I argue. "Aren't you supposed to be all-seeing, all-knowing, and all-powerful?"

He doesn't take offense, only grinning as though I'd told him he has the largest cock out of all his friends. "I am. Just not when I haven't activated my soul b—" He stops abruptly, his face turning to stone and snapping his mouth shut.

"Your what?" I yank the metal free and toss it on the small pile we've collected on the rug.

"Nothing," he says, quickly changing the subject. "Let's get started."

I watch as Aggonid fashions a small set of silver tools from the scraps of sanguimetal. We work together, chipping away at the metal and melting it down to form a disc. It's a slow and tedious process, but we need enough of the metal to amplify the portal and get back home.

Once we have enough, we tightly cram the metal disc into a tiny pouch and race through the hallway, invisibility cloak intact, and our heartbeats drowning out the sound of our soft footsteps echoing off the cold stone floor.

We narrowly escape detection from the guards patrolling the castle as we dart between pools of darkness, where the shadows help hide the faint glimmer these cloaks give the air to the trained eye.

I stumble forward, my ankle twisting painfully beneath me, alerting anyone within eyesight to our presence. Aggonid curses and frantically flings his hands in a desperate attempt to reestablish his magical veil, but he's too late. For a split second, our location is exposed in a brilliant flash of limbs before his magic cloaks us once more.

"I can help you," a tiny voice whispers, hobbling along with us, and I tug on Aggonid's arm to stop him.

Aggonid scowls at me as I grab hold of Oceana, bringing her under our cloak. "We don't need help," he hisses.

"Please," she begs. "I can't run away, but I can help you. I know a secret way out of the castle, and where they keep the amplifiers for the Luna magic. You'll need them to activate the portal."

Aggonid glances at me, and I nod, urging him to understand that I trust this merfae. Maybe even feel a certain kinship with her. Her temperament is so much like Wilder's mother.

We don't have time to waste, and if Oceana knows something that could help us, we'll take it.

"Lead the way," Aggonid grumbles.

Oceana gives a small nod and starts hobbling down a hidden passage. The musty smell of damp stone wafts up from the dark, winding corridor, and the silence around us is deafening. It's as if the castle is holding its breath, waiting for us to make a misstep. I clutch the pouch tightly to my chest, sweat beading on my forehead as we follow the merfae deeper into the labyrinth of hallways.

As we round a corner, a sudden burst of light fills the corridor ahead, and we freeze in fear. Aggonid grips my arm, ready to protect me, but it's only a guard, patrolling the area. He passes us without a second glance, his expression hidden behind a silver mask.

We continue, heartbeats pounding in our ears, until we finally reach the courtyard. The portal looms in the center, a massive, swirling vortex of light and energy. It's mesmerizing, and I have to shake my head to clear it.

Where are the amplifiers she's talking about? I scan the area, but it's mostly empty except for a few statues and benches. There must be something here that—

And then I see it. A tall, black obelisk, its surface covered in carvings and symbols.

Oceana hobbles over to it, revealing a hidden lever at its base.

"This is it," she says. "The amplifiers are inside, but they're bright, and will alert everyone in the castle as soon as I pull this."

We can't risk being caught, but the amplifiers are essential. Our gazes meet in a silent understanding. Aggonid will fend off the guards while Oceana and I sneak away with the amplifiers.

A streak of flame crashes into the massive statue of King Valtorious, sending chunks of marble everywhere and echoing shouts of alarm in its wake. Aggonid strides into the chaos, his face an expression of pure confidence. He raises his arm, and a blade of shadows materializes in his hand, ready for battle.

Oceana and I dart around the edge of the fight, and I pull on the hidden lever. An obelisk at our feet thrums to life, radiating a brilliant blue light.

"Stop them!" A guard's cry rips through the air as all eyes turn to us.

Without hesitation, Oceana slides open a secret panel beneath the obelisk's base. Inside are six mysterious triangular pieces of sanguimetal inscribed with powerful symbols and runes.

"Quick!" She shoves the pieces into my hands and hustles me away. We hurry as fast as our magic-less legs can take us, and Oceana stumbles several times when the ropes around her ankles trip her up. I barely make out the sounds of Aggonid fighting off the guards over the wild thrashing of my heartbeat in my eardrums.

As we reach the portal, a guard barrels into me, sending me crashing to the ground, scattering the amplifiers. He shouts in agony, and I flip over to my back to scramble away, a huge grin on my face as I touch the protection amulet at my neck.

Their own metal used against them.

I've got no weapons and no magic, and neither does Oceana, but I still put myself in front of her as guards converge on us. I swoop down to grab two amplifiers, handing one off to Oceana, and we use them to swing at the men surrounding us.

A blinding flash of light erupts from the courtyard, piercing through the darkness and searing our eyes. King Valtorious strides forward, the divine sword of molten gold glimmering in his hand as his face contorts with unbridled rage. "Stop!" he roars, unleashing a deafening echo that silences all in attendance.

Every eye turns away from the king and towards the devil himself. Aggonid stands victorious atop a mound of fallen guards, his arms spread wide, a grin plastering his face. His body is slick with sweat and the blood of his enemies, and his eyes burn with ruby red intensity.

He laughs, gesturing to the hushed chaos around us. "I am a God." He smirks. "I stop when I wish and not a second sooner."

With a single gesture, he throws an impenetrable darkness across the courtyard that claws through the air and wraps itself around a guard standing behind me, squeezing the life out of him in a flurry of screams and prayer. Before I can even process what's happening, the guard falls limp to the ground, leaving me breathless in the wake of his terrifying power.

Like a sea serpent traveling through waves, he sends another straight for King Valtorious, who shouts and jumps out of the way just in time. The king lands in a roll and stares up at Aggonid with a defiant gaze.

"You cannot WIN!" Valtorious roars.

Aggonid only smiles, standing tall before the full assembly of the Romarie guard and declares, "I am Legion." He strikes another guard dead with a shadow puppet. "I am source." Another one drops at the king's feet. "I am legend." Another. "I am the monster under your beds." A row of thirty guards grab for their throats, their eyes bulging. "I am the father of hell, and the keeper of souls!" His hands fly out, sending a hundred shadows to find their targets, only the thump of bodies and the shrieks of the survivors fleeing can be heard in the garden.

He stalks towards where King Valtorious trembles on the stone path. "And I will enjoy torturing anyone who defies me for the rest of eternity." He reaches down, grabbing Ollin by the neck and dragging him to his feet. "Especially you."

The king screams and begs for mercy, a wet spot blooming at the crotch of his pants before traveling down his leg, but Aggonid only smiles. He drops him to the ground with a thud, but doesn't kill him, and turns to me, eyes locking with mine.

"I think I'll keep him alive, so he can spend the rest of his miserable life looking for me in the shadows, knowing that I can come at any time to take his soul. What do you think, Morte?"

I stare at Aggonid, struggling to understand the expression on his face. The mask of cruelty has been torn away and replaced with a look of sorrow and exhaustion.

While the king lies trembling at Aggonid's feet, I can't help but wonder if this was all for show—to prove to the people of Romarie no one messes with the devil without facing his wrath.

"Why are you keeping him alive?" I ask, still clutching a sanguimetal amplifier tightly in my hand.

Aggonid's gaze flickers over to me, then back to the prone form of King Valtorious. "Let's just say he's more useful to me alive than dead," he says, his voice tinged with amusement.

I nod slowly, still unsure of what's happening. Oceana tugs at my sleeve, her expression wary. Her teal hair has come loose from the long braid that hangs to her waist, and it gives a wild edge to her beauty. "You should go," she says.

I turn to face her fully and shake my head. "You can't stay here, Oceana." Panic rises in my chest. "He'll kill you for helping us!" This merfae might not know my best friend, but every merfae I know are kind and loyal.

She gestures to the binds around her ankles. "These prevent me from leaving." She shoves the amplifier into my hand. "Go!"

I whip around towards Aggonid. "You can remove these, can't you?"

He crouches low, examining the binds. "Yeah, this is weak enough." He snaps his fingers, and the binds dissolve into nothing.

Oceana scrambles up and takes off running, not looking back as she flees from the grounds.

I watch her go before turning to face the devil again. "Will she be safe here? In Romarie?"

"As long as she gets to the sea in time, she'll be fine." Aggonid sounds certain, and the worry in me eases.

Gratitude chokes me, tears pricking at my eyes as I study Aggonid's softened features. He's so different like this. Less 'I'm going to use my shadow puppets to destroy the entire realm' and more 'I'll use my shadow puppets to destroy your enemies if only you promise to be mine.'

The devil nods before standing up, his eyes serious once more as he gestures to the portal. "Let's go," he says, urgency lacing his words. "We need to hurry. I'm under no illusion Ollin was keeping us here to stall for something."

I follow him towards the portal, my mind racing with questions and confusion. Aggonid's behavior towards me has been erratic, and I still don't know why he's keeping the king alive. But I don't have time to ponder on these thoughts as we approach the swirling vortex of light and energy.

Aggonid steps forward, his hands raised as he begins to chant in a language I've never heard before. The air around us shimmers and warps, and the portal grows wider as if responding to his incantations.

"Come on," he says, motioning for me to follow. "We have to go now."

I take a deep breath and step through the portal, feeling a rush of energy coursing through my body. The world around me shifts and morphs into a dark, twisted hallway different than the one we entered from. It's now a landscape of jagged rocks and fiery pits. The air is thick with the scent of sulfur and brimstone, and the distant howls of demonic creatures echo through the abyss.

Aggonid lands beside me, his eyes scanning the surroundings. I study him, wondering what he plans to do now that we're here. He takes off towards the end of the tunnel, and I have no choice but to follow him.

"What is this place?" I trail my fingers along the damp walls, avoiding the glowing fungi.

"This is the back entrance beneath Hellwing," he murmurs, his steps hesitant.

"Why did it take us here?"

"It shouldn't have. There's no portal beneath the castle, or at least there never used to be."

A loud crash echoes through the dark and damp tunnel, causing Aggonid to freeze. The sound seems to come from deep within the bowels of the earth, and it sends a chill down my spine. The devil's hand moves instinctively to his sword of shadows, and I take a defensive stance, my eyes scanning the tunnel for any sign of movement.

As we wait, I become aware of the musty smell of the underworld, mixed with the scent of damp stone and mold. The air is heavy, making it difficult to breathe. There's a faint humming sound in the distance, almost like a low, steady vibration, that seems to be coming from the walls themselves.

Suddenly, Caius appears at the end of the hallway, battle-ready with armor and a battle axe held in one hand. His surprise at seeing Aggonid quickly gives way to relief, and he rushes over to embrace his mate, the weapon clattering to the ground. As they exchange murmurs of love and worry, I take a moment to study the tunnels around us.

The walls are made of rough-hewn stone, and there are occasional torches mounted on brackets, casting flickering shadows on the uneven surfaces. I catch a glimpse of something moving in the darkness, and I realize with a jolt that we are close to the dungeons.

Caius interrupts my thoughts with a sharp exclamation. "You guys were gone for twenty-six days!"

Aggonid's eyes widen in shock, and he releases Caius to stare at me. "It felt like two nights," he whispers.

I glance between the two of them. "We slept twice, right? Or was it three times? How is this possible?"

Caius's brow furrows in confusion. "What do you mean?"

Aggonid sighs heavily and begins to explain what happened in Romarie as we make our way towards the main part of the castle. As we walk, I can hear the distant sounds of running water and the echoes of footsteps in the empty tunnels.

As we approach the end of the corridor, Caius throws an arm around my waist. "You doing okay?" he whispers to me.

I nod, grateful for his concern. "As good as I can be, I guess."

Aggonid loops his arm around both of us, and a second later, we're back in their bedroom.

I glance around, feeling shy at the memory of this place. Spinning around, I face Aggonid. "You promised you'd give me my magic back if I came back with you."

"You weren't planning on coming back?" Hurt flashes across Caius' face. "I thought you liked it here."

I cross to the bathroom, calling behind me. "Yeah, I love over-bearing demons who try to trick me into their beds and not being able to use my magic."

When I emerge from a quick bath, I find the two of them talking in hushed whispers near the window. If I had my magic, I could hear them fine from the other room.

"Well?" I stand with my hands on my hips, my damp hair dripping onto their floor. "Pay up, Ag."

A grin crosses Caius' face at the nickname before turning his attention back to his mate. "Aww, our little bird gave you a pet name. I love it."

"Our? I'm not 'our' anything."

Aggonid looks between us and gives a small sigh. "Don't you even start," he grumbles as he stalks towards me.

His lips crash to mine in a heat of passion, awakening a warmth that spreads to every inch of my being, restoring my power and igniting a spark within my soul. He pulls slowly away from me, a satisfied smirk tugging at the corner of his mouth.

"What the hell was that for?" I sway back, stunned by the intensity of the kiss as I hold tight to the towel wrapped around me.

"You wanted your magic back, didn't you?" His voice is seductive, as though he were speaking of tangled limbs and crumpled sheets as he stares at me.

It's an intense experience staring into the deep pools of ruby that make up his eyes, like endless oceans of emotion and power.

I nod ever so slightly, still trying to process the whiplash he gives me. "Yes, of course I did, but ..."

"Then I kissed you because I wanted to." He breathes out, his gaze smoldering with desire.

Caius chuckles, "So is this a thing between you two now?"

"No!" I take a step back.

"It should be." He circles me, as though studying how to crack me open and spill all my secrets. "Just imagine the fun we can have, little bird."

"I'm going to bed," I declare. My voice is weary as I utter the words and my heavy sigh echoes in the stillness of the room.

While magic helps fuel my energy, getting all of it back in seconds has me drained. My steps are leaden as I walk towards the bed, creaking floorboards groaning beneath me.

There's a weariness in my bones, a heaviness that I can't shake. The kind that comes before a storm.

CHAPTER TWENTY-FOUR

AGGONID

The Underworld

The moment I was handed the parchment that sealed my fate thousands of years ago, before I took the throne, I began my research on phoenixes. Tethers, as I understand it, are sentimental, fickle things. Give it the slightest bit of attention, and the little beasty latches on, desperate for love and attention.

Remove the tether, and you can kill the phoenix. Some might describe a tether as the will to live, but I believe it runs deeper than that.

I thought by seducing Morte, I could get her to trigger the fae promise she'd made with Caius about her virginity, thereby eliminating my problem. What I hadn't considered was how, in doing so, her phoenix was tethering itself to me.

I feel it there, a waif of a thing, steadying my hand, softening my tone as I interact with her. It blooms in my chest, pawing at the beast inside me, getting me to let my guard down.

When she's near, a tranquil hum of energy fills the room, like a lullaby that soothes my soul. A calm melody that brings peace to my heart and makes me feel safe and secure. It's a gentle whisper, a subtle reminder of something that I can't quite place. The words it speaks are lost in the air, but the feeling it evokes is clear—warmth and comfort.

Weakening me.

I realize my mistake now, as I watch her soar through the clouds above Hellwing. She slept for several days after we returned, and now her magic is at full-force, and she's expending some of the energy.

She's a dazzling sight as she soars, her wings spanning wide, her body glimmering in the sun. Her skin is luminous, and her eyes have that sheen that tells me her beast is in control right now. She dives and twists, a feathered beauty, a graceful acrobat, turning and looping in the air like a dancer in flight.

Though it pains me to do so, I've got to get her to hate me, sever this tether, then send Caius away to another realm for a few days while I kill her.

No doubt he's a tether, too. And maybe I'll need to send Azazel and Emeric away.

I've got Caius across the forest torturing all the new arrivals I killed in the courtyard in Romarie. He's head over heels for Morte, so I'll have to make it look like an accident.

Sending a shadow into the sky, it curls around Morte, engulfing her in an inescapable net. She struggles within the misty prison, but the more she fights, the tighter it gets. Her shrieks are lost in the air as the wind rushes past her, carrying with it a whistling sound as I drag her back to the ground. She's not hurt, so the protection necklace she wears does nothing.

She hurls magic at me with reckless abandon, each spell she casts hurling a blistering fireball or freezing spike in my direction. I dodge and weave, narrowly evading every deadly projectile. When her feet touch the ground, I'm ready and primed with a power that pulses through my veins. I stare her down, unblinking, as the rage in my soul boils over.

Roaring with a fury barely contained, I demand, "Morte! You may have won the hunt, but you belong to me! Kneel before me and accept your fate."

She responds with a haughty laugh. "No," she replies, her voice low and steady, though hurt flashes across her face. "I won't bow. I'll never bow to you."

Her beauty is an affront to my eye, a glowing reminder of my own weakness. I spin around, dragging her along by her arm, shadows snaking around us like a serpent. Fury and bitter hatred burning inside me, I roar for Irid like a battle cry, pushing through the garden doors in a feral rage.

"Yes, my Lord?" Irid bows before me, her voice echoing against the walls.

"Take this one to muck the dungeons, and when she's done there, chain her to the wall. She's gotten too comfortable and needs to realize her place."

"Yes, my Lord." Irid bows again.

Morte's eyes flare with rage, her fists clenched tight as if she ready to strike. But Irid's grasp on her arm is unyielding and her screams and curses are met only with a stern expression.

Her resistance ebbs away at last and she's led away, her protests now muted.

I stand there, my jaw clenched and my heart thundering in my chest, a poisonous thing that leaches into every cell in my body, begging me to bring her back and make things right. This is necessary. If I had to build a prison against my own soul and feed it to the death-wings, I'd do it just the same.

Morte

TERROR GRIPS my throat as I sit chained in this dank dungeon. The oppressive heat is cloying, though not as bad as it was when I first arrived, thanks to Caius' magic, and cold droplets of water from the cavern ceiling fall onto me, only adding to my distress. The metal encasing my wrists and ankles does little to abate the fear that has taken ahold of me as I realize why Aggonid needs King Valtorious alive: to provide all these cursed magic suppressant items—chains, bracelets, and necklaces designed to smother the power of others.

The devil torments me with his cruel mind games, luring me in with a false sense of security before taking it away as soon as I succumb to his persuasive trap. My heart is drawn to him like a fae fly to a flame and it singes my soul each time he tramples on my emotions and leaves me feeling broken.

I deserve every ounce of it.

I slump against the wall, my mind reeling and my heart splitting in two. Monsters end up in hell.

And I'm the worst of them all.

~

Nearly 200 Years Ago

I SPRINT to the coastal dunes north of Convectus castle, my heart racing with anticipation. I can feel the heat of the sun burning on my skin as I sink into the white, powder-soft sand and roll onto my back. The crashing waves reverberate in my ears like an orchestra of distant drums.

With my eyes closed, I tilt my head skyward and relish in the warmth radiating from above. A satisfied smile creeps across my face. I'm early, just like I planned. Wilder should be here after he finishes helping his parents.

Scorching sun rays beat down on me as I lay half-asleep, and in the blink of an eye dark shadows eclipse the warmth, covering my shivering body. My eyes fly open, and a sinister chill runs through me.

Amidst the jovial voices surrounding me, I jump to my feet, reaching for the dagger concealed beneath my sleeve. The men standing in front of me chuckle at my panicked state, bearing their pearly white teeth.

I'm ready to unsheathe my hidden blade and fight, but then one of them speaks up and holds his hands outstretched in a placating move.

"Hey now," he begins softly, "you're okay." He turns to his friends with a glint in his eye. "Mind if we join you?"

Sheltered under Castanea most of my life, I don't know most of the fae orders that make up Bedlam. I can't make out what these men are, but one thing is for certain—they're using a glamor to disguise their true faces. I can see it in the way the light shimmers over their skin. I'm sure most people can't tell, but I've perfected glamours to keep the people of Castanea safe for thousands of years. I know it when I see one, just as I know the face in my own mirror.

Eight men with wildly varying appearances stand before me— from the darkest ebony hair to the lightest flaxen locks, they are all exquisite. Clothed in muted hues that somehow manage to remain trendsetting, they seem formidable yet inviting. A sweet and musky scent fills my senses as the waves crash rhythmically behind them. Their low conversations interspersed with occasional laughter makes me wonder—what secrets do these mysterious men hold? Are they uglier than they let on? Some of the less attractive Tolden glamor themselves to appear more attractive when makeup can't achieve it.

"Okay," I hedge, glancing around the barren beach for anyone else. We're alone.

The sun-warmed sand shifts beneath my feet as they come closer, the coarse texture scratching my bare toes as they plop down next to my picnic spot. The blond, ruddy-skinned one with a high voice pulls out a flask and thrusts it in my face. I take it slowly, my nose inhaling its contents. A wave of sweet elixir floods my nostrils—the faintest hint of Fae wine, a drink so rare that we have to risk our lives by crossing the Wastelands and entering Convectus for it—though not as rare as absinthe. I take a swig, reveling in the liquid gold that spreads across my mouth like wildfire. The taste is both familiar and foreign, sending shockwaves through my veins as if lit ablaze.

My stomach churns as I feel the brunette's gaze on me. My throat is dry, my heart hammering against my chest.

"Your accent is different," he says, plucking the flask from my grasp and slipping it into his pocket. "Where are you from?"

I struggle to keep a smile on my face as I rack my brain for the rehearsed answer I'd practiced with Wilder. "Oh, I grew up in Sundahlia amongst the humans." The lie sticks like glue on my tongue. "Where are you from?" I hear myself ask before the silence could become too awkward.

The men regard each other with a fierce intensity, their breath quickening as the energy in the air shifts. Their faces morph into a mask of dark menace, and I can almost feel their bloodlust radiating from them in waves.

The red-haired one speaks, his voice ripe with anticipation. "We come from all corners of Bedlam."

"We've seen you around." The blond one steals a piece of cheese from my picnic, grinning.

"Oh?" I squeak. Alarms go off inside me, but I can't put my finger on it. I should get out of here.

I leap to my feet, sand spraying in all directions. My heart pounds as I take a step back, only for someone to wrap their arms around me from behind. I scream and spin around to face him. His inky-black hair nearly glows blue in the sunlight, and the chains draped across his hands sparkle like stars against a night sky.

"Tolden," he snarls at me. "We've been hunting you for months."

My stomach churns with terror, and my chest feels like it's being split in two.

They know about Castanea.

Fury and panic swell within me and I shriek as more hands grab me from behind. "What do you want?" I demand.

I'm outmatched, and I'd rather die than let these men bring me back to Castanea.

"You're going to take us to your little Tolden hideaway," the brunette hisses as he and his friend manhandle me. Chains clink menacingly in their hands.

"Please, why are you doing this?!" I cry, my futile struggles only serving to make them grip on tighter.

"The black market for Tolden hearts has made its name rather well-known," he snarls with cold brutality. "And you're going to be our ticket, girl."

My heart pounds against my ribcage like a wild beast desperate to escape as they drag me away from the beach, towards a fate that's more horrid than death itself. I can't let them find Castanea, my home, my people.

With a wild surge of energy, I wheel around, sending a sharp elbow into the brunette's stomach and a well-placed kick to the blond one's shin. The two crash to the ground with a howl of agony, while their comrades swarm around me like a plague of locusts.

I summon my inner phoenix, feeling its fire blaze through my veins and it carries me up into the air with wings of flame. But before I can make my escape, an iron chain snatches at my feathers, yanking me back down to the scorching sand below.

Rage builds inside me until I'm filled with a seething fury; flames lick out of my mouth in an inferno that boils the sand beneath my feet and sends the attackers scrambling for cover in panic. With time precious, I use my power to fling balls of pure fire at them, driving them further away as I plan my next move.

These people have been following me for months. If they find their way into Castanea, all my people are at risk—we've been hidden away for millennia, away from the werewolves who can use our hearts for their cure.

My heart lurches in my chest as I realize what must be done. Innocents depend on me, and I can't let them down no matter the cost. Without another thought, I descend towards the sand and shift into my fae form. Fury courses through my veins and I grit my teeth with determination.

I march towards my enemies, hands outstretched in a white-hot ball of flame. They cower before me in fear and plead for their lives, but I refuse to relent in my onslaught until they are all nothing more than smoldering ash.

This is the price I must pay to keep those I love safe, and by the stars above, I will pay it.

After scanning their remains, my stomach drops as I count them. One, two, three ... seven. *There are only seven here.*

I whirl around, panicked as I look for the eighth member. I find him crawling on his stomach through tall grass, his lower half completely severed from the rest of himself. Charging towards him, I sweep my hand down to grab him by the back of his torn shirt and haul him upright, so he dangles from my grip.

A strangled cry escapes me at the face I see below the glamor, his magic no longer able to keep the façade as his life drains from him. Tears pour from my cheeks as I shriek, "Why?!" They blur my vision and cause me to stagger until I crash to my knees, but there's no mistaking the tiny features of the boy I now cradle in my hands.

This is no man.

He is a child.

"Why?!" I wail again, trying desperately to heal him. "I thought you were men!" My screeches are animal-like as they tear from my throat.

"We … were starving," he chokes out, agony marring his little face. "Orphans. I'm sorry," he breathes, his small chest heaving one more time as I clutch his tiny, battered hand in mine. His eyes, hazy, glossy, and so desperately sad as a sole dark tear glitters like jewels down his pale cheek.

Releasing my wings, I rip feathers from my body, trembling hands pressing the bloodied plumage to this little boy's skin, begging the gods not to take him, for a frantic, last-ditch miracle. To let him live, like they let me live so many times.

But fae feathers cannot save children from the grips of death, only delay its march.

I gasp for air desperately, feeling as if I am drowning in an unbearably heavy tide of such an unforgivable act.

Monster.

Wilder finds me on my knees amidst the carnage, his eyes burning with a fierce intensity as the smile slips from his face. He pulls water from the sea to shroud us in a blanket of rain, hidden from view of a group of people rushing down the beach.

He tightly clutches me in a powerful embrace, the musky scent of mint and ocean wafting through the air. His intense gaze pierces into my soul as I tell him every harrowing detail, causing icy dread to crawl down my spine. My throat dries up in terror as my actions replay in my mind.

"Children," I sob. "I killed children."

He cradles my face in his hands, and I feel all the love and determination pour out of him as he speaks. "You didn't know."

"They'll investigate, and they'll find out about the Tolden. What am I going to do?" Raw agony bleeds through my voice.

"I won't let that happen, Morte."

"I can't let them find Castanea," I wail.

As the warmth seeps into my skin, I'm enveloped in a deep calm. Wilder's eyes brim with tears as he unleashes his magic on me. "Listen to me carefully," he whispers. "I will take the blame for what happened here today."

"No!" I scream, frantically grabbing onto his shirt, trying to anchor myself to reality.

But his spell is too strong, immobilizing me completely. He continues in an eerily detached voice, "When they ask you about what happened, you will tell them you watched me kill these people. You were an innocent bystander. If they ask for my motive, you will tell them these children were trying to kill you for your feathers."

Horrified, I feel Wilder's magic coat my tongue and infiltrate my soul until all I can do is cry fat tears of despair.

"I love you, Morte," Wilder murmurs softly, his eyes darkening with pain as he brings his spell to an end, as if his words aren't poison that will destroy everything we've ever built together.

Shouts echo around me as the curtain of secrecy Wilder had woven to protect us is torn asunder. The authorities appear with lightning speed and snatch Wilder away, while I can do nothing but stand there in terror, my mouth agape and my screams heard by no one.

CHAPTER TWENTY-FIVE

AGGONID

*T*he late evening sun casts an eerie light against the walls of the library, painting it an ethereal blue, the air heavy with a thick, oppressive atmosphere.

The quiet is pierced by the sound of Morte and Irid entering the library. Their footsteps are heavy and labored, as if they're carrying a great weight on their shoulders, and faint scraping of metal links from the chains binding Morte's wrists and ankles.

I pause my hand on the bookshelf I'm perusing to face them. My little phoenix is filthy, her once-crimson tresses now a drab brown with dirt, and her dress is torn and tattered. Her once vibrant aura diminished, replaced with a thick wave of misery. Tear tracks streak her cheeks, yet she no longer holds any of the grief in her eyes. Instead, fury pools in those depths.

A whiff of dampness hangs in the air, mingled with the combination of sweat and soil from Morte's dirt-caked body. Beneath that, a faint trace of smoke from outside, carried in on the evening wind.

A fire of longing sears through my veins, urging me to go to her and embrace her, whispering promises of safety and security. Yet I remain still, knowing if I give into my desires, I will bring destruction upon us all. My heart screams in anguish, as though it could pierce the hollow silence that falters between us.

"My Lord." Irid bows. "If she doesn't eat, I'll have to drag her upstairs, and her necklace won't like that."

Exhaustion mars Morte's features, and her once supple lips are now cracked and bleeding. But there's a flare of anger beneath the hurt expression on her face, and that's what I use to fuel my ire.

"Go hose her off before she gets an infection and get her a slice of bread and a cup of water," I order.

"Yes, my Lord." Irid bows her head in resignation and ushers Morte away. I'm left standing in the silence, the weight of my emotions almost too heavy to bare. My vision blurs as tears threaten to spill over, but I remain standing until they're long gone. When the echoes of their voices have faded away I finally collapse to the ground, sobs shaking my body as I confront the truth of what I must do. I know Morte needs to hate me, but it doesn't ease the ache in my heart.

My knuckles turn white as I clench my jaw, desperately trying to hold back my sobs. My tears form a river of salty despair that burn deep trails down my cheeks, no matter how tightly I press my palms against my face. I feel like my heart is slowly being torn in two and the pain is almost too much to bear, but I eventually gather the last of my strength and make myself stand tall.

Morte's eyes are dull and distant when she saunters back into the library, her lips sealed together with a determination that could cut concrete. Even after Irid leaves, Morte still refuses to say a single word to me, her silence echoing in the vastness of the room like a screaming thunderclap.

"I made the mistake of promising that you can sleep in our bed while you're here for the next few days, one I regret immensely, but—"

"Then I'll go back to my hut in the woods," she spits, holding up the chain around her ankle. "Let me out of this and I'll leave now."

The air around us sizzles with tension as I snap, "So quick to give up on me already? Good riddance." My magic swirls around me as I let out an icy laugh and I hurl a shadow at her that sends her chains flying off her body. Before she can make for the door, I thrust my arms forward and use my power to slam the door shut with a reverberating thud that shakes the walls of the room. Morte stands there, trapped, fear and panic in her eyes.

"Not so fast." I stalk towards her. "Tomorrow is the Wild Pursuit. Keep your doors locked." Just because I can't have her, doesn't mean I want anyone else to have her, either. Least of all any of my fucking demons.

"Nah, I think I'll let your mate take my virginity, actually."

Her words leave me so stunned, I don't stop her when she rips the door open and sprints out into the night.

I stand in the doorway, my fists clenched at my sides and tears shining in my eyes as I let the door slam shut behind her.

Morte

I STUMBLE INTO MY SMALL, dark abode a few hours before midnight, my heart heavy with grief and my mind racing with worry. Aggonid's treatment of me has been nothing short of a nightmare. The god who was once so good to me in Romarie now acts as though I am nothing but a burden, a nuisance he can barely tolerate.

He had me mucking stalls like a common servant, and then chained me like a prisoner. The memory of his disdainful gaze and cruel words still haunts me, sending dread down my spine. How could he treat me this way, after everything we've been through together?

I know I can't stay here much longer. I'd rather take my chances in Romarie, where at least King Valtorious didn't hurt me. But even that is a daunting prospect, given the current state of affairs in the kingdom. I'd need to convince him to release good people like Oceana from his captivity.

My thoughts swirl in a dizzying blur as I lock the door behind me, cutting myself off from the outside world. If Finn can't come through for me, I don't know what I'm going to do. But one thing is clear: I can't stay here under Aggonid's thumb any longer.

from my throat, unbidden, and a surge of energy takes over my body as my beast takes control.

The call of freedom and lust sings through my veins, and the scent of my desire trails behind me as I rush down the hallway and slam the bedroom door shut. I dive onto the bed, heart pounding and breathing harsh, knowing that only one thing can ease the burning ache inside of me.

Them.

The heavy wooden door explodes from its hinges and crashes to the ground with a deafening boom. Three handsome fae stand in the doorway and I feel their power reverberate through me, igniting a primal pulse of desire deep in my core.

Az leads, and Emeric and Caius move around him like graceful predators. I can hardly contain my beast as it preens beneath their unwavering gazes, begging them to take whatever they wish of me. I lie back on the bed, panting and practically trembling with need. My body aches and begs to be taken, but I won't give in completely.

I shudder as I recognize the inevitability of what I've been running towards, and away from, all this time.

Az snatches me from the bed, and his lips descend on mine with an insatiable hunger that seems to consume my very soul. His hands roam across my body, setting it aflame with an unquenchable passion, as if he's a man possessed. As though I am both his poison and his antidote.

I can't help but respond to his touch, stretching out beneath him. The sensations he stirs in me are like nothing I've ever experienced before, a heady mix of desire and fear that leaves me dizzy with need. As he kisses me, I feel my resistance crumbling, my defenses giving way to the raw power of our connection. My beast is at the helm, but I am a willing passenger.

He wrenches my clothes from my body with a force that leaves me gasping, ripping the fabric like it's his own enemy. My eyes never leaving the contours of his body as he does the same to his, I can feel the steam radiating from his heated skin as every inch of his toned, tattooed body is exposed to me. His muscles quiver with raw want as he moves closer to me.

A scalding fire engulfs my soul, and I'm overcome with a craving for him to consume me and claim me as his own. His voice is like an earthquake, shaking me with its depth and power, as he growls out, "Mine."

The feral beast within me is unleashed with a devilish smirk on my face as I challenge him, "Prove it."

He enters me slowly, filling me inch by inch, and though the pain is brief it's intense enough for me to let out a strangled gasp. He pauses for a moment, allowing my body to adjust before pushing himself further in. His gaze never leaves mine and his body vibrates from the effort he's making not to let his beast take over completely.

But then something changes in his expression, and I can feel it radiating from his body; something primal and feral takes over him and he thrusts himself into me powerfully, as if staking his claim beyond all doubt. His eyes take on a wild intensity, more monster than man.

A delicious sear of pain and pleasure floods every inch of my being, setting off sparks throughout my body with each thrust of his hips into mine. My breath comes in tight gasps as the intensity builds higher and higher.

Caius and Emeric crowd around us, adding their own touches, sweat slicking our skin. Their hands and mouths explore me, and a primal scream escapes my throat as my body shakes, the climax sweeping through me as Azazel's fangs pierce my neck.

The act draws pleasure from a deep well inside me. Both my fangs and claws elongate, sinking into his flesh as though I were cutting silk. Az's blood fills my mouth, and the taste is euphoric and familiar all at once, a sense of comfort settling in my chest.

Mine.

My beast drinks hungrily, gorging on him as he roars his release inside me. I can feel the power coursing through my veins, his essence mixing with mine in a delicious blend. His eyes flicker with a wild intensity that only deepens when I meet his gaze.

In that moment, we are bound together beyond words or under-standing.

When his hips still, his mouth meets mine before he's torn off me. I'm vaguely aware of the sound of a feral wail outside, and the entire house shakes as Caius plunges into me.

More.

I recognize the voice now. It's my beast, wanting to sink her claws into any worthy man that draws near.

Caius' mouth trails my neck, his breath hot against my skin before he snarls his pleasure and bites down hard on my shoulder. His fangs draw blood from me, but the pain only brings more euphoria with it. Az follows suit, sinking his fangs into the other shoulder as Emeric licks and kisses up my arm until he reaches my earlobe.

I claw and mark Caius, my instincts taking over as I flip us so I'm on top, dragging my hips against his. My mind narrows to only one focus; riding him and consuming every sensation my beast demands of him.

I feel no pain, the adrenaline of my beast dulling any aches and heightening all pleasure.

Caius growls and sits up, drawing my mouth to his neck. "Mark me."

His demand sends a thrilling shock through me, my body begging for more. My fangs sink into his flesh, eliciting a chorus of moans from both of us. His claws dig deep into my shoulders, anchoring me to him as I drink deeply from his vein.

Heat floods my core as he spills his seed in me, and I let out a feral cry as pleasure takes me over the edge, too.

The moment of euphoria is broken when the roar of a god rents the air, like a crack of thunder, and Aggonid barrels into the room, his eyes no longer ruby, but a soulless black. Shadows pour off him, filling the room with an oppressive power. His hair braided close to his scalp, it hangs long over his bare shoulders, glass beads glinting off it in the dim light.

More.

Aggonid stalks towards the bed, ignoring Az and Emeric, and pulls me out of Caius' embrace, crushing me to his chest. His lips seal against mine, the force of it searing through me. My eyelids flutter closed as his tongue invades my mouth. His kiss is all-consuming, a possession of the deepest kind.

My back meets the mattress, the silk comforter sticking to my sweat-slick skin as Aggonid lowers himself over me. His eyes are wide with a primal need, all the measure of the god in his depthless gaze. He devours my mouth with his own and my fingers work at his belt, but my beast grows frustrated and burns his pants and belt off him with a flare of fire that doesn't singe him.

A wicked grin settles on his face when he pulls back to see what I've done. My pulse hammers in my veins as his fingertips trace my body with aching slowness, sending sparks of pleasure through me with each stroke. His hand wraps around my hip as he lowers himself between my legs, the head of his hard arousal pressing against me.

I'm vaguely aware of Caius and Az on either side of me, lust-filled gaze heavy on where Aggonid rolls my nipple between his fingers. I feel Emeric somewhere in the room, too, but abandon the thought when Aggonid speaks.

He stares down at me, desire and a possessiveness in his black eyes. "Mine," he growls like a vow as he pushes inside me in one long thrust.

My magic flares to life, pouring from my core like a river, and flowing into him. It illuminates the room in a brilliant display of crimson and gold, not snuffing out his shadows, but dancing around them as though greeting a long-lost love.

Aggonid grabs my hand, weaving our fingers together as he slams into me again. I scream in pleasure and awaken to the true nature of what it's like to be fucked by a god. His animalistic growls and my blissful cries fill the room, echoing off the walls. The sound of our bodies meeting is like thunder rolling through the air, creating a rhythm that only we can move to.

As we move together, something stirs between us, an elusive force that draws us closer with each passing moment. It's like a spark of magic, shimmering and ethereal, that ignites with each thrust and deepens our connection in ways I cannot comprehend.

There's a sense of inevitability to it all, as if our souls are slowly melding together, fusing into one entity. I'm lost in the sensation, swept up in a tide of feeling that threatens to overwhelm me.

Yet even as I surrender to the moment, I can't ignore the sense of foreboding that lingers at the edge of my consciousness. There is power in what we share, but also a danger that I can't fully grasp. All I know is that this bond between us is both beautiful and terrifying, a dance of light and shadow that threatens to consume us both.

But my beast is at the helm, and she will not be denied.

He moves faster now, his own voice joining mine in cries of passion as our bodies move in perfect synchronicity. I feel something deep inside me, a rush of warmth that pools beneath my skin and causes goosebumps to break out along my flesh. His lips ghost along my jawline and down my neck before hovering over the pulse point at the base of my throat.

Aggonid growls hungrily as his teeth graze my skin, sending shivers of anticipation racing through me. I gasp as he sinks his fangs into me, the throbbing pleasure almost too much to bear as I'm filled with desire for more of him. His thrusts become more urgent, pulling me deeper and deeper into a pleasure-filled abyss that threatens to consume me entirely. Our climax is explosive, a cataclysmic wave of sensation that crashes into us both and leaves us trembling with exhaustion in its wake.

CHAPTER TWENTY-SIX

CAIUS

*F*atigue pulls at me, but things don't feel right. I glance at the four others slumbering in this bed, replaying the sequence of events from the night.

I'd been called to find Morte, which was easy enough. She was always going to be mine. I knew it. She knew it. Our beasts did, too. So how is it that Azazel, *a prisoner of this realm*, came to claim her first?

The Wild Pursuit always values power above all else. So when the hunt began, I should've been the one who took Morte's virginity. But neither my beast, nor any of the others, recognized mine as the most powerful.

Once Aggonid showed up, all of us took a back seat—as expected —but I'm his mate, which should make me the *second* most powerful fae in this entire realm.

Eyeing the giant fae in a new light, I catalog his features; thick, black hair hangs to his waist in loose waves, and all manner of piercings adorn his face and body. His wings are tucked away, but if memory serves me, they're some of the most lethal pair I've ever seen.

Even in his sleep, his strength is almost palpable. A gnawing uneasiness creeps up my spine and settles in the pit of my stomach, though I can't put my finger on it.

But what really catches my attention is the tiny drop of blood at the corner of his mouth and the way Morte clings to him even in sleep. I can feel their connection, the same one that sits in my chest.

Does she even know?

This was all I ever wanted, though the addition of Az is ... unexpected. And I'm sure if Aggonid hadn't shown up, Emeric would've been part of this, too. Maybe he still will be.

He's been good to us, so I decide as long as he continues to be, I won't stand in the way if this is what Morte wants.

Metal adorns this entire room, in various shapes and sizes, yet I find a certain beauty in it. It's fitting for this place and the people within it—dangerous, yet captivating.

I slide out of bed when an urgent knock sounds at the front door. No one else stirs; we're weak after solidifying our mating bonds. Although Emeric is probably just being lazy—dogs are like that.

I'm still zipping my pants up when I reach the door. Sensing who is behind it, I relax, finish dressing, and open it.

My jaw clenched, I yank open the door to find my sister standing there, her eyes filled with fear and despair.

"What is it?" I grab her by the arm and usher her in.

She staggers towards me, her skin as white as death, and I'm stunned by the sheer amount of blood covering her from head to toe. In a voice filled with desperation, she gasps "Aggonid has to get back to the castle now!" and she collapses into my arms with her legs unable to support her weight. Incredulous, I quickly shut the door in fear of who could've done this to one of our toughest warriors.

The others, hearing the commotion, come barreling into the living room in various states of dress.

"What the hell is going on?" Aggonid strides over, his voice a mask of anger.

Iris's eyes pause briefly on Azazel before returning to Aggonid's. "Someone came through a portal below the castle." She winces as she clutches her side, so I shift my hold. "Demanded to speak with you or they'd kill your mates."

"Mates?" Morte squeaks, her face paling even more.

"Don't be daft now, girl," Irid snaps, and a growl rumbles from my chest as I set her down and move to get between her and Morte.

Aggonid huffs in frustration before turning towards us. "Keep her safe for me." He presses a kiss to my lips before giving Morte one.

"What?" Her eyes are wide, shock clear on her face, making Aggonid chuckle before he turns and sifts out with Irid in tow. She trains her eyes on the spot they were standing in, worry engraved into her features. "Is he going to be okay?"

I give her a lazy grin, enjoying the change in her attitude towards him as I pull her into my arms and place a kiss to her temple. "He's a god." I chuckle. "They'll sift to the castle, dispatch the intruder and be back—"

A searing, burning pain spreads from my stomach and I collapse, Morte voicing the same agony as she crumples to the floor. Pain radiates from my abdomen like a hot knife slicing through me. Agony so intense I can't scream.

Az shouts, falling to his knees in front of Morte, checking for injuries while Emeric shifts into his beast, searching for an attacker.

"What's going on?" Az's voice is frantic as he moves his hands over Morte's body, turning her arms over. "Tell me where it hurts!"

Another slice of pain lashes my chest, robbing my lungs of breath as Morte wails.

My mind is so scrambled from pain it takes me a while to register I'm not actually injured. "Aggonid." I climb to my feet, stumbling when my vision goes black. "He's hurt," I gasp, shock and fear making my voice tremble. My eyesight clears, and I blink, swaying as I try to right the room.

Az's head snaps towards me, his expression hardening. "I'll keep her safe. Go."

Emeric shifts back into his fae form, his clothes shredded at his feet. "I'll come with you."

"No." Az shakes his head. "I need backup in case someone comes here."

I pull Morte into a chaste kiss before I sift out.

Morte

MY WORLD DISSOLVES INTO AGONY, a pain so fierce it feels like an inferno raging inside me. A scream bursts out of my mouth, raw and animalistic, as if some wild creature has taken hold of me. I curl in on myself, gasping for breath but finding none. Every nerve ending is alight with searing flames, and each beat of my heart a hammer blow against my chest. This is pain beyond anything I've ever felt; beyond anything I could have imagined. It's as if my very essence is being consumed by a fire that can't be extinguished.

Az's grip on my arms tightens, holding me up as I convulse. He's saying something, but the words are lost in the deafening roar of pain that floods my senses. Every fiber of my being is consumed by the torment, as if I am the one being flayed alive.

It takes what feels like an eternity for the excruciating sensation to ebb to a crushing ache, and for my mind to clear enough for coherent thought. Gasping for breath, I manage to choke out a question. "Why do I feel his pain?"

Emeric's voice is barely a whisper as he crouches down to meet my gaze. "Pretty sure he's your soul bonded mate," he says gently, his expression softening with sympathy.

My mind is still reeling from Emeric's words when the pain returns with a vengeance, a searing hot poker through my chest. I can barely breathe, let alone stand, as I cling to Emeric and Az for support. "He needs help," I gasp out, desperation clawing at me. "Please, come with me."

"I don't think that's a good idea, Morte," Az says, his voice heavy with concern.

"Don't think I don't feel you in here, too!" I slam my flat palm against Az's chest, stunning him. "Do it for me!"

Az's expression softens, understanding dawning on his face. "Alright," he says, his voice quiet. "We'll go."

The three of us sift to the castle, the urgency of the crisis evident.

My chest tightens with a sudden pull, drawing me towards the throne room like a fae fly to a flame. With each step, the fear and dread inside me grows until it feels like I'm drowning in a sea of emotion.

As we burst through the doors, I'm struck by the scene before us. Aggonid and Caius are on their knees, their faces grim with fear. They are held down by impenetrable metal bands that shine like platinum, extending from their wrists to the floor. The material appears to be unbreakable, and its silver hue stands out against the darkness of the castle's interior. Romarie guards surround them, wearing uniforms of blue and black, weapons raised, and menacing eyes fixed firmly on the two prisoners.

The room is filled with an eerie silence broken only by the clank of metal and the murmur of voices as the guards exchange orders. Then all I can hear is the rustle of clothing as they shift, the clicking of weapons being primed, and the deep breaths taken by Aggonid and Caius.

Az and Emeric keep a firm grip on my shoulders, holding me back from rushing towards the men who've suddenly become the center of my world. Confusion and fear war inside me as I try to make sense of what's in front of me.

And then I see her.

Her blue flesh is pale in the torchlight, but the runes flash on her skin when she turns her attention towards me. Irid stands poised in front of my mates, a sword in each hand, her face painted with a wicked smile. Her eyes glimmer with malicious intent and her gaze is fixed firmly on me now.

Her long, dark blue hair cascades in waves over her shoulders and her body is draped in midnight leathers that give her an intimidating presence. "Welcome to the family, sis." Irid's voice carries a deadly tone that silences the other guards as she speaks. Each word is uttered with calculated intent, dripping with malice and disdain. "My brother is going to need someone to help him through his grief. Not that he gave me the same consideration."

The memory of one of our first conversations comes filtering back to me. *"Your survival benefits us both. I need the Wild Pursuit to end. And you are my only chance of making sure it does."*

My breath hitches in my chest as dread curls in my stomach. The guilt and unspoken words between Aggonid and I roil around us like a tempestuous sea, drowning me in its depths. I meet his ruby gaze, and I can see the same regret mirrored in his eyes.

Deeper than the ocean, and more powerful than a hurricane, our regrets ebb and flow between us until I'm nearly overwhelmed by the weight of it all.

Forgive me. Aggonid's voice echoes in my mind, as though he were whispering the words right in my ear, burrowing them right into my soul.

Before I can even begin to mutter the words of a spell, Irid's blade falls with a sickening thud, crushing through bone and flesh, cleaving Aggonid's head from his body with a sound that echoes through eternity. I'm rooted to the spot in shock and disbelief, unable to comprehend what has just occurred in a split second. My eyes fill with tears that stream down my face as I choke on a scream of pure anguish and crash to my knees, agony slicing my chest.

CHAPTER TWENTY-SEVEN

MORTE

*T*he gruesome sight of what just transpired replays over and over in my head as my world shatters into a million pieces.

The room blurs in a nauseating spiral around me, and Emeric and Az's arms feel like a leaden weight on my shoulders. I can barely breathe, barely think, as I stare at Aggonid's motionless form in front of me, the agony of it as though my soul has been torn from my chest.

Wails erupt from Caius, and my shrieking continues far past the shredding of my eardrums.

My heart shatters like glass until every bit of me has been broken. As my tears fall like rain, I see Irid turn menacingly to Caius and something inside me clenches with sheer terror and hopelessness.

My head erupts in a fiery rage as my sanity is shattered, surrendering my mind and body to the darkness that has taken over. My beast roars to life, its presence taking control of my being, plunging me into a never-ending abyss of despair as she surges across the room.

"I am the queen of fire and ash now." Irid stands triumphant over my mates.

Words, unbidden, flow out of me as though pulling from beneath the earth. "You speak of fire and ash as if it's a passing fancy, a fleeting flame that you can easily extinguish or control. But I was born in it, raised by it, and molded by its unyielding strength. Fire is not just a part of me; it is me."

Irid's eyes barely have time to widen in terror before I lunge at her with a deafening screech and sink my claws deep into her chest, piercing through her flesh and winding around her heart like a vice grip, the darkness seeping into my veins like a poison.

Romarie guards rush at me, shouting, and I slash at them with my talons as I continue to tear into Irid. I rip her apart one piece at a time, my fury and thirst for revenge so deep that nothing can stop me now.

The last of the Romarie guards falls to the ground, beaten and wounded, and I drop to my knees. I scramble for Aggonid's head, slipping in the blood beneath me before I can take it in my hands.

An animalistic shriek tears from my throat, and wails rent the air as I cradle him to my chest, low keening sounds coming from me in waves of despair.

I can feel the energy inside me warping as my beast fades back into the shadows within my soul, her grief too great to be part of this reality now. Even when I hated him, she loved him.

She knew long before I did who this god is to me.

Was to me.

They say a soul bond is the greatest marker of love. It transcends all reason and logic and is born from the most beautiful and terrible parts of our hearts and souls. And I can feel that bond now, even though he is gone.

My body is wracked with sobs, and I lay beside him, my tears washing away the blood beneath us and merging with the lifeforce staining his features. My fingers brush against his cold cheeks, tracing the ridges of his still handsome face.

The faint sound of clanking metal reaches me just as Caius is freed from his binds. His arms wrap around my shoulders, and together, our giant, heaving bawls quake the air around us.

For millennia, Caius and Aggonid had been inseparable, their souls intertwined in a love that transcended time and space. But now, with

Aggonid's lifeless body lying at our feet, it feels like the world has come crashing down around us.

I can feel Caius' pain like a physical weight on my chest, his sorrow so palpable that it feels like a tangible thing in the throne room we're in. As he clings desperately to me, I wrap my arms around his broad shoulders and hold him close. I don't know what to say to him; how to ease the crushing ache that threatens to consume us both.

How can I justify my pain when he's had thousands of years to love the devil?

For a moment, words fail me. Nothing will ever be the same again.

Emeric kneels beside us, his eyes red and wet, and places a palm on either of our shoulders in a silent display of comfort. Azazel drags the Romarie bodies away, his face lined with sorrow when he returns to my side.

As the sky starts to lighten, I gaze up at the stars winking out of existence one-by-one, like a shadowy curtain drawn over the throne room's majestic moon-roof. The moonlight creeps away like a thief in the night, leaving me in a darkness more profound than ever before. Though the sun shines, and the birds sing, everything feels dead inside me.

Emeric and Az redirect traffic so everyone stays away from this end of the castle. No one but those in this room know the fierce ruler of this realm is dead.

Did he know before the Wild Pursuit that I was his soul bonded mate? Is that why he pushed me away for so long?

I want to believe he did and that this was his way of protecting me from the truth—whatever his truth is. Despite the awfulness of our last moments, I can't help but feel relieved that he accepted me in the end, and that he knew I was his. Even if it was too late.

So many questions, but too few answers.

Now all I have is the brief echo of his love.

Emeric and Az don't try to move us or rush us along. They stand sentry while Caius and I drown in our grief.

I feel like a fraud; my memory of him too short and punctuated by violence to be real. But tell that to my soul, which lies in tatters at my feet, bleeding out for a god it loved with every fiber of its being, even when its host cursed his name.

The sun comes and goes, and I no longer feel the cool press of the sticky floor against my cheek, nor the ache in my bones from where I still lie next to Aggonid's body. I don't hear the words my other mate whispers in my ear, though I bear his grief inside my chest, and there's a small measure of comfort knowing I'm not as alone as I feel.

Some of the servants try to come clean his body for burial, but I lash out at them, my emotions riding the edge of feral in my grief. Though Emeric isn't my mate—we'd been interrupted before anything could consummate—my beast seems to recognize him as a safe person and allows his proximity to help comfort me.

As I lie there next to Aggonid's lifeless body, the weight of his absence crushes me. It's as if a piece of me has been ripped away, leaving me raw and bleeding. My mind races with memories of our time together, the good and the bad, the moments of love and the moments of hate. Love and hate are like two sides of the same coin, and I've been flipping it for too long without knowing which one I truly wanted.

But now, all I feel is the emptiness of his loss, and how badly I wish I could take back all the time I wasted hating him.

Caius clings to me, his own grief pouring out in heaving sobs. I don't know how long we lay there, holding onto each other for dear life. Az and Emeric's comforting presence are the only things that keeps me from completely losing myself to the darkness. All my feathers litter the ground around us, unspent as I tried to bring him back to me.

To us.

But he's a demon. The God of them. And in the end, not even my feathers do the gods deem worthy.

As the hours pass, I become aware of a flicker of light just outside of my periphery. It's a small flame, moving slowly closer. As it comes into focus, I realize it's Azazel holding a torch, his face etched with sorrow. He approaches us with slow, measured steps, the light casting flickering shadows across Aggonid's still form.

I watch in a daze as Azazel kneels down beside us, his expression pained. "Morte," he says softly, "we need to move him."

I resist the urge to lash out at him, to scream and rage against the injustice of it all. Instead, I simply nod, my body feeling heavy and unresponsive. Together, we lift Aggonid's body, carrying him with the utmost care. As we make our way out of the throne room, I can feel the weight of his absence pressing down on me with each step.

We carry him to the master bedroom, a place where we can mourn him in private. Emeric joins us there, his presence a comfort even without a bond to tie us together. We spend the rest of the day and night in that room, grieving for Aggonid and the love that we've lost.

But as the hours pass, something begins to change. I can feel a warmth spreading through my body, a growing sense of hope. It's a feeling I can't explain, but it's as if Aggonid is still with me, somehow.

The next morning, I awaken to an even stranger sensation. It's as if a fire burns within me, but not one of grief and despair. This flame is different, warmer, and brighter, and it fills me with a sense of purpose.

I rise from the bed, my limbs still heavy with sorrow, but my mind clear. I make my way to the window and look out at the world beyond. It's a new day, a fresh start, and for the first time since Aggonid's death, I feel as if there's something worth fighting for.

I turn back to the room and see Emeric and Azazel standing near the bed, their expressions somber as they help a near-catatonic Caius pull a shirt over his head. I approach them, feeling a new strength within me. "We need to do something," I say, my voice brittle from crying.

Emeric raises an eyebrow but doesn't protest. "What do you have in mind?" he asks.

"I want to honor Aggonid." I help Caius put some pants on, pausing to wipe tears from my cheeks. "I want to give him a proper send-off."

Azazel nods in agreement. "We can do that. Is there something in particular you want to do for him?"

I close my eyes and take a deep breath, letting the energy within me surge forward. When I open my eyes again, they're glowing with a fierce light. "We'll burn his body," I say. "In Castanea, we'd been hidden underground for millennia, so we'd burn our dead to keep the bodies from piling up."

Emeric and Azazel exchange a look, but they don't argue. Instead, they help me gather the necessary ritual materials: oil, kindling, and a wooden pyre. We carry Aggonid's body outside to a clearing, and Caius pours the oil over him, repeating the sacred words I've uttered so many times before.

But this time, it's different. This time, it's not just about the flames. It's about the ritual, the honoring of more than a fallen comrade. I light the pyre, and we step back to watch as the flames begin to rise. They lick at Aggonid's body, and I watch in silence, my eyes fixed on the pyre as the inferno grows. It's hot and bright, and it consumes him with a ferocity that makes my heart ache, though I barely feel the heat. The weight of my grief presses down on me with a force that threatens to break me.

It shouldn't be like this.

I'd known he was my soul bonded mate for mere hours. He's the one person in the world who was supposed to love me unconditionally, and I was supposed to love him just as fiercely in return. And now he's gone, consumed by the flames that I set alight.

My mind feels numb, my body a mere shell that's being dragged along by the others as they move around me. Emeric and Azazel stand nearby, their heads bowed in respect. Caius is a few feet away, his body hunched over as he sobs uncontrollably.

I feel a surge of anger and bitterness, emotions that are directed not at them, but at Aggonid. He had to have known I was his soul bond, it's the only thing that can explain his extreme hot and cold behavior towards me. What secrets did he keep? And why did he have to die, leaving me with nothing but this unbearable pain?

But as the flames reach their peak and begin to die down, a strange sense of calm settles over me. It's a feeling I can't explain, but it's as if a weight has been lifted from my shoulders. Maybe it's because I know he's at peace now, his soul finally released from the constraints of his mortal body.

I watch as the last embers flicker out, leaving nothing but ash and charred bone. The others move away, leaving Caius and me alone with the remnants of what should've been the love of my life. I kneel and sift through the ashes, searching for any sign of him.

An old habit.

But there's nothing there. Nothing but the vestiges of a life that's been snuffed out too soon.

I rise to my feet, my heart heavy with grief. This is not how it was supposed to end, but it's all I have left. The memories of a love that burned bright, quick, and fierce, but ultimately could not withstand the cruel hand of fate.

I turn away from the pyre, my eyes fixed on the horizon. The sun is setting, casting the sky in shades of red and gold. It's a beautiful sight, but I can't find it in me to appreciate it.

All I can think of is the emptiness that now fills the void where Aggonid once stood. And I wonder if I'll ever be able to fill it again.

Caius slides his hand in mine, and a thousand words die on my tongue. There is too much to say. Too much to feel.

The faintest breeze blows our way, as though the weather, too, knows we can't take anymore. With it comes the acrid scent of smoke, carrying a hint of Aggonid's vetiver and tobacco essence.

I close my eyes, and for a moment, I can almost feel his arms around me. Even the faint chuckle of his deep, mellow laughter carries on the wind. But then the moment passes, and I open my eyes, tears streaming down my cheeks as reality sets in once more.

Aggonid is gone, and he's never coming back.

CHAPTER TWENTY-EIGHT

MORTE

A tug on my shoulder causes my steps to falter, and Caius must feel it, too, because a gasp shoots out of his throat before he steadies himself.

Slowly, as though the world has tilted on its axis and we are a millimeter away from flying into the sun, we turn around, too stunned and too heartbroken to hold onto hope.

Aggonid stands there, his eyes alight with a burning fire that was extinguished in all of us. Alive as ever, a radiant smile graces his inky lips.

Like warm honey poured over smooth whiskey, his laughter ignites something in all of us, filling the void he left behind and banishing the darkness that'd taken residence inside our hearts. "Can't get rid of me that easily." He grins.

Caius is the first to recover, throwing his arms around our mate's neck, sobbing a broken, "You're alive."

I stumble forward, my hand brushing against his as our eyes meet over Caius' shoulder, and a wave of pure emotion overwhelms us. We all collapse into each other's embrace, feeling more alive than ever before, relief washing over us like a soothing balm.

We cling to him like lifelines, and it is only when Emeric lightly clears his throat that we break apart—but not too far, as none of us can seem to let go.

"How?" Caius croaks out.

"Yeah, care to explain how you came back from the dead?" Az crosses his arms, appearing skeptical.

Aggonid only laughs, the sound ringing with a hint of something magical and mysterious. "In every world, in every form, I will find them. Not even death can keep me from my mates."

"So what is this, you think you can treat her like shit, die, and she'll suddenly forget everything you did to her?" Az throws his hands up, fury blazing in his eyes.

"No, death can't make her forget," Aggonid says, his voice softening as he places a gentle kiss to my forehead. "But it did give me the chance to make it right."

I take a step back, sinking into Azazel's warmth while I study Aggonid. He's completely unmarred. "You came back because you're the soul bond of a phoenix fae."

"It appears so." Emotion swims in his depths and he nods. "You see, my dear Morte, you are built for darkness. You were made to thrive in the chaos and destruction of the Underworld, just as I was made to rule it. But you need someone to guide you, to teach you how to use your power for our greater purpose."

"How long did you know?" I fold Az's arm around my chest, hugging it to me like a shield. As though I could protect myself from the fallout of this conversation.

He glances around us, avoiding my eyes. "Let's have this conversation inside." He watches the retinue of guards standing sentry on the hill. "I don't know who I can and can't trust."

We all trundle inside, the crackling fire in the hearth strangely comforting in the quiet evening. Aggonid sits in a chair, fingers steepled in front of him as he stares deep into the flames.

"How long did you know?" I repeat my question, refusing to let him dodge it as I nestle between Az's thighs on the bed, our fingers intertwined.

A large part of me always hoped I'd be Wilder's soul bonded mate. But it'd been Aggonid this whole time.

The tension in the air is thick and palpable as he begins to speak. "I knew before I even ascended the throne."

As though I'd been sucker punched in the gut, I gasp, my heart lurching in my throat. "But you killed me." My voice comes out tiny, broken. The ache in my chest spreads until it feels like I'm choking on it.

"What?!" shouts of outrage fill the room.

Caius sinks to his haunches in front of Aggonid, crestfallen. "Is this true?"

He nods, a pained expression crossing his features as if he too was hurt by this revelation.

"Why?" Emeric threads his hand through mine, resting it on Azazel's thigh.

"I'd like to know that, too. How could you torture and kill the one person you were meant to love and protect?" Tears pour down my cheeks.

Aggonid stands, crossing the room to me, before kneeling between my thighs.

My breathing is shallow, the ache of my heartbreak too great to take deep breaths.

"I interpreted a prophecy wrong, and you were the casualty of it. It's something I'll spend the rest of our lives making up to you."

"What prophecy?" Caius looks up from where his hands are cradled in his head in front of the fireplace.

> *"When a virgin phoenix falls,*
> *Her blood does hold a hidden call,*
> *To those who taste its flaming hue,*
> *Their bond forever true.*
> *But not all who taste her flame,*
> *Will feel this bond and take its name,*
> *Only the chosen few will see,*
> *The bond that's meant to be.*

Loathing consumes one lover whole,
And he plots to take control,
He schemes to end her fate,
With a wicked, malevolent hate.
As he's distracted by this strife,
His enemies plot to take his life,
Leaving him to face the fight,
All on his own, with all his might."

His words are spoken with such feeling that I can practically feel his shame radiating off him.

I place my hands on either side of his face, wiping away the tears that have gathered in his eyes.

So I was sent here—not because what I did was irredeemable—but because I have a destiny to fulfill? I swallow hard and my heart quivers with hope.

"That's why you tortured me?" I breathe, and he nods, his eyes blazing with regret.

"Irid was the conspiring with the enemy this entire time," he whispers. "I'm so sorry, Morte."

"Does this mean you're done being mean to me?"

His shadows coil around my ankles, yanking me so I slide off the bed and into his lap with a startled yelp. He cups my cheeks, pressing his forehead to mine.

"Morte, I never claimed to be a good man. I torture and kill people with little regard for their feelings. But know that I will never hurt you ever again, and I'll kill anyone who tries. Starting with my sister-in-law."

"I tore her to pieces."

"You what?" He pulls back, studying me.

"Well, my phoenix did ..." I wince. "But yeah, she's dead."

He stares at me, his face unreadable. Then he exhales, a slight smirk appearing on his lips.

"Good," he says softly. "I was going to have to do it anyway."

His arms wrap around me, and I feel the warmth of his love seep into my skin. We sit there in silence, embracing one another, until he pulls away and brushes a gentle thumb over my cheek.

"I'm sorry—"

The air shifts, an enormous pressure taking up the bedroom as a wind comes out of nowhere. Lightning strikes in quick succession just outside the window, and the shutters fly open, the curtains whipping violently in the gale.

I look up, my eyes widening as a figure appears in the center of the room. She is tall and slender, a luminescent blue, clad in a gown of stars. Her hair is a cascade of white, framing her regal face. She takes a single step forward and holds out her hand.

"Luna, no!" Aggonid's roar echoes within the confines of the bedroom, slamming against the walls like a wave crashing into rocks, scrambling for me as my body involuntarily floats towards the goddess. "You can't have her!"

The shutters rattle in the gust of the wind that comes from everywhere and nowhere, sounding like thunder that builds and builds.

"My son paid a very heavy price to bring her back. I'm sorry, but she's going back to Bedlam."

An acrid tang of burned ozone lingers in the air as lightning dances around the figure in the center of the room.

The fear starts as a chill that grips tight around my heart, and I watch in horror as Finn's mother unleashes her power. I see the swirl of blue energy that crackles with electricity, engulfing my mates and Emeric in a force field of energy. They are unable to move, held against the walls of the bedroom, unable to do anything but watch as she takes me away with her.

As Luna's grasp tightens around me, I feel my heart thrashing in my chest. The world around us blurs into nothingness, and I am left alone with this god, a stranger to me but a powerful force that could shatter everything I've known.

Her voice echoes in my mind, resonating with a strange magic that sends chills down my spine. "You have a destiny to fulfill, sweet phoenix. One that cannot be accomplished in the underworld."

I struggle against her grip, but it's like fighting against a hurricane.

My mates' shouts and screams are muffled by the howling wind, and I'm torn between the safety of their embrace and the unknown that Luna promises.

"I won't let you take her!" Aggonid's voice rings out, but it's distant, like he's speaking from the other end of a tunnel.

Luna's grip tightens, and I feel myself being pulled away from the men I didn't want to fall in love with, but did anyway, just like I hadn't mean to fall in love with my best friend.

I close my eyes, tears streaming down my face, and I whisper a silent plea to the gods that I'll see my mates again.

"Do not resist, child. Embrace your fate."

MORTE HAS FINALLY FOUND her mates, but fate has cruelly separated them. Now back in Bedlam, she is haunted by the question of whether she will ever see them again. Can she find a way to reunite with Aggonid, Az, Caius, Emeric, and even Wilder, who remains locked away in prison? Meanwhile, King Valtorious looms on the horizon, threatening the fragile peace in the realms. Follow Morte's journey in **A Realm of Dreams and Shadows (Aggonid's Realm Book 2)** to discover the fate of her love, her mates, and the world they inhabit.

Want some of the backstory about what actually happened with the boon between Aggonid and High King Finian Drake? This happens in book three of the #1 bestselling series, **Bedlam Moon Trilogy**, but you'll have to start with Bedlam Moon (book one) for the full story. It follows the story of Lana and her paramours and features tropes like found family, one bed in an inn, hidden powers, captive romance, evil cults, and a time traveling witch hellbent on making things difficult for them all.

Wondering which supernatural order you'd be in Bedlam? **Take the quiz at kathyhaan.com/quiz** and see if you're a vampire, witch, or shifter. Share your result in our brand new Facebook group, **The Bedlam Fae Society.**

ACKNOWLEDGMENTS

I would like to express my deepest gratitude to the following people who have supported and encouraged me throughout the writing of this book:

• **Kirk**, for their unwavering love and support, and for putting up with me during long hours of writing and editing.

• **My family**, for their constant encouragement and for always believing in me.

• **My friends,** for their invaluable feedback and encouragement, and for always cheering me on.

• **My editor,** Jess, for their guidance, expertise, and invaluable feedback, which helped shape this book into its final form.

And finally, **my readers.** Your obsession with the world I've created is *my* obsession, and it warms my heart to know you love my characters as much as I do.

Without the support and encouragement of each of you, this book would not have been possible. Thank you for your unwavering support, your patience, and your belief in me. You have all made a profound difference in my life, and I am forever grateful.

ABOUT THE AUTHOR

As a blood descendant of literary greats like Jane Austen and Emily Dickinson, and from a long line of artists and creators, #1 bestselling author Kathy Haan believes that the secret to telling a great story is living one. The second youngest, in a massive horde of children between her parents, she did her best to gain attention and kept everyone entertained with jokes and wild stories.

She lives a life of adventure with her hunky husband, three children, and Great Pyrenees in the Midwest, United States. While this is her third series, you might've seen her work in Forbes or US News, where she's a regular contributor. Or, in Notoriety Network's 12x international award-winning documentary, #SHEROproject.

CHAPTER ONE

BEDLAM MOON (BOOK ONE, BEDLAM MOON TRILOGY)

*T*ime is a funny thing. The worst moment of my life is so fresh in my memory, but twenty-six years is an entire lifetime to be away from her. I was eight years old when she vanished. Long enough to remember her, but not long enough to hang on to the details.

There's a sign outside the entrance to the long, overgrown driveway that leads to the cabin. It reads, *"NO TRE3PA33ING"* with inverted S's. Below the sign is a little alien ship attacking Earth, although I'm not sure how ominous any would-be trespassers think it is.

I turn my Jeep off the main logging road and drive down the gravel entrance, which snakes around giant pine trees and wildflowers. Weeds grow amongst the rocks, cracking them apart and taking their place. After the last set of evergreens, the vegetation thins out, and the driveway opens up into a clearing in front of the cabin. The old place sits on a hill overlooking a small pond that ripples in the early summer breeze.

My hands shake involuntarily as I pull the Jeep next to the cedar log cabin. The old beams of sunlight stream through the branches of the pines and oaks, creating an oasis of light in a patchwork of darkness. I place the vehicle in park and shut off the engine. *So many years.* I slide my trembling hands under my thighs in an attempt to steady them and lean against the headrest before closing my eyes.

I thought I'd never come back here again, let alone find the place, but somehow my heart knew the way. The police tape around the weather-warped porch has faded to a warm, soft yellow color reminiscent of a baby chick.

This is where I last saw Mom.

She went out to catch breakfast at the little bluegill-stocked pond on our property. She hadn't returned by the time I woke up, so I went to look for her. The fish was good that time of year, and she wanted to fry up a batch of fresh fish cakes for dinner that night. Her fishing pole and tackle box sat next to her chair, but she wasn't there. They never found my mom, and with no dad around, they sent me to foster care.

Now I'm back at the place where my entire world fell apart.

But there's a bud of hope blooming in my chest when I open my eyes and turn my gaze to the small brown package, still untouched, sitting on my front passenger seat.

Whenever I'm traveling the world, my best friend Hannah receives mail for me and lets me know what bills I have. When she got this package, she forwarded it to the concierge at the Minneapolis airport so I could fly back from the Amazon and see if this leads me to more clues at the cabin.

When I relax my hands and slow my breathing, I reach for the box and place the parcel on my lap. After taking a few deep breaths—like my former therapist taught me—I use the Jeep key to pierce the packing tape Hannah placed around it. I pull out the white slip of paper and worry my lip while reading the scrawling print.

Lana,

I'm sorry I didn't send this to you sooner. This was in your mother's things, and Annabelle would want you to have it now.

Love,
D

The handwriting is unfamiliar. I set the mysterious letter on my seat and unfold the cream-colored tissue paper at the bottom of the box. Nestled within it is the key that Hannah told me about. The new key in my hand is strange; its handle a deep, dark metal with a pattern of blue and red gemstones embedded in the surface, too many to count. It almost seems to vibrate with energy, ricocheting through my limbs.

Not an ordinary key, indeed.

I turn it over in my hand and trace the intricate details with my finger. Tilting my head back against the headrest, I vaguely remember my mom having a similar key, but this isn't hers.

I remember little about hers, other than its weight and the pearly sheen that glimmered in the light. When I had friends over, we'd spark our imaginations, dreaming up stories of how her key could open any door in any house. Mom wasn't too keen on my fascination with it and would insist I be gentle with it.

Now, I have a similar key of my own, but who sent it? An array of small, vibrant blue and red gems adorns the entire handle. There are far too many to count, and I have a strange suspicion these might not be ordinary gems.

Palming the key in my hand, I grab my backpack from the floor of the passenger seat and toss the letter, box, and tissue paper inside. Stepping out of the Jeep, my gaze lands on the aged humble abode I spent every summer in during my youth. After twenty-six years of neglect, the wood is weathering, and a pang of guilt hits my stomach that I haven't been back to look after the place.

I grip the police tape and ball it up before shoving it into my jacket pocket, cursing as thunder cracks in the distance. I look up. The sky is blue, but along the horizon, storm clouds threaten to drop a lot of rain.

I cup my hand over my eyes as I peer into the glass on the wooden door. Inside the cabin everything is just as it was when I left it; in the kitchen is an oak table where my mom and I would roll out dough for biscuits. One of the legs is a little shorter than the others and makes a wobbling sound when you rest your elbows on it. Part of me thought Mom did that on purpose so I wouldn't.

Standing back from the door again, I eye the keyhole, slightly larger than a dime. The door is a dark green, with a large brass knob in the center. I've come too far not to try it.

I position the key against the hole, not sure if it will fit. The key feels warm and tingles in my hand. What is happening?

A black barrel sprouts from the bottom of the keyhole and darts around like an insect. It starts to spin faster and faster, like a drill bit, the sound of metal sliding against metal. Just as quickly as it began, it stops, exhaling a puff of smoke and leaving a hole large enough for me to fit my pinky finger through. I glance around the property in disbelief, wondering how someone pulled such an elaborate prank on me. And *why*?

At first, the key doesn't look like it will fit. I push on it anyway, and the bit shrinks and slides into the keyhole perfectly. I turn the key, and it rotates smoothly in my hand as the door unlocks. I push the door open, and it creaks with almost three years of disuse.

No ordinary key, indeed, I think again before placing it in my jacket pocket.

With my hand on the doorknob, I step over the threshold and close the rustic, wooden door behind me as I take in my familiar surroundings. It's like stepping into a time capsule: the worn pine floorboards, the fieldstone fireplace with lopsided cinder blocks for hearthstones, and the red and purple oval rug made from old t-shirts draped in front of it. On particularly chilly nights, I'd fall asleep on the rug while playing with my dolls. By morning, my mom had scooped me up and placed me in bed.

I glance over at the kitchen. The old oak table that had been covered in so much spilled food and craft projects as a child is still here, and the cabinet with glass doors is still above it. Inside there are all my old school photos, ribbons, and medals.

I step over to my rocking chair and stare at the ashes in the hearth, long cold, as a melancholic ache crushes my chest. In front of the fireplace is my white stuffed gorilla I named Kongo after watching it in theaters. Thinking back on it, I was far too young to see it, but Mom let me anyway. She'd given this to me when I got my tonsils and adenoids taken out. It kept me company through many late-night bedtime stories, where she'd read me R.L. Stine books until I was old enough to read them myself. All of my Barbie dolls are still stacked next to it in an unceremonious heap.

The cabin isn't huge but it's big enough for two people; a tiny kitchen, a Queen-sized bed, a twin-sized bed, and a couple of rocking chairs placed in front of the fireplace along the opposite wall.

The entire property is off-grid, and there are still a few logs in the holder next to the fireplace, but I will need to gather some more firewood if I plan on being comfortable tonight. This far North, thunderstorms can often welcome evenings just on this side of cold. After bringing in the rest of my bags and the supplies, I look for the ax we kept here for chopping wood and I find it in our tall cabinet in the kitchen.

Walking outside, a dark gray rain jacket on, and new hiking boots squeaking on the soggy overgrown path that wraps around the cabin, I make a mental note to clean the leaves off it in the morning.

In the shed I find protective glasses and a splitting wedge, which will make my job a lot easier. With the storm headed this way, I don't have much time to get the job done. I'm happy to find a felled black walnut tree nearby. Mom always hated them, and not because they dropped huge green husks that fell from them and clogged up our push mower.

I spend forty-five minutes chopping wood, resting on my knees every thirty seconds. It's the same thing I do when I travel so people don't see me huffing and puffing while climbing the hills of Riomaggiore. Only then, I turn around and snap pictures so it looks like I'm meaning to stop, and not just out of breath.

So, I might be a little more than out of shape.

The sky darkens until it's difficult to tell when one log splits into two, and that's when I give myself permission to stop. The first of the raindrops hit my cheeks, helping cool my overheated skin. Exhaustion takes over me after the back-breaking labor and carrying the split logs into the cabin to nestle in the wood holder next to the fireplace. I contemplate heading straight to bed, but a rumble in my stomach warns me otherwise.

I didn't know how hungry I was until I smell the smoky, spiced scent that now tickles my nostrils. I follow the odor around the side of the cabin, straining to find the source of the smell. And then I whip my head up when I hear the crunch of gravel out front.

As I approach the front of the cabin, I spy a tall, shadowy figure stalking up the driveway, and I freeze mid-stride. Ice bubbling to the surface of my blood, I stand still, like a deer caught in the sights of a predator, more afraid than I've ever been. I'm in the middle of nowhere, and the fading light of day, coupled with the storm right near us, gives the area an ominous feel.

Who on Earth is here?

"I'm sorry for frightening you, *Sahira.*" He has an accent that I can't quite place, and his voice is like liquid honey.

"Who ... who are you?" I fumble to turn on the flashlight on my phone.

I point the beam of light at the figure, slowly closing the gap between us. In front of me is a man built like a granite mountain, and I glance around for any sign of another person.

The second I determine he's alone, my eyes lock onto him, drinking in every detail as if my life depended on it—and it might— his jet-black hair resting across his forehead, terra cotta skin, and dark eyelashes that frame striking blue eyes, like gemstones caught in the light of the setting sun.

He appears to be in his early thirties, his complexion flawless enough to pass for a professional model on any magazine cover. Paired with his tailored suit, so at odds with the Northern woods, he appears as though someone plucked him from the pages and deposited him in my path.

My heart thrashes in my chest at the intensity radiating from his gaze. Raw emotion flashes across his face, as though I were the answer to every question, prayer, and hope he's ever had. I feel undressed in front of him, like my soul is laid bare before him and he cradles it carefully in his hands. I'm overpowered by a flood of emotions so powerful I can barely breathe.

I should be afraid and curse myself for leaving my ax by the chopping block. Instead, I continue to freeze where I'm at, staring far longer than is acceptable for a first encounter.

The man standing before me is more than just beautiful. He's exquisite. My mouth hangs open slightly as I take in his well-defined arms hidden underneath his tight two-piece suit, his lean waist, and the way his strong legs take root in the ground below him. He must be well over six feet, and his broad shoulders hold a confidence I don't feel right now.

My eyes travel to his face. He has a dark, sun-drenched look to him that makes me think he's from the Middle East, although his blue eyes suggest I might not understand what the hell I'm talking about.

Is he an investigator? Did Hannah let them know about the box I received?

The corners of his mouth curl up, revealing a brilliant straight set of teeth, radiating kindness. Like a warm embrace, I'm overcome with a feeling of peace, one I don't fully understand. How could his smile be so captivating and comforting? Was it the soft twinkle in his eye or the slight curve of his lips? I'm aware I should be afraid, but instead, I feel a strange sense of safety, especially as the intensity in his eyes fades.

I angle my body toward the man on the driveway, giving a little wave as I push my long, tangled hair behind my ears. My rain jacket hangs open, and that's when I notice my oversized t-shirt and black leggings are covered in dust and small bits of wood. I desperately need a shower and my muscles ache from chopping wood. I should run for the ax, not get lost in this stranger's eyes.

"I'm Osgood Finlandian, but you can call me Oz. I own a cabin down the road and thought I'd check out the place after I drove by and saw tire tracks leading here. No one's been here in a good twenty-five years, so I wanted to make sure people weren't breaking in."

Twenty-five years? While true, the man in front of me can't be over thirty-five or forty. I don't recall any other kids living nearby when I was little. Unless you count the occasional family staying at the campgrounds between here and the entrance to the forest.

"Thanks for looking in on the place. I'm Lana Chapman-Sawyer. This is my cabin, but I haven't been here since I was a kid." I'm still wary of the stranger in front of me.

"Ah, okay." He runs a hand through his thick, jaw-length hair. "You're the woman whose mom disappeared here ... I'm sorry."

And there it is—the inevitable moment when people remember the scared little girl whose mom vanished. My stomach flip-flops at the idea that this beautiful stranger knows about the absolute worst event of my entire life. It broke me, and I've spent the rest of my life trying to find the pieces again.

"Yeah." I absentmindedly toe gravel at my feet. "I was eight when she disappeared. I'm back to piece together what might have happened to her." No sense in hiding the story; he already knows it.

Everyone did.

"Would you like some help? My family has owned a lot of this forest for several centuries, and I don't think there's another person alive who can navigate these woods better than I do."

I think about that for a moment, digesting Oz's offer, and consider the odds. Investigators spent years trying to figure out what happened to Mom, to no avail, so I could use the help. Besides, despite being startled when Oz first arrived, I believe I can trust this man. My intuition has never steered me wrong before.

"Actually, that would be great. Thank you. Uh ... I'd invite you in, but I haven't settled in yet, and I'm still trying to find my bearings." Glancing at the storm, I wince. The nice thing would be to invite him in, especially as the rain picks up, but I'm still hesitant.

While I don't have a lot of belongings, my stuff litters the table and both of the beds. I'm also very certain that the bra I'd taken off and flung across the room as soon as I got in the cabin is on full display somewhere on the floor. With that realization, I throw my arms over my chest and zip my jacket.

Oz averts his eyes. "Not a problem, Lana. Would you like to come over to my place, and we can map out a game plan? I've got a hot shower. You can freshen up while I make us something to eat. You've had a long day from the looks of it."

Ouch. Was he admitting I look like shit? Despite my embarrassment over my disheveled state, the idea of being close to him stirs up something inside me.

"I'd kill for a hot shower, thank you. Let me grab a few things really quick." I start walking away but hesitate, turning back to meet his gaze. "Just wait here, okay?"

He inclines his head, and I pivot on one leg before bolting up the creaking porch steps to the cabin, taking them two at a time. Adrenaline courses through me as I slip on the top step, and in a horrifying second, I stumble. My arms stretch outward, desperate for something to grab onto, but instead of the unforgiving ground, my hands meet those of a stranger. He catches me as I trip, his muscled arms holding me steady. His skin is cold, but his touch sears through me like fire, blazing a path through my chest before pooling low in my belly.

Oz helps right me, and I dust myself off. He saves my dignity and doesn't say a word. Mortified, I run into the cabin to grab my stuff, and after shutting the door, I shrink down against it.

Well, that was freaking embarrassing.

I collect myself against the door, but then I remember Oz is still waiting outside for me, so I dart across the room, grabbing clean clothes and some toiletries. I pause my hand over my makeup bag and consider whether I should bother putting on makeup after I shower. He's seen me at my worst, and it is late in the evening. I don't want him thinking that I'm trying to impress him.

I mean, I *am* trying to impress him, but I don't want him actually *knowing* that.

Who am I kidding? Of course I'm going to put makeup on. Sure, he's probably not interested, but I can always bring my best self, right?

Maybe this man likes thick chicks, and we'll spend the evening rutting in the woods.

A wicked grin crosses my face, and I grab the makeup bag and toss it in my backpack. *Careful, Oz; I'm a man-eater when I have my hair and makeup done.* With that thought still on my mind, I exit the cabin, locking the door behind me.

A grin spreads across Oz's face, and his two eyebrows rise in unison. "All set?"

The air between us is perfumed sweet with a hint of spice and vanilla, so I take a deep breath through my nose before I respond. Perhaps it's the wildflowers at the side of the house.

I give him a nod, and we start down the long driveway. Now that I'm side-by-side with Oz, a breeze sends another aroma up my nose of Earth and elemental, which is likely the storm that seems to be holding out on us. I can't help but take a deep breath to inhale more.

As the leaves and gravel crunch beneath our feet, I gaze down at Oz's leather shoes. Why is he dressed so nicely out here? They're huge and had to have cost more than my entire outfit combined.

"Size fifteen." Oz quirks an eyebrow at me.

I glance down at my boots. "I thought I had big feet."

He smirks. "Where were you before you came back to the cabin?"

Do I explain that after my adoptive parents died, I had an early mid-life crisis and sold everything I owned so I could escape and travel the world? That, since then, I've traveled through much of Europe, Central, and South America, hitching rides on boats and buses and clinging to the sides of trucks? I'm not sure if he's ready for that level of crazy yet. Instead, I tell him about South America.

"I was traveling in Colombia for a bit, and I stayed near Leticia in the Amazon Rainforest, right off the Amazon River."

"I spent a lot of time in that area, so I'm familiar with the Amazon. ¿Habla Español?"

"No. I took Spanish, but I remember little. Are you fluent?"

"I speak a few languages, and I've done a lot of traveling. I have business dealings all over the world."

As a free-spirited person, I feel even more inadequate learning those things about Oz, and I can only imagine what he thinks of me now. The gal who got an MBA only to give up a lucrative corporate job in pursuit of adventure.

The rain starts, and I pull my hood up. Oz plucks a black umbrella out of the inside pocket of his coat. We continue small talk and walk another half mile, wedged together under his umbrella until we reach the entrance to his cabin's driveway. He starts up the pavement, and I follow suit, but there's no cabin in view at all, although I spy light through the trees. My nerves stir a little.

"It's about a quarter-mile walk. Are you going to be alright?" He eyes my obviously brand-new, never-been-scuffed-before hiking boots.

I tell him to press on, although my heels are chafing.

Eventually, the "cabin" comes into view. The only word that comes close to describing this place is "compound." His definition of cabin and my definition of cabin differ wildly. His definition is grand, mine simple; he focuses on what you can see, I on what you cannot but feel.

The jack pine trees standing between me and the lodge-like building are so tall that I can't see their canopy in the dark. Each window of the place is at least twenty feet high, and a single door—just as big—sits at the front.

It's beautiful, and it fits him. Though, the idea of Oz living here, alone, in this seclusion doesn't make sense to me. Where are his friends? His family? If anything, it stirs a deep sadness in my chest.

Is he alone, too?

Embarrassed, Oz admits he got a little carried away when designing the place.

His cabin is resplendent in forest green with warm wooden beams. I step back and crane my neck to take it all in. The wood is stained a deep oak color, and the roof is made of cedar, which softens the security lights that filter through the trees. Scents of dirt and moss tickle my nose.

I can't breathe, can't think of anything but the big, lonely home in front of me. Yes, it's warm and inviting, but are the halls hollow and free of the pitter patter of little feet? Do the walls hold a lifetime of memories, or secrets of sorrow, too?

The wooden front door and the window frames, even the roof beams look as if they've been whittled by hand. Understanding dawns on me now. Each and every square inch of this place is meticulously crafted, with a heart and an artisan's soul. Details I'd been too naïve to notice now come alive. From the driveway, this place is foreboding and a little cold. But up close? At the heart of it?

This is Oz.

My feet carry me up the stairs, and my heart places me somewhere I never thought I'd be again—home.

Wait, *home?* I shake my head. What the hell is wrong with me? I don't know this man, nor have I ever been inside his home. And I definitely didn't know this place sat right next door until today.

He holds the door open. "After you."

As I step inside, a cool gust of wind rushes through the side of my hair, billowing it back. Oz steps around me and takes my jacket from me, and places it in a closet near the front door. A glow of firelight warms the cold moisture off the marble floor as I step in.

I am at his *house.* This is a *big* house, but I can feel the warmth from the decor, which echoes sentiments of an old world gone by. A vintage chandelier, its beaded chain dripping with crystals, hangs from the vaulted ceiling and casts light upon the entry. All around the walls hang artwork, its curator one with a unique eye for the past and how it could inform the present.

My eye catches a painting across the foyer, and I step closer to capture a better look at the artwork. The painting is of a curvy woman, dressed in nothing but a sheer blanket draped around her ample bosom and tiny waist. My face heats at the signature in the bottom right corner of the canvas—*O. Finlandian,* painted in big loopy swoops.

He painted this woman, stroke by stroke, with such passion she seems to come alive under his brush.

Lucky girl. I pull at my filthy shirt, feeling like an intruder in my dirty clothes, and ask Oz to show me to the bathroom so I can shower.

He walks me past the expansive kitchen, where I inhale the smells of baking bread, up the wooden stairs, and down to the bathroom at the end of the hallway. It has a standalone, deep jetted tub along one wall and a marble-tiled walk-in shower along the other.

Oz flicks on the towel warmer and sets a very fluffy bath sheet along the top bar. "Do you want a towel for your hair, too?"

He must spend a lot of time around long-haired women, but probably not enough time around curly-haired ones. "No thanks. Because I have curly hair, I usually wrap it in a t-shirt to dry."

At that, he inclines his head, leaves the room, and returns with one of his t-shirts.

"Oh, you don't have to … "

"I insist." He extends his arm towards me, the t-shirt clutched in his hand.

I reluctantly take his shirt from him and set it on top of the towel, giving my thanks. He leaves the room, and I lock the door.

Foolish to be here, in a stranger's house using their shower, but let's not push it by leaving the door unlocked. I won't make it easier for him to murder me.

After undressing, I pick up his shirt, hold it up to my face, and inhale deeply. *It was him earlier;* that intoxicating aroma of earth, vanilla, spice, and an elemental sort of scent reminding me of thunderstorms.

My mind races with a million questions. What kind of crazy am I, drawn to a stranger like this? I want to trust him, but at the same time, he has that irresistible charm that all the women in true crime documentaries fall for. Still, he has a lovely Burberry-scented body and a face that could make even an angel cry.

Or sin.

Those pants of his hug his sculpted thighs so tightly, and I'd be a fool to not be attracted to him. I wonder if he's as into me as I am him?

Gods help me.

Read the **Bedlam Moon Trilogy**, starting with Bedlam Moon (book one) for the full story. It follows the story of Lana and her paramours and features tropes like found family, one bed in an inn, hidden powers, captive romance, evil cults, and a time traveling witch hellbent on making things difficult for them all.

ALSO BY KATHY HAAN

Bedlam Moon Trilogy (Complete)

Lana sets out to find the truth about her past, and when a hot vampire begins to unravel it for her, she's caught up in the web of an evil cult, prophecies, and curses. All while falling for the King of Vampires and his royal court. This is a why choose romance.

Bedlam Moon (Book One)

Tales of Bedlam (Book Two)

Wicked Bedlam (Book Three)

Fae Academia Series (Incomplete, 8 planned)

A spin-off of the Bedlam Moon Trilogy, we follow Lana's daughter, Rose, while she attends a magical university. The summer before college is perfect until the family begins to receive threats, and Rose ends up getting into a different college from her twin brother and her boyfriend. A male roommate, his hot friends, and a sexy professor all find themselves eager to win her affection. This is a why choose romance.

Bedlam Academy (Book One)

Arcane Scholar (Book Two, May 2023)

Forbidden Rose (Book Three, ETA Q4 2023)

Aggonid's Realm Series (Incomplete)

A Realm of Fire and Ash (Book One)

A Realm of Dreams and Shadows (Book Two, ETA Q4 2023)

When the commander of an elite group of phoenixes ends up dead for real, she tries to convince the fae devil there's been a huge mistake. Can she convince him to let her go before he snags her heart? This is an enemies to lovers why choose romance.

Fae Gods (Incomplete)

Fae Gods (April 2023)

Fae Guardians (TBA)

They watched their charge her entire life, completely invisible to her and only intervening when necessary. When they get fed up with her miserable marriage, Jocelyn's fae god watchers decide to help. After all, no fae of royal lineage deserves to be left to wilt away on Earth. They devise a plan to reveal their true selves to her, calling themselves the Marriage Doctors. But what happens when, during the course of their live-in lessons, the infallible gods fall for their off-limits charge? This is a why choose romance.

Bedlam Penitentiary (Incomplete)

Bedlam Penitentiary (ETA end of Q4 2023)

At the most ruthless prison in the fae realm, you're either at the top of the magical food chain, or you've got to form alliances with those with the most power. Because at a prison where you must expend your magic or you'll die, it's a no man's land full of dangerous criminals. This is a why choose romance.

Made in United States
Troutdale, OR
09/26/2024

23174230R00192